# AT THE
# END OF THE
# WORLD

# AT THE END OF THE WORLD

by

# CHARLES E. GANNON

Set in the Black Tide Rising world
created by

# JOHN RINGO

AT THE END OF THE WORLD

This is a work of fiction. All the characters and events portrayed in this book are fictional, and any resemblance to real people or incidents is purely coincidental.

Copyright © 2020 by Charles E. Gannon

A Baen Books Original

Baen Publishing Enterprises
P.O. Box 1403
Riverdale, NY 10471
www.baen.com

ISBN: 978-1-9821-2469-4

Cover art by Kurt Miller

First printing, July 2020

Distributed by Simon & Schuster
1230 Avenue of the Americas
New York, NY 10020

Library of Congress Cataloging-in-Publication Data

Names: Gannon, Charles E., author.
Title: At the end of the world / by Charles E. Gannon.
Description: Riverdale, NY : Baen, [2020] | Series: Black tide rising
Identifiers: LCCN 2020015895 | ISBN 9781982124694 (hardcover)
Subjects: GSAFD: Fantasy fiction.
Classification: LCC PS3607.A556 A95 2020 | DDC 813/.6—dc23
LC record available at https://lccn.loc.gov/2020015895

Pages by Joy Freeman (www.pagesbyjoy.com)
Printed in the United States of America
10  9  8  7  6  5  4  3  2  1

Truly excellent authors thrill and even startle us with the singular creativity and unique vision that spills from their pages. But in many cases, they cannot or will not take the risk of allowing others to work within their world.

However, many of the very best of these excellent authors do not merely permit, but invite and encourage colleagues to expand that original edifice of imagination. This is because they possess the confidence and wisdom to recognize that these enthusiastic additions only serve to enrich and adorn the world they brought into being. And in so doing, honor it.

This book is dedicated to one of those very best excellent authors:

John Ringo

Thanks for letting me play in your outstanding sandbox, John.

## Part One

# AT THE END OF THE WORLD

# My Journal, 2012

**May 29 (revised)**

My mom always had a knack for making friends. Friends who were men. If you know what I mean.

That's probably not the best way to start the first journal I've ever kept. But if I don't lead with and explain that, you'll get the wrong impression of her and of how I came to be on a ship when the plague hit.

See, she didn't want to leave me on my own in Los Angeles for a few weeks, but it was really the best move. For both of us. Ever since I was born, it was just the two of us. The deadbeat who was my biological father was out of the picture six months before I popped into the world. Then Mom's otherwise super-religious Catholic family did a role reversal and tried to convince her that I shouldn't be allowed to exist at all. Because: racism. They were worried I might have darker skin than theirs, apparently. Which is kind of weird, considering they were victims of discrimination their whole lives. But before they could disown my mom and me, she disowned them.

We managed to hang on in New York until I was about eight. Mom didn't start out with a great job, but between weekends at the closest community college and a few online courses, she managed to earn an associate's degree. That allowed her to get into executive assistant positions, at which she was pretty darn good.

And at every job, she always seemed to find friends. Friends who were men. It's not like any of them took a lot of interest in me, but that was cool, because I knew what the deal was before I knew the words for it.

Now it's easy to make all sorts of nasty assumptions about a person who will approach their career that way. But here's the deal. Mom got better jobs by changing employers. And every time she got a new job, she needed a new ally, somebody who could keep her from being a victim of office politics or other bullshit. And while she always liked the men she dated at her job, this wasn't the life she would have chosen for herself. I mean, with me along and no family, she didn't have any margin for error.

But Mom never said word one about that. She made sure I always had a quiet place to study, a patient ear to talk to, and, when needed, a single spank to set me straight when I was in danger of steering wrong. There was always food on the table, always a shoulder to cry on, always a person to take care of the cuts and bruises that I got from all the fights. Which I didn't win very often, cuz I'm not a big guy.

So it was kind of a surprise when we had to pick up and move out to L.A. I'm not sure why things went south so quickly at her last job. She didn't say much, which was unlike her. She usually tried to explain things to me like I was a grown up, but this wasn't one of those times. Looking back, I'm guessing her man-friend at the last job got married and his new wife couldn't stand him having his former squeeze in the same building. Which meant she squeezed my mom out of her job. And that put us on a bus to the sunny City of Angels.

I wasn't too surprised that we didn't see any angels. Instead, the real surprise was the cold climate we encountered in the Hispanic community. It hadn't been like that back in New York. Maybe that was because there you were always surrounded by other ethnic groups and—since they are seen as the competition—you tended to be tightest with the people who came from the same culture and spoke the same language.

That wasn't the case in California. In our neighborhood, you almost never saw anyone from any other culture. Where my mom worked, almost everybody at her level was a Latino or Latina— just not as skilled or experienced as she was. She was willing to share what she knew and to pay her dues, but they didn't want her help or her friendship. They just wanted her out of the way.

Except there was one little problem with that. My mom was

smarter and tougher than all of them put together. In just four years, she was working as an office manager. And of course, as she got better positions with each new change of employer, she always made new friends. Yeah, friends who were men.

Me, I wasn't so lucky with our new home. My school was like her first workplace: wall-to-wall Latino and Latina. And, like my mom, I was The Outsider, the kid from the wrong Coast, the kid who didn't fit, and the kid who was so small that he was pretty much sure to lose any fight he got into. Which the other boys spent a lot of time proving my first year there. However, unlike my mom, I couldn't change my gig.

That's why I got involved in aikido. I didn't let anybody at school know about it because it had zero street cred. It didn't look cool like kung fu or karate. And I was just one guy. So they didn't notice any change, and I didn't make any waves about it.

But when I got to high school, the guys with stubble on their chin decided to make me their punching bag again. I guess it was to prove that their *cojones* were as big as their egos. Bad surprise for them. But I had to be smart about when and where I was willing to let something get physical.

See, if you think there's any honor left in big-city public high schools, you clearly haven't been in one recently. That's why I had to keep the fights as private as possible: one or two bystanders at most. That way, when a bully got dumped on his ass by a pipsqueak like me, almost no one saw or heard about it. And if I didn't open my yap, he sure wasn't going to either. Which, in turn, made him less willing to take a second chance at it.

So by the time I was ready to graduate, I was pretty much left alone. I'd been an okay swimmer, a pretty fair soccer player by any standard outside of the Latin and Jamaican communities, and yeah, I did pretty well in school. Salutatorian, with A's in pretty much everything except art. My rendering of the human form really hadn't improved much since I was about four. Maybe it had gotten worse. Frankly, I didn't much care.

However, there was going to be one problem with that long-envisioned moment where I sat bored at graduation, not envying the valedictorian. And that problem was because—you guessed it—my mom had made a new friend.

But this time it was different. She met this guy while he was consulting for her company for three months. He was a Brit, had a cool accent, was funny, kind, and seemed to genuinely like me. But if the relationship was going to have any chance to develop into something serious, Mom had to follow him back to London for a while.

There was a professional angle to this situation, too. She had exactly what his company lacked, and really wanted, in their London office: an American woman with native Spanish fluency to help in their international marketing division. So this was a huge step up for Mom.

The only hitch was that she had to go over in late May. That meant that she wasn't going to be around for my graduation, and that I'd be on my own in La-La Land for better than a month afterward.

So we put our heads together and found a way for me to get out of town after only two or three days on my own and get her even more time to prove her value on the job in London. It was one of a set of packaged trips chartered through some company called Sail to Discovery. They sent kids on supposedly educational sea journeys to places like the Galapagos Islands, the reefs off Cancun and Cozumel, and other sexy and cool places where there's lots of sun and a reasonable chance of underage drinking, at least by American standards.

Unfortunately, a latecomer like myself, who needed as much financial support as possible, couldn't exactly pick and choose destinations. Particularly not when the really cool ones had been booked solid for almost half a year. So my ultimate destination— after shooting down the western side of South America and going around Cape Horn—was the oceanic ass-end of nowhere: South Georgia Island.

Never heard of it? Neither had I. There's good reason for that. It's a fucking shit hole. Correction: it's a fucking *cold* shit hole. But, because it was under-booked, and the charter company was able to save tax dollars by offering some berths on the cruise as scholarships for inner-city students, I was able to go for a fraction of the usual cost: it averaged out to only twelve dollars a day. Hell, there was no way I could have lived for that low a rate in L.A., so it was a done deal.

Which meant that, two days after Mom made a big batch of empanadas, kissed me, and then took off for England, I walked out the door to catch the bus that would take me to San Diego and Sail to Discovery. And to begin my journey to a part of the world where, in the old days, the maps only had a blank space and a legend such as, "Here be dragons," or "Ultima Thule."

And that's why I wasn't around to see everything go to hell in a handbasket.

Thanks to my mom and her knack for making friends.

This package to South Georgia advertised that over the twelve weeks, the journey would "make every Discoverer an experienced sailor." So of course, the first part of the trip didn't have a damned thing to do with sailing. We got shipped down to the Galapagos on what the company called a "liner." I think a more accurate term would be "partially refurbished freighter." The cabins, if you could call them that, were not much more than sections of the hold that had been partitioned into closet-sized bunks. The "amenities" and food were like the cabins: total crap.

It's not like the Galapagos has a huge marine terminal or anything like that, but it was the first stop on every "Sail to Discovery" itinerary. It's where you went to hook up with your particular charter's boat. Within two hours of arriving, I was being ferried out to the hull that was actually going to take me a third of the way around the world. The ship, the *Crosscurrent Voyager*, was a long-hulled pilot house ketch. She was seventy feet at the waterline and made for long-distance ocean sailing. Accommodations were still cramped, but well-designed, not refitted for the purpose. It wasn't the best painted or shiniest ship, but it looked sturdy and the deck felt solid underfoot.

And that's where I met Chloe.

Now, I have to be honest: when I first saw Chloe from behind, I wasn't sure if she was a guy or a girl: she was, as the saying has it, sturdily built. Don't misunderstand: that is not at all a euphemism for being overweight. Let's put it this way: if I had to make draft choices for a woman's rugby team, she would be my very first pick. Probably be in my top three picks for a men's team, in fact.

First time I saw her, she had her back towards me and was wearing jeans and a T-shirt. She was lifting one of the yardarms with two of the other people who were part of our Sailing to Discovery group. Then she turned around, and I realized my mistake in identifying her as male.

No, I'm not talking about female body features. Well, I'm not *just* talking about those. What I mean is that she looked like one of the women you'd see in a Spanish painting of angels or their earthly assistants. At least that's what I thought of when I saw the heart-shaped face, the almost feline eyes with long lashes that looked like they had been genetically altered to always have mascara on them, and lips that my mom's co-workers in L.A. got from plastic surgeons. The first words out of Chloe's mouth were utterly characteristic of who I learned her to be:

"What the hell are you staring at?"

Yep, that was a typical Chloe greeting. Although, once I got to know her, I realized that this was a pretty mild introduction. She used language so inventively obscene that, had I used it, I'm pretty sure my mom would have thrown me off the top of our apartment building. It was the sort of stuff you just didn't say where other people could hear. But Chloe did. All the time. That's just who she is.

I blame her appearance and first words for what I did next, which made it quite clear to everyone else how totally at home I felt on the deck of the *Crosscurrent Voyager*. Because, you know, I'd read about ships. I'd watched YouTube videos about rigging and how you're supposed to work the lines and catch the wind and all that crap. Which meant, of course, that I didn't know shit about sailing.

It was about thirty feet from the accommodation ladder at the stern to the knot of people standing amidships. In the process of covering that span of deck, I managed to whack my head into the davits for the dinghy, almost get hit by the now-swinging yard, and step into an unspooling line that tangled around my foot. Yeah, I cut a real cool nautical figure.

Chloe laughed harder and louder than the rest, shook her head, and called me *pequeño*. Which just did wonders for my ego.

In fact, I was so busy nursing my wounded pride that I didn't notice that the line around my foot was tightening and preparing to saw through my ankle. But before that could happen, the Great Ghoul of the Ocean-Sea rose up out of nowhere to put me out of my misery.

Okay, so the captain wasn't actually a ghoul, but he sure as hell looked like one. Even stooped, he still stood an inch or two over six foot, and everything about him was long. His face, his beard, his eyebrows, his legs, and his stares. The last of which he fixed upon me with undead intensity as I tried to untangle myself from the rope. I couldn't tell if he was annoyed or just waiting for it to amputate my foot. So that I couldn't run away before he devoured me. Prior to full exsanguination, naturally.

Instead, without even looking, he reached to the side, grabbed a gaff, somehow got it into the tiny, shrinking gap between my foot and the spinning rope. Then, with only a directional nod of his head, he coached me into the one move that allowed me to escape a ring of rope burn that might have cut down to the bone.

I looked at him, knowing I should say thanks, but all I could do was stare at him. I guess he saw gratitude in my eyes; he nodded and said, "Never on a boat before?"

Now, I pride myself on having reasonable skill with words. I like to think that on first meeting somebody, I'll have a remark or a quip which leaves them with a positive impression of me. I certainly displayed that skill on this day. Still looking straight into his eyes, I responded, "Um, um, yes, I mean, no, sir. I mean, never on a boat. Until now. Except the one that brought us down. Sir." If I could have looked and sounded more like a jackass, I don't know how I would have done it.

Behind me, I heard Chloe crack up. I have to say, her laugh was the least pretty thing about her that day. She sounded like a cross between a hyena and a banshee.

The Great Ghoul of the Ocean-Sea just kept looking at me and his mouth moved. I think that was a smile. Whatever it was, he hooked a cadaverous finger in my direction and led me back into the ship's bridge. Well, pilot house, on this ship. It's fully enclosed and is kind of perched over the weather deck, putting it a bit high for most sailboats. But, given where we were sailing, I guess that made a lot of sense; the weather around Tierra del Fuego is said to be some of the worst.

Once the pilot house door was closed, he pointed to a table where old-fashioned paper maps were laid out. It's not like he didn't have electronic gadgets all over the place. From what I could tell, there were three different kinds of radar and two different kinds of positioning systems. But he just folded his arms, looked me up and down, and said, "You are Alvaro, right?"

"Yes, sir," I answered. A simple sentence, but a distinct improvement over the last one. I was proud of myself.

He nodded. A very small motion. Almost as though he feared his neck vertebrae were so brittle that they'd crack. "So, you did pretty well in school, didn't you?"

What, was this a test? An ID check? Making sure he was about to indulge his undead penchant for eating only high IQ schoolkids? But all I said was, "Yes, sir."

"Good. I want to see what you can do with these maps, that calculator, and the charts."

I was this dumb. I said, "Do what—er, Captain?"

He sighed. It was like the exhalation of a dying vole. "I want to see you chart the first leg of our course. Think you can get us to Valparaiso, on the Chilean coast?"

I looked at all the papers and devices which had not looked intimidating only five seconds before. "I'm not sure, Captain," I said. "I might need a little help."

He looked out the window (it's not round so I guessed you couldn't call it a porthole), and answered, "I expected as much. Let's get to work."

## June 14

It's a good thing I'm enjoying life on *Voyager*, because we don't have a lot of interaction with the outside world. No Wi-Fi, no phone signal, not even much on the radio. And The Great Ghoul of the Ocean-Sea is pretty negative about us listening to the radio. As he puts it, we are on the sea to be with the sea. The chatter from the land prevents you from developing your sea legs because, according to him, it keeps your head from getting in tune with the swells.

I kinda wonder if he says that to all his passengers on what we now call the Misfit Cruise, or if this was just special for us. On a couple of occasions, when he's turned off the radio really quickly, I've wondered if there might be something going down in the Big Wide World that he's trying to keep from us. Particularly since, for all of his lectures about being in tune with the sea and staying away from the radio, he's started huddling over that little glowing box a whole lot more during the last few evenings. Which we're not supposed to know, I guess, but you know how it is: someone has to hit the head and sees the light shining down the aft companionway, creeps a little closer. But either we never got lucky or he has some freaky excellent hearing, because by the time anyone goes close enough to overhear, the radio is off.

Otherwise, our first two weeks on the *Voyager* have been pretty uneventful, unless you count the fight I almost got into. Which was unlike any other fight I have been in. Because it was with a girl. Specifically, with Chloe. The whole thing was really stupid. It was all because of knots. Except, not really.

Okay, I'd better explain. I had started to teach myself all the maritime knots I could find in the *Voyager*'s seamanship books. Which I'd finished reading after ploughing through all the other books on the ship: about thirty. That took me about twelve days, so yeah, I am a fairly quick reader. Just lucky, I guess.

So, when the Great Ghoul discovered I was not only done with all the navigation guides and handbooks but had made pretty decent progress teaching myself a ton of the more common knots, he decided I was the guy to teach them to others. It didn't bother me, because it gave me something new to do.

Anyway, Rodney and Giselle were my first two students. They are the brightest kids on the ship, but the sad fact of the matter was that they are as unfortunate in their knot tying as they were in the names that their parents hung on them.

Chloe had nicknamed Giselle "Gazelle" within the first seventy-two hours. Giselle has that body type that clearly craves carbohydrates but is unwilling to surrender them up as metabolic fuel. If you get my drift.

Rodney's name was simply shortened to Rod, which didn't seem too offensive on the face of it. He's long and skinny as a pole, so it seemed to suit him. However, Chloe emphasized it in such a way that you could tell that, every time she said it, she was calling him a dickhead. And unfortunately, poor Rodney is about as socially adept and comfortable as a thirteen-year-old forced to go to a middle school dance with his older sister.

So today I was teaching them the intricacies of the sheet bend. Giselle was catching on pretty quickly, but Rod was having a difficult time, as he often did. Smart kid, but he suffers from a bad case of nerves which sometimes makes him slow to understand things that are really very simple. Halfway through the lesson, Chloe came along, trailed by her friend-without-benefits, Blake. Chloe saw that Rod was struggling, made a crack about him "having a hard time." Rod got flustered, and they pretended to talk about him like he wasn't there, about how he'd probably keep having a hard time as long as he wasn't the one sharing Giselle's bunk.

Rod blushed almost as red as a boiled lobster. It's pretty much common knowledge that he developed a crush on Giselle within his first forty-eight hours on board. Just to be clear, it wasn't that Giselle rejected Rod's interest: she just didn't know about it. What made it extra cringe-worthy was that the guy she *did* wind up shagging for a few days—Johnnie—is unquestionably *Voyager*'s least intelligent inhabitant. That statement would be no less true even if we had a retarded chinchilla aboard.

So Giselle sees Rod dying of shame, drops her rope, and tells Chloe to butt out: that it's none of her business and she's just being mean. It wasn't the most eloquent remonstration I'd ever heard, but it certainly got the point across.

And it certainly got Chloe angry. Her complexion darkened. She looked Giselle up and down and said, "So, little Gazelle, you trying to get torn apart by a lion?" The way she was leaning forward made it quite clear that Chloe was nominating herself as the king—well, I guess the queen—of the beasts on our ship.

I gotta give Giselle credit: she didn't back down an inch. Probably because she is Rod's devoted friend. And more than that, it's pretty clear that she had a crush on him, too. Which of course *he* would never see on his own, not unless she did something a little less subtle than blushing when their eyes met. Like maybe tackling him and jumping his bones.

But given Giselle's defiance and Chloe's darkening complexion, I had a suspicion that this confrontation might not end with words. There wasn't much room separating these two sizable ladies, but I saw—and jumped into—the little bit of daylight still between them and planted myself there. Only then did I realize that I didn't have any clever lines to go along with my bold move. So all that came out of my dumb-ass mouth was, "Ladies, let's not fight."

That got Chloe to lean back. But not because she was intimidated; she was just surprised. Then she really leaned back—to laugh. "And who's going to stop us 'ladies'?" she taunted. "You?"

I managed not to swallow, even though I wanted to. Not because I was scared, but because the last thing I wanted to do was fight a girl or young woman or whatever you call somebody who's eighteen and acting like she's four. And besides, I really do kind of like Chloe, which is stupid and hormonal, but there you go. I was also pretty capable of acting like I was four. Or maybe as old as twelve, on this occasion.

I just nodded at her. "I'll stop you if I have to. And I don't want to have to."

Chloe's eyebrows shot halfway up to her widow's peak. Then

she laughed again and quick—like a striking snake and surprising for her size—she snapped her head forward and yelled, "Then get out of my way, runt!" and she poked her index finger into my chest.

Except her index finger never got there. Reflex took over before I could even think to just let her poke me. Because this is what you train for in aikido: to be able to react faster than you can think. And that's what I did.

I got her index finger twisted so that her wrist had to roll along with it. My other hand came up and grabbed her wrist on the opposite side. I turned it so her palm was facing upward and then bent it towards her hard, the back of her hand facing me.

If you know what that does in aikido, then you know that despite being both surprised and angry, Chloe was a lot more aware of the profound discomfort in her wrist, with the promise of serious agony lurking right behind it. She went down to one knee, as they usually do, and emitted a surprisingly shrill, "Ow!" After a quiet moment, she said in a low, very serious voice, "I'm going to kill you."

What she did next was what a lot of people caught in that position do. She tried to make a grab for my foot with her free hand, trying to pull me over or trip me. But because that's what an untrained opponent usually does, it's also one of the moves aikido teaches you to react to. The moment I saw her free hand in motion, I sidestepped, then pushed and twisted her hand some more. From the position she was already in, it was easy to chicken-wing her so that she ended up on both knees, her face more than halfway down to the deck.

I waited another second. "Are we done now?"

It was two seconds before she answered. "I'm going to kill you," she repeated.

"I don't think so," I replied. "At least not from that position. And I'm not going to let you go until you take back that threat. And convince me that you're not lying."

She looked around before she answered, and I realized what was making the situation even more complicated than it already was. Most of the other kids on the ship had gathered around. They were all surprised, some slightly amused, and one or two were kind of scared. Probably because—with the captain still chasing us away from the radio while remaining riveted to it himself—we're increasingly worried that something bad might be going down back home. And that makes people more sensitive about anything that might ruin the already weak cohesion of our group.

But right then, Chloe was simply getting darker. "I'm not promising you anything, pipsqueak," she said.

I sighed. "Well then, we've got a real problem. I'm not going to let you up until you give me your word that this ends here. Because, seriously: you're pretty strong and pretty dangerous."

She paused for a long time. By the time she spoke, her voice sounded a little bit surprised, a little bit grateful, but still a whole lot pissed. "Nice of you to notice," she said. "Won't save you, though. You should have minded your own business and let the ladies work it out."

"Yeah, well, it looked like your version of 'working it out' meant you were going to pound Giselle's face into the deck. I won't have that."

"Then what you have is a new enemy."

"Can't see as how you were anything but that already, Chloe. Wish it wasn't like that."

She was quiet for about four seconds this time. When she spoke again, her voice was very changed. "Well, isn't that a shame. Because when you let me go—and eventually you'll have to—you are never going to know when I might come up behind you and—"

"Enough," said a voice that sounded like a rifle going off.

We all jumped. Except for Chloe that is. She jerked in surprise, which made her yelp: I kept her hand twisted.

The Great Ghoul of the Ocean-Sea was glowering at us, standing next to the hatchway from which he'd emerged. "There will be no fighting on board this ship. Especially not between men and women. I see something like this again and I will flog the lot of you." He managed to say this in a tone of such disgust and anger that I think everybody but me looked down. Chloe had no choice in the matter; I still had her chicken-winged. He stared at me hard for a moment, but then his lower eyelids drooped. Which actually made him look younger.

"I'm sorry, sir," I said.

He nodded, half in acknowledgment and half toward Chloe. "That's enough," he muttered. I let her go. She pulled away sharply.

He glared at her—she looked down again quickly—and then

he stared all around the group. "You should all be ashamed." He snorted disdain. "I don't care who did what. Or who is right and who is wrong. I will have no more of that shite on this ship. Is that clear?"

The mumbled replies were vaguely affirmative.

"IS—THAT—CLEAR?" He shouted each word so that it sounded like a sentence unto itself.

The other kids all looked up pretty much simultaneously. Almost as a chorus, they answered, "Yes, sir," quietly but clearly.

One last undead glower. "Then get back to your work. All of you." He glanced at me, jerked his head toward Rodney and Giselle. "Are they done learning knots?"

"Not just yet, sir."

"Well then, stop lazing about and get them finished. I need you people to be able to handle a ship. On your own, if need be." That got everybody moving.

Except me. Was I—and am I still—the only one who heard something ominous in that last short sentence of his?

## June 15

I spent a lot of time in the pilot house today, charting a new course. Originally, we were supposed to stop at Valparaiso for fresh water, which would have been pretty tight by the time we got to South Georgia Island. But the captain had refurbished the *Voyager*'s condensers only a few months earlier, and they were keeping up with the demand, so the captain decided to make straight for Cape Horn. Leaving me with the job of plotting our approach to Tierra del Fuego.

My head was so deep in the maps and numbers that I just about jumped out of my skin when a voice behind me said, "We need another navigator." It was the Ghoul himself.

"Yes . . . I mean aye, um, I mean aye aye, Captain," I said. When I look at that on paper, it only reads half as stupid as it sounded.

"You'll be doing the teaching."

"Me?" I don't think my voice has broken that way since I was thirteen. "But I hardly know how to navigate, myself!"

Already halfway out the door to the weather deck, he turned back. "Tell me," he said quietly, "what's a rhumb line?"

"A line on the surface of the earth making the same oblique angle with all meridians," I snapped back at him. I figured this was some sort of test, and I wanted to make up for sounding stupid and having my voice break. For the first time in my life, I cared about somebody's opinion of me other than my mom's.

He nodded. "And what's the solstitial colure?"

"The great circle of the celestial sphere where the sun passes through the celestial poles and the solstices."

"And swirl error?"

"The additional error in the reading of a magnetic compass during a turn, due to friction in the compass liquid." I could do this all day.

The captain stared at me through narrowed eyes. "And what's the third topic heading in the sixth chapter of *Knight's Seamanship*?" he asked me.

"Which edition, sir?" There were two on board.

"The old one." He stopped to think. "Tenth edition."

That seemed like a pretty arbitrary piece of information, but I knew it. "'The Azimuth Circle.'"

He looked at me. "So you say you don't know how to be a navigator."

"Well," I explained, "I mean, I can do it a little. But most of that is just book learning, and I—"

"Bollocks, boy." I think that may have been the first time he ever interrupted me. "You've been charting courses without any help for three days. And you didn't need my help for the four days before that. I've never seen anyone learn these principles so quickly. But then, you get on pretty well with books, don't you?"

I felt my face get hot. "Pretty well," I admitted.

The left side of his mouth twitched in what might have been, for him, a broad shit-eating grin. "Pretty well, indeed. I'll wager that if I asked you to give me a few entries on the celestial navigation tables, you could do that sitting right there, without cracking the cover." He stared at me. "Couldn't you?"

"Maybe," I lied.

He leaned forward. "No, you *could*. And I know it. And we don't have the time or the freedom for this kind of faffing about. The plain fact is that you have a photographic memory. Oh, you're sharp enough as well, I warrant. But see here: a captain must know all the assets at his disposal, all of the resources upon which he can count. So when were you going to do the right thing and let me know about this little skill of yours?"

I shrugged. "Hadn't thought about it really, sir." And it was true. School is bad enough when you're the pint-sized outsider who's always getting the best grades. God knows how much worse it would have been if they'd known I was some kind of freak who remembered everything he saw and heard. Without really trying.

The captain must have seen some of that old dread flash past in my eyes. He leaned back. "Right, then. I can see it might not have always been a skill you were glad to have. But now, we could have need of it. These are treacherous waters." He looked away. "And this can be a dangerous world." He paused, as though he intended to add something, but instead got up and left. Like he was in a hurry.

It's the first time the captain ever said or did anything that struck me as evasive. And suddenly, for reasons that I cannot fully identify, I am now terrified. If something gives the Great Ghoul of the Ocean-Sea even a moment's pause, I figure that it has to be pretty damned serious.

Like Armageddon. Or worse.

## June 16

"So," the captain resumed the next day in the pilot house, like we'd never stopped talking. "Resources. There are only two people on *Voyager* who can navigate her. That's not enough. So you're going to start training another one today."

I had thought about it since yesterday. It didn't sound so bad, particularly not if it was somebody like Rodney or Giselle. They had pretty good heads on their shoulders, even if the brains inside didn't always work to get them the best social outcomes. "Sure," I replied. "Actually, I think that either Rodney or Giselle would—"

"I asked you to train a navigator, not recruit one. I've already done that." He called down the companionway. "Come up here." It sounded like he was talking to a misbehaving pet.

He moved out of the way so that the new navigator-in-training could get up the stairs and past him. It was Chloe.

I looked at him. And this time he really did grin a little. "Have fun you two," he said. And left.

Chloe looked at me and I looked at her. We did that for a while. Strangely enough, she was the first one to look away.

"Look," I said in a low voice, "do you have any idea why he—?"

"You're asking me?" she said, turning to glare at me. "You're his Golden Boy. You'd know, if anyone."

The notion of being the Great Ghoul's Golden Boy left me speechless for a few seconds. Then: "Well, if I'm his favorite, he has a damn strange way of showing it. I didn't know he even wanted another navigator, much less expected me to train one. And I can assure you, if he'd given me a choice of who—" I heard myself and stopped.

Too late.

She turned toward me. "The only thing worse than having you teach me is having you near me. So, let's start with some ground rules. You stay on the opposite side of this chart table. Maybe that way I won't puke."

I should have been able to shrug that off, to just smile, lean back, and say, "Whatever. Let's get to work." But no. Instead, I blurted out the first response that came to mind, a tit-for-tat reflex. "Of all the things you need to worry about, me wanting to get close to you is not remotely among them."

She wasn't out of grade-school ammunition yet. "Why? Because you're afraid I might pick you up and break you?"

"No, because you're a nasty, selfish bitch, and I wouldn't get with you if you were the last female on earth."

Yes, I went there. And yes, I was totally in the wrong. And what had come out of my mouth shocked me speechless.

Her, too. For a moment I thought the odds were even that she was either going to cry or scream. However, I could see that the odds were much better than either that she was going to smack my face—and I wouldn't have stopped her even if I could have.

But she stopped herself. I don't know if it was a memory of what happened the last time she tried coming after me, her fear of the Great Ghoul, or some still vulnerable part of her that my retort had hit, punctured, and sunk. For a moment, it looked like she might fold in on herself, but then her jaw came forward and locked in place. "Right," she said. "Let's get to work."

## July 6

It turns out that Chloe had problems in school. Discipline problems, mostly, but they spilled over into her academics. If she works too long, or runs into a dead end, she gets tense, which means she gets snippy and then resentful if you try to keep her at it.

Frankly, she's okay at math. In fact, she's better than average at almost everything. It's her attitude that sucks. On the first day, she was so hostile that I figured I'd better start by finding her comfort zone. So I asked her what subject she liked best when she was in school.

"Gym," she answered without batting a lash. And they are very long lashes.

Okay, I should have seen that coming. "So what made everything else so crappy? A school full of lousy teachers?"

She shook her head. "No. I just don't like to re—to work."

I shrugged and didn't let on how I noticed that, at the last minute, she'd shifted away from saying "I just don't like to *read*." Instead, I got her started on the material we had to cover for navigation: basic math. At which she was okay, once I walked her through it. But when I asked her to go over some written instructions about procedures, we didn't get anywhere.

We stopped early and I went to find the captain. Who was apparently waiting for me in his cabin. "Sir, I'm not sure that Chloe is going to prove the best choice for a back-up navigator."

He folded his long, thin arms, and leaned back. "Is that a fact?" His tone was mild, almost amused.

Everything became a lot more clear. "So you already knew that she—"

"Quiet. My question was rhetorical. And yes, I still think she'll be a good navigator. And yes, I do think you'll be able to teach her to read. And no, I don't bloody care that it will take longer, or that you're likely to consider suicide before it's over." The last was hyperbole. I think.

"Yes, sir, but—"

"—But why is it worth all the trouble? Because, if you haven't noticed, she's healthy, reasonably smart, and jolly well the most aggressive of you all. Traits which mark her as a survivor."

"A . . . survivor, sir?"

"Yes. The sort of person who will be useful in any situa—in any walk of life. Just needs a bit of work, a bit of fixing, to her education."

That was the first time that I didn't just suspect the Great Ghoul of the Ocean-Sea was bullshitting me: I knew it. Something was wrong. Really, big-time wrong. My palms suddenly felt cold. I couldn't call the captain on it, but I needed to find out why it was so important that Chloe was a survivor. "Well, I'll do my best, sir. Any particular subjects you want me to push her toward, in addition to the navigation?"

He speared me with his eyes. "Don't be so clever, lad. I'm not her—what do you call them in the States?—her 'guidance counselor.' But you should know this: I get a file on each of you from the charter company."

I couldn't keep my eyebrows from raising.

"Nothing particularly revealing, usually. But in her case—" He shook his head and leaned forward. "Some of you come from pretty hard backgrounds. We get a little extra information on those. Just in case." He waited for me to nod before he went on. "Her parents never married. Split up when she was young. Father tried, but fell down a bottle—the way only an Inuit can, according to the report. The mother either started as or became an addict; wasn't even in Alaska, let alone Juneau, half of the time." He stood, which, since it was his cabin, made it pretty clear that my time was up. "She had to raise—and protect—herself," he muttered. "I just want her to have the tools she'll need. For the future."

Until today, I had never heard anyone utter the word "future" like it was part of a eulogy for the present.

## July 11

We should have been at our current location weeks ago, but the captain's insistence on making us competent sailors has cost us speed and time. A few of us have wondered, out loud, how we'll get back home when we're supposed to. He just looks at the mounting swells beyond the bow and, after a few moments, recites the same tired explanation, "We'll worry about that when Tierra del Fuego is behind us."

Which is really no explanation at all. Which everyone else noticed, as well.

We've also noticed that he doesn't hang on to the radio the way he used to. Now, he keeps it off. And it's been almost a week since we've seen another ship, even though the Chilean coast is just beyond the eastern horizon.

A month ago, when I first noticed that the captain was starting to say some dire stuff, everyone else thought I was nuts, that there was no need to talk about how he might be acting a little hinky.

Now, they don't talk about anything else.

## July 17

So today, as soon as Tierra del Fuego disappeared behind us, the captain tried to raise Port Stanley, capital of the Falklands. What he got back was fevered gibberish. While it lasted. He turned the dial, retuned, tried to raise our destination: King Edward Point, the small sub-Antarctic station the Brits maintain on South Georgia Island. No reply.

He turned off the radio slowly, then sat back. I waited for what was, according to the clock above the wheel, slightly more than three minutes. When he spoke, he did not look over at me. "Alvaro, we're going to keep trying those stations. So, until someone replies, we're not going to tell the others what we just heard—or didn't. Your mates are far too twitchy already."

I just nodded. Which made me complicit in agreeing to what he was really saying: "we're going to keep this between the two of us until and unless there's proof that the whole world has gone to shit." Or as he would have said, "has gone pear-shaped."

"Next steps, sir?" I asked.

He looked at me. "You don't rattle easy, do you, Alvaro?"

"I try not to, sir."

"That's good." From him, this was unthinkably high praise. "Do you know how to fish?"

"I know there's a hook involved. Other than that, not a clue, sir."

His jaw seemed to experience a momentary tic: whether that was a spasm of disappointment or amusement, I couldn't tell. "Well, find someone who does. I suspect Chloe will have some experience. Tell them to meet me astern at 1400. We're going to go off prepared foods for a while."

"I see, sir. Anything you want moved into the ship's locker?" Which meant, effectively, placed under lock and key.

He nodded. "Vitamins. Bottled water. Canned goods. Spare batteries." He stood. "There will be more. But we will take this one step at a time. Eventually, we'll need to collect any personal medical supplies—ibuprofen, acetaminophen, aspirin—and anything else we might need to ration." He finally looked at me. "Where's your family, Alvaro?"

"My mom is in England. On business. Mostly. She's my only family."

He nodded, walked to the door: beyond it, the grey South Atlantic tossed fitfully, as if, far below, thousands of whales were having bad dreams. "From now on, whenever I'm not using it, the radio is unplugged and off limits. You understand."

"I do, sir. And yes, sir."

He went through to the weather deck looking like he had aged another ten years.

## July 20

I didn't know I'd have trouble writing this entry, but when I finally got to my bunk and picked up my pen, my hand started shaking. This is the third try. I hope I can get it all down.

The day started normally enough. The captain was up first, as always. And he went to the place that was now his full-time station: the radio. With the exception of a short trip down to the condensers, he kept tuning through the dial, again and again. And every time he caught a scratchy snippet of some signal, he would drop the volume. As if the others didn't know what that meant: that he didn't want the rest of us to hear it.

But apparently, while the captain was down checking on the condensers, and I was busy giving a hand with the sheets, Blake slipped into the radio room. It was in the compartment at the bottom of the pilot house's companionway. He hooked up the set, fiddled with the dial himself. Then, when the Great Ghoul of the Ocean-Sea came thumping up the companionway, he realized he couldn't get out in time, so he ducked into the bridge locker, which was mostly empty except for signal flags, spare rope, buoys, and some chandlery odds and ends.

The first sign that something had gone wrong was Blake's long scream: "WHAAAT? NO! That's bullshit! That's totally bull—" and then a thump and a long silence. I was the only one who didn't come running.

Not like I missed a lot by walking, though. Blake was still sprawled on the floor, staring up at the captain in shock. "You bastard," he whispered. "You've been hiding it from us. All this time."

Chloe was frowning. "Hiding what?"

Before Blake could answer, the captain stepped between them. "That's enough. This is not a bloody democracy." He turned toward Blake. "Mr. Worley, you disobeyed my express orders about the radio. You will be disciplined. When I am done."

Even Chloe looked worried. "Done with what?"

"Done explaining what has been going on back home and how it bears upon our voyage."

Blake made a sound that was partly a bark of laughter and partly a sob of panic. "Yeah, it bears, all right."

The captain's eyes were on Blake. "One more outburst and I will confine you to your cabin."

The pilot house was dead quiet.

The captain leaned upon the pilot's console. "A little over three weeks ago, coastal radio stations started reporting the outbreak of some new strain of flu. It started in the U.S.—Los Angeles, in fact—but shortly afterward, began breaking out elsewhere. About twenty-five percent of all infections are eventually fatal. Quite a few more never recover."

"Jesus," Rodney breathed.

"It spread through the developed nations first, but they have had better luck containing it. When it hit the less developed nations—such as those of Central or South America—it ran wild." He paused, looked around the group. "There is no known vaccine, and it is racing ahead of conventional quarantine and isolation efforts."

Suddenly, all I could think of, or see, or hear, was memories of my mom.

Rodney had raised his hand. At any other time, it would have just added to his image as a doofus and a loser, but suddenly, it seemed appropriate. The way we liked to envision ourselves—as adults—had just gone out the window. There was only one real adult aboard. He had the dope on what was going on in the world. Without him, each and every one of us were as screwed as a nymphomaniac mink. These were the simple facts, and right then, the only ones that mattered. The captain nodded at Rodney's raised hand.

"Captain, you said that the virus is twenty-five percent fatal, but that even more don't recover. What happens to them?"

The captain frowned. "I can't tell you exactly because the

radio transmissions have become so infrequent and . . . bizarre. It seems that more than half of those who survive suffer permanent brain damage that reduces them to mindless savagery. Including cannibalism."

If the pilot house had been quiet before, it was tomblike now. And because at that moment death seemed to close in all around us, I found myself making note of all the other kids on the trip in a way I never had before: as if they might be the last people on Earth.

That in turn made me realize I have never even bothered to mention them all in this journal. Like the passersby we see in the course of any regular day, they were sort of like extras: faces that inhabit the movie of our lives without having any role to play other than populating it. Suddenly I had a sharp awareness of them as individuals, along with a tangle of feelings that mostly grouped around two opposed poles. First, horror at the thought that this handful of teenagers was going to propagate whatever grim new Eden the globe became and that I'd have to participate in that process. Second, a surge of manic relief that somehow, by the strangest of all coincidences, I happened to be among their number. That I, out of all the millions on Earth, might be one of the few who had chanced to survive.

I had to admit, looking around the group, that my first thought was, "We're pretty lucky to have Chloe." Yes, she has the disposition of a badger with a toothache, and yes, she might not be at the highest point of the bell-curve for smarts. But on the other hand, she doesn't fall too far below that high point and she dwells at the very peak when it comes to nerve and aggressiveness. In short, the traits that had, thus far, made her a total pain in the ass now make her one of the stand-out members of our crew.

Rodney and Giselle might not be the most impressive physical specimens, but they are kind of a two-part brain-trust, and I got the feeling that both of their awkward social identities were about to slough off like old skins. Shit was real now, and neither of them was recoiling from it. They were leaning forward, attentive, late teenage angst dropping behind as fast as the grey ocean swells.

Blake was the one that worried me. His eyes were open a little wider than normal and he hadn't blinked since the captain started explaining how the world was dying around us. His pronounced Adam's apple was cycling regularly, and he simultaneously looked like he wanted to be anywhere other than in the pilot house and yet also wanted to dive back in the locker with the signal flags I doubted we'd ever use again.

Johnnie, Giselle's former squeeze, worried me for the opposite reason. He just sat there, his habitual smile a little dimmer, his mouth hanging open a bit. Frankly, a little bit of anxiety or a sudden sharpening of attention would have been reassuring. But no, Johnnie's good nature was there in part because he was disinterested in, and not particularly adept at, anything too complex or too serious. It's fortunate that he is physically larger than average, because on the mental aptitude side . . . well, I guess you could say he seemed to be on the back slope of the bell curve and if the current situation didn't sharpen his focus, nothing would.

Steve, the quietest of the group, is something of a wild card. Just like in all our other meetings, he sat cross-legged, eyes staring at the floor. It looked like he was listening very carefully, but I couldn't see how the information was hitting him. In general, he was composed, competent, unremarkable: that kind of person who was likely to go through life never making a particularly big stir. In the world we'd left, he would have grown up to be that guy who'd do his job, get his paycheck, receive a minimum raise each year like clockwork. How that personality would translate into our new reality was a complete unknown. Maybe he'd just keep tick-tocking along. Or maybe he'd wig out.

Willow, the barefoot scientist, just listened to the captain while her eyes grew shiny and even bigger than they usually were. And then, in a few minutes, she was back to normal. Willow is like that. She's one of those people who not only marches to the beat of a different drum, but doesn't seem to hear or care about the dominant rhythm. She had become the most popular person on the boat because she clearly didn't care about popularity and was always friendly to everyone. Willow's default expression is a big, toothy smile with absolutely no agenda behind it. She knows what she wants, focuses on that, and is happy to encounter whoever and whatever else shows up along the way. Hell, she was the only one of us that really wanted to be on *Voyager.* So far, she had spent all her time studying fish, or studying books on the ecosystems of the Falklands and South Georgia like they were the coolest things on the planet. That she had now promptly grieved for the loss of all the people on that planet—and then, was ready to get down to business—was pure Willow. I suddenly wished I had spent more time getting to know her and not discount her as a weirdo flower-child.

The last crewmember is Lice. Which is short for Alice, but she spends so much time scratching at the dark brown rat's nest on her head that I had almost forgotten her real name. Lice is how she introduced herself, and she seems to take pride in that, along with the other weird behaviors and clothes that kind of make her emo and punk at the same time. Unfortunately, that combo means she never tells you—or even shows you—what she really thinks. She rolls her eyes at everything. Especially anything that involves her parents. I figured the odds were equal that she'd feel personally liberated by the death of the world, that she'd fold in even more, or just wouldn't care.

We sat there for at least half a minute, staring at the deck and sneaking glances at each other, before Steve observed, "So, this is pretty much like *The Walking Dead*."

The captain, whose English accent was becoming more pronounced all the time, closed his eyes patiently, started with, "Now don't be daft. The infected haven't died. They're just—"

Blake jumped up. "Don't shit us, man. Don't shit us. It's like Steve says. Whether they're dead or not, we *are* in the middle of *The Walking Dead*. Wherever we get off this boat, they're going to be there, waiting for us. Ready to eat us. Probably won't have had any fresh meat in weeks or—"

The captain had never touched any of us, for any reason, until that moment. He grabbed Blake by the arm and pulled him off the deck. "Leave off," he snapped. "This isn't a bloody TV fantasy. This is real. If you kill the infected, they stay dead. And the rest can't roam around forever. We can ride this out. And we won't be the only ones. There's no end of ships that might have—"

"Captain," said Willow.

"Damn it—what?"

"Alice is gone."

When no one was looking, she had just gone to the side and climbed over.

Using the engine for the first time in weeks, it took less than three minutes to get to her. Even so, she was damn near frozen by the time we did.

## July 24

I've wanted to write in this journal for a while now, but we've been short-handed. It's been so busy that I just fall asleep as soon as I hit my bunk.

Lice only got back to work today. Captain kept her below deck since we fished her out of the ocean four days ago, shaking through the borderline hypothermia before she finally went limp as a rag. Since then she hasn't done much of anything except stare at the bulkhead in her cabin. She eats, drinks, follows simple instructions (which is a change for the better, actually), but that's it. He never said it, but it's pretty obvious that this was the closest thing to a suicide watch that the captain could manage on a small working ship like *Crosscurrent Voyager*. It's hard to tell if Lice is really any better—she was never much of a talker—but now she's gone mute and there's a lot of work to do.

Part of that increased labor is because of the captain himself: he seems even more gaunt, if that's possible, and I think he's getting weaker. What I do know is that he spends more time catching his breath and talking us through increasingly complicated sailing maneuvers and skills rather than showing us by example.

I don't know if the others have noticed it yet. Everyone except Willow has burrowed into themselves since we learned of what Rod has dubbed The Walking Non-Dead. We had just started to really work together as a team when the apocalyptic shit hit the fan and short-circuited whatever bonds were growing between us. Besides, the days down here are grey and quiet, and with the southern hemisphere's winter deepening, the high seas and the constant cold don't put anyone in a particularly cheery mood.

It was getting on toward dinner when I dropped by the pilot house, nodded at the captain, glanced at the charts. What I saw there made me check again.

The captain looked away.

"Captain, aren't we going to the Falklands?"

"Why do you ask?"

"Because if we wanted to get to Port Stanley, we should have pulled up out of the Antarctic circumpolar current." I eyeballed the map more closely. "At least a day ago. Sir."

"Two days," he corrected. "You read a chart passably well."

I laid my hand upon the wheel. I suppressed the wild vision of heeling us over to port, regardless of the wind, and heading north toward the Falklands, the equator, to anywhere other than the endless grey peaks and troughs of the winter waves. "Sir, what are we doing?"

"Making for South Georgia Island."

"But that's—"

"—over a thousand miles away across open ocean. Yes. I'm surprised you didn't suss it out sooner, while you were playing teacher with Chloe in here."

The derisive tone he'd slipped into when he said "playing teacher with Chloe" was like a slap in the face. The captain wasn't a warm man, but he was never sarcastic—or hadn't been until now. "Not much of our work is in navigation anymore, sir. Mostly reading and writing."

My tone was stiff enough to make him look up. When he did, his eyes were angry, but as I met them, his glare thawed into something like sadness. "I was a right pillock just now, Alvaro. Don't mind me. You've done a fine job helping Chloe." He looked out at the next high swell the *Voyager* would have to climb.

I nodded. "Why are we skipping Port Stanley, sir?"

"Because the Falklands have gone completely off the air. There were three different radio operators there in the past week, out in smaller towns and coves. Each one started out by sending distress signals but ended by going mad as a hatter. And now, dead air for the last forty-eight hours. Not even a carrier wave. They're done."

I scanned along the revised course he had plotted. "So, King Edward Point?"

The captain rubbed his lower lip. "Maybe. I hope so. Depends upon whether the last supply run by the *Pharos* included infected crewpersons or not. If not, then—well, we'll see. The staff at King Edward Point may not be as welcoming as we'd like."

"You mean, they might think *we're* carrying the virus?"

He looked out over the waves again. "They shouldn't. They're a research outpost, so they should have heard and understood what I have: that the asymptomatic contagion phase is, at most, about a week and a half. We haven't met up with anyone since leaving the Galapagos in early June, so there shouldn't be any worry that we're a plague ship. But I know some of the personalities at King Edward Point. They might have a different—perception of their duty, in these circumstances." Still looking out over the waves, he moved his body so that his back was facing me.

I wanted to ask what different sense of duty might prevail at King Edward Point, and how he had such detailed knowledge of its staff, but his body language told me that, for now, our conversation had ended.

I went below to help Chloe cook dinner. She isn't a half-bad cook, but, like all the rest, her taste buds run toward white-bread bland. I'm the guy who has to sneak in a little adobo, recaito, or just a dash of cayenne and cumin when no one else is looking.

And then they wonder why it tastes better.

## August 5

We had following seas and the wind astern all the way to South Georgia Island. That was a good, but not great, combo. The wind coming from directly behind meant we had to tack a bit, which, all told, probably cost us an extra day. But the seas became calmer as we edged a bit north, and the grey line of clouds to the south receded. From the Galapagos onward, the captain had warned us that this could be the roughest part of the voyage. But once we were hugging Tierra del Fuego, he added the caveat that the weather and seas had remained mild this year. Which made all of us pretty glad that we weren't going through in typical weather, because it was still plenty rough and the water was cold enough to kill you in a few minutes if you went overboard.

South Georgia Island's glacial peaks popped over the horizon just as the light was starting to dim. I eyeballed the distance, added the time it would take to hook around the south end of the island and swing up along the eastern coast. "We could just make it."

The captain locked off the wheel, stepped down from the helmsman's platform and opened the pilot house's starboard door. "Reef the main." By the time the door was swinging closed, Chloe had gone forward, Rod had started securing the boom, and Willow had gone below to get two of the others on deck to secure the canvas with bungee cords.

Our speed began dropping, and the *Voyager* heeled a little less. We were obviously not trying for King Edward Point by nightfall. "Risky navigating Cumberland Bay at dusk?" I guessed.

"Daylight is better," is all he said.

He didn't speak for the rest of the night. Which, at the outset of our journey, wouldn't have been too unusual. But ever since we had pulled beyond Tierra del Fuego, the captain had become slightly more talkative, even if he hadn't become more personally communicative. Instead, he reviewed our seamanship in greater detail and started drilling us on all the features of the *Voyager*—and I mean all of them.

But this night, as soon as dinner was done, he simply set the watches and went aft to his cabin without another word. That excited some speculation among the others, which kept them busy until midnight.

I just went to my bunk, wrote this, and wondered if we'll learn tomorrow why he became so quiet tonight.

## August 6 (first entry)

As we approached the entrance to Cumberland Bay, the captain jutted his bony chin to the north. "That further gap in the shoreline. That's the mouth of Stromness Bay. Remember it."

I didn't even need to hear his tone anymore to know that he was not going to tell me why I needed to remember it. Instead, I turned us half a point to port and made sure we didn't need to adjust the rig too much. The foresail swelled slightly; *Voyager* pushed through the water more briskly.

Almost everyone was on deck: captain's orders. Most of them were gawking at the towering, snow-blanketed mountain ridge that seemed to fly up out of the water to north/starboard. As we followed that granite-toothed wall southward, I leaned forward over the wheel, craning my neck to get a look at the very top of it, if I could.

The captain shifted in his seat. "Just over thirteen hundred feet at the highest." He stared at the sails, particularly the telltales that fluttered along their edge. "We'll reach the station in eight minutes. Up ahead, where the mountain sweeps away to starboard, follow its curve. The station is right there." He reached up, threw the test switch for the boat horn; it glowed green.

I glanced at it.

"You eager to toot the horn?" he asked.

I shook my head. "No, sir. Just wondering."

"What?"

"Why you intend to announce us ahead of time. If the station has been infected—"

"Then that's all the more reason to sound the horn. Infected or not, I want to see who—or what—comes out to greet us before we approach the dock too closely. And if they're still uninfected, I want them to get a good look at us. That way, everyone is less likely to do anything stupid."

Which made good enough sense to me.

Captain sounded the horn. One short blast, one long.

A few flakes were starting to drift down when we made our long, slow starboard turn, speed dropping as we pulled into the lee of the mountain and I got my first glimpse of King Edward Point. It was larger than I'd imagined. The first building I saw was damn close to a hundred yards long, paralleling the water: the doors looked like it was a combination warehouse and operations site. It, and most of the others, were white with red roofs, all lined up along the edge of a small, flat spur that stuck out from the side of the mountain. It took some careful sailing to swing sharply again to starboard and come up alongside the deep-water mooring at the end of the short concrete pier on the far western side of the base.

Three figures, wearing surprisingly light down jackets, were waiting for us, hands in their pockets.

One of them stepped forward, looked up at the pilot house as the captain stepped out. "Took a chance coming here, you did, Alan."

"Alan" nodded. "Everywhere is chancy now, Larry."

The other nodded back. "True enough. Where was your last landfall?"

"Galapagos."

The man on the shore scanned us kids. "That's your crew?"

"It is. They are fair enough hands. Now."

"Yanks, all?"

"Every one."

The man shrugged. "Well, you might as well make fast and come in for a cuppa."

And that was our dramatic arrival at King Edward Point, or KEP, as the folks here call it.

## August 6 (second entry)

I had to stop writing because there is some serious shit going down. I thought everyone was done for the day, after catching a drink together in the pub—well, the room the station team has decorated to look like one. But then I heard the captain slip back out of the house where they've put us up. So I slipped off my bed and crept out the door after him, toward the outbuildings and the pier.

Okay, I just read what I wrote, and realized it won't make any sense to anyone else who might read this. Hell, if I read it a few months or years from now, it might not even make sense to me.

Once we'd made the *Voyager* fast at the end of the pier, we started a walking tour of the station. But the captain missed a step when he heard there were only nine staff at KEP. "Who's missing?" he asked.

The man who'd spoken to us before—Lawrence Keywood, the station leader—shrugged, "Robertson."

"The Government Officer? Why?"

Keywood shrugged. "He has family on the Falklands, so when the comms from Port Stanley started getting odd, he packed up and left on *Pharos*. That was six weeks ago." He sighed; the snow crunched under foot. "I told him that, to my mind, he was heading the wrong way. But it was his family. He had to try."

"You never heard from him?"

"No. About four days after *Pharos* left, the Commissioner's Office sent a coded general directive over the emergency frequency. No further transmissions from any settlements or bases other than their own station at Port Stanley."

Our captain just nodded. It was Willow who asked, "Why?"

Keywood tried to act like her uncle and did a lousy job; he'd watched too much Masterpiece Theater, I guess. "My dear girl, they did not say."

Captain looked sideways at the station leader with the same expression he had used back when we were still making beginners' mistakes at sailing. "They need the facts, Larry."

"Larry" got flustered, then annoyed. "The fact, Alan, is that Port Stanley did not say why we were to stop transmitting."

"They didn't have to say. You knew."

Willow looked at the captain. She was getting more, not less confused. "He knew what?"

"That Port Stanley was trying to protect the other communities, keep them from pointing to themselves with radio transmissions." When the captain saw that half of our group still didn't get it, he threw a long, bony hand back in the direction of South America. "Plagues breed pirates, bandits. Not the kind who are after money, but who are after resources. And any place operating a radio is a target for them. It's a place where the infected haven't overrun everything, a place they might not have found. Nothing is worth more than that, right now."

Keywood nodded. "That's the gist of it. There's always a few veterans in every dodgy lot, and they're likely to recognize our call signs, and figure out that this plague might not have reached us. And as the bodies pile up around them, there will be little to stop them from grabbing a ship and seeing for themselves. That's why we didn't answer your transmissions, Alan. Orders. And we couldn't take the chance of encouraging them."

The captain seemed to be sucking at something caught in his teeth. "Won't help, you know."

"Now, Alan—"

"Don't try to cod me, Keywood. I know this part of the world. I know how many fishing boats come to these waters from Argentina, Chile, even Brazil. They won't forget about KEP just because you go off the air." The captain stopped as we drew abreast of the long warehouse. "There's one inhabited spot on this whole bloody island: right here. And a thousand miles of frigid water and dodgy weather protect it from plagues better than the *Ark Royal* and Royal Marines could do."

"Are you saying that pirates are *sure* to come here?" Blake sounded like he might wet his pants.

"I'm saying that there are thousands of people who work the fishing boats, and who served in the various navies of South America, and that there won't be anyone or anything to stop them from commandeering a trawler, or some naval auxiliary. They all know how to run a ship, know of KEP's existence, and won't be shy about travelling to South Georgia Island. So we have to be ready to defend ourselves." He looked around. "And from what I can tell, Keywood, you haven't given much thought to that."

Larry bristled. "In fact, I've given it a great deal of thought. But unlike you, I'm not in a rush to arm ourselves with boat hooks and knives against pirates who will probably be carrying assault rifles that used to belong to the police or army. I know a losing fight when I see one, Alan. We need to consider a different approach."

The captain rarely sneered, probably because it required too much facial flexibility. But he did now. "There's only one approach that works against raiders, Keywood, and it does not involve negotiation or barter."

Keywood shook his head. "You never change, Alan. It's been— what? thirty years?—and you're still trying to re-fight that bloody war against anybody who'll give you cause. Well, come on, then; we won't settle this here and you need to have a look at what we've done."

As we walked, my understanding of the captain was undergoing a major change. Specifically, there was only one war that had ever involved this part of the world since World War II, and that was the 1982 Falklands War. So that had to be the war that Keywood was referring to. Which meant that the captain had probably been sailing here, on and off, since then. That's why he seemed to know everyone at the station, as well as the staff who'd been here before, often many years earlier. And probably why he had some of the skills he had.

Keywood showed us the station's boats, snowmobiles, warehouses, droned through what he called an abbreviated list of their stores. Then it was time for a tour of their dinky clinic and office space, and lastly, the housing for the summer staff, which was where they told us to crash.

At lunch, we met the rest of Keywood's team. They are pretty evenly split between folks who are here to handle practical operations and those who are here to conduct scientific and environmental monitoring. There's one fisheries scientist, one zoological field assistant (she's all about seals and penguins), two boating officers, one electrician, one mechanic, and a station operations manager whose only job seems to be making sure that Keywood's orders get carried out.

After lunch, Keywood took us out again to show us all the booby traps we'd missed—and that had been right under our noses—at various key storage points and even next to the clinic. Most were cans of fuel with homemade electric igniters, all slaved to the same activation switch. The captain was unsurprised; it was pretty clear he'd seen them all the first time.

Giselle, standing in the middle of the largest warehouse space after being shown the fourth booby trap there, turned through a full three hundred sixty degrees, eyes wide. "Why?"

Captain got his reply in before Keywood; his first two words were as sharp as thunder claps. "Larry *thinks*," he began, "that these booby traps will deter the raiders. That once they learn that all the supplies will be destroyed if they misbehave, then they will be keen to cut a deal. Which is rubbish."

Keywood glowered. "Of course you'd say that. Anything to ensure that there's more shooting. Except our side doesn't have any guns."

"Piss off, Larry. You're being soft-headed about who you'll be dealing with. And you've got at least one scoped rifle. Left from the elk eradications, just in case any survivors are sighted."

Keywood's eyes widened for a moment—at the captain catching him in his lie, not at the insulting tone—then he put his hands on his hips and his brow came down. "And just what are we going to do with one rifle, Alan, if, as you think, we'll be dealing with a shipload of pirates? Get ourselves all killed, is what. So forgive me if I plan to control them by controlling access to what they really want: our goods."

The captain barked out a hoarse scoff. "Right. Because they're going to pull up to the pier like we did and announce their intentions. So that you, in turn, can tell them that you have all your supplies rigged. Two little problems with that plan, Larry. Small one first: they know you can't get along without those supplies. So yes, they want what you've got—but they're also not so dim to overlook that the same bomb that will destroy what they want will destroy you, too. And they'll bet that not all of you will have the nerve to commit suicide rather than try to cut a deal—a deal that sells out the rest of you.

"But here's the bigger problem. Unless they are all potty, they're not going to announce their arrival by steaming up to the pier, as bold as you please. Some of them will know the lay of the land here. They'll send a small group ashore to take a dekko at the grounds and maybe nick whoever's out on guard or taking a pee. And so they'll learn about the booby traps, because they won't stop at waterboarding captives, of that you can be sure. And how brassed will your lot be when the pirates finally come ashore at the pier, all armed with rifles, and hand you a bag of your mate's fingers?"

Keywood put up his chin, but his voice was shaky. "And if we refuse to cooperate?"

Alan's smile was mirthless. "Why, they'll just climb back in their boat, and tell you to think it over, because they'll be back in a few hours with a few more fingers—or maybe an even more interesting extremity. Because they know that your team will tear itself to pieces over what to do next and that not all of you will be made of stern enough stuff to hold to the course you've set. Why, they might bring your fingerless mate to shore and, waving around a pair of bolt-cutters, tell you that they're going to start removing more pieces at a steady rate—which you can stop any time. Any time one of you is willing to show them around to disarm the booby traps, that is. And someone will. You know that, Larry. Your crew are compassionate, good people. Too good to play out the kind of game to which you're committing them."

Keywood had grown very red. "You talk this tripe in front of my people, Alan, and I'll—"

"You'll what? What will you do to me, Larry? What *can* you do?"

Keywood folded his arms. "Don't make this more difficult than it has to be, Alan."

"I'm still waiting to hear how *you're* going to make it difficult for me and mine. It's you who have a hard road ahead, unless you face facts."

"We have faced facts. And the facts are that we do not have the training, or the weapons, to fight back."

"Not as you are, no. And not from this location."

"What are you talking about?"

The captain took a half step toward Keywood; it looked like

a prelude to a plea, rather than a threat. "Anyone coming out here will know where KEP is, but they won't have gone to the other bays. They won't know to look for us at—"

Keywood stepped back. "No. That's madness. This is the only facility big enough to hold us. And we could never move enough of the stores in time. Besides, this is about you and that bloody glacier again. What is it, Alan? A death wish of some kind?"

"I don't give a tinker's damn about the glacier. I'm talking about Husvik."

Keywood shook his head. "Totally daft. We'd be cheek by jowl in the manager's house and we've got no way to store everything there."

"Not everything, no, but enough, and they'll never look for us there. Besides, if they did, they'd be on unfamiliar ground in a very dodgy environment."

Keywood began walking back to the main house. "I won't say more and embarrass you in front of these—in front of your crew, Alan. But this conversation is ended."

When Keywood had walked away, we all looked at the captain. He didn't look back; he just nodded at the door. "You'll want to follow the station leader. Get a cup of tea or broth. Go."

The others filed out.

He glanced sideways at me. "You deaf?"

I shook my head. "What's Husvik, Captain?"

"None of your look-out," he snapped. He started toward the doors, turned to mutter over his shoulder. "Not yet. Now don't diddle about; let's warm our feet indoors."

Tea turned into early dinner. I think Keywood and his operations manager, Lewis, were trying to bring the day to a quick end. I could understand why; every attempt to start a harmless conversation took a wrong turn.

For instance, while we were picking at some canned—they called it "tinned"—meat, the captain tried to make (what sounded like) small talk. "So, no more elk after the fifty you bagged last season?"

Lewis shrugged. "We haven't seen any more, but we found some of their scat. So however good a job the hunters did, it is certainly not complete. They'll have to come back."

The captain stopped eating. "Come back? The hunters?"

Lewis nodded. "Yes. I suppose it could be a while, of course.

A while before anyone is thinking about such things, even once the plague has passed. But we've left the hunters' weather sheds out there. For when they return."

And I thought, *"What planet are you living on?"*

The captain was more discreet. "So you're still following your environmental mission?"

Lewis shrugged. "Have to. Last orders from Port Stanley."

Keywood shifted uneasily in his seat. The captain glanced at him, then looked back at Lewis. "The last orders you got from Port Stanley were that you should still be conducting elk surveys and your other... other scientific tasks?"

"Well, yes. In a manner of speaking." Lewis shrugged. "I didn't hear the message, of course. That was Larry and Simms." He jerked a finger back at the electrician. "The acting commissioner told us to 'carry on.' So that's what we'll do." Lewis' lips smiled and his eyes were wide. They didn't blink. That's when I realized that he had gone quietly and totally nuts.

Rodney had stopped eating, and before either Chloe or Giselle could stop him, he blurted out what all of us were wondering. "Don't you know what's going on back in the world?"

Lewis blinked, the right eye a little slower than the left. "I've—I've heard enough. Larry keeps us up to date. It's a bad business, right enough, but they'll get the measure of this bug. We're just lucky to be here."

No one was looking at Lewis by the time he finished; we were all looking at Keywood. Chloe's face had darkened; she started leaning across the table.

The captain leaned in first, preempting her. "So, you oversee all the radio traffic."

Keywood kept a pleasant smile on his face, but his jaw set. "Simms and I, yes, we did." He nodded toward the electrician, who nodded back but kept his eyes on us. "Back when there was any traffic to monitor."

I remembered when we drifted past the radio room as part of our walking tour; all the lights were off. Keywood had said they were just saving power and wear and tear on the equipment. Now I wondered if that was the case, and how long it had been since the radio had been turned on.

Chloe wasn't wondering; she was standing up. "Haven't you told them—?"

"They know how bad things are," Keywood interrupted. I managed not to shout "liar!" "We just didn't need to hear the same sad reports, over and over."

The captain turned his ghoul-gaze on Chloe. She sat down again, out of respect for, not fear of, him.

And now I understood why Keywood wanted to hurry the day to a close. If he didn't, then whatever we kids knew about how bad things were in the world might get revealed and his team might wig out. Some of them already looked close to that point. The seal and penguin expert—Diana Paley—had started leaning close against the electrician Simms, her eyes frightened, bracketed by crows-foot crinkles. Simms put an arm around her, looked daggers at Chloe and the rest of us. And then I understood something else: Simms had already looked into the abyss and seen their death. The death of the whole world. He had accepted that fate. So he was just trying to take care of Diana until the final curtain fell, to keep her from having to face the reality he had.

The captain had noticed the same thing. He released one of his mouse-sized sighs. "Thank you for the meal. Nice change from fish."

"You out of supplies already?" Keywood sounded surprised, maybe worried.

"No, just supplementing them with catch. Make them last longer." He rose. "Time for us to get some kip. First time we've bunked on dry land in months."

We all heard the cue—even Johnnie—got up, and filed out. As we did, Keywood called after the captain, "Have a dram, in a bit?"

The captain just nodded, shrugged into his coat as we prepared to brave the short walk to our rooms. Once outside, we discovered it was already below freezing.

"Captain," started Giselle.

"No questions. Not tonight. In the morning. Before breakfast."

We walked through the dark and the snow, which swallowed up the sound of our footsteps and everything else.

It really did feel like we were the last people on Earth.

When we got to our rooms—with real beds, not bunks!—I didn't even take off my clothes: I just dropped down on the blanket and started today's first journal entry. Then, about fifteen minutes later, I heard soft footsteps in the corridor. Since my room was closest to the outside door, it meant that someone either wanted to sneak in on me or was about to leave the barracks. But I didn't hear the door to the outside open. Nor did anyone knock on my door or try the knob.

So I waited. Almost certainly, it was the captain, going back to the main house for his "dram." I was pretty sure that meant whiskey; I heard it in an English movie, once. I popped my head out into the corridor. No one. But there were boot prints on the floor; big ones. Yup; that was the captain all right. But how the hell had he gone past making less sound than a kid in fluffy slippers, to say nothing of opening and shutting the door? Serious ninja skills.

Serious enough for me to realize that if he had the skills to get out of the barracks without making a sound, he probably also had the skills to wait to see if anyone was trailing him. So I waited for two minutes that felt like an hour. Then I slipped my coat back on and followed him.

Of course, he was gone by the time I poked my head out into the cold—and I mean *cold*—but mad ninja moves or not, he couldn't keep from leaving tracks in the snow, and there was just enough light to make them out.

I followed them back to the main house. I was just realizing that I didn't have any way to get inside without attracting the attention of everyone in their "pub" when the door opened. I tucked back around the near corner of the main house, heard low voices: the captain and Keywood. Feet crunched in the snow, heading toward the opposite/western corner of the house. Just before they moved out of hearing, I stepped out and followed them.

I kept my distance, not wanting to wind up on the captain's ninja radar. He and Keywood ultimately slipped into the marine stores shed, just a little bit east of the boathouse that fronted on the pier. I went around to the rear of the huge "shed" and eased open the back door.

I had missed the opening part of the conversation, but I had no trouble picking up the topic.

"—so I don't want to have to pull rank, Alan, but this time, you can't make your decision as a free agent."

"You don't have enough rank to pull, Larry. I'm still in the reserves and since I am the only military authority in the area, I am activating myself. Which leaves us at an impasse. If I'm being charitable."

"What do you mean?"

"Well, you haven't shared all of what you heard from Port Stanley, but I'd be gobsmacked if the commissioner didn't declare martial law before he went 'round the bend. Hell, the old girl back in Buckingham might have sent that word herself, for the whole of the UK and its territories. In which case, I rank *you*, Larry."

Keywood was silent for a long moment. "As you say, we seem to be at an impasse. But I can't have you corking off about the state of things out there, any more than I can allow you to fill my team's heads with any of this Husvik nonsense."

"It's not nonsense, Larry."

"No? There's a month of winter left. Don't know what you plan to do for heat. You can't have much food left, and I'm not giving you any of our supplies. Might as well throw them in the bay."

"We'll be fine, Larry. But we won't be at Husvik now, so if you and your lot are still alive come spring, don't bother to look for us there."

"So where will you be, then?"

"As if I'd tell you, now."

"You won't tell me? Why not?"

The captain paused for a moment. Then: "When your visitors from the mainland arrive and you find yourself taped to a chair with one of your snowmobiles' batteries wired to your balls, you'll understand why I wouldn't tell you."

"Damn it, Alan, that's paranoid. The odds are *at least* even that there won't be any raiders willing to come across a thousand miles of winter ocean. In which case, you and those poor young people will all have died for nothing." Keywood paused; he may have stepped closer. "Come on, Alan: give it up. She didn't die because of you, and those helicopters weren't your fault. It's time to let that go and stay with us. We have plenty of beds here, plenty of supplies. And come spring, you can—"

"Come spring, anyone who stays here will be dead. It's a bloody miracle that a boatload of cutthroats hasn't already arrived from Buenos Aires or Montevideo or some Brazilian pest hole to winter over here and wait out the plague. And your own people know it. Just look at Lewis. He's barking mad, he is. Playing at the old stiff upper lip until things return to normal. Which they never will. And you know it."

"Of course I know it. But what would you have me do? For now, that belief is all that keeps them going."

"That's total shite, Larry. Deep down, they know that the world is gone. But they'll deny it to each other and themselves as long as you let them ignore the facts. Right up until the Argies come steaming in and your plan for holding them at arm's length goes fatally pear-shaped. But you've decided to believe your own lies, so this is pointless."

It sounded like the captain was preparing to leave. Keywood's voice was urgent. "Very well; so we can't agree. But I need to know: what do you mean to do?"

The captain paused for a few very long seconds. "Tomorrow, I am going to wake my lot—my crew—up early and tell them they have a choice: stay here or come with me. I will not minimize the hardships they can expect if they come with me. I don't want any hangers-on who aren't fully committed to pulling their own weight. They'll have about an hour to think it over. They'll tell us what they've decided to do right after breakfast. Fair enough?"

"Damn it, you owe them better than that, Alan. If you want to go out into the wilds, to do battle with whatever guilt and demons have been inside you since Paraquet, that's your affair, your life to lose. But not theirs. They deserve to have a reasonable chance at survival."

"And that's precisely what I'm offering them. Goodbye, Larry. Don't come looking if you change your mind. You won't find us."

The captain started moving again. I slipped out the back door, tried to make a stealthy getaway and then realized I was totally busted: I'd left footprints in the snow, too.

So I just ran like hell back to the barracks.

## August 7

As always, the captain was as good as his word. Got us all up before there was a glow in the east. Sat us down in the commons room and spelled out the choices: stay at KEP or go with him to some other place on South Georgia where we'd have limited shelter, have to get our own food, and we'd likely have to use up the last of the boat's fuel for generating heat. We couldn't live on the boat because it was too dangerous: it wasn't likely in the last month of winter, but if the shallows froze up, it could be trapped, or even crushed—and us in it.

It was a pretty bleak picture he painted, and while he painted it, he kept looking over at me. Probably wondered if I was going to say anything about what I'd heard the prior night. But I'd learned this much: when the captain was in his "commander-in-chief" mode, you didn't speak unless asked to do so. So I didn't.

When he finished, he asked if there were questions. Giselle nodded, leaned forward. "What about this place you spoke about with Mr. Keywood—Husvik, I think? Are we going there?"

The captain folded his hands. "I told Mr. Keywood that I have rethought that decision, and that we are not going to Husvik. If someone comes here and tortures him for information, he could have pointed them at us. Any other questions?"

There weren't any. He looked at me again—a long, hard look—and then stood up. "Breakfast in an hour. Don't be late."

We weren't. Breakfast was served promptly. Barely a word was spoken. When we'd all sipped down the last of our tea, the captain pushed back from the table. "I spoke to my crew about an hour and a half ago. They know the choice they have to make."

He looked around the ring of faces in the room. "If anyone is worried that my presence will exert undue influence, I shall step out." He looked squarely at Keywood when he said it.

The station leader pouted, as if considering, then shook his head. "Not necessary. I believe these young people know what is at stake and will speak their minds." He looked at me. "Mr. Casillas, what do you—?"

I didn't even let him finish. "I'm going with the captain." Chloe, who was sitting across the table from me, blinked, then frowned.

Keywood nodded. "I understand. Your respect for Lieutenant Haskins is obvious, and he—"

"Mr. Keywood, I do respect the cap—er, Lieutenant Haskins. But that's not why I'm going with him. I just think he's right. On the way down here, I heard some of what was on the radio. People were getting desperate. Crazy desperate. Maybe no one will think to come all the way to South Georgia Island. But I kind of doubt that. And if they make the trip, they're going to come right here to King Edward Point." I leaned back, crossed my arms. "So right here is where I *don't* want to be."

Keywood frowned, then shrugged and went on around the table. Rod and Giselle answered as a couple: they were sticking with the captain, but they didn't elaborate. Willow said the same. Johnnie just smiled at her and said, "Me, too." Steve shrugged, then nodded.

It was Lice's turn next. She was looking down in her lap and was very pale, even for her. Keywood was about to ask again when she very slowly shook her head.

"So, you don't want to go?" Keywood asked.

"No," Lice whispered. "I don't want to go."

Giselle leaned across the table, reached out her hand. Lice just shook her head again.

I have to admit I wasn't surprised. Ever since we pulled Lice out of the water, she avoided group talks, particularly those which focused on our future. Sometimes, when we were on deck, I'd see her looking at the water and I couldn't help suspecting that she regretted not having the courage to take a lungful before we got to her. And in just the last twenty-four hours, she'd kind of detached from us. She'd spent most of her time hanging around the station team, who had reached out to her like they were trying to tempt a lost kitten to jump into their car. And now she had.

Blake stared at her, stunned. The two of them had only one thing in common—they trash-talked their parents nonstop—but, at this moment, I'm pretty sure it was their need for parents that motivated them. Staying with the station team meant staying with surrogate moms and dads in a nice, cozy environment. Blake's mouth opened, but no sound came out. With a helpless look on his face, he turned toward Chloe.

Who, I discovered, was looking straight at me. But "looking" isn't the right word. It was like she was dissecting me with her eyes. I couldn't tell if that was a good thing, a bad thing, or a bit of both.

I shrugged, and I guess I smiled as I did it. "Hey, somebody's gotta keep calling me *pequeño* behind my back."

Her face changed really fast; I thought she was on the verge of either laughing or getting angry. But instead, she took a deep breath, got really calm, and looked at Keywood. "I'm going with them."

"Me, too." Blake exhaled. He sounded simultaneously relieved and desperate.

"Well, that settles it," Keywood said through a long sigh. "If you change your minds, you know where to find us. But getting back here might be rather difficult." That was an insane understatement: without *Voyager*, return was absolutely impossible until late spring.

The captain stood; we did too. Except Lice. "Alice," he said, "I promised I wouldn't try to talk anyone out of their decision. But we're leaving directly. Be sure this is what you want."

Lice either nodded, convulsed her way through a few silent sobs, or both; she was hunched over so far, I couldn't see her face.

The captain walked around the table and placed a very gentle hand on the back of her head. "I'm sorry, Alice-girl," he almost whispered, "I'll miss you."

The rest of us murmured something similar and filed out after him.

Last to leave, I looked back: Lice was almost doubled over now and was shaking: whether from tears or terror, I could not tell.

## August 8

About half of the crew stood at the stern, watching King Edward Point dwindle in the distance. I wasn't among them. I was at the wheel on the weather deck and was glad to be there.

Despite everything that had happened, this was the moment when it all grabbed me by the balls. Knowing that the world was going down the toilet faster and faster, realizing I'd never see my mom again, learning more practical skills in a few weeks than I'd learned in my whole life, finding myself having to make a life-and-death choice more serious than most adults ever had to: somehow, each of those felt like steps toward the edge of a cliff. But now, I had stepped off and was free-falling into uncertainty. KEP was the last vestige of the old world, and I'd left it. This—whatever was before me—was all that was left. I was so terrified and so aware of being alive that I shook. No, I didn't want to watch King Edward Point drop behind us: for me, it was already gone.

Getting out of East Cumberland Bay was a dull job. The wind from the east that had brought us in yesterday was now in our faces, so I had to tack my way up to where the east bay met the west bay and then slip out into open water. Once there, we had the wind almost directly athwart the beam, so we picked up speed. We stuck close to the coast, though; the captain was aiming for Stromness Bay by 2 PM, at which point we would only have a few hours of light left.

Lunch was cold fish, which probably had more than a few of us wondering if we couldn't have stolen some food from the warehouse at KEP before leaving. Snow started as we angled into Stromness Bay. The captain got out a pair of binoculars and started scanning the shore.

"What are you looking for?" I asked.

"Seal. Elephant, but fur would do. Penguins. Seabirds."

Willow heard this, came bouncing away from the sheets. "Oooo! Can I see?"

"When there is something to see, yes," the captain muttered. "But I'm not sure you'll want to make too close an acquaintance with any of the animals."

"Captain, I came here to *study* those species!"

"Ironic. Now you'll be eating them."

"Sir?"

The captain's jaw set. "You're a very smart young lady. I have to believe you've figured it out by now. We need more food, and we don't have a net to fish with or enough fuel to trail one. And we can't live on fish forever. On the other hand, the animals here are completely without fear of humans. If we take only outliers, and take them quickly, we shouldn't even scare the others off."

Instead of recoiling, Willow seemed to lean forward into his words. At the end she nodded. "That's true: we'll need some red meat. So, we'll have to hunt seal. But what about greens?"

The captain nodded, probably more in approval of her rapid shift to practicality than anything she had said. "That's the tough part. That's why I haven't let you young marauders near the power bars and why I've locked up the vitamins along with the meds. We'll have to supplement very carefully. There is some edible—*marginally* edible—seaweed to be had, but remember: no one planted a colony here because you can't survive on the local foodstuffs alone."

Willow looked along the coast. "So: seals. We're looking for beaches, then. Particularly any that run back into valleys or grassy gaps. They always like a little extra room to waddle."

The captain looked at her like he'd found a one hundred dollar bill on the pavement. "So, you really have studied South Georgia's wildlife."

"Ever since I knew I was going to come down here." Her smile dimmed. "Although I think my plans to become a marine biologist are pretty much over."

Captain shook his head. "Maybe, but I suspect that knowledge will benefit more people than it would have before. Not many persons know the habits of these creatures. You do. And we have to be able to hunt them effectively. Starting tomorrow."

Willow sighed. "Okay. Tell me when your eyes need a rest."

I caught him smiling as she returned to her position near the mainsail. He caught my eye. "A *good* pilot only watches the swells and the tell-tales," he muttered.

"I'm doing so, sir. Question, though."

"Ask."

"How do you plan to hunt elephant seals, sir? I'm pretty sure I recall reading that the males average close to fifteen feet long and weigh in at over three tons."

By way of answer, he stalked past me, walking as easily and steadily as if he was crossing his living room, despite the swells. He went down the companionway, but emerged from it less than thirty seconds later. In his right hand he held a long, smooth-looking rifle with a big, squarish magazine protruding out from under it. "Ever fire one of these?"

"No, sir," I answered. Which was a true statement whether he meant that particular rifle or any gun at all. Hey, I grew up in New York City and L.A. Not a lot of legal opportunities.

But Chloe must have been staring back in our direction because she comes flying back from the bow, her lips wide, and her deck-coat flapping. I swear, you could dress her in three layers of shag carpet and you'd *still* know she was a woman.

The captain looks up, sees her rushing over, frowns, then almost smiles again when he realizes her eyes are locked on the gun.

"A FAL, right? .308. Well, 7.62 NATO. Great gun for deer, even elk or bear if you've got some distance and a brass set."

The captain did not have a wide range of emotions that he displayed. I think this was his version of being "charmed." "You've fired one?"

"Damn, I wish! Uh...sir. But a neighbor had one, and we used to hunt together sometimes. But that was, uh...a while ago." She looked away as she said it, and then quickly up at me. Don't ask me why, but judging from that look, I suspect that as Chloe had come closer to womanhood, her neighbor's choice of prey had probably undergone a dire change.

The captain tucked the weapon back under his arm. "I'm glad you're familiar with rifles. You're going to be familiar with this one, too, by the end of the week."

Chloe only nodded, but her eyes looked like her brain was yelling, "yippee!"

I could see the mouth of Stromness Bay, now. "Once in the bay, what's my course, Captain?"

"Due west. To Husvik."

Chloe and I looked at each other, then at him. "Sir, did you say Husvik?"

"I did."

Giselle had heard and came stumbling over. "You mean the place you told Mr. Keywood we *weren't* going to?"

"Yes."

The others started gathering around the pilot house. "Captain, you lied to us!"

He turned on Giselle very quickly. "I did not lie to you. I lied to *Keywood*."

"But you told us—"

"I know exactly what I said, and it was this: 'I told Mr. Keywood that I have rethought that decision, and that we are not going to Husvik.' So, when you asked if we were going to Husvik, I only repeated *what I told Mr. Keywood*."

So the captain was not only a ninja; he was a shyster-lawyer, too.

He must have seen the look on my face. "You had to believe it, too, at least until we left the station. Because I couldn't take any chance that he believed we might still go to Husvik." He looked away. "Not that it will necessarily do us much good."

Rod was frowning, but not like he was angry: he was confused. "What do you mean?"

The captain glanced over at me. "He can tell you. He decided to eavesdrop on Larry and me last night."

Everyone looked at me.

"What did you hear?" Chloe asked.

I told them what the captain had said about the odds of KEP making it to spring without a visit from pirates, and how, since he'd mentioned Husvik to Keywood, that it was now the one place he *wouldn't* take us.

Giselle was frowning like Rod by the time I finished. She looked back at the captain. "So, are you worried that Keywood didn't believe you when you said you wouldn't go to Husvik? Is that why it won't do us much good?"

The captain shrugged. "No, Keywood believed me. But by then, it was Hobson's choice when it came to Husvik. Once I mentioned it, torture would pull it out of him. But even after I denied it, torture just as surely will make him swear that we *can't* be found there. Even a half-brained pirate will wonder if that can be believed. And if I hadn't said anything? Well, they might have twisted him for other places we might winter over—and again, Husvik would have been high on the list. There's a modern building there, as well as another original one that's been kept up. The only inhabitable structures on the island, besides KEP itself."

"So we were probably screwed, no matter what," Silent Steve summarized.

The captain shrugged. "When it comes to being found? Possibly. But not when it comes to surviving." He glanced at me. "Run to the end of the bay. Husvik is the last inlet on the starboard side. Make straight for it."

## August 12

I have never been so tired in all my life.

We reached Husvik right before the light started fading four days ago. It is every bit as desolate and dismal as the captain said. Like the other abandoned whaling stations we passed at Leith and Stromness, it's mostly a pile of rusting tanks and half-collapsed buildings. At Husvik, though, the so-called manager's house was in good shape, as well as the radio house not too far away, but we couldn't move in that night. It was too dark and too risky to get things on shore, particularly since falling in the water is an open invitation to hypothermia and frostbite, at least until we get the heat going in the two houses.

If anything, dawn was even worse: Husvik really does look like it's at the ends of the earth. But we didn't have enough time to get depressed: the captain was at us right away. And he hasn't let up since.

As soon as we had moved all the gear and supplies into the manager's house—which is actually pretty damned nice inside—we started sprawling around, thinking about lunch. Nope. Captain had us back on our feet. First we had to throw together a makeshift launch ramp for the dinghy. Then two of us had to tap eighty percent of the fuel out of *Voyager*'s tank and store it in pretty much every container we had, including some of Husvik's old try pots. He sent another few of us to walk around the perimeter of the old whaling station and make a crude map of what they could see, marking any places with a lot of fallen wood that weren't completely filled in with snow. And he, Chloe, and Willow went on a nature walk. Translation: they went off to find where the seals, penguins, and other birds hung out.

We didn't eat until dinner, at which point we were so hungry I suspect we'd have considered chowing down on some of that half-dry wood that the map-makers had prospected. Instead, the captain had bagged a fur seal and found a nest of emperor penguin eggs. By the time we came staggering back from our jobs, he had set up a kind of small furnace in one of the half-collapsed buildings that was mostly made out of steel sheeting. He was using some of the wood for a fire, which was boiling a small try pot of water that had started out as upland snow.

But when we started to huddle around the fire, Chloe came at us with a stick. "What are you, a bunch of idiots? That's treated wood."

"What do you mean, treated?" said Blake. He was that ignorant.

"It's been soaked in creosote or even worse stuff." When Blake's expression didn't change very much, Chloe rolled her eyes. "It's poison, asshole. Once the fire's going, you've got to stand back or cover your mouth and nose. That's why captain has covered the pot and has those red-hot iron bars leading straight out of the fire to a little makeshift camp stove: so we don't all die or become retards."

"Not very efficient," Silent Steve observed.

"Plenty efficient if you want to stay alive, geek-boy. Now, get out!"

Captain almost smiled as we filed out.

If he kept up with these displays of emotion, he was going to start weeping at old movies, soon.

The next two days were very much the same and entirely different. Yes, I meant what I wrote. Our jobs all changed, but we wound up just as hungry and exhausted as we had the day before.

The captain took Chloe and Willow on a bona fide hunting trip, this time on the *Voyager*, scouting for elephant seals. He set almost everyone else to surveying Husvik, filling in the map and keeping our eyes out for useful metal objects, which was a pretty broad definition. However, Rod and I got the strangest job: crawling up and into an abandoned ship called the *Karrakatta*.

I gotta say, that was pretty cool. It was an old steamship that dated to the turn of the last century, and which had been laid up on a slipway at some point between the world wars. They just left it there but had cut through the hull in two places to get to the fuel and the boiler, respectively. Despite all that, it was in surprisingly good shape. Our job was to find out what, if anything, had been left aboard. The captain's hunch was that, when they originally put her up on the slipway, they had probably intended to come back for her; if she hadn't been seaworthy, it seemed unlikely they would have gone to all the trouble to raise her up out of the water.

You had to be careful in there, though. While everything beneath the weather deck was actually in better shape than the interiors of any of the buildings (the deck of a twentieth-century steamship is a whole lot tougher than sheet steel roofing), water tended to pool and there was a lot of junk lying around. Sharp rusty junk, now, some of which was concealed under puddles of slush. And once we were inside, the captain had insisted we use the surgical masks he pulled out of the *Voyager*'s medical stores: they used a lot of asbestos back when the *Karrakatta* was built. On the one hand, I was grateful for the protection. On the other, I had to wonder if any of us were now going to live long enough for mesothelioma or any of the other asbestos-based cancers to catch up with us. But I wore the surgical mask; hell, I'm an optimist at heart.

At the end of that very long day, we gathered in the radio house while the furnace in the remains of the primary processing plant got hot enough to cook dinner. But we couldn't wait, because we were starving again. So hard-boiled penguin eggs were passed around.

Now let me tell you two things about penguin eggs. One is pretty predictable; the other is pretty bizarre. The predictable: they taste pretty much like fish. I mean, they are just this side of awful. But when you're hungry enough—well, you'll pretty much eat anything. The bizarre: their "whites" are absolutely clear. Like colorless acrylic. You can see straight through to the yolk. Which is green. It's like eating food from another planet.

But soon after we finished the eggs, we could look forward to some slow-roasted seal-meat. Slow roasting in the iron stove was the only kind of cooking we were going to see other than boiling, since we had to keep the oven so far away from the fire that it took a long time to get the iron bars really hot.

The captain considered the day a success. He and his female naturalists found a small colony of elephant seals just two miles to the east, halfway to the foot of Jason Peak. They showed no fear of humans, and some of the smaller males had been banished to the fringe by the bigger harem bosses: perfect targets. The biggest problem: hauling a carcass back. On the positive side, the temperature hadn't been higher than four degrees centigrade in days, so it wasn't as if the meat was going to go bad, and the rat extermination on the island had been pretty thorough. But how were we going to cut up the carcass, even if we meant to take it in pieces?

The scrounger group had the answers. In several of Husvik's better preserved buildings—but particularly the machine shop, the laundry, and the "slop house"—they found all sorts of abandoned tools. Most of them had either gone to rust or their handles had rotted away, but there were all-iron boning axes—curved, heavy sons of bitches—that were apparently made to cut apart whales. Some experimental sharpening had shown that they could be restored to a condition good enough to handle an elephant seal, at least.

They also discovered a few boat knives and what looked like machetes with either regular or extra-long handles. Captain told us they were called flensing knives.

Rod just shrugged. "I just call them whaler's glaives." Which was a perfectly good name, particularly once Rod reminded me exactly what a glaive was (he'd apparently played more Dungeons and Dragons than I ever had. A *whole* lot more.)

"Why?" the captain asked Rod. "Did you find some on the *Karrakatta*?"

That was the "smart-ass reveal" moment that Rod and I had been waiting for. We unveiled what we had found in the rusted hulk: almost a dozen big, well-preserved flensing knives, most with five-foot handles and blades almost half as long again. But the handier ones were shorter: three-foot handles with two-foot blades. Like a really beefy machete mounted on a short axe haft. And some were just, well, beefy machetes. They all had a coating of rust, but that's all it was: a coating. A few minutes of work and there was the metal, shining out from underneath.

The captain nodded gravely. "Good finds. Were they in the ship's locker?"

"Mostly," Rod gushed through a big gap-toothed grin. "There were some up near the crew's quarters, too, in personal lockers. Must have been overlooked. The lockers were still closed and the water never got into them. Some of the tools were still wrapped."

The captain's nod was actually perceptible. "With the hole they cut to tap her fuel tanks and use her boilers, the water didn't stay inside her. Ran out the lower decks." He eyed the flensing knives more closely. "Those will make short work of whatever seal we take. The smaller ones look to be handy close-quarters weapons, too. Anything else?"

"Oh," said I casually, "just these." I got off of the box I had been sitting on, and reached inside. Pulled out two damn near pristine boat knives. Scrimshaw handles, still intact. And then, like a magician pulling a rabbit out of a hat very, very slowly, I produced the Find of the Day: a flare gun with five rounds.

The captain scowled. But his eyes were fixed on it. "And where did you find that? At the bottom of a puddle?" *Voyager's* flare gun had gone missing the same time he had dropped off the prior group of kids at Galapagos: not much mystery there. He had meant to replace it in Valparaiso, but hey: apocalyptic shit happens.

Rod was shaking his head. "It was in a closed metal box— water-tight—that was on the highest shelf of the pilot house's ready locker."

One of the captain's eyebrows rose slightly. He made a reaching motion toward one of the flares. I handed it to him. He sniffed it like a wine critic who'd just opened a precious bottle that might have gone vinegary.

His other eyebrow rose. "No sign of moisture?"

"Not a bit."

He pocketed the flare. "We'll test it later. Now what about the chains?"

"The whats?" Rod and I asked in unison.

"The anchor chains?"

Oh, yeah: he'd asked us to look for those. "All there. A little rusty, but in good shape. Why? Are they important?"

"Only the most important single piece of gear in Husvik."

We all looked at the captain as he started handing out the seal meat. Finally, Chloe asked, "Why are the anchor chains so important?"

He shook his head. "We'll go into that later. For now, here's tomorrow's assignments: if you're not on the hunting team, you're carrying the chain."

"Carry *that* chain? How?"

"You don't carry it all at once. Every anchor chain has removable links. Find them, remove them. Carry the sections. Leave them in the main plant. Close to the bay."

"It's going to be hard, getting them apart. They're rusty."

"Excellent. You can all use the exercise."

I don't really remember much of the next day. Seemed like I was working before I was fully awake. Blake, Steve, Rod, Giselle, and I cleaned rusty tools until it grew light, then we carried links of chain, then carted more wood into the furnace-house to dry out (any time you didn't have something else to do, that was your job). We were dragging our sweaty, dirty asses back to the radio house when *Voyager* showed up. The captain docked her at the long pier that ran out from the main plant: its pilings were solid but the rest of it was pretty rickety.

We spent the next two hours getting big chunks of elephant seal off the boat and into the machine shop, which was still pretty intact. But however tired the rest of us were, Johnnie was actually staggering with exhaustion: he'd been swinging one of those boning axes since they'd made the kill.

"How many shots did it take?" I asked him.

Chloe overheard. "Three," she murmured.

"Why are you whispering?"

"Because the captain was pissed. Even though he's got a crate of ammo for that FAL."

I'd read about how fast you can put a hundred rounds down range in an honest-to-god firefight and didn't say a word. This one time, I think I had a good idea of what the captain might have been thinking and why he begrudged using every single bullet.

I remember finally making it back to the radio house after that, eating some fish, part of an energy bar, swallowing a quarter of a multi-vitamin...

And then I woke up here in my bunk. I figure I got back here myself. I figure I slept about ten hours. The only thing I can't figure out is how I got to sleep. Because between the stale blood, fish, and sweat stink on me, I'm thinking of fashioning nose plugs. And we're still two days away from "wash day": the day we spend enough fuel to get indoor hot water and clean both our clothes and our bodies.

And god knows, we need it.

## August 14

We had a light day yesterday; we didn't have to do anything other than move more wood to dry out for cooking and washing clothes. We don't have enough soap, but boiling water does a fair (if brutal) job on its own. Problem is, none of us have that many sets of clothes, so we've got to wear each one about four days running—because in this cold, that's about how long it takes to dry after they get ladled out of the wash pot. So in the course of twelve days, each of us go through the three sets of clothes we were each told to pack by the Sail to Discovery folks. At this rate, I suspect we'll be wearing rags by March. Or sooner.

But today was a real change of pace. Might even call it a day of revelations. Because two things happened that put a new spin on things. Again.

Firstly, most of us who had been on scrounge-and-carry duty for two days in a row got a change of scenery. Captain wanted to sail up to Leith, the whaling station closest to the mouth of Stromness Bay. Everyone else got left behind to lug pieces of tin roofing back into the plant. Once the corrugated metal sheets were there, Johnnie swung the back-spike on the biggest boning axe to put a hole in them. Captain didn't take the time to tell us why that was important, but he was deadly serious about it being done. Then the captain, Steve, Blake, Chloe, and I set sail, as the rest started in on that job. Which made life on a chain-gang look both easier and more meaningful.

Arriving at Leith, I realized how much more welcoming Husvik already was, even though we'd been there less than a week. There was usually a fire going now, and you could smell the wood and the meat and the seal blubber being rendered, as well as seal dung being dried for fuel. But, even if you didn't have a sense of smell, you'd know someone lived there. Pathways in the snow led to and from the buildings we used; piles of wood or gathered tools were near all of them; and as long as there was light in the sky, there were the sounds of people at work: hammering, bashing, shouting, even laughing.

But Leith was deader than dead. Blanketed under snow, it was utterly noiseless, and the only smell was the faint tang of the salt water. We pulled up to the best pier—the one that led to the old guano processing plant—and got out in silence, surrounded by hollow, windowless buildings and rusting scrap. The captain had a backpack and was carrying a folding shovel—he called it an "entrenching tool"—that I'd never seen before; must have kept it in his cabin. He handed the rest of us empty back packs, as well.

But when Chloe, who was the last to get to the side, made to hop up to the pier, the captain shook his head. "Stay with the boat."

"What?" she said.

"Get the FAL. Watch the mouth of the bay. Use the ship's radio if you see anything coming in." He pulled a small walkie-talkie out of his parka, turned it on. "I'll be listening."

Her almond-shaped eyes got very wide, then she looked over at me. I raised my eyebrows and shrugged. I mean, what else could I do?

We walked through Leith, not even stopping to look for salvage until we came to a shed. There was nothing special about it, except that its door was intact and the captain had headed towards it like it had a homing beacon. He opened the door, pulled out two long-handled tools that were kind of like really sharp and really heavy garden hoes. "Originally for pulling off strips of blubber or meat that got stuck to the bone itself or burned on to the side of the ovens. You'll use them to dig."

"To dig?"

He nodded and started walking again, up toward the slowly rising field of snow that reached up into the mountains hemming in Leith Bay.

We found ourselves moving westward, staying between a stream that ran down to the harbor on the extreme south side of the whaling station, and a hundred-foot ridge to our north. After a few hundred yards, the captain veered toward a spot where the side of the ridge flattened out a bit and became less steep. After five minutes of stomping our way upward through the snow, we got to level ground again. Less than a minute later, we made a quick button hook into a tight little gap in a rocky outcropping that rose ten feet above the mini-plateau.

What we found in the back of that notch wasn't exactly a cave, but it sure made for a nice little shelter: unless the wind could somehow blow uphill, and then downhill, and change direction by about one hundred and ten degrees while it did so, you were in a totally calm cubbyhole.

"Cool," muttered Blake, huddling into the space. "Good to get out of that wind and get warm."

"You'll be warmer, still, when you start using that tool I gave you," the captain observed, setting down his backpack.

"What?" Blake said after a speechless moment.

The captain pointed at the ground underfoot—which was actually packed dirt, almost totally free of snow. "We have about four inches of digging to do. Although it won't be digging so much as hacking; the ground is frozen solid. Once you get an inch or so broken up, I'll shovel it out. Then you go back at it."

Blake looked irritated. Steve looked at him. I looked at the ground, and then at the captain. "Here in the center?"

He nodded. "Yes. We'll need to clear about a yard in diameter."

I kept looking at him.

"Well?" he asked.

"A cache? From the war?"

One of his eyebrows may have risen slightly. "Why do you think that?"

I shrugged. "Because it's obvious you were here back then. It's obvious something went wrong. And I remember something about the British having to abandon or destroy things on South Georgia." Which was pretty much all I remembered.

The captain leaned against the wall. "Did you ever read about something called Operation Paraquet?"

I shook my head. Steve and Blake squatted down, eyes on the captain.

He sighed. "Before the invasion of the Falklands, the Argies— Argentinians—first came here. Right here. About fifty 'salvage workers' brought by the *Bahía Buen Suceso* to collect scrap metal from Leith. But there were Marines in among them and they raised the Argentine flag. People forget it, but that was the opening gambit of the Falklands War."

"And you were here when they did?"

"Me? No, but I already had orders to come to South Georgia. My cover was to provide additional security for two nature photographers who were shooting a wildlife documentary on the island, Annie Price and her boss, Lucinda Buxton. Who just happened to be the third child of Lord Buxton, so that assignment was pretty convincing cover for my actual mission."

"Your actual mission?" I asked. For once, I was talking less than he was. I hadn't thought that was possible.

"Advance recon and operational support for what became Operation Paraquet. I was dropped off separately from the Royal Marines that were shipped into KEP. They didn't even know I was aboard the inbound supply ship; I had signed on at Port Stanley as a new crewman."

"So what happened?"

"I was put ashore a few miles away from the documentary team and linked up with the security operative that was already on overwatch. I informed the operative I was in place and then moved on to my actual objective."

"Here?"

"Right. Had to look in on what the Argies were doing. Of course, the aggro between London and Buenos Aires was rising by the hour, so I finished my recon and checked back on the actual safety of the birdwatchers. I was there less than a day before their security operative and I were both assigned to help set up for the first attempt to insert troops here: Operation Paraquet. By that time, the Argies had grabbed the Falklands, and had set up housekeeping in KEP."

"And where did your troops insert?"

The captain hooked a thumb behind him, to the west. "Fortuna Glacier. It was madness. It was April 21 and the weather was awful. The task force leader was dead set on sending 19 Troop in, despite the shite visibility and winds coming from three points of the compass. I told him what the conditions were like, but he kept pressing. So I gave the go-ahead, made the call they wanted to hear.

"I was a damned fool. Two helicopters went down. Everyone

survived. Miracle that. Then they had to shelter until the last helo could fly in and recover them."

"And what did you do in the meantime?"

"Not bloody much. There was nothing for it except to stay on top of that bloody glacier with them. Gave them all my rations, used my camp heater until it ran out. That might have made a difference. Might not have."

"And what about the other person—the one who had been security for the filmmakers?"

"Right there, doing the same thing. Until the weather cleared enough for the last helo to come and try to get those poor blokes back out. Took three tries. Damn near crashed every time. They were flying on instruments, navigating these bleeding fjords with radar that had been designed for sub-chasing. So naturally we had to get out there and help."

"Help how?" Blake's voice was hushed.

"Sending radio signals. The security operative and I both had small sets. We set up on either end of what looked like the best landing zone. Direction finding on our signals gave the last helo some crude triangulation capability. And they needed all the help they could get. If the weather closed over once they started their final approach, the only way they knew if they were nearing the ground was if we signaled that we had spotted their lights, or saw their rotors kicking around the snow."

"And did the chopper crash?"

"No; it came in hard but straight, and two helicopters'-worth of my mates managed to cram themselves into that little Wessex 3. It was like a bunch of bloody weightlifters packed into a clown car."

"Then...what went wrong?"

The captain looked away. "Everything seemed fine. The helo went up, got out over the water, and was headed back toward the ship. I turned to find the person I'd been working with." He stopped for a moment. "No sign. I looked for days. Found a hand-held landing light at the edge of a crevasse. Nothing else."

I could hear how careful the captain was every time he spoke about this security operative who'd been lost on the glacier, but I wasn't going to ask him any questions about that, particularly not with the other two gawking at him. "So if the story ends at the glacier, why is this gear down here?"

"Because the story doesn't end on the glacier. Once I was done there, I had to come back to Leith to keep an eye on the Argie Marines. They just sat here. But when my mates retook KEP, then it was time to let the invaders here know that they had to give it up, as well. Took a day of pretty testy negotiation."

"Why?" Blake seemed outraged at the notion that the Argentinians wouldn't give up immediately. "They must have known you guys would slaughter them, otherwise."

"Probably, but their commander wanted to sign a separate surrender and save his skin."

"I don't understand," said Steve.

The captain nodded. "Their commander was a right swine by the name of Alfredo Astriz. Sadistic strongman for the Argie military government. Disappeared all sorts of people, including some Swedes and French nuns. He knew that London would want him extradited, right enough. So he made a separate peace, you might say. Took an extra day."

"And you were part of those, um, negotiations."

"I was just the messenger. If it had been up to me, I'd have shot the bastard."

I poked at the frozen ground. "And so . . . this?"

"I was ordered to stay on. Keep an eye peeled, make sure the Argies hadn't left anyone behind. Then came orders to destroy what was left of the two helicopters. And the kit that the Argies left behind."

"How did you do that?"

"The weapons and vehicles got what you Yanks call a willie pete and that was the end of 'em. But it seemed a bloody waste to destroy perfectly good rations and vitamins." He pronounced it "vittemens."

I started scratching the outline of the hole we had to dig. "Okay, but why bury them here?"

The captain shrugged. "Back in those days, no one knew if the war might flare up again in a month, or maybe a year. Seemed like a fair enough idea to have a cache on hand, if that happened. Afterwards"—he shrugged again—"never had a reason to dig them up. And, in case some tosser in Moscow or Washington decided to push the button and end the world, I figured I might run here for a few months, let all that fallout blow over."

I stared at the ground. "You think they're still good?"

He nodded. "It's in plastic. In metal containers. In ground that never gets warmer than about ten degrees centigrade. And all of it has expiration dates measured in decades, not weeks or months. So get digging."

We did.

When we came back to the *Voyager*, I thought Chloe would lay into us with questions about our brimming backpacks. But instead, she was waiting aboard, gun in her hands, fidgeting from foot to foot.

"Captain!" she called when we got within fifty yards. "Someone was on the radio."

He started walking faster. "Who was it?"

"Don't know, but I'm pretty sure they were speaking Spanish. And I think they were sending a lot of numbers."

The captain's brow lowered a bit.

"Coordinates, course, speed? Response frequencies?" I asked.

He shrugged. "Possibly all of that." To Chloe: "You didn't respond, did you?"

"Captain! You've given orders not to. And I'm not stupid, you know."

He nodded as he climbed back aboard. "Let's get home. Quickly." He turned to me. "You take us out. I'm going to search the dial."

I don't think any of us said a single word, all the way back to Husvik. The captain was out of the boat before we'd even heaved a line up to the pier. "Did you get all that scrap collected?" he asked loudly.

Giselle and Willow had emerged from the machine shop. They nodded together. "Probably a ton's worth."

"Good. Keep working." He turned to those of us in the *Voyager*. "Start helping the others to relink the anchor chains. Two equal lengths. Keep them in the plant, near the fire. They must stay dry and warm." He went back to the radio.

Normally, when we got jobs like these, we groused once the captain had stalked off. We didn't do that today. We knew the captain was worried. And that meant we were worried, too.

We were all pretty tired by the time we got together back in the radio house for a meal and news from the captain. He heard more of the radio traffic about an hour after we got back. According to him, the senders identified themselves as the crew of a fishing boat that, returning to Montevideo, found chaos, and turned around without making port. Now they were trying to raise KEP to get news of safe harbors. "Which," the captain finished, "is all a load of shite. They give their position as a few hundred miles away." He shook his head. "Any boat that turned its back on the mainland wouldn't have gone steaming over five hundred miles into the middle of the wintertime South Atlantic before trying to find out if there was anyone at home at King Edward Point. That and some of the terms they used, their radio habits: they aren't fishermen."

"So they're coming for us," Rod said quietly.

"Hard to say. But I suspect they'll at least go to KEP. Whether they know the island well enough to have heard about Husvik, or whether they, erm, debrief the staff at KEP, that's another matter. No point in speculating: we assume they will. Which is why we've been getting ready since we got here."

"Getting ready?" Johnnie asked earnestly.

Blake rolled his eyes.

Which pissed me off. "Okay, Blake, so if you understand the point of everything the captain has had us doing, why don't you explain it to us all?"

Blake flushed bright red. "We're getting weapons together and . . . and getting ready to feed ourselves for as long as it takes."

"How does that explain the chain, and the pieces of steel sheet that everyone else was gathering today, and that Johnnie was punching holes in?"

"Shut up, Alvaro."

"You're free to try and make me, Blake."

The captain stood. "That's enough. The only fighting I'll permit is against the Argie thugs. As for how we'll defend ourselves, I'll explain that tomorrow. We're in no rush. They've got a way to go and we are certainly not their first port of call. Now see if your next change of clothes is dry yet and get to your bunks. All of you."

I thought that's where the day was going to end, except I hung behind in the radio house to clean up: I had kitchen duty that day. Just as I was finishing, the door opens and Chloe slips in.

She looks at me, then at the floor, then at me again. Not her usual, bold-as-brass self.

"Hi," she says.

"IIi," I say back. "Leave something behind?"

She shook her head, and—I swear to god—she scuffed one of her shoes against the floor. "You're a good teacher, Alvaro."

I'm pretty sure I just stood staring at her for a minute. I couldn't decide what shocked me more: that she thought I was a good teacher, or that she had called me by my first name. "Thanks," I eventually replied in a virtuoso display of eloquence.

She looked around the room. "We're going to be in it soon, I guess." She nodded out at the bay. I knew she was really nodding toward an approaching trawler full of probable pirates, bobbing like a cork on the cold, dark waves at least two hundred miles west of us. "Things could get bad."

"Sure could," I agreed, continuing to showcase my rhetorical gifts.

"So I want more training."

I think I blinked. "Chloe, you've done a fine job. Better than that, actually. You can handle any boating task as well as I can, now." Well, that wasn't quite true, but hell, no reason not to build some extra morale. "And your reading—"

"Screw that. I want you to teach me how to fight. The way you do."

This time I *know* I blinked. "You want me to teach you aikido?"

"Yeah. That."

"Um. Why?"

She looked away again. "Look, I know I talk a lot of shit, but I'm no fool. A really big guy who knows how to fight—he's gonna roll right over me. I won't let that happen." Her eyes and voice changed when she added that last sentence. The only adjective that comes to mind is that she looked and sounded "haunted." Then she snapped back to the here and now. "So I want to learn to fight dirty. Like you do. In case I can't beat them with strength alone."

So: Chloe wanted me to teach her how to fight . . . but because I knew how to fight dirty. Talk about leaving me with mixed emotions. "Even if we get in an hour of practice a day, you're only going to have a few of the basics," I warned her.

"I figured. I don't care. I'll take any edge I can get. Now teach."

So I did. For all of ten minutes. Then she stood back. "I don't want to do all this dancy stuff."

"Chloe, this 'dancy stuff' will teach you how to move so that—"

"Damn it, I need you to skip to the part where I can keep someone from tackling me. From holding me down." She didn't look away; her eyes were wide and defiant. But they were also a little shiny.

*Oh.* I looked down. I knew she wouldn't want to see the realization in my own eyes. "Okay. So, that means two things. Learning how to keep from getting knocked down. And how to keep from getting pinned down, if you're already on the ground."

She nodded. "Right. Let's go."

I figured we'd go over the basics, although this wasn't really aikido, anymore; it was a really limited number of aikido moves converted into a basic self-defense course. She learned how to dodge, sidestep, even trip an onrushing attacker. How well she'd be able to use it—well, that was a different story. Then, to end the evening, I went over how she could break free from someone who was trying to grab her and hold her down.

On the second run-through, when I grabbed for her, she didn't dodge. And instead of twisting my wrist and trying to shove me off to her left while she rolled up to her feet on the right, she just held my hand. I found myself looking down into her eyes, not quite a foot away.

It's crazy how fast human situations can change. One minute you're working on self-defense, and the next, you're looking into each other's eyes and wondering—really, really wondering—what it would be like to have sex with each other. And you don't have to say it to know it. In fact, saying anything kind of destroys it. So we just looked at each other. I don't know for how long.

"Thank you," she said eventually.

I doubt there's anything else she could have said that would startle me out of my sex-obsessed thoughts, but that did it. "Uh, sure. For what?"

"For sticking up for Johnnie today—and for the others."

I guess my surprise showed on my face.

She can apparently read my mind, too. "Yeah, yeah, I know: I was a pain in the ass early in the trip. I went around making people feel like shit. I do that when I'm scar—when I'm with new people. Want to let them know I won't take any of *their* shit."

"Well, you got your point across." I couldn't help smiling.

She spent a moment studying my expression. I guess she decided I wasn't sticking it to her, because she smiled, too. "What

I'm trying to say is you kind of look out for all of us. Even the ones you don't like too much. Like me." The last sentence was cautious.

"I don't dislike you," I said, falling desperately short of the truth.

"I gave you plenty of reason."

I smiled again. "Yeah, but since then, you've given me plenty of reasons not to. Plenty of really good reasons to like you, in fact."

And again, something changed. Her hand grew tense in mine, but not like she was going to fight. Quite the opposite. She was looking at me really steadily now, and although she was smiling a little less, it wasn't because she was less happy. I was pretty sure that Chloe's state of mind had gone well beyond "happy" . . .

The door to the radio house banged open. Johnnie barged into the other room, yelling. "Alvaro? Chloe?"

Who chucked me off her like a bag of rice. Which was fortunate: that way, we were picking ourselves up from opposite walls. Johnnie stared back and forth at us. "What are you guys doing here?"

"Practicing," Chloe said. She blushed ferociously as she said it.

"Aikido," I added. Then I translated for Johnnie: "Self-defense. What's up?"

"Chatter on the radio again. Captain wants you."

"Why?"

"Your Spanish is better than his."

I was careful not to look back at Chloe. I'm pretty sure she was careful not to look at me as I raced out.

And I'm pretty sure we each remained intensely aware of exactly where the other was for the rest of that night. I almost thought I could hear her breathing as I lay in my bunk.

Not sleeping.

## August 18

Haven't heard any more transmissions. Wouldn't mind much if we had: too tired to care.

For the past four days, we've been working like dogs. Most of it has been readying more sheets of punctured steel siding and roofing. There's also been a lot of dragging old struts and pipes and even light girders into the plant, all to hold up the I-beam support that braces the big doorway which opens out to the pier. It's gonna have to hold a lot of weight.

We've also been building a pair of platforms, one on either side of the I-beam so that they flank the access lane that runs right out onto the pier. We're building these platforms like they are stools: solid and able to hold up a lot of weight at their center—unless you pull away one of their legs. Which seems to be the plan.

Meanwhile, poor Johnnie's been out on the shallows in the *Voyager*'s dinghy, lashed to either one of two sets of pilings about forty yards out along the pier. He's been whacking away at them almost all day long, every day, with the biggest of the whale boning axes. He's got them whittled down so much that I wouldn't stand on that stretch of the pier on a bet.

Silent Steve and I had hard days of a different kind: hiking with the captain. Although he gets winded sometimes—more and more, it seems—he can set a pretty exhausting pace for a while. He led us through two lowland valleys to the hunters' shelters he'd asked about at KEP. Damned if he didn't have more stashes there. Apparently he'd had some war souvenirs that some of the hunters had been so crazy about that they'd traded away some of their own stuff to get them. So in addition to what we expected to find in each shed—a portable camp-stove, a lot of wood-pellet fuel, blanket, oil lamp, some canned and dry goods—in one of them, he lifted up the floorboards to reveal a .308 bolt-action with a scope. At the other, it was a .44 revolver. The rifle had plenty of ammunition; the pistol not so much. It was a gun for putting wounded animals out of their misery, apparently.

With all the caches pulled in, the captain has become a little more generous with the vitamins and other "fortified foods." Damned if I don't have more energy, feel more alert, wake up more quickly.

But it seems to be having the opposite effect on the captain. He's okay in the middle of the day, but mornings seem to be a little harder for him now, and he racks out a little earlier every night. I never really thought about it, but despite his being as tough as shoe leather, he's just not that young anymore. Best I can figure, he's almost sixty.

I'd write more, but there really isn't anything more to write about. I spend a lot of time looking at Chloe; she spends a lot of time looking at me. We don't say anything. But Willow spends a lot of time looking back and forth between us and smiling like she was just given a puppy for her fourth birthday.

God, is that annoying. Almost as annoying as knowing that tomorrow, we're going to get up and work ourselves until we're falling down tired.

Again.

## August 21

The radio got lively again this afternoon. Same ship and voice, but the transmissions were a lot more clear. They kept repeating that, if they did not get a reply, they were going to steer clear of KEP for fear that the plague had hit there, too.

No one replied.

The captain sat thinking for a long time.

"You think they might be legit?" Blake asked.

He shook his head. "No. They're trying to be sly."

"How so?"

Giselle spread her hands. "Blake, c'mon. They're trying to sound like they are just a scared bunch of fishermen. Who just might be the last ship that could help the staff at King Edward ever get off South Georgia."

"Wait." Johnnie was frowning. "I thought people were trying to get *to* South Georgia, not get *away* from it."

Giselle nodded. "Well, they do want to get here—for a while. But eventually, we all need to get off this island. Like the captain pointed out, there's no way to live here forever. There's food, but it's not balanced, doesn't have all the nutrients we need. And unless we want to burn seal blubber and dried dung forever, there's no fuel for fires, either. So we might be safe from the plague, but without a way off, we would eventually die because of the environment. And the pirates know that the station team is aware of that. They're hoping that someone at KEP will get scared and reply, will ask them to come. It will make their job that much easier."

Which seemed to shoot the captain out of his chair. "They shall find it anything but easy if they decide to test us here.

Everyone: you know your jobs. Get to them. I want them done today, so we can start resting up tomorrow."

"Resting up?" Willow asked. "For what?"

"For giving these brutes a proper reception if they come nosing around here."

And yeah, we worked. We looped the chains around the pilings that Johnnie had almost hacked through, threw the chains' other ends over the plant entry's reinforced I-beam so that each of them lay on one of the platforms. Then we started threading those chain ends through dozens upon dozens of the hole-punched sheets of steel, the way kids make necklaces out of Cheerios or Froot Loops. Or used to, anyway.

The captain disappeared with Chloe for a good part of the morning, and we heard rifle shots—maybe a dozen—up the cut that ran into the mountains behind Husvik. Zeroing the new scoped rifle, I guessed.

When we were done threading the sheet steel on the chains, we fastened their ends to some of the big, rusty try pots for boiling blubber, almost like they were replacement anchors. By the time we were done, the platforms had started to sag under the weight.

Meanwhile, Willow and Steve had been pouring boiled blubber on that part of the pier that was just landward of the pilings Johnnie had been hacking at. Sounds like an easy job, but it's not. Try carrying a bucket of melted fat, sometime. Then try spreading it around with a couple of old planks.

By that time, the captain and Chloe were back. He oversaw our assembly of some more perforated steel sheeting, but this time, just one or two with a light girder or other steel support sticking up through them. Then we had to load them in the *Voyager* and all of us took turns dumping them heavy-side down in the shallows, most of them along approaches where a small boat might try to run up to the shore in front of the manager's house.

It was getting dark by the time the captain had us go to the positions he'd chosen for us, told us what to do, ran us through drills, almost spat in frustration, and told us to go inside and get dinner, get seconds, and then get to bed.

We were pretty surprised. Seconds on food? And a mandatory "lights out?" Willow wondered, purposely loud, why the captain was giving those orders?

"Because you're going to need all your strength tomorrow. And the next day. And every day until you get it right."

"Get what right?"

"The drills you failed to perform properly today. Tomorrow you're going to do it right. And you're going to keep doing it until you keep getting it right. Every time. Now go."

We did. We ate. We didn't talk too much. Because we knew that we were all wondering the same thing:

When will the pirates arrive?

## August 27

It feels strange to write in a journal, particularly someone else's. I haven't written in one of my own since I was eight, or maybe nine.

So. My name is Willow Lassiter and I am writing in Alvaro's journal because Captain Haskins asked me to. He said that if you want a record of what happened during a fight, then you need to write it down as soon as you can. He says it's very easy to forget exactly what happened, particularly once you've slept on the memories. Fighting is so fast and chaotic that our minds try to make sense of it in retrospect, and so we start remembering things in a more sensible order than they might have actually occurred. So I agreed to write what the captain insists on calling this "after action report."

The pirates didn't surprise us. Starting three days ago, Captain Haskins put us on a rotating schedule of watches. One hour each, starting an hour before dawn, and going until sunset. He wasn't worried about night-time. The possibility that any of the pirates had ever visited Stromness Bay was very low; the chance that they'd be confident navigating it in the dark was about equal to our chances of being hit by a meteor.

Long before they came into sight, we could see the smoke from their ship. They had probably seen ours, too; there really isn't any effective way to hide it, and we can't do without it.

Steve was the one watching when they came into sight, clearing the headland just west of Busen Point about an hour after dawn. It was precisely when and where the captain told us to expect them, if they came. From about a mile to our southeast, Steve shone the captain's emergency flashlight on a mirror we had taken from *Voyager*, and which he kept angled away from the harbor. Within one minute, the captain was on the radio with him, getting a report. After hearing it, he told Steve to keep observing and stay there until the ship drew abreast of Tönsberg Point, which was about three miles from Husvik. Then he was to slip back to us along the mostly-concealed path we'd marked. He'd be pretty much invisible doing it: he was wearing a white wrap made from a torn sail. Even if they were using binoculars, they'd have to be pretty sharp-eyed and lucky to see him from three miles away.

By now, we could get into position very quickly. Chloe and I had the longest run; all the way to the *Karrakatta* and up to its pilot house, which was still intact. We listened on the radio; no update from Steve, which meant that the ship hadn't put any other boats in the water to land anywhere else and so, outmaneuver, or "flank," us as Captain Haskins likes to say.

I settled into my perch behind the multiple layers of iron plate with which we had lined the inside of the pilot house. I was the scout and spotter. Chloe would be too busy with her rifle to see everything that might be going on in the places other than where she was preparing to shoot. So watching was my job. So, because I had been given one of the two pairs of binoculars, I was the first one to get a good look at the ship that had come to attack us.

It was an old, rusty trawler, but a big one, what the captain called a multi-purpose fishing vessel. As it moved past some of the orientation points we had ranged and marked in the water—rocks, debris—I estimated it to be slightly under one hundred and fifty feet in overall length. It had a superstructure, not just a pilot house, and it had a side door in its hull, just aft of the bridge. The midship gunwale was more than a yard lower than the bow. I reported what I saw to the captain.

I must have sounded a little excited or nervous. The captain's response was slow, like he was trying to calm an animal or a little child. "That's very good, Willow. Now I need you to tell me how many people you see and what they are carrying."

"I think I see three on the bridge. There are a few on top of the superstructure. They are all carrying guns." I squinted hard. "I think two are the military assault rifles you spoke about, two more are AK's, and maybe two are short shotguns."

"How short?"

"Police cruiser, not sawed off." I was pretty proud that I had managed to memorize all these facts about guns.

"Good job. But no one on the weather deck, up near the bow?"

"No, sir." That was the first hint that something about this ship was odd, but it didn't seem particularly important just then. Besides, we had more important things to do.

"Anything else worth reporting?"

"They have two small boats, sir. Back near the stern. And sir, I think they are wearing the same cold-weather clothing that the team at KEP wore."

There was a long pause. "The same kind of clothing, or exactly the same?"

"British Antarctic Service colors and patches, Captain."

We all knew what that meant: station leader Keywood and all the other members were almost certainly dead and the base and all its supplies were gone.

The ship clattered and clanked closer—the engine sounded like it was about to break down at any moment—standing off from the shore a bit. It slowed, sounded its horn. The pirates waited. One of them scanned the end of the bay with a pair of binoculars. He seemed to be particularly interested in the *Voyager*, which was anchored well down the shore from his other point of interest: the manager's house. Although we didn't have a fire going, it hardly mattered. There was no way to hide the deep trenches our comings and goings had cut in the snow, any more than we could conceal that there was no snow on its roof, or that of the radio house: they always stayed warm enough so that it tended to melt and slide off.

We had thought that seeing an obviously inhabited whaling station with no people in sight might give them pause. It certainly would have made any of us consider our next move very carefully. But not them. When no one responded to a second sounding of its horn, the pirate ship chugged out a little more black smoke and made for the end of Husvik's only remaining deep water access: the end of the pier. I swept my binoculars to the rear of the ship: no activity among the dinghies there.

That was a little surprising, too. We expected that while their main hull pulled up to the pier, they'd also put teams out in any smaller boats they had. That way they'd be threatening us at two or three different locations. But that didn't seem to concern them. After changing to the second radio frequency, I reported what I was seeing.

The captain was as puzzled and worried as I was. "Keep watching them, Willow. And stay on this channel."

"If they are monitoring, they might hear."

"They might. So it's time to switch to Russian."

"*Da*, Captain." I said. In the weeks leading up to this day, the captain had asked us all sorts of interesting questions, many of which initially seemed odd. But eventually, we understood the importance of all of them. In my case, he had discovered we shared a language that was not likely to be spoken by many South Americans, unless they were holdovers from the Cold War days. At any rate, it was a better bet than English (too common), French (common enough and too many common root words), and none of us spoke German, Chinese, or Arabic (including Captain Haskins).

The fishing ship started backing engines as it approached the end of the pier, then swung its stern around very slowly so that the side of its hull gently kissed the remains of the bumpers. Specifically, they were aligning their hull-side door with the end of the pier. "It looks like they are ready to land a raiding team," I muttered to Captain Haskins.

"Looks like it," he agreed. "Alvaro?"

"Yeah?" said Alvaro, who just used English; he didn't know Russian.

"Your motor is idling reliably?"

"It is."

"Good. Standby."

"We're ready. *Voyager* out."

The ship's side door slid aside, which the crew managed to do with some kind of winch they had rigged from the superstructure. Odd: was the door's main mechanism broken, somehow? The pilot gently pulsed the engines, keeping the hull snugged against the pier so closely that it creaked and groaned. Much more pressure and it was likely to splinter.

We all waited, and for several seconds, there was no activity around the open door: just a lightless rectangular hole in the side of the ship. Then there was a sudden rushing noise—steam gushed from the open doorway—followed immediately by screams.

Wild, chaotic screams that came out along with the raiders as they fled the steam.

Except that these weren't raiders. Not the kind we had thought about and prepared for.

Naked people came scrambling out on to the pier, their hair matted, their eyes wild and insanely intense. And they kept pouring out.

All of us realized what we were seeing at the same time.

"Sod it!" the captain shouted, not bothering with Russian. I swung the binoculars over to his "fighting position:" snugged behind the raised concrete foundation of the foremen's barracks and protected on either side by old iron try pots. He reached up, pulled a line taken from the *Voyager*. From atop the ruin of a chimney behind him—the only part of the barracks still standing—a large metal gear toppled down to hit a shallow iron bowl. It rang loudly.

There was enough of a gap in the roof of the main plant that I could see Blake, Rod, and now Steve count to three together, and then swing homemade mallets at the rear legs of the two platforms holding up the weighted chains.

Both platforms tilted for a moment and then—the three boys scattering away—they came down with a crash Chloe and I could hear almost two hundred and fifty yards away. Without the support of the platforms, the weights on the two lengths of anchor-chain plummeted. The chains were yanked down hard, went taut; their other ends were looped and straining around the pier's much-hacked pilings. For a second, the pilings held.

But only for a second. Cut almost all the way through, the pilings snapped, one after the other, loud enough to make even the forty-odd zombies—because that's what they looked like—stop in the middle of their headlong rush toward land. They stared as twelve feet of the pier was half-pulled and half-fell down into the water. Some of them started to howl at the unsupported planking that now sloped down into the frigid water only eight feet away, but most turned to look back at the ship.

The door in the side of the hull shut quickly, and smoke started coming out of the funnel.

The zombies grabbed at the suddenly receding ship, their hands slipping as they tried to get a hold of its sheer sides. Two fell into the water. Two more looked at the gunwale that began at the base of the superstructure, a few yards forward of the door. One of them tried to jump the widening distance. She got half her body over the side, scrabbling to pull herself all the way onto the weather deck. But her desperate handhold had apparently been upon a coil of spooled rope: it unwound and she went down. The other two were already sinking, gurgling and uttering wordless yowls as the water closed over their heads.

One of the others on the severed pier roared and took a running leap at the collapsed length of planking that slanted down into the water. Surprisingly, he reached it—but his first attempt to scramble up that ramp was also his first contact with the seal fat that had been slathered upon it. He seemed to run in place for a moment, then screeched in fury as he pitched backward into the low swells. The water wasn't quite over his head, but that didn't matter; if anything, the zombie's reaction to that sub-zero cold was more rapid and severe than ours. After a few seconds of highly agitated thrashing, his limbs began to slow down, looked like they were stiffening.

Chloe had to poke my ribs to get me to stop watching the zombies; it was important to see how they differed from us, and observing species is what I do best.

"Willow. What's happening?"

I swept the binoculars from the captain's position to the raider ship and then over to *Voyager*. "Nothing much. Wait. The pirates are backing engines."

"What? Why?"

"Don't know. Wait. It's the spikes we put in the water; they're steering away from them. And there's activity at the stern. I think they're preparing to put a boat in the water. Maybe both of them."

"Bet on both of them," Chloe muttered, slowly angling the muzzle of the bolt action rifle over in that direction.

A lot of howling brought my attention back to the pier. Some of the now stranded zombies had pushed some of their front rank over the edge, apparently in the primal hope that they could crawl over them to get to the pier. And from the corner of my eye, I saw what had focused their aggression enough to do so.

After dropping the weight that collapsed the weakened span of the pier, Blake, Rod, and Steve were under orders to grab flensing knives—more like machetes or swords, actually—and hang back in the shadows of the plant. If anyone still got over the pier, they were to ambush them as best they could. A dangerous job, but we only had three guns. Besides, we were pretty sure that our enemies would be unable to cross the gap, and we had the captain to shoot at any who tried.

But Blake had stepped out of the shadows of the plant, taunting the zombies. I doubt they understood his words any more than his obscene gestures, but I guess seeing him dancing on shore, so close and yet so far, made some of them a little extra crazy. Which is why some pushed their own kind into the water, intending to scramble over and reach the greased ramp that led up to the pier.

One of them actually got a hold of those half-submerged planks and then—either out of pure dumb luck or intent—found himself clinging to one of the pier's intact pilings. Which he started climbing.

"Captain..." I said in Russian.

"I see him," Captain Haskins muttered back. "Tell me what the raiders are doing."

I looked back at the fishing ship. "They are preparing to lower two dinghies into the water, about four people per boat."

"Bloody hell. I'm going to sort out the bugger trying to crawl atop the pier. Tell Chloe to wait until I start firing."

I did so, then watched as the long barrel of the captain's FAL eased out from between the try pots. The captain started firing. A moment later, Chloe did as well—which pretty much deafened me. Even though the pilot house didn't have windows anymore, a lot of the sound was still trapped in that small room.

The captain had told us that if shooting started, we wouldn't be able to think straight and that we certainly wouldn't be able to keep track of everything going on around us. The noise, the threat, the fact that everyone would be either hiding or moving or shooting: it would just be too much. "Sensory overload," is how he explained it. "It takes getting used to."

I distinctly remember nodding at his explanation, but still thinking, "That's other people. That's not me. I have always been calm and collected in crises. I might be a little distracted, but it will not be so bad."

I was wrong. So very, very wrong. When Chloe started firing her rifle just a few feet away from my head, I suddenly couldn't think of anything. I thought I might scream. I'm not sure why.

But I managed to remember that my job was to watch what was going on. So I did.

Captain Haskins had already withdrawn behind his two try pots. The zombie that had reached the shortened pier was dead in the water and sinking. One man at the stern of the pirate ship was lying face down. Another was holding his leg with one hand and dragging himself back to the rear hatchway with the other. The rest had taken cover: they had either run around the far side of the superstructure or were crouching just within the aft hatchway. They were looking around uncertainly, scanning the roofs of the whaling station, the *Karrakatta*, even some of the hills behind us.

As Chloe reloaded, I reported what I saw to the captain. He acknowledged, added, "You're a cool one, Willow."

*I'm about to vomit from nerves*, I wanted to reply. But I said, "Thanks. Now what?"

"Now we take the fight to them. Is the bow still empty?"

"Yes, sir. And I think I see why they didn't have anyone out there before."

"Why so?"

"The hatch cover to the fish bin has been damaged; it can't close. If there's a communicating passage between the bin and the side-door, then—"

"Yes: that was how they controlled the infected. Kept them in the fish-hold. The buggers stayed below to keep out of the cold wind, but if there had been movement on the forward weather deck, they would have swarmed up." The captain paused, as if he was thinking. "*Voyager*, this is the moment to intercept."

"Roger that," answered Alvaro. "Just give the word."

"The word is given."

"Aye, sir. Releasing the anchor line. Leaving the mic open." Alvaro leaned away from the pick-up, shouted, "Johnnie! Get on deck but stay under the gunwale. Are the containers ready?"

"Still nice and warm."

The sound of a motor rose up quickly from what had been an almost inaudible background idling.

Out in Husvik Bay, *Voyager* started moving very slowly, no longer attached to its anchor. If any of the pirates saw its change of position, they gave no sign of it.

Instead, a bunch of them came running out of the super- structure and set up around the forward weather deck, from the waist to the bow. They were scanning the high points behind their ship. Including, of course, the *Karrakatta*. A moment later, the men who had ducked back into the rear hatch came rushing back out; three of them kept sweeping their weapons back and forth across the same high points. The rest set to work on lowering the two dinghies. "Captain—" I started.

"I see it. They're readying the boats at the taffrail again?"

"Yes, sir."

"The others are all looking for Chloe. They know they can't land safely without suppressing her."

"So what do we do?"

"You wait until I start my diversion."

"Your what?"

Chloe had overheard. "His diversion."

Everything seemed to happen at once. The captain started firing at the men lining the bow of the ship. He didn't hit any—the range was more than two hundred yards—but he came close and certainly got their attention. They leaned their weapons over the bow toward the captain—

Two of the zombies stuck on the isolated length of pier started pushing and shoving to get a better look at what was happening around them—and fell into the water. Blake, who had been watching them from the edge of the main plant's shadows, whooped and shouted something at them, waving his flensing knife in their direction—

The two raiders on that side of the bow swung their weapons over at him and started firing. One of them had a real AK-47, a machine gun.

Blake turned, took one running step backward and then sprawled, his flensing knife flying away, that hand now clutching his hip.

It happened so fast, I didn't even gasp. And the next second, Chloe fired. One shot. Then she ducked down as she worked the bolt. "I missed again. Shit."

"One miss is to be expected at this ra—"

"Willow. I fired five shots the first time. And only two hits." She rose up slowly; I scanned the back of the ship. Although she hadn't hit anyone with her shot, they were all crouching down, still scanning. One of them was pointing in our direction, seemed pretty convinced the shot had come from *Karrakatta*. Two of the others were focused on an elevated overseer's office at the eastern end of the plant. "They're going to see you next time," I told Chloe. And then I remembered. "They hit Blake."

"Shit," she said, blew out a long breath and prepared to rise into her armored sniper's notch for another attack.

I slipped over into my back-up spotter's slot—never be in the same place twice—and realized that the bridge crew had seen that the *Voyager* was not only moving, but angling toward them. "Their ship is turning to port, Chloe. The guys at the stern are looking around, surprised. The two on the far right are looking back through the hatchway—"

Fully in the shadows, Chloe rose up carefully, settled the rifle on her sawdust-filled sandbag, began staring down the scope.

The riflemen up at the bow seemed to get instructions from the bridge; they started moving across to the port bow, where they might get a shot at *Voyager*.

Captain Haskins evidently saw that; his FAL began banging away again. Five fast rounds: one of the raiders went down, twisting on the deck. Then he fired once every other second or so. The raiders who had been moving along the bow stopped where they were, sheltered, did what the captain had told us most pirates will do: rather than following orders, they stopped to shoot back at whoever was shooting at them. They all emptied their magazines at the captain's position, reloaded, did so again.

*Voyager* edged closer.

The bridge crew blew their horn, probably to get the attention of their team up at the bow.

Chloe exhaled, took her next shot.

I swiveled back to look at the stern of the ship.

One of the raiders was down on his back, arms wide, a dark puddle spreading around him. The others ducked behind their two dinghies, started yelling. Two jabbed their index fingers fiercely at *Karrakatta*.

Chloe had already worked the bolt of her rifle, was snugging it against her round cheek. "Time to die, bastard." She squeezed the trigger.

She missed, but it put a hole in one of the dinghies. They all started firing at us.

I thought we were going to be dead in the first few seconds. But initially, they didn't even hit the pilot house. And since we were in the shadow of its overhanging roof, they had no way of actually seeing us, unless they saw the flash from Chloe's gun.

Chloe took three seconds to reload, her frown deepening. "I've fucking had it," she growled, rose up and didn't even wait for me to spot for her.

Three times she squeezed the trigger and worked the bolt. I got my binoculars over in time to see one raider drop his rifle and clutch his arm, and then another fall back with a red smear where his right collarbone used to be. Chloe ducked back; the return fire was closer now, going through the weathered wood of the pilot house and ringing against the improvised iron plating like we were hidden inside a church bell.

I slipped back into my first spotter's position, watched the pirates pull back inside the aft hatchway again, dragging their wounded in after them. They weren't getting their boats down in the water anytime soon, now. I had one moment to wonder how badly Blake had been hit when the captain started shooting faster again and shouting, "Willow! Chloe! The bastards at the bow are moving portside." He coughed; his throat sounded tight, constricted. "I can't get shots at them anymore. And Alvaro and Johnnie are—"

I looked beyond the waist of the pirate ship's weather deck; the *Voyager* was sweeping in and slowing.

"Chloe?"

By the time she was on her feet, the *Voyager* had maneuvered to come parallel and drift alongside the enemy ship—and big, broad-shouldered Johnnie jumped up and slung an industrial garbage bag of liquid fat onto the fishing ship's weather deck. As it broke, splattering and spreading, the riflemen rushed to that side. Alvaro, steering from the deck-wheel, raised the revolver in his right hand and fired three times at them.

They ducked, but it was more like a bobbing reflex; they were already rising again the moment he was done shooting.

Chloe choked out a sobbing curse, yanked the gun around with a sudden desperation that I had never seen in her before.

Johnnie hurled another container over on to the ship's deck— this one a ten-gallon jerrican—swinging it away from him with both arms, like he was throwing the hammer in the Olympics. The jerrican trailed a spout of oil as it cleared the enemy's gunwale—and Johnnie dove for the deck.

Alvaro, being agile and fast, had already leaped up the stairs to the top of the pilot house. He fired three more times at the riflemen who poked up over the port bow; they hunched back down, shooting blindly. With everyone ducking and firing at the same time, no one seemed to be hitting anyone else, even though they were barely fifteen feet apart.

Alvaro dropped the revolver.

A rifleman stood to get a better shot at him...

Chloe screamed, "Fucker!" and fired.

The rifleman went down.

Alvaro had pulled another gun from his belt: the flare gun. He aimed it carefully, his waist on level with the enemy's deck.

Chloe's rifle fired at the same time that the other two riflemen at the bow popped up to shoot at Alvaro.

Who fired the flare gun and then fell off the pilot house, hit by one or more bullets.

And suddenly I could not hear. Not because of Chloe's gun—that was loud and steady enough—but because of her banshee screams. Somehow she seemed to be crying and shrieking and shooting and cursing all at the same time.

A second gunman went down at the bow; the other one scrambled to a blind spot in the lee of the superstructure, having to skirt the spreading oil as he did so.

Johnnie got up, heaved another, smaller jerrican of the oil on the deck. I could see its puddle spreading to where the flare was still burning.

The men at the stern came out of the hatchway again, crouching. Chloe, who was now deathly quiet, let one get out, then caught the second one with a shot in the chest right as he cleared the coaming. By the time the next one was clambering over him, she had worked the action and fired again. That one went backward—whether hit in the leg or trying to fling himself out of the line of fire, I couldn't tell. Then she nudged her gun over to where the first pirate, the one she had allowed to exit the hatch, was hiding. Finally summoning the nerve to fight back, he popped up.

"Chloe—"

"How's Alvaro?"

The raider fired twice then ducked back down. One shot rang off the pilot-house's iron plate.

"Chloe, I can't see if Alvaro is—"

"Then shut up."

The pirate rose again, bolder; a head-and-shoulders target. He started firing.

Chloe let him get off three rounds, let him get more confident, rise up a little more.

"Sniper's triangle," she whispered and squeezed the trigger.

The man slumped back with a dark hole at the base of this throat. He did not move.

I had to put the pen down for a while; my hand was shaking. I don't know if it was because I was holding it so hard and writing so fast for so long, or if it was because it was the first time I thought back through all of what happened.

The rest was anti-climactic. Although Alvaro's flare overshot the oil, Johnnie's last container of liquid blubber flooded along the deck to where the flare had come to a stop. In a second, half of the weather deck was obscured by a low, dim, sheet of flame: blubber, even if it is refined again and again in try pots, does not burn like motor oil or gasoline.

But the captain was right when he assured us that the thing a ship's crew fears the most is fire. Any fire. Whatever organization was left on the pirate ship disintegrated. Some came out to try to fight the fire; Chloe gunned them down, along with some help from the captain. In fact, when they finally put their hands up to surrender, he had to shout at her over the radio—hard and loud—to get her to stop.

Johnnie had taken over the *Voyager*'s wheel. Although he's not our best hand with the boat, he brought it around and stood off thirty yards from the ship. Using the radio, I talked him through what he should do: instruct the enemy survivors to go to the stern, pile all their guns there, leave in their dinghies, and remind them that Chloe's gun would be on them the whole time.

As that was taking place, Steve and Rod pulled *Voyager*'s own dinghy out from behind a pile of rusting tanks, got it down to the water, where the captain joined them. He was moving slowly, looked like he might stumble. "Captain?"

"No time to talk. Need to get these Argies sorted."

"Then can you give the handset to Giselle?"

He did not reply. But a moment later, the circuit opened again and Giselle asked, "Willow? Are you all right up there?"

"We're fine. But how's Blake? And the captain?" I wasn't going to ask about Alvaro, not as long as Chloe had the pirates in her sights. She never did take her unblinking eye from that scope.

Giselle's voice was hushed. "Blake is dead. They hit him a bunch of times. Rod saw him pass out after about half a minute. They couldn't get to him without leaving cover and getting shot themselves."

"And the captain?"

"He's in bad shape, Willow. Freak hit. I was down here, reloading magazines for him, heard one of the try pots kind of snap and ring at the same time—and there he was on his back. Apparently, a bullet hit the side of one of the pots, cracked it, bounced back, hit him in the left shoulder."

"So he'll be all right?"

"I hope so. When I tried to put a dressing on the wound, I saw more blood. All along the left side of his neck." She was silent for a moment. "The bullet cracked chunks off the pot—spalling, I think it's called? Pieces cut into his neck, into his arm, one into his armpit."

"Can you see them, get them out?"

"You're the biology and premed type, Willow, not me. I can't see anything, because the fragments didn't really make holes; they made slits, almost like he'd been cut with a razor. I packed them as well as I can, but they keep soaking the gauze."

What little I knew about surgery and wounds told me that did not sound good. But I didn't say that—not yet.

It took us about two hours to get everyone together again, and the prisoners locked up in the gunpowder house: not much more than an unfurnished, unheated shack on a stone foundation. We took turns guarding them with their own guns: Johnnie had shinnied up the ship's davit ropes and got their weapons.

For which he caught hell from the captain while he was shinnying back down. "You damned fool! You can't know that ship is safe. They might all be contagious. They probably are!"

Which scared us all because it became pretty clear pretty quickly that the captain had heard more about the plague than he had let on, probably before we had even come around Tierra del Fuego.

But there was no time to ask him—or even think—about that. We had a lot to do. Alvaro had been shot through the thigh:

no broken bones, but he lost a lot of blood and the fall stunned him. Chloe alternated between hovering over the little guy and then leaping to her feet, eyes full of hellfire, ready to go out to the gunpowder house and shoot the Argentinian survivors.

Not that they didn't deserve it, but the captain insisted that they had to be debriefed. He waved off my attempts to check his wounds even though he became very pale.

By two o'clock, Alvaro was caning around, and we were ready to talk to the prisoners. There were only eight left, four of whom were badly wounded. We stood outside the gunpowder house, pushed in a camp stove. They were grateful for the heat, asked for food, which only got them stares; it was pretty clear they had been eating a lot better than us.

Alvaro and the captain did most of the talking; the captain because he had clearly done this kind of thing before, Alvaro because Spanish was as much his first language as English.

The pirates weren't eager to share information, but they weren't eager to die, either. It also turned out that the alert ones didn't care what happened to their wounded, or really, each other. But what were we willing to give them in exchange for cooperation?

Captain Haskins told them he'd provide the best care for the wounded that he could, and that, furthermore, he would let them join our community if they were willing to go back on board their ship and unload the supplies for all of us to share. Alvaro got very dark when the captain forced him to offer that. The Argentinians could barely keep from smiling; that deal was obviously fine with them. I think we were all silently wondering if the captain had gone, as he put it, around the bend. The raiders almost certainly had some weapons left on board their ship, and even if they couldn't fight all of us, once aboard and unsupervised, there wouldn't be much we could do to keep them from motoring away. We couldn't even be sure they hadn't left someone—or something—aboard as a backup: it was a plague ship, so we weren't about to search it. The only reason we thought it was probably empty was because the raiders had all been so eager to get off, away from the fire. Which ultimately did a lot of superficial damage, but burned out before the whole ship caught flame.

Our worst fears about the team at KEP were confirmed. As the captain had expected, rather than making a direct approach, the raiders had tried sneaking into the warehouses. They set off the booby traps and almost all the supplies had burned. They were evasive about how they'd known to travel to Husvik, but it was clear that Keywood and his staff had not given us up easily, if at all. According to the pirate leader, they had died of exposure after breaking out of the building in which they had been locked.

Captain Haskins ended by getting their assurance that their story was complete and honest, pointing out that the penalties for lying were extremely severe in our group. The pirates swore to their truthfulness on Bibles they had never read, and on the souls of mothers that they had probably abandoned to squalor and disease by the time they were fifteen.

The only really useful information we got was about the plague itself. We learned more details about the various stages of the disease, about how contagious it was, and which were the most likely ways to catch it. But ultimately, what none of them knew was how long you had to wait before going back into an area where all the infected had died. In fact, it was that uncertainty which had led them to grab the ship about two months ago: a conglomeration of semi-allied gangs that had one leader smart enough to realize that the only way they were going to live was by getting away from all possible sites of infection. But during their weeks at sea, most of them had turned anyhow and ultimately became the survivors' zombie shock troops.

The captain motioned them to get up; it was time to unload their ship. Alvaro stared at Captain Haskins, who only stared back and used a boat hook to pull out the camp stove once the four unwounded pirates had exited.

The captain had us tow the Argentinians back to their ship in a separate dinghy, then shocked us by being the first to board, even though he clearly had difficulty ascending the rope ladder that Johnnie had left hanging from the stern. He disappeared into the aft hatch, was gone for a few minutes. When he returned, he confirmed that he had found no traps and motioned the first two Argentinians to come aboard. Once they were, he had them hold the ladder steady while the last two clambered up.

When the second pair was just a few feet away from the taff-rail, the captain quietly drew the revolver that Alvaro had used earlier and put a bullet into the back of first one raider's head and then the other. As they fell, he yanked the knots holding the rope ladder: the last two raiders plunged down into the water, screaming as soon as they surfaced.

I don't think anyone spoke or moved for a full second. Then, reflex took over and we went into rescue mode. We started grabbing for boat hooks and life preservers.

"No," shouted the captain. "Leave them."

"Leave them?" I shouted back. "They'll die!"

"As they should. Care to guess what I found on their ship?"

I shook my head.

"The gnawed remains of Larry Keywood and Diane Paley."

It took us a second to realize the full significance of that: the raiders had used the station team as fodder for their zombies.

So we watched the two dog-paddling Argentinians plead and pray and shiver and sputter, growing more pale, growing more listless. Finally, unable to even tread water, they sank beneath the grey swells without so much as a ripple.

The captain had watched from the ship's taffrail. "They were warned about the penalty for lying. They've paid the price. Wait there."

He made five trips into the ship's interior, emerging with large, bulging plastic trash bags. He also ran a fuel hose over the side, told us that it was for tapping one of the fuel tanks. Then he lowered the bags into the dinghy in which we'd brought along the Argentinians and climbed down into it himself. At that point, he was as pale as the men who'd drowned a half hour before. He mumbled for a line. We tossed him one and then towed him to shore.

Once there, he snarled at us if we came close. He dragged the bags out of the dinghy, upended them all on the scree beach, careful not to touch anything that fell out, and spun on his heel toward the radio house, wobbling as he went.

"What are you doing?" Giselle shouted after him. Her voice was angry, frightened, hurt.

"Putting myself in quarantine," he said. "No one comes in. We speak through the door. Burn their dinghy. Burn the bags. Filter masks on when you handle what I salvaged. Even though I never touched it directly, everything goes in boiling water. Even the ammunition. Can't take a chance. And Johnnie?"

"Sir?"

"You're going to stay in the end room of the manager's house. You went on the ship, so no contact with the others. Not safe."

He turned and locked himself in the radio house after giving us strict orders to stay away from the wounded pirates in the gunpowder house. Earlier in the day, we would have argued against just leaving them to freeze overnight, which they would certainly do. Now, death by slipping from semi-consciousness into sleep and on into hypothermia seemed like a fairly mild form of justice. Besides, no one was willing to expose themselves to whatever virus the prisoners had been living next to for weeks or months.

Alvaro limped away someplace, trailing blood in the snow. Chloe made to go after him, but Giselle put a hand on her arm and shook her head. When Alvaro came back, he looked okay, but his eyes were red. He insisted, almost violently, that he was going to take the captain's dinner out to him. No one argued.

By the time Alvaro came back, he was too tired to do anything except tell me that the captain wanted to speak to me.

I went out to the radio house, knocked on the door. It opened a crack. "Stay back." The captain sounded terrible.

"Captain, what is it? What can I—?"

"Two things. First, I left a manila envelope under my bed. In it, you'll find everything I ever learned about this bloody virus. It's not complete, but it has some additional details about what to avoid and how long it takes to become symptomatic under different conditions. Second: write down what happened today. Not just the action against the raiders: everything. Everything we learned from them, everything you observed. You—we'll need it." But his correction to "we'll" sounded like an after-thought, the kind of thing people say when they are trying to pretend that they'll live as long as their kids or are trying to act confident about surviving a dangerous surgery.

So I just said, "Yes, Captain," and went back to the manager's house.

I have done as he has asked. I have written everything down. And now I want to sleep and not think about tomorrow. Or anything that comes after.

## August 28

Now that Willow went and recorded her report in my journal, it doesn't really feel like my journal anymore. But maybe that's okay. I started it for myself, but now, I have to wonder: is this journal just about me, anymore? Or is it the story of us? And if so, maybe I have to rethink who gets to write in, and read, it.

We wanted to bury Blake, but with the ground frozen, there just wasn't any way to do it. So we put him to rest in the whaling station's graveyard and piled stones on top of him. When it came time to say a few words, everyone looked at me. Don't know why, except maybe I reek of Recovering Catholic. Anyhow, I was the only one who'd spent any time in a church.

We tried checking in on the captain on the way to the graveyard, but when we opened the door a crack, we heard snoring. So we backed off. When we tried on the way back, he answered our first knock. He had to be talked into some food, which I brought back out with Willow.

He sounded very weak. Told us to leave the food on the step, that he'd pick it up. Willow asked him if she could come in just a step or two, to see how he was doing. He refused. She threatened to push on in anyhow.

The captain replied in his ice-cold authority voice. "If you do, I will not be able to allow you to leave. You'll have to stay in here with me. For weeks, maybe months. So don't come through that door." By the end, his voice had faded to a pleading whisper.

Willow tried to say something, choked back the words along with a sob, turned on her heel and walked back to the manager's house. Really quickly.

I didn't know what to do or say, but about a minute after she left, the captain spoke. His voice was low. "Alvaro, things are going to get more difficult."

"More difficult than a ship full of raiders?"

He may have chuckled; he just may have been coughing and gurgling. "Fair point. Let's say things are going to get difficult in a new way."

"Well, that's good to hear. The old way was getting boring."

"I knew you had some cheek in you. But hard facts, now, Alvaro. I'm never leaving the radio house."

"Captain, if you haven't come down with the virus in a month—"

"Alvaro: think. You're smarter than that."

He was right. Deep down, I knew better.

He evidently knew my silence meant I realized he was right. "Don't feel badly, lad. I knew I was dead when I climbed up the ladder to the stern of that ship."

"What do you mean? Your wounds aren't—"

"Alvaro: it has nothing to do with my wounds, although they will accelerate my—my outcome. As it is, you're going to have to go through all my kit soon, anyway. So when you get back to the manager's house, go in my room. Go look at the bottles in my medicine cabinet. That will tell you what you need to know. I was the only one who could risk going on their ship, because I'll be dead before I can, er...can 'turn.' Assuming I'm infected at all."

"Captain, whatever is wrong with you, you can't be sure—"

"Yes, I *can* be sure. What's wrong with me is not going to get better. And even if I had some miraculous reversal, I can't risk staying near you lot, lest I *do* turn. This is the way it has to be. But there's a harder patch ahead."

Now I knew what he meant. "Johnnie."

"Yes. He's a good lad, but it will be hard having him living in a separate room in the manager's house. So, when I—no longer have need of my bunk here, this is where he should be."

"So this becomes the plague house."

"Yes. So, listen now: here's what you have to do."

He talked me through the necessary steps in about five minutes. He had it all thought out, down to the last detail. By the end, he had gotten hoarse. "Now go. Talking makes me tired."

I heard him shuffle away, deeper into the radio house.

When I got back to the manager's house, I went into his room; everyone stared at me as I did. Everyone except Willow, that is. She just looked real sad.

I learned a lot of things. Like what a bastard I was for calling him the Great Ghoul of the Ocean-Sea and other smart-ass shit like that. The first of those orange prescription med bottles I picked up had this on its label: "Methotrexate—for advanced Non-Hodgkin's Lymphoma." I didn't see the dosage or anything; I didn't need to. There was Lieutenant—no, *Captain*—Alan Haskins' death sentence, written out as calm and plain and small as the bullshit you read on the label of Flintstone's vitamins.

And then I saw that the bottle was empty, and that the "next refill date"—in Valparaiso—was May 30, 2015. Almost three months ago. So, whatever the captain had heard on the radio by mid-June made him skip going to Valparaiso for his meds. Going through the rest of the prescription bottles (which included interferon, Welbutrin, and a bunch of opioids), I found another empty methotrexate, this one from Port Stanley. Clearly, a pharmacy there was his back-up plan. But by that time, no one was dispensing any meds—or anything else—in the Falklands.

The only bottle that didn't make sense at first was a prescription for Vyvanse, made out for someone named Phillip Grover. Then Willow walked in and solved the mystery.

Looking over my shoulder, she scanned the bottle and said, "Huh. Sure."

"What?"

"It's why the captain perked up over the last week. That's some kid's ADHD meds. Vyvanse is an amphetamine. Must have been left behind on some cruise."

"Damn it," I muttered. "The captain, he—he deserved better than this."

She nodded. "He's had a hard life. Unfair."

"Unfair?"

She shrugged, went to the nightstand. There was an open manila folder on it. "He had me get this out from under his bed last night: all the data he ever collected on the virus that's causing this plague. But I found something else under there." She took what looked like an oversized jewelry box off his nightstand and handed it to me.

Inside was a square silver cross. It was hanging from a white ribbon with a purple stripe running down its center. It took me a moment to realize I was looking at a medal. "Holy shit. What do you think it is? The Victoria Cross or something?"

She handed me a much folded letter on royal—*royal?*—stationery that had gone with the medal. It was the Military Cross, awarded for gallantry to Lieutenant Alan P. Haskins of the—

I looked up. "He's friggin' SAS?"

She nodded as I put it down. "I wonder how long we would have survived if anyone else had been the captain of *Voyager.*"

For a moment, I couldn't decide whether I felt we were the luckiest people on the planet for having had him with us, or the unluckiest for losing him and never knowing who or what he was until now. I guess if we hadn't all been such a bunch of self-involved kids with our heads up our asses and obsessing over first-world problems, we might have seen him more clearly.

Tucked under the medal box were letters. The addresses were written in a female hand. Judging from the postmarks, they were probably from the woman Keywood had mentioned. Who seemed to be one and the same as the security operative he had lost on Fortuna Glacier, according to some of the security stamps on a few of the envelopes: evidently, she been assigned to Port Stanley from the Foreign Office. I put the medal box back on top of the letters: I couldn't open them any more than Willow had been able to when she found them.

We wandered out into the next room. Everyone was there, look-ing at us. Because now we had morphed into a combined surrogate-captain; we were the ones who shared out the information, set the next course. I thought I might shit my pants right there.

I started to speak. Before I had the first word out, Giselle put up her hand. Yes, she put up her friggin' hand. I just nodded.

"What about Johnnie? He needs to hear what's going on, too."

I answered carefully. "We'll catch him up. As soon as we're done here. But captain had some—orders—about Johnnie. And himself." Which I explained in stomach-sinking detail.

After that, we had to review the new equipment we'd added to our collection. Although a lot of the raiders' guns had gone overboard, there were the bunch Johnnie had pulled off the ship, and then a few more the captain had stuffed into the bags he'd brought out. There were four Argentine FALs, three Rexio pump shotguns, and two AKs that looked like they had been well-chewed and spat out by the backstreets of half the cities in South America. There was about an equal number of handguns: a few Tauruses and Browning Hi-Powers, but most were .38 Special knock-offs.

The other things that the captain had scavenged for us—mostly food, water, vitamins, medical supplies—were all in sealed plastic: the only reason he had picked them up. In addition to a pair of toolboxes, that was pretty much it.

When I was done, everyone sat for a while. Then Rod looked up. "Okay, but what are we gonna do next?"

I sighed, couldn't believe I was going to say what I was about to say. "We start getting ready to leave."

"Whoa, whoa!" shouted Silent Steve—who'd really found his voice in the past twenty-four hours. "That's not for a few months, though, right?"

I shook my head. "Captain says there's a change of plans. We leave within the week. Have to."

"What? Why?"

"Because of the plague."

"But we've got the captain and Johnnie quarantined. And if they're okay—"

"We won't know until it's too late, Steve. What do you want to do, tape them to their chairs for the next month—assuming that's long enough? Except how do we restrain them without also getting too close to them? According to the reports, when the infected turn, they turn fast. Really fast. And—worst news—the two people who've been exposed and are currently quarantined are also the two largest, strongest people in the group."

Steve eyed the guns leaning in the corner next to the door.

"Really?" I asked. "You think you could shoot either of them? And do you think they'd make it easy?" I thought I might throw up. "Captain thought this through. Winter is just about done down here. In a week, if the weather is good, we start out. If not, we wait for it to turn, watching the ocean from Leith Harbor."

"And what?" Giselle gasped. "Just leave the captain and Johnnie here?"

I sighed and looked straight at her. "That's what the captain says. And if you have a better solution, one that allows us to keep them with us, but safely in quarantine, I am all ears." I kept myself from adding, *I don't like this any better than you do. Probably a lot less.*

Giselle's chin came out: she wasn't going down without a fight. "There's the other ship. We could put them on that."

I shook my head. "It's a good thought, but it won't work. Running that ship requires a lot of hard work and a lot more than two crew. Unfortunately, the captain can barely hold a teacup. And Johnnie—well, he'd need a lot of hands-on guidance." In order to make that sound better, I added. "Any of us would." Which was true enough. "Look: the captain is right. We can only take one ship: *Voyager*. So we refuel her from the raider's tanks, and take as much more as we can hold in the containers we have. But all of that is for emergencies: for close maneuvers, outrunning bad weather, whatever. We aren't experienced sailors like the captain, but he taught us a lot more than the basics. As he pointed out, we ran the ship on our own from the time we got around Tierra del Fuego."

Chloe frowned. "Ugh. I'm not looking forward to going back through there."

I smiled at her and her frown went away. Hell, she even smiled back. "You won't have to. Because we aren't going that way."

Rod nodded. "If we head toward Africa, we can jump from one current after the other over toward Brazil. Then we can coast-follow all the way up to the Caribbean."

"To do what?" Steve asked. "None of us have spent any real time on the East Coast. The West Coast is all we know."

Willow shook her head. "Actually, Steve, we *don't* know the West Coast. Not anymore. Every place is an unknown, now. But if we tried sailing back to California, we'd have headwinds for a thousand miles to the west and then a hard tack up along South America's Pacific coast. But if we go north, we can follow the Benguela Current up to the South Equatorial Current and catch a ride all the way to the Spanish Main and the Caribbean."

Steve smirked. "Yeah, just in time for hurricane season."

Chloe shrugged. "Hey, if you know a perfectly safe place these days, tell me and I'll go. But if not—damn, there are a lot of ports up that way. A lot of places to look for survivors."

I nodded. "And the captain pointed out that there are a lot of sub pens that face on the Atlantic. If anyone in the world got away from this virus, it would be sub crews. So we want to get up there and get our radio in range: not just to pick up their transmissions, but to trade information, join them."

Giselle sighed. "We're not the only people who will go to the Caribbean. Which, if I recall my history, was a hot spot for pirates until the last century."

I smiled. "Well, we certainly don't have a shortage of guns or ammunition this time. We even have enough to get in some practice."

"On the open ocean?"

"Could. Or if we scout out some of the islands that have remained uninhabited. We might make landfall there."

Steve screwed up his face. "What uninhabited islands?"

"There are some everyplace you go. Usually small ones that don't have any springs or rivers of their own and are so small that any decent hurricane will put them underwater for a while."

"So we're going to stop there just to practice shooting?"

I shook my head. "Fish gather in their shallows. There are fruit trees. We get a chance to feel our feet on the ground. And yes, we also get to practice our marksmanship."

Rod nodded. "Captain really did have it all figured out."

I smiled, didn't let on that the last couple of ideas were my own. Then I noticed Willow smiling a Mona Lisa smile at me. Well, yeah, okay: *she* knew they were my ideas. After all, she's friggin' Willow.

It was she who got up first. "I'm going to go tell Johnnie."

No one volunteered to come with her, to talk through the door to tell the biggest, most good-natured of us all that we were going to maroon him here with a dying SAS lieutenant who just might go whacko and kill him before the first week was out.

I felt like a shit.

## August 29

Just when you think you've got things under control, you realize that control is an illusion. Because the world takes all your fine ideas and solutions and flushes them down the crapper.

Here's how it happened.

I was one of the first people up. We'd ended the prior day making some initial preparations for the journey, figuring out how many and what kind of rations to leave behind for the captain and Johnnie, which weapons, how much ammo. Made us feel lower than dogs the whole time we were doing it. And we stayed up pretty late. Except Willow. She participated through dinner then went to her bunk. She looked depressed or maybe very thoughtful or—hell, I don't know. Because: Willow.

So next morning, as soon as I pulled on my clothes, I went to check on the captain. No response to a light knock and no snoring. Either he was still sleeping or he had died, which was always on our minds, now. But I calmed myself down and walked back to the manager's house, figuring it was time for us to bite the bullet and eat some more of those godawful penguin eggs. They were protein and they wouldn't stay good forever, so what the hell.

When I walked in, Chloe and Rod were already up. He was heating water. She had already grabbed one of the penguin eggs from our makeshift "fridge" outside.

I sidled over to Chloe. "Hey."

She smiled sideways at me. "Hey." She leaned close enough that our bodies were touching all the way down the side. It felt great. Then it felt more than great. Her smile widened. "So," she asks, all innocent as she changed the unspoken subject, "where's Willow?"

"What do you mean?"

Chloe's smile dimmed. "She's not with you, checking on the captain?"

Giselle's head popped out from under her blankets.

"No, I went there alone—"

"Damn it!" shouted Giselle, who leaped out of bed and ran down the hall to the room at the end of the hall, the one with a separate outside entrance. Johnnie's room.

She hammered on the door. "Johnnie, Johnnie? Is Willow—?"

"I'm in here," Willow said through a loud yawn. "And we'd like to sleep a little more."

Johnnie actually giggled when she said the word "sleep."

Giselle nodded, walked away from the door and started to cry. Rod held her, and I'm not sure his eyes were dry either.

Chloe had grown very pale. "No," she whispered. "This can't be happening."

"Oh, it's happened all right," muttered Steve. "Shit."

In retrospect, I should have seen it coming. We all felt that way, particularly Giselle, who was the only one of us who had noticed that Willow always seemed to find extra time to spend alone with Johnnie. On the surface of it, you'd think there couldn't be a more mismatched couple, but in a crazy sort of way, it made sense. Although Willow was arguably the most grown-up of us, Johnnie was the most uncomplicated and comfortable with himself. Which we had sometimes mistaken for stupidity, I guess. Granted, he wasn't the sharpest knife in the drawer, but what we were really seeing was that Johnnie wasn't a worrier. He took things as they came and always with a cheery attitude. That's just who he was, and when someone was cruel to someone else, you always got the sense he didn't quite understand it—as if we were behaving like people from another planet.

So Willow had made her choice. And there was obviously no going back. She didn't do it to try to get us to lift the quarantine; she did it to stay with Johnnie. Kind of the weirdest and scariest Adam and Eve reboot you could ever imagine. She knew the dangers. She knew that a balanced diet was going to be a big challenge for them. She knew all of it. But as she calmly, patiently explained through the door, she knew that we'd leave them a good supply, she knew which seaweed she could use to supplement their other nutrient needs, and she knew the wildlife of South Georgia well enough to help them get by. And with Johnnie, she certainly had a strong pair of arms to help her. And with all the diesel left in the ship, they'd have heat and electricity for a long time, as long as they only used it when they needed to.

"Besides," she said in that eighteen-going-on-fifty-eight voice of hers, "if we don't catch the virus, it means we've learned some important things about the vectors of contagion. And then if we wait for, say, a month or so, we can try going back aboard the ship, scout out more of the supplies. Also, it's certainly got a better and more powerful radio than we have here. So, you see, if all of you find the world dead out there, you can always come back here. Because we'll either be safely dead and frozen solid, or we'll be alive and with plenty of room for all of you."

I wanted to find a flaw in her reasoning, but I couldn't. I also couldn't help envying her for how much of an adult she already was. I suspect she was born that way.

So after pushing back the sense of loss, of how much our group had shrunk, we went back to the radio shed with the captain's breakfast. Once again, he didn't reply. We knocked hard. Still nothing. We pushed open the door with a flensing knife. He was in his bed, staring at the ceiling.

And beyond it into eternity, I guess.

## September 6

It is still hard for me to write. I have to say the words first and then spell them one by one. But I like doing it. Because now I will not be "dum Chloe" any more.

Alvaro could'nt write today. He was so tired. He steered the ship out of the bay and far out into the ocian. He never took a brake.

It was hard waving good by to Willo and Jonny. I will miss them. But they are happy and I am glad for them.

And the five of us who are leaving have a new addvenchur. We are sailing to the Caribeen. The wether is good, we have enough suplies, and we are healthy. And I remember what the captain told me when Alvaro was first teaching me to write. That I shoud keep one eye on the wether, one eye on the radio, and both eyes on tomorro.

I just never gessed I woud see tomorro whenever I looked at Alvaro and my frends. But now, that's what I see.

Because they are all my tomorros. And I am theirs.

## Part Two

# AT THE END
# OF THE LINE

## October 13

When we got hit by a storm on October 11, about nine hundred miles south of the Ivory Coast, somebody must not have secured the pilot house's aft deck door. I suppose that "somebody" could have been me, but remembering routines (or anything else) isn't usually one of my problems. On the other hand, after a month at sea on the same boat, the stuff you do lots of times every day begins to blur together.

None of this would even be worth mentioning if, toward the end of the storm, we hadn't been hit by a following gust that whipped through and around the pilot house and scooped out a bunch of papers. We lost some charts, but fortunately, we have backups of all the working maps. But we have no way to replace the last twenty-seven days of my—well, *our*—journal.

Not that it was riveting reading or anything. But it's kind of like having a hole gouged out of our story. I mean we still have the log book, although not everybody keeps the records of our course and speed as carefully as they might. And now that I've written that where everyone else can see it, I will stop grumbling about it. Well, I'll *try* to stop grumbling about it.

Besides, it's my fault for not making myself an even bigger pain in the ass by insisting that we *never* leave the journal topside. Meaning that losing it is on me as much or more than it is on anyone else. So it's up to me to make good on that loss as best I can.

Here's what I remember of the last five weeks:

Only two days out from South Georgia Island, our radio went dead, and none of us knew why. Captain was the expert and all he had showed us was how to operate it. Hell, he barely had enough time to make us semi-competent sailors. So I took a dive into the user's manual. I didn't get very far.

Unfortunately, that was farther than anyone else got. As a result, our daily coded contact with Willow and Johnnie—timed and date-patterned squelch-breaks that we used to tell each other that we were okay—ended almost as soon as it began.

A difficult discussion followed: do we go back and see if we can repair the radio from spares at Husvik? Giselle wanted to tack back to South Georgia. Rod was unable to make up his mind. And so, for once, was Chloe. Whereas hers had always been the most ruthlessly practical voice, I think that after fighting the pirates at Husvik she had turned some kind of psychological corner. It's as though she had adopted us—all of us—as surrogates for the family she'd never really had. And let me tell you, as I've learned many times since, Chloe doesn't do anything half-assed. If she says she's all in, she means she's ALL in. And this choice damn near tore her apart. The practical side of her sided with me: we'd have to fight our way back against both wind and current and that meant more time before we reached our first destination—St. Helena—to replenish our slim supplies of food. Besides, the odds were poor that we'd find any spare parts for the radio at Husvik. Assuming we could figure out which ones we needed to fix it.

On the other hand, Chloe nodded every time Jeeza (Chloe's new, improved name for Giselle) insisted that we at least let Willow and Johnnie know that we hadn't gone off the air because we'd died at sea. Jeeza got wet-eyed every time she reminded us that the two of them were all alone at the far end of the world. They needed to know that we were still out there, too. Which I sympathized with and felt like a bastard arguing against.

But in the end, it was Silent Steve who smacked the ass of the elephant in the room. "We can't take the chance," he said, not looking up from where he was sitting cross-legged on the crew deck that night. "They've been all over Husvik now. Including the radio house. And we don't know how contagious the virus is or how long it stays that way. So we couldn't even help them look for parts to fix the radio. All we could do is holler at them from the middle of the inlet, then turn around and sail back out. With less food and even less time to find more." He looked at Jeeza. "I'm sorry." He rose and went to the head.

No one said anything after that. No one had to. He was right. The risks just didn't justify whatever good we might do by letting them know we were still alive. One by one, everyone left our new crew commons: the Captain's cluttered stateroom. We could have cleaned it up, but it had already become a shrine. Leaving it as he'd had it made it a little bit like having the Captain there, listening in on our discussions.

It was lonely without him. And to be dead honest, it was terrifying. Don't get me wrong; he'd trained us well. But damn it, four months and one whole world ago, our biggest worry had been meeting our new roommates at the freshman dorms we never got to.

So we didn't go back to Husvik and spent two weeks feeling pretty lousy about it. That was also when we steered away from the uppermost margins of the Antarctic circumpolar current (the same one that helped push us from Tierra del Fuego to South Georgia) and nosed northward into the Benguela current. We paralleled the western coast of southern Africa for ten days, then sheared off, heading northwest for St. Helena.

After making that turn, the winds were brisk but changeable, so we spent an extra day or two tacking to hold course. Thank god GPS is still working, because with all that back and forth, there were about a dozen times I wasn't entirely sure if we were on the right heading. Twice we weren't. Not huge errors, but this is the South Atlantic. No landmarks because, well, no land. If your numbers aren't "spot on" (as the Captain put it), then you are shit out of luck.

But GPS gave us those one- or two-degree corrections when we needed them and thirty-one days after leaving South Georgia, we saw a rocky hump profiled low on the horizon, the setting sun dropping behind it. So we all celebrated a bit, then a bit more, and for the first time in weeks, I was able to relax and get a good night's sleep.

But as we made our final approach the next day, we found ourselves facing new uncertainties, because we knew damn little about St. Helena.

For instance, it was entirely possible that whatever was left of its small population might be staggering around like extras from a zombie flick. If that was the case, what would we do? Kill them all? Yeah, we had brought most of the guns and ammo, but would that be enough? And would anything useful be left, or would the early survivors have gone through all the supplies before finally turning and tearing each other to pieces? As we sailed for that looming sea-surrounded mesa, we couldn't ignore the possibility that, after coming all this way, we might find St. Helena to be not only our first, but our last, port of call.

But soon after we swung around the northeast shoulder of the island, we saw white-hulled boats out in the water. They were spread in a thin fan around the small bay that fronted the port capital of Jamestown. Several were under sail. Four miles farther out, a big ship was riding at anchor. A quick look through binoculars showed it to be the Royal Mail ship that cycled between the island and Cape Town.

But before we got within two miles of the port, two of the sailboats heeled over and started waving us off. So we stopped near what our map told us was Sugar Loaf Point and started with the signal flags.

I don't think I've ever been as grateful for my memory as I was when I saw their first flag: catty-corner yellow and black squares. That was Lima. Meaning: stop immediately. Pretty much the greeting you'd expect in a world blanketed by a plague.

I told Jeeza to come around slowly and angle away from the coast as I rummaged for a half-blue, half-red flag: Echo, or "altering course to starboard." I held it aloft, followed it with another that was half a vertical yellow bar, half a vertical blue bar: Kilo, or "I wish to communicate."

Don't know what they were expecting, but it sure wasn't that. They reset their yards, slowing their approach. But no flags.

"What are they doing?" I shouted at Steve, who was up near the bow with a pair of binoculars.

"Talking with each other."

"Anything else?"

"Just talking. A lot."

Made sense. From the look of it, they might never have had any visitors at all. So while they figured how to respond to our request, I flipped through the rest of the flags in the box and had the nagging sensation that the Captain was right behind me, his lips seamed by the grimace he called a smile. (And when the hell did I start capitalizing "Captain" like that?)

He had known I wasn't into learning the flags and spent only one morning going over them. But he drilled me on each flag several times, enough to fix it forever in my head, whether I liked it or not. And now that skill was saving my ass. So I guess his ghost had reason to gloat.

Eventually, the folks on one of the boats started responding, but it was semaphore this time. And that took a lot longer. After about fifteen minutes and about twice as many mistakes, I got the basic message across: we'd never been exposed to the virus, we'd been at sea for four weeks, and we meant to trade and sail on. Another minute or two and then more semaphore from them: we were to backtrack to St. Helena's east coast and head to a small ramp of rock sticking out of the water just off its southernmost point: George Island. They'd meet us ashore. "At distance," they added.

We turned around and headed back south. It was a short coastal sail, about eight nautical miles. But having become accustomed to being on the open water, we weren't eager to get too close to the brown and tan cliffs of St. Helena. But the depth charts and sonar reassured us that, as with most sea mounts, this one fell away into the depths really quickly.

Navigating near the rendezvous point was a different story. There was no telling where submerged crags were waiting to rip out the bottom of *Voyager*. So we decided to stand off, reef sails, and use our trawling motor to push over to George Island.

I had to stop after I wrote the words "George Island." Otherwise, I might have laughed and awakened Chloe. Everything about that little scrap of rock was a joke. Beside the Brits' apparent reflex to work the word "George" into most of their islands' names, it hardly deserved the label "island." It was just a bigger-than-average rock-spur shaped like a launch ramp, barely two hundred yards long and seventy wide. Except for birds, there was nothing living on it. Probably because it was damn hard to get a boat close enough to land safely. One moment you were in a rising swell and had a full fathom of water under you; the next, you were bottoming out only a hand's width from submerged volcanic teeth.

The two boats from Jamestown arrived half an hour after Rod, Jeeza, and I climbed out of *Voyager's* dinghy. And because they knew right where to approach and how to time the risers, they got ashore in less than two minutes. But the moment we started approaching, they made shooing gestures and used a megaphone to get us to stop. Unfortunately, we'd lost our megaphone back when we were making the southern passage, so "communicating" on George Island meant shouting through cupped hands until we got hoarse.

At first, the Saints—that's what the locals call themselves—didn't believe that we had no desire to stay on St. Helena or that we had completely avoided contact with the virus. They kept returning to questions about where we'd been since the plague hit, and where we'd just come from, and how long it been since we left there. In their place, I'm not sure I'd have done any different. Eventually, though, they accepted that we really didn't want to live on St. Helena, but, instead, meant to sail all the way to the Caribbean.

So, why had we come to St. Helena? And we repeated, "to trade." I wanted to add "like we told you earlier." But I didn't. We needed supplies a lot more than I needed to get in my weekly ration of snark.

That sent them into another long confab, which ended with them apologizing for taking so long (so veddy, veddy English). Not counting the Royal Mail ship, we were the first boat to reach them. Which isn't particularly surprising. St. Helena is only useful as a waypoint across the emptiness of the South Atlantic. They had decided to turn away all refugees but had never considered traders.

Which actually sped things up. Since they didn't have any scripted bargaining strategy, they just asked, "What do you have, and what do you want?"

Now it was our turn to realize how little we'd prepared for this. No matter how fair your trading partner is, you *never* let them know that you need something in order to survive. Because no matter how ethical they are, you just told them how to squeeze you dry. So we replied that we wanted to pick up some additional food. We didn't let on how desperate we were for it, particularly carbohydrates and anything green.

Carbs had been a problem from day one, even though we left South Georgia with more than our fair share. Willow was confident that if she and Johnnie didn't get infected, the food the Captain had seen on the pirates' trawler—mostly dry and canned goods from King Edward Point—would last a long time. Willow even had a solid plan for getting to those supplies in a few weeks: douse the compartments with water and wait for it to freeze. That would entomb anything harboring the virus in ice that could then be broken up and tossed overboard. It was a typical Willow plan: practical, smart, elegant. But even with those supplies, and her having identified the edible seaweeds on South Georgia, getting the right foods (and enough of them) was still gonna be dicey. At best.

We were in pretty much the same situation. We'd rationed our carbs but, after more than a month at sea, had already gone through ninety percent of them. Vitamins weren't as big a worry; we had enough tablets to hold us through to the new year.

But humans need nutrients and minerals that you don't find in over-the-counter supplements. Which is why, if we had lost *only* the carbs from our diet, we might have been okay. Yeah, we'd have found out what full-blown ketosis is like (I'd never heard of it until Willow explained it), but we could've managed that. What we couldn't manage was a diet that was just protein and fat. That kind of malnutrition would prove fatal. Most likely because of being woozy and making stupid sailing mistakes long before our bodies physically shut down.

The Saints were even more unwilling than we were to admit what they needed most. But one old guy finally got impatient, grabbed their megaphone, and howled: "Prophylactics!"

He shouted it three times. And then, maybe because we didn't reply right away, he made it even more clear:

"RUBBERS!"

Rod was the first to snicker. "So I guess asking us for rubbers was ... was really *hard*."

I managed not to roll my eyes.

Jeeza giggled, added, "Yeah, they sure were ... beating around the *bush*."

Rod chortled.

And then—yeah, I'll admit it—so did I.

Look: you had to be there. First, imagine five teenagers alone in the post-apocalyptic world and punch-drunk with early-stage ketosis. Now add a bunch of veddy proper Englishfolk called "Saints" who start bellowing through a bullhorn that their most desperate need is a crate of Trojans.

Right out of Monty Python.

But once we shook off the brief reversion to really bad tween-aged sex jokes (wait: is there any other kind?), the locals' need for condoms actually started to make sense. It was all about surviving their own greatest danger: a baby boom and major population spike.

Clearly, the Saints had come through the plague by learning to subsist on what they could grow and catch and by avoiding both community meltdowns and unwanted visitors. The mail ship moored way off shore had been their only outside contact and, with just one lifeboat missing and a lot of the portholes and doors open to the wind and the rain, we could fill in its story. The virus had broken out during its cruise up from Cape Town and the Saints hadn't let anyone off. So RMS *St. Helena* ended her days as a permanently quarantined plague ship. Otherwise, the Saints would have stripped her.

But the same isolation that had kept them safe also made it impossible to meet needs they couldn't supply locally: in this case, birth control. After they hushed the old guy howling about rubbers, the other Saints explained that they would not survive a population increase until they found ways to make the arable parts of the island more productive and determined how and when to safely venture out into the world again.

We explained that we had no solutions to those long-term issues, but that we did happen to have a lot of condoms. For which we were, once again, in the Captain's debt. Other than guns, ammo, and food, the only thing he dragged off the pirate trawler was a small crate of condoms.

We never learned why. Maybe it was foresight, ensuring that a bunch of scared teenagers didn't add babies to the other challenges of their post-apocalyptic existence. Or maybe the Captain was just obeying decades of military reflex: always grab the major consumables. Food, water, booze, smokes, ammo, and rubbers. Not always in that order.

Why did Argentinian pirates have a crate full of condoms? No way to know. However, since they had chosen a profession without health benefits and where a pension would be pointless because you'd never live to collect it, I don't think they were concerned with safe sex. My guess is that they just grabbed every box they could carry out of some *farmacia*, figuring that one day they'd have a use for most of it.

It took twenty minutes to arrive at a deal with the Saints: a couple hundred condoms for about a hundred kilos of fresh produce, exchange set for the following morning.

The next day, I almost drooled (for real) when they showed up with crates—*crates*—of pumpkins, bananas, yams, tomatoes, and—my personal favorites—onions and hot peppers. No garlic, but hey, at last I had a chance to make something other than bland *gringo* food.

They topped us up on fresh water, too: as much as we could carry in every empty container aboard *Voyager*. It's not just that it would give our condenser a break; it was the taste. You might not believe it, but something as simple as the taste of fresh water can be a huge morale boost when you've been living on what comes out of a purifier.

We asked about radio parts but got nowhere with that. The few of them who had our particular model refused to trade even the smallest components. Which made sense: none of that stuff will be manufactured again in our lifetimes.

After several hours of moving all the food and water through the choppy waters to *Voyager*, we waved farewell and set sail. We had more than half a day of light left and wanted to get a good start. The Saints seemed both sad and relieved when we weighed anchor and started west for Ascension Island. Where, it turns out, most of the civilian population hails from St. Helena.

By the time that high rocky loaf of an island finally dropped below the horizon astern, our excitement over the new food and fresh water had faded. Quiet followed. Not until we were sticking our forks into our first fresh meal in weeks did we discover we'd all been reflecting on how far we'd come in the past month. For us, the new food symbolized our success as sailors and survivors, so we felt pretty pleased with ourselves. Chuffed, as the Captain would have said.

And he would have been laughing as he said it because soon after celebrating how mature and capable we were, the ocean reminded us that we were just as small and vulnerable as ever.

Two days out, the wind began to rise and clouds started gathering to the southwest: right between us and St. Helena. So no going back. Two days after that, the storm hit. And toward the end of it, the wind came in and took away the complete story of our journey since leaving Willow and Johnnie at Husvik.

Fortunately, the Captain proved right again. He had told us that major storm systems don't often form in the South Atlantic. The region's strong vertical wind shear pretty much tears them apart. I guess that's what happened with this one. It slowly got worse over thirty-six hours and then just died away.

Still, even though we didn't lose any sails or spars, we'd never seen waves that big. But thanks to the Captain's training, we knew when and how to put our bowsprit into those curling walls of water and ride them. Now we're about two days out from Ascension Island, which, the Saints warned us, has been radio silent for months.

They also warned us that Ascension is a very different kind of island. Far more barren than St. Helena, but far more trafficked, also. The Brits share (well, probably *shared*) a base with us there. A communications hub and tracking for space missions, according to the mostly crap references we have on board. So, it's likely that the base will have at least *some* working radios.

Assuming that the plague didn't drive everyone there into a frenzy of total destruction.

I guess we'll find out which it is soon enough.

## October 15

First thing you think when you see Ascension Island is, "This place is going to suck." Then you land and . . . and—

Look: do you remember how your parents and teachers told you that "appearances can be deceiving?" Well, sometimes they're not.

Ascension Island is almost all volcanic rock and cinder stumps, more moonscape than landscape. We could see green up on the one major mountain/cone at the other end of the island, but aside from that, it was a picture from the apocalypse we'd all grown up expecting: the nuclear kind.

The port was small, with a stone pier and one crane. A boat came out, waved us to sail parallel to the coast. Once we'd complied, they closed to hailing distance, asked where we'd come from, asked how long it had been since we had been either on land or another ship. We gave them the facts, then passed on news and messages from St. Helena.

They hadn't been very suspicious to begin with, but the moment the names and news of the Saints flowed, they waved us in so that we could spill everything we'd heard or seen there.

On the one hand, it was great to set foot on real land again and to be surrounded by people who didn't presume we were plague carriers. But on the other hand, news of our arrival spread so quickly that within five minutes, we could barely get off the boat because the crowd lining the pier was three deep. It was chaos until Jeeza put on her war face, pushed her way on to the dock, climbed atop an old crate, and started reeling off the names of the Saints we'd met, and from whom we were carrying messages.

Me, I was holding back a little, because there were some folks in the crowd with guns. Not sure what you call that kind; it's one of the types with the magazine behind the pistol grip, the one you see carried by Brit soldiers. I could see more folks carrying them as they wandered around the streets. Well, not wandering, exactly; more like a casual walking patrol.

And then there were the dogs. Dozens of them, doing their doggy things: sniffing everyone, barking, tails wagging, tongues hanging out, and generally being excited by having so many people in one place at one time. They seemed to know every person on the pier but didn't seem to belong to anyone in particular. I couldn't figure it out.

But Chloe did. From back in the pilot house, where she held one of the fully automatic AKs below the level of the helm console, she muttered, "Ten to one there are infected on this island somewhere."

"Huh? 'Cause of all the guns?"

"Naw. The dogs. Lookit 'em. Almost three quarters are only a few months old. And every bitch in the bunch is fat with more." When I didn't show instant understanding, she raised an eyebrow.

"Look," I explained, "I never had a dog. Not a lot of my friends did either. In my neighborhood, it was mostly old ladies who had dogs. The kind that fit in their purses. Or cleavage."

Chloe made a face. "I think I just threw up in my mouth. Listen, the dogs here are protection. For everyone. They're not pets; they're part of the town."

I looked back out and saw the whole scene differently. "And that's why all the guns are out. Not special for us; just part of the everyday scenery."

"Yup," she agreed. "These people have some real nasty neighbors."

"Infected, probably."

"Try, 'infected, for sure.'"

"You seem pretty sure you're right."

Chloe smiled. "I'm always right. Seriously though, dogs are better than sentries. Particularly if something doesn't smell right. And I mean that literally, 'cause those zombies we saw back at Husvik—they were seriously messed up. Skin all peeling and skeevy. Dogs will smell that almost as far as they can see it. So, at night—"

"—dogs are the best alarm system."

She hefted the gun so it rested on her lap. Which was a little less wide than when we had left South Georgia, even more so compared to when I first met her. She stared at me staring at her. "Whatcha lookin' at?"

"You don't know?"

She rolled her eyes but smiled. "Down boy. You wanted to trade with the locals, so go to it."

"You coming?"

Her grin widened. "It's always about sex with you, isn't it?" Which was kind of a weird thing for her to say. I just smiled back. She shook her head, still grinning. "Like you always tell the rest of us, we work and *then* play."

"I don't say that. Much."

Both her eyebrows rose high.

I must sound like a prick a lot of the time.

I went ashore, mingled with the locals, and thought about what we could trade with them.

Mostly.

The moment we'd shared the last of our news from St. Helena, the crowd didn't just disperse; it vanished. I imagined that's what it was like to be a "one-hit wonder" band. Back when such things existed.

A few final stragglers mentioned that we could probably find a meal at the Obsidian Hotel, the only spot ever built for tourists. We trailed after them.

The owners were nice enough, but the restaurant was just a bar, now. No reason to serve food when it was going to be the same as what everyone was eating at home: fish, turtle meat, turtle eggs, and occasionally—very occasionally—vegetables from rooftop gardens. We saw the same signs of borderline malnutrition we'd seen in ourselves about two weeks before reaching St. Helena. But the tap-room was pretty full because the Obsidian Hotel was still serving drinks.

Actually, there was only *one* drink to have and it was awful. Not that I could tell good liquor from bad, but hell, I grew up in a poor neighborhood and the only booze that cash-strapped teens can score for parties is crap. But this was so much worse that I wondered if a little actual shit hadn't been mixed in. For taste.

The locals had run out of real booze months ago, so they were making this sorry substitute out of carrot peelings and something else that none of us had the nerve to ask about. Still, everyone in the bar was sipping that vinegar-and-old-socks poison. But no one just tossed it back: doing shots was not a good plan unless you wanted to encounter your dinner again.

A minute or two after we finished shuddering down the first tiny taste, we started making small talk, the way you do when you want to be sociable but really don't have much of anything to say. So we started by asking about the town.

First thing they told us was its name: Georgetown. GEORGE town.

I swear: for one second, I really did think about going back to the boat. Was this whole part of the world named George?

But the barkeep didn't miss a beat telling us about how Ascension had started out as a military base back in Napoleon's day and that nothing much grew here until some botanist came in and made it his personal mission to change that. He'd succeeded. Maybe we'd noticed that the slopes of the old volcano were mostly green?

Before we could reply, the next local picked up the tale. Others chimed in. By the end, we had a far more detailed picture than we needed. Or wanted.

Here are the useful high points. Ascension is just under eight miles east to west and not quite six north to south. It became strategically important as soon as the European empires started spreading by sea, because it was the only land for thousands of miles in any direction. (Okay, if you head due north, it's "only" nine hundred miles to Africa). So the island was a natural stopover point for ships and, later, aircraft.

For much the same reason, it became a listening post and rebroadcasting hub for radio and television throughout that part of the world. During the Cold War, the island was also a major site for spook-work: intel gathering, eavesdropping, signals assessment. The space race brought the addition of a downrange tracking and telemetry station for anything launched from Kennedy Space Center. Later on, those services mostly switched over to monitoring and communicating with the rockets that went up from the ESA's facility in French Guiana.

So although Ascension Island was in the middle of nowhere, it was a stop on the way to almost every place else. Which was why we made landfall there, ourselves.

The weirdest thing was that despite being inhabited since the

Brits built Georgetown, it never had a permanent population. There was no private ownership of land, of buildings, of anything except personal items. Everyone was contract labor, so it wasn't really anyone's "home." They just happened to be stranded together on that splinter of volcanic rock when the world ended.

The locals didn't put it that way, of course. They told the story of their island with a bland version of English good cheer tinged with a creepy mix of "we're all in it together" and "stiff upper lip." Even their weak smiles seemed to assert that:

1) shit happens,
2) particularly to them,
3) and they can even taste it in their booze.

They asked a few questions, showed a momentary spark of interest about our fight with the pirates and infected (they call them "stalkers") in Husvik, and then drifted off.

Once they were out of earshot, Jeeza frowned and asked, "Is it just me who was tempted to ask why they haven't returned to St. Helena?"

Rod nodded. "Yeah, 'cause sailing between the islands isn't hard. Hell, we just did it."

I decided not to mention the storm. "Maybe they wouldn't have been welcome back there."

"Not just that," Chloe added. "Why did these guys go radio-silent on the Saints? Something doesn't add up."

As they batted possible explanations back and forth, I noticed a guy sitting alone. The only solo patron in the Obsidian. Nobody even glanced at him. And he didn't look at anyone. Except us.

I nodded at him. He nodded back. I pushed away from the table, opening up a spot for another chair. As the Captain used to say, a wink is as good as a nod.

The solitary guy did in fact nod, picked up his shot glass, and joined us. He was as tall as Rod—so about 5'10" or so—and thin. I mean, all of the locals were thin, but his arms and legs and shoulders looked like they'd always been light. I thought he might be three years older than us. At most.

As he slid his nonexistent butt into a chair he'd pulled from an empty table, he asked, "You lot certain about this?"

"About what?"

"About being seen sharing a glass with the local pariah."

I shrugged. "We drink with whoever we choose."

"Besides," added Chloe, "we're moving on soon."

"Looks like you might be interested in doing the same," Silent Steve added.

I managed to keep myself from staring at Steve in surprise. However, to use one of Rod's favorite gamer terms, he and Chloe failed their saving throw at him. Silent Steve typically saved his words for crucial moments.

But he might have been on to something. The Brit smiled slowly. "Sometimes, you Yanks are a bit too blunt. But sometimes"—he nodded at Steve in what looked like gratitude—"it is very welcome." He leaned back. "I might be considering a change of location, but perhaps we should get acquainted first."

*Yeah, we should* definitely *get acquainted first,* I thought. But I just nodded and introduced myself after the others had.

When we'd finished, he leaned forward. "I am Percival Halethorpe. Ex-Her Majesty's Royal Air Force, ex-Edinburgh student on deferral, ex-everything. Except being The Reviled of the Earth, here on Ascension. That I can still claim without doubt or debate."

"And why are you 'The Reviled of the Earth' here?" Jeeza asked, propping her chin on her palm. She was clearly infatuated with the guy's accent and use of the word "reviled."

"Because I am the architect of all the misery suffered by the good people of this island." To say that his tone was facetious would be like saying that the pre-plague world was a slightly nicer place to live.

"Sounds like you've got a story to tell," I observed.

"A timeless one, in fact. It's called, 'Blame the Outsider.'"

Rod frowned. "But—you're all English here. More or less."

Halethorpe cocked a wry eyebrow. "Be that as it may—and I underscore *may*—I was, and remain, the living symbol of how the plague came to our inhospitable shores. No one says as much, of course. They're all too proper. Too *English*—more or less," he concluded with a wink at Rod.

Chloe folded her arms. "As a blunt American, I gotta tell ya: I don't know what the hell you're getting at."

Halethorpe's smile was genuine, even appreciative. "What I am getting at is that it was the military that brought the plague here, my dear girl."

"Okay," Chloe answered. "But since you ain't my daddy, I ain't your 'dear girl.'"

That surprised him for a moment. Then he smiled widely—which showed us why England used to be such a cash market for orthodontists. "Fair enough, Chloe," he agreed. "I will try to be less cryptic. But old habits die hard."

"So what do we call you?" asked the no-longer-Silent Steve. "I mean, you don't go by 'Percival'—do you?"

Rod stared at Steve. "You think 'Percy' is any better?"

"Guys," I interrupted. "In case you've forgotten, the man in question is sitting right here." I turned to Halethorpe. "Sorry. We don't get out much. So what did they call you at home?"

"Nothing at all," Halethorpe answered brightly. "Since I was never there."

"Never off duty?"

"Never welcome."

"Oh." *Shit.* "Sorry."

He smiled. "No harm done. And I should have spoken plainly, rather than leading you up the garden path to where my family and titanic irony intersect."

Chloe shook her head. "I know you're speaking English, but it still sounds like a foreign language." She frowned. "It also sounds like you had it pretty rough at home. And here, too, I guess."

He shrugged. "I can't honestly complain. After all, I'm not dead—or what might be worse." He began glancing westward over his shoulder, stopped himself, downed his drink instead.

"Is that where your base is?"

"Was," he corrected. "My mates—and your lot—all became stalkers. Or meals for them."

"What do you mean, 'your lot?'"

He stared. "I guess your welcoming committee didn't mention that there were only thirty of Her Majesty's Finest on the island when the plague deplaned. Because that is almost certainly how it arrived. And almost certainly from your Air Force's weekly flight from Patrick AFB in Florida. It was the last flight that ever came in and it was almost full." He shrugged at our dubious stares. "You had almost three hundred personnel here, most from the 45th Space Wing."

Jeeza stuttered. "A-and the town blamed *you?*"

Halethorpe shrugged. "It wasn't you Yanks who brought it

into Georgetown proper. And to their credit, your officers closed the airfield and base. No one in or out."

"Why didn't your commander do the same?" Chloe asked.

He sighed. "We didn't live on base. Most of us rented rooms here in town or stayed in barracks out at Two Boats. Probably wouldn't have mattered, though. It spread so rapidly. A few of the aircrew from Florida felt a bit dodgy on the pub night we hosted a few days after they arrived. The first few who turned overran the rest." His eyes seemed to stop seeing our faces or the bar of the Obsidian. "Two weeks later, most of my best friends in the world were dead. And there was no time left for anything but remaining alive. Which was a pretty grim business."

"What do you mean?" Jeeza's voice was hushed.

Halethorpe stared down at the tabletop. "Families locking each other in attics, in basements. The healthy having to kill their turned relatives, friends. If they didn't turn before they could bear to pull the trigger. By the third week, everyone that wasn't a stalker had barricaded themselves in."

His gaze rose up from the tabletop. "And since no one is truly a resident, there was no true community to rely upon. Not in the sense of people who'd grown up around each other. After most of the children were gone, it was every man and woman for themselves."

We were quiet for what felt like a long time. It probably wasn't more than ten seconds. But when you've been talking and then everyone stops all at once, the only thing you notice is every moment that passes in complete silence.

Even though we'd heard about the onset of the plague, we'd never seen, or even had to think about, it in this kind of detail. But now it was like waking up in a deserted movie theater where the screen was still showing a horror flick of all the misery we'd missed. All because we were among the lucky few who hadn't been there for the grand premiere of the end of the world.

Percival told us how, like sirens in a big city at night, the screams never stopped. And you never knew the cause of the screaming. Maybe someone was being killed by a loved one. Maybe it was because they were having to kill a loved one. Or maybe they were just losing their shit, because there's only so much terror and loss and hopelessness that most people can take.

But some people, most of who wound up surviving, became

nearly as silent as the corpses around them. Their bodies were still alive, but their ability to feel and react—that died. At least until the worst of the madness was past. Because the insanity of the plague either broke you into pieces, or your emotions became like a ghost: all the horror just drifted through. Like you weren't there. Because, in a way, you weren't.

Those people survived. Whether what remained of their existence could be called "living"—well, that was another matter.

On the other hand, you could say that we were more spoiled than when we'd boarded *Voyager*. Yes, we'd lost people: probably everyone. But we'd been spared seeing all the mad shit that kept on going down until there was no one sane left to see it. Just stalkers, hermits, and survivors who had holes where their hearts used to be.

Halethorpe pushed back from the table. "Sorry. Damn dull talk."

"Not to us," I assured him. "But there's still something I don't understand."

Percival nodded. "Of course: why we didn't all evacuate to St. Helena." He rolled his empty shot glass between pale palms. "To make a long story brutally short, the Saints were glad to talk to us over the radio, but not eager to have us show up at their island."

"B-but, most of the people here—they're *from* there," Rod objected as if personally offended.

Halethorpe nodded. "Yes. But on this end, it was an all-or-nothing proposition. The civilian council decided that if any significant number of us left, it would mean the death of everyone who didn't get to go."

Chloe frowned. "And everyone agreed to that?"

Halethorpe's smile was crooked. "It sounds a great deal more democratic than it actually was. The guns were mostly in the hands of lads from other branches of the Royal government: support for the RAF facility and the comms station, mostly. Not a Saint among them. Nor among most of the boat-owners; they're ex-pats who provided charters and yacht servicing.

"Mind you, even the Saints here weren't in lockstep on the issue." (He pronounced it "iss-yoo.") "Nearly half wanted to stay away for the same reason that their relatives weren't keen to have them back: the possibility of contagion. So St. Helena's government dictated that we should 'shelter in place for the duration of the outbreak.'"

Giselle's voice was almost a squeak. "Seriously? They said that? Who are they to give orders to the people here?"

Percival shrugged. "They are the duly appointed authorities of what is known as the Overseas Territory of St. Helena, Ascension, and Tristan da Cunha. Would you care to guess where the governor resides?"

I shrugged back. "Biggest population center: St. Helena."

"Got it in one. So you see, the Saints really did have the first and last word." Halethorpe stared at the boarded windows of the taproom. "Can't say I blame the governor. Or even think he was wrong." Another silence threatened to suffocate the table. Percival straightened in his seat. "Right. So why did you come to Ascension?"

I managed not to blink at the sudden change of tone and topic. "To trade. And to stop over. We've got a long stretch of open sea once we leave here."

"So, back to the New World." He thought for a moment. "Next stop, Fernando de Noronha?"

*Wow, that was fast.* "I didn't think our destination would be so obvious."

"Wouldn't be, except that your stop at St. Helena suggests a pattern."

"What pattern?" Steve asked.

I answered before Percival could. "That we're island hopping back to the New World. More than that: our accent tells him we're from the U.S., but *Voyager*'s stern shows its port of registry as Port Stanley, Falklands. And instead of retracing our steps, we are headed north for a transatlantic crossing. So logically, we are taking a different—and easier—path back to the States."

Halethorpe's grin was genuine. "Also, it's a safe bet that whoever taught you to sail that boat also warned you that the mainland of South America was sure to have gone completely pear-shaped. So, since you can't safely stop there on your way to America, you're going to the closest off-shore waypoint: Fernando de Noronha." He frowned. "Still, its pre-plague population was larger than St. Helena's, and it was a vacation spot. When the virus struck, its population would have included tourists."

I shrugged. "We're not planning on clearing it. Just getting some water, some food, some fuel. And then moving on."

Halethorpe leaned back. His smile wasn't condescending, but it was certainly ironic. "As if such simple plans are ever truly simple in this Brave New World."

"Yeah, but it's still the only plan that makes any sense... Prospero." Hell, not only did that nickname riff on his own Shakespeare reference, but "Prospero" kinda sounded like Percival. If you had a speech impediment and lisped a lot. Halethorpe blinked at the name. He didn't say anything, but I saw the surprise in his eyes.

And I thought, *Yeah, so you hear the barrio accent and simple words and you think I can't read and understand your precious Bard? Homes, you don't know me.* I'll give him this, though: he looked happy-surprised. Like he was relieved.

Halethorpe smiled. "Sorry; no sorcery credentials, I'm afraid. But I am glad to meet you all. Very glad."

"Yeah, so you let on. Why?"

Percival upended his shot glass. The locals looked over, reacted as though they'd swallowed vinegar. Which would have been an improvement on what they were drinking. "That question," he announced, "is an excellent place to resume tomorrow. Which is, I take it, when you hoped to find persons with whom to trade. Same basic needs, I presume? Water, food, fuel?"

"Got it in one." I smiled. "Prospero."

He smiled back. Good-natured. "I can assist with that. Indeed, I suspect I can help you get most of what you need without even having to trade for it."

"What? You mean, for free?"

"Another topic best left until tomorrow. For now, let's find you a safe house to sleep in."

Steve sounded suspicious: "What's it cost?"

Percival shook his head. "Nothing. There's no housing shortage here. But do bring weapons."

"Why?" Chloe asked. "Infected come knocking here in town?"

"Not usually," Percival replied as he led the way out of the Obsidian's taproom.

## October 16

About 3:30 AM, I wake up. There's a sound like trash cans being mauled by raccoons. But big ones. And far away. So I slip out from under Chloe's arm, out of bed, and pad over to look through a gap between the boards across the window. Like in the rest of the town, our bedrooms are on the second floor. (The locals reserve the ground floor for traps and dogs.)

Way to the south, from behind the naked volcanic cone they call Cross Hill, I can see occasional flashes of light. It's the same place the sounds are coming from. After a few minutes, it stops. I watch for a while, but nada; show's over.

When we met Prospero for breakfast down by the bay, I asked him about what I'd seen.

"Oh, that," he says. "That's just a few stalkers having a go at the funhouse."

I'm not sure what creeped me out more: what Prospero said, or the casual tone in which he said it. "Funhouse?" I repeated.

He nodded, chewing a hard-boiled turtle egg. "A little play-ground we made for our unsavory neighbors. Some lights and a turntable with rusted pots and pans and old trash-bin lids. If any of the stalkers come close to town during the night, the watch throws a switch and *voila*: instant diversion."

"Cool. But how is it powered?"

"Solar cells charge a dedicated battery." He nodded at the roofs behind us. "Lots of solar here, particularly after your Air Force brought it in, not long after they installed wind turbines back in—oh, 1996, I think it was."

Steve was eating slivers of his own turtle egg. Slowly. "And how do you know when the infected—I mean, stalkers—are getting too close to town?"

Prospero shrugged. "The dogs. They get restless." He waved beyond the town limits. "We kennel a few in abandoned houses on the outskirts, keep an active baby monitor in each. When we hear the dogs start to whine and whinge, that's when the night watch taps the switch for the funhouse. Have to do it before the dogs bark. Otherwise, the stalkers go towards them—and, likely, us—rather than the decoy."

"And that works all the time?"

Prospero tilted his head from side to side. "Nothing is perfect, but it reduces the problem. We still get one a week or so. Usually a loner, when the wind is out of the north. Carries their scent away from the dogs."

"Still, a pretty smart system. Who thought it up?" I was pretty sure I knew the answer.

"We like to call everything a community effort, here on Ascension Island," Prospero explained with a shit-eating grin.

I nodded, grinned back. "Yeah, I thought so. But if wind out of the north carries their scent away from the dogs, doesn't it carry the scent of you—and the fish you catch—towards the stalkers, sometimes?"

He picked a fragment of tortoise shell out of his eggs. "We're careful what we do, and when. No cooking when the wind is blowing south. The fish and turtles are gutted and fileted out on the water: no blood smell ashore. And living right next to the waves drowns out the day-to-day sounds."

I nodded, waited for him to finish his scrambled eggs.

He glanced at me. "You either have a most unusual fixation with my dining etiquette, or you have a more pointed question."

"A few, actually. But they can wait until you're done."

"Very polite, but do carry on."

"How many survivors are there? We gotta know who, and how many, we're trading with."

Prospero nodded. "Before the plague arrived in economy class, the population here in town was about six hundred fifty. Fifty or sixty at Two Boat, out near the school. Maybe another fifty who preferred living out in the rough."

Giselle nodded. "So, seven hundred fifty. Give or take."

"And now?" I persisted.

"Two hundred and sixty-nine, as of three days ago." His smile was very small and very ironic. "Not that we are counting, of course."

"Almost two-thirds dead," Rod murmured, horrified.

"Dead or worse," Prospero corrected. "Some of the last to turn wandered off into the wastes when they couldn't force their way into the barricaded houses."

"How many?"

He shrugged. "Twenty, thirty. Maybe more. No one was keeping a tally, those days."

"What about the bases? Did anyone survive except you?"

Prospero stared out over the bay. "No. Which certainly didn't help diminish my pariah status. Some persons still believe I survived because I ran out on my mates."

Chloe leaned forward. "Did you?"

Prospero was clearly starting to get used to her; he just shook his head and smiled. "Ms. Tukkiapik, you are the most refreshingly direct human I have met in . . . well, in many, many years."

"Thanks. Now: *did* you run away?"

He shook his head. "I did not. I was in town with a . . . a friend. I returned to my—the British—facility when reports started coming in about people turning. I arrived just after my leftenant returned from his briefing with the Yank commander. He updated me, sent me back to my billet.

"I hadn't been there long enough to get a cuppa when one of my Yank mates calls me. Seems just after I left, he'd gone up to the Golf Ball and found the leftenant snarling and taking pieces out of the duty staff. He'd already wrecked the bloody ops center. Half of the desktops were smashed, and there were guts all over. Even inside the mainframe, which my chum was trying to salvage before the leftenant went after him, too."

"And?"

"My mate got his rifle in hand before the leftenant got him. I grabbed my kit, a pair of birdwatching binoculars that my . . . my in-town friend kept at my place, and drove back to the Golf Ball. No luck; my mate had locked up the facility and didn't answer his phone. I drove to another rise overlooking the Yank base. They were shooting each other in the lanes between their tidy little prefab billets." He shrugged. "Nothing to be done, except take a rough count. Then I came back here. Had to make sure the locals knew what was happening."

Giselle had folded her hands, was looking down. "And your in-town friend? The one you were with when you heard?"

Prospero glanced back at the rugged, barren wilds behind Georgetown. "Gone. Maybe turned. Maybe eaten. Maybe drove back to Two Boats and died of the virus. Anything is possible."

Rod sounded like he might throw up. "You never went looking...to find out if...if—?"

"No, I did not," Prospero said firmly. "At first, no one could risk leaving. Not until the stalkers finally decided that it was easier to get at the sheep, donkeys, and rabbits on Green Mountain than into our barricaded houses.

"After a few weeks, a few optimistic survivors reasoned that the danger had passed. They went out looking for missing friends. None of them came back. Not one. Since then, no one travels overland, except to ensure that the funhouse remains operational."

I nodded. "So, since you know how many locals are left, and you've got a good idea of how many were killed, what's your guess on how many turned?"

Prospero smiled. "That is the question isn't it? I'm guessing at least two thirds of the U.S. base, initially. Add about thirty civilians."

"Sounds like two hundred and thirty, total?"

"Initially, but we've seen the buggers devour each other, particularly if one is wounded. And we've killed any who come snuffing around here."

"So, your estimate of remaining infected is...?"

"Is utterly unreliable. But the council believes that, after three months, there couldn't be more than one hundred."

I frowned. "And you don't agree with the council."

"The logic behind their calculation is reasonable, but I don't believe it is complete. Not enough to rely on for future planning."

Chloe frowned. "What kind of plans are they making?"

Prospero steepled his hands. "The council have concluded that since the stalkers are indiscriminate reflex predators, they will reduce their own numbers to a point where we can take the fight to them and clear the island."

"You don't sound convinced," Chloe said, folding her arms.

"I'm not."

"Why?"

Prospero hunched forward. "Basic math. We know how much a normal human has to eat to remain alive. Now, modify that by the amount of energy stalkers expend and that they eat meat almost exclusively. That gives us a rough estimate of how many pounds of meat the average stalker has to consume every day."

"And?"

"And they should almost all be dead by now. But they aren't. And they still travel in packs. Which they wouldn't do if every other stalker is an imminent threat."

"So where are they getting all the extra meat?" Rod muttered.

I thought I saw where Prospero might be going with all this, but before I could say anything, Chloe leaned toward him. "You think the council is missing something."

"I do."

"Such as?"

Prospero nodded. "Well, no one knows a bloody thing about stalker behavior when they're not trying to devour us. But no creature can sustain full-on homicidal aggression all the time. It would be utterly exhausting and far too expensive in terms of energy."

Rod blinked. "So you're saying that the infected, uh, take a lot of naps?"

Prospero smiled. "More than that. I believe that if they go long enough without detecting prey, they become torpid."

Chloe sighed, her long eyelashes half-closing. "English, please."

"He means they go dormant," I translated, nodding.

"You agree with him?" Chloe asked.

I shrugged. "It's a damn sight more logical than what the councilors are presuming. According to them, only one hundred infected were running around after the first month or so. That's about eighty days ago. So, in the past eighty days, those one hundred zombies had a total requirement of eight thousand days' worth of food."

"I figure they each need about four pounds of meat every day," Chloe nodded. "That's about what a wolf needs to get by. Barely."

"Which means," I continued, "that a population of one hundred infected would need thirty-two thousand pounds of meat to continue to function for eighty days."

"I think I'm going to throw up," Giselle muttered thickly.

"Then Jeeza, you won't want to stay around for this." I gave her a moment to move to a chunder-friendly spot, but she stayed put. "So, were thirty-two thousand pounds of meat available to the stalkers during the past eighty days?"

Rod nodded. "Okay, let's start by subtracting the, uh, meat mass, of anyone who could *not* have been part of that total."

"Right. So: subtract the two hundred and seventy survivors here in town, and the one hundred infected. So that's three hundred seventy humans we know they *didn't* eat." I turned to Prospero. "And how many corpses did you...dispose of?"

Prospero stared off. "Almost four hundred, between the flu deaths, the stalkers we killed, and their victims. All burned where we found them."

I nodded. "Okay. So, from the one thousand people we started with, we subtract two hundred seventy healthy survivors, one hundred infected, and four hundred corpses. That leaves about two hundred and thirty bodies the infected could feed on."

"That's still a lot of meat," Jeeza observed.

"Not as much as you might expect," Chloe said with a shake of her head. "Predators like the infected, or us, aren't very efficient. Scavengers, like worms or beetles? Different story. But bigger critters leave a lot behind. If they didn't, carrion eaters—like crows and rodents—wouldn't have enough to live on."

Prospero was staring at Chloe. "And how did you become familiar with such matters, if I may ask?"

"Living in Alaska. Hunting to put food on the table. And watching what actual predators like wolves and bears leave behind. Which was usually close to thirty percent, give or take."

"Okay," I agreed. "So we start with two hundred thirty bodies. Call the average weight one hundred and fifty pounds. About twenty percent of that is bone and other inedibles. Say only twenty percent is lost to inefficient eating. So only sixty percent of the body mass is useful, or about ninety pounds per body. So two hundred and thirty bodies at ninety pounds each is—"

"Twenty thousand seven hundred pounds," Rod supplied quietly, just as quickly as I could have.

I nodded. "That's only about two-thirds of what's needed."

"Sixty-four percent," Rod murmured almost apologetically. "A massive shortfall."

I turned to Prospero. "Could meat from the feral animal populations make up that difference?"

He shook his head. "Fifteen thousand pounds of meat? Only if the last environment survey was off by fifty percent."

"And even then," Chloe added, nodding, "realize that four

pounds of meat per infected per day is a really, *really* low estimate. So I'm with you, English. The council's numbers don't wash."

"Which is why they've had to revise their die-off estimate three times," Jeeza concluded.

Prospero was looking around the circle of our faces. "I knew I was going to like you lot."

I got up from our seaside table. "So, this island is more screwed than your leaders think. Is that why you want off?"

His expression became what old novels call "calculating." "That is a longer topic. Best left until the day's business is done."

"You mean, after we finish trading?"

"My advice to you is *not* to trade at all until your position is stronger."

"And how are we going to manage that? Hell, we gotta know what your people want, what they need." I stopped, thought. "Since you guys have to stay so close to home, how do *you* get enough to eat?"

Prospero's answer was a lot more detailed than it needed to be. Here's what it boiled down to: Georgetown got most of its food from the sea, even more than St. Helena. Not just fish, but turtles and their eggs. But like us, they were in real need of carbs. That's why the council was trying to outlast the stalkers; there were plenty of basic carbs growing on Green Mountain.

But while they waited for the stalkers to die off, they were also running out of everything else. Unlike the Saints, who had ten times the population and a free run of their entire island, Ascension's survivors were living on whatever supplies had been in Georgetown when the virus hit. They were also limited to the water they caught in roof cisterns or purified with solar stills.

"At least the dogs can make do by lapping up whatever dew collects on the road or the rocks," Prospero concluded. "Don't know how they, or the stalkers, stomach that, but they do."

Chloe sat straighter. "The stalkers? They drink water from the road?"

Prospero sighed. "Oh, they do better than that. They drink the water that collects on the runways at Wideawake Field. Probably why they haven't all gone over to Green Mountain. The runways are actually the best source of fresh water on the island. Damned inconvenient."

Steve frowned. "Because it keeps a lot of them close to town?"

"Not just that. It keeps them sitting on top of the answer to all our problems."

"You mean, the base?"

"Exactly. Its warehoused supplies would meet every need Georgetown has."

Jeeza frowned. "That presumes that the infected haven't torn everything apart, the way they did your communications and tracking building."

Prospero shook his head. "They haven't. I drove up there for the first few weeks. It was a good position from which to watch. Stalkers aren't superhuman. They can't smell tinned meat, for instance. And they can't break into safe-rooms, or padlocked warehouses, or hangars.

"Furthermore, they don't stop for gardens. Inside houses, they ignore most grain-based products. As far as machinery goes, they might scat on it or just as likely might not. It's meaningless to them. The only reason the comm building looked like a tip was because it isn't much bigger than the inside of a freight wagon and there had been a life-and death struggle in it."

Steve was looking at his hands. "Still. The base was small. How much would be there to start with?"

Prospero smiled. "You Yanks are obsessed with always having more than you need, so you shipped goods in quarterly and flew in additional supplies on every plane. Also, since the base was tasked to maintain readiness for providing logistical support to expeditionary forces—a lesson we learned from the Falklands War—there was always a stock of extras on hand to support combat operations."

I nodded. "All of which will look like a well-stocked department store to survivors of an apocalypse. But there's one small problem."

"Which is?"

"According to you, the place is crawling with zombies."

He nodded. "Which is why it's too early for you to open negotiations with the council. If you are patient, you will be able to meet at least half of your needs without having to trade for them."

I shook my head. "How? By leveraging our charm and good looks?"

"No, by leveraging what you *really* have to offer."

I still didn't get what he was driving at. "You don't even know what we're carrying in our boat."

"I don't have to."

"Why?"

"Because your most important commodity is your ability to undertake actions that will restore hope to everyone on this miserable little island."

*Actions?* "Wait a minute; you said we could get what we need for *free.*"

"No: I said that you could probably get most of what you need without having to pay with your own goods."

"So what deed is going to get us anything we want? Besides, how will the locals swing it? You just said this island is in short supply of everything."

"It is. But that will change once you've retaken the base."

Really, I should have seen it coming. Chloe had. She was already smiling and shaking her head by the time I was able to reply. "That's—that's nuts! There are just five of us."

"I'd be with you," Prospero countered.

Which I waved away. "There are dozens of people here who can probably shoot a gun. Why not them? If this is such a great idea, why haven't they already made it happen?"

"Because, Alvaro, they lack three things that you lot have in ample supply. The right weapons, plentiful ammunition, and sheer nerve."

Well, he was right about the first two—but: "Hey, how do you know what guns we have and how much ammo?"

"I was on the pier when you came in. I heard Giselle tell the story of what happened at Husvik. Assuming that was not a fiction to preempt misbehavior by the locals, I am impressed. So were the locals."

"Yeah. Impressed enough that they ought to be ready to make us some sweet offers for military rifles and ammunition. So they can take care of their own problems *themselves.*"

Prospero leaned back, glanced toward the west end of town, where the road wound south toward the base and, on the way, connected to a side road that went inland/east, all the way over to Cross Hill. A middle-aged woman was patrolling there with one of those Brit assault rifles hanging from her shoulder. "As you can see, we already have military rifles, although we could use a little more ammunition. But tell me, Giselle, did you detect the faintest hint of envy, of desire, when you let slip you had more than enough of both?"

Jeeza was about to reply but stopped with her mouth open.

"No," Steve answered.

"And you won't," Prospero affirmed with a nod. "You will not catch anything with that bait, not here." He leaned forward. "It's not equipment that is lacking here. It is the qualities that you lot have. Nerve. Determination. Experience. And solid training from a captain who sounds like he might have earned that title from a career as something other than the owner of a charter boat."

Rod blurted out what I was thinking. "Yeah? Well what about you? Why haven't you led them back to the base? You're military!"

Prospero's smile was as bitter as any he'd shown so far. "I am—was—a signals and sensor specialist, Rodney. We qualify on weapons—barely—but I have never been in a firefight. I have shot a few stalkers, but they were hunting me, not me them. And although this community suffers my occasional advice, they'd salute a tuna before they'd take orders from me."

"So, English," asked Chloe quietly, "do you have a plan, or do we provide that, too?"

Prospero turned quickly. "I rather thought you would be the one who would *like* this idea."

"Didn't say I don't. But if you think I'd be on board just because I've shot more than my share of wild creatures—human or otherwise—then you'd better think again."

I wanted to kiss her. Long and hard. Right there.

Instead, I leaned into the space between them. "Just because we have killed doesn't mean we want to make that a permanent activity. We're not mercenaries." I paused. "On the other hand..."

I looked around the group. I saw a lot of indecision in Rod and Jeeza. Couldn't read Steve; then again, who can? But Chloe? I'm not sure that she got the gene that enables indecision; she was all in.

"...on the other hand, I'm not sure if it's possible to keep our hands clean in this world. Maybe this is what the survivors have to do, if they want to stay alive. If they want to have a chance of rebuilding this world, somehow."

"So we become killers." Now Jeeza sounded like she really might hurl.

*I can't sugarcoat this.* "Giselle, if the infected were willing to negotiate or receive sensitivity training, I'd be all over that option." Even though the words were playful, I kept my tone serious; there was a fine line to walk, here. "But we have to face facts. We've got two choices: stay on a truly deserted island for the rest of our lives or be prepared to kill. At least until we make some safe places. Then, maybe, we can find that deserted island."

But in my heart, I knew I would never do that. This world is supposed to belong to thinking, feeling, hurting, hoping human beings, not rabid eating machines. And the globe's few survivors couldn't afford to make the same decision that Ascension's councilors had: to wait it out. For all we knew, the infected might be able to breed. And if they could, then the only way we could retake this island (or any other) was by removing them from it. One at a time, if need be, but better in bunches. Big bunches.

I cut to the conclusion. "Here's the bottom line: if we want to take this planet back, we can't do it by hiding." I straightened. "So for me, the job starts here. And the job means killing the infected.

"What's more, if any of us can't do that job, it means everyone else has to carry that load. And that's not right. In time, it would tear the group apart. And staying together as a group is Job One. So, it's all in or no go." I looked around at the only four friends I had on the planet. "What do you say?"

It was Steve who broke the silence. "I once read a scifi book about soldiers who jumped out of spaceships to fight aliens. A lot of the book was kinda confusing—there was a lot of talking—but one line was real clear: 'everybody drops, everybody fights.' That's the only way they could depend on each other. They had to feel like they were—I dunno, like a clan, or a family. Sorta. Sorta like us."

Rod and Jeeza looked at each other a long time. They had questions in their eyes, but different ones. His eyes were asking, "Will you?" Hers were asking "Must we?" After the longest three seconds I've ever lived through, Jeeza looked away and nodded. "Yes. I will."

Once it was clear that we weren't going to be torn apart by this decision, I wondered if anyone else left in the world even got to *choose?* In most places, you had to kill the infected and keep killing them until you got to safety. By that time, the whole "will I or won't I kill?" question was kinda moot.

Yeah, we were still spoiled kids—but that was changing.

Fast.

## October 17

Damn if Prospero wasn't right about the reaction of the councilors. At today's meeting, they almost wrung their hands in gratitude and eagerness when we offered to step in and work as, well, exterminators.

The only near-misstep was when Prospero and I both started explaining how they'd screwed up their projections of stalker die-off. But Jeeza saw it coming, and before the two sides could get into a pissing match over whose speculative zoology was correct, she gave us a withering "the customer is always right" look. Then she turned the sweetest smile upon the town leaders and pointed out that:

a)  in the event that some undefined (but surely *minimal*) number of the stalkers slipped into torpor to some undefined degree, then
b)  this would of course have made it *impossible* for the councilors to accurately gauge the time (and therefore supplies) that Georgetown had left before the infected finally turned on each other, and that, consequently,
c)  the same variation in stalker torpidity meant that the present die-off strategy presented a new and unforeseen risk to Georgetown's survivors.

How so? asked the wide-eyed town-fathers and -mothers.

"Well," she explained as if she was selling them a new bedroom set, "if some of the stalkers remain in torpor, then how can you ever be sure that all of them have been killed off by the others? How can you eliminate the possibility that a dormant stalker is hidden someplace the others miss? And that, being missed, it might then reactivate weeks or months after you believed the crisis was past? Because just one reawakened stalker could start a whole new wave of infection. Far better to hunt the stalkers actively now. And what better place to start than their single most dense area of concentration: the airbase?"

"In fact," Rod ad-libbed in an unfortunately high-pitched voice, "we've been working on strategies to bait the other stalkers off Green Mountain. That way, their total numbers would be so low that the rest could be eliminated with a few weeks of aggressive patrols and baited traps."

It was like selling a bunch of starving kids a crate of chocolate bars. They were willing to promise us fifty percent of everything that could be removed from the airbase. That was actually a lot less generous than it sounded, since they knew we didn't have the lading capacity to take more than a fraction of that haul away with us. Until, that is, Steve pointed out that we would be happy to take that 50/50 deal if they provided in perpetuity warehousing of our share for an additional five percent. So a 45/55 split, with us having permanent storage for whatever we couldn't sail away with.

Everyone, including us, stared at Steve, who hadn't said anything in the two-hour meeting. You could see the councilors' deal-making gears spinning behind their eyes. If they accepted Steve's modification, they'd wind up with far fewer goods than they expected and would have us as their only and much-wealthier trading partners, who might or might not be around when they needed us to extend them some "credit" from our stash. Of course, we could always give them the freedom to take what they needed "on account," but they knew we'd reserve the exclusive right to determine "fair compensation" for every bit of it.

In the long run, they countered with a "first pick" proposal. In short, we would only take away what we could carry, but we had first choice of everything we found.

And so the deal was struck. And we went to get the equipment we'd need from the town and to scout the approaches to the base for the first part of our multi-phase plan.

Because Georgetown was so depopulated and we weren't asking for food or water, there were spares of everything we asked for. Either that, or it didn't exist.

For instance, for our ride, we chose a Range Rover that the local police had tricked out to function as an anti-zombie vehicle during the first few weeks of the plague. We could see it from inside their headquarters building: all the glass in the passenger compartment had been removed and replaced with what looked like sections from shark-diving cages. Chain link fencing had been fastened between them and the body of the car, so grasping hands couldn't get through. The wheel wells were covered with sheet metal, down to about five inches ground clearance. The front and back bumpers had been turned into a cross between weapons and cow-catchers; they were equal parts abatis and porcupine. We looked at each other and asked that the biggest spikes be removed: more likely that the infected would grab on to them than get torn to pieces. We also asked for another layer of the chain link fencing: not being able to shoot out the windows didn't worry us. Because if we ever found ourselves that close to the infected, our only concern was to make sure they couldn't touch us.

Which was uppermost in everyone's mind. There were no hazmat suits except at the airport, probably. But they'd have been nonstarters even if they were available. I'd rather try moving and fighting in a clown costume. All that protection won't do you a damn bit of good if someone is actively chasing and tearing at you. Better you stay fast, agile, and harder to catch. Just like aikido.

What I would have liked was biker leathers. Now that is something where you got a lot more protection in exchange for a small loss of flexibility. But this was Ascension Island; no biker gangs here. Nor were there any football helmets, or hockey equipment, or fireman's coats. Actually, there was plenty of firefighting gear on Ascension but, again, it was out at the airfield. We did score some pretty heavy-duty boots, and not just the hiking variety. There were serious anglers among the locals, and some of their footwear is built plenty tough. Unused hiking gear was most useful for all the belts and straps that you could hang ammo pouches on. There was also a good amount of eye-protection available, as well.

At the clinic, the other anti-infection precaution—surgical masks—had all been used up, but I considered that a blessing in disguise. Yes, wearing a surgical mask meant we were less likely to breathe in the virus or get infected spittle or blood in our mouths or noses. But I was pretty sure that it would prove more important to be able to shout and be understood; clear communication could prove key to organizing ourselves enough to maintain maximum distance between us and the infected. That was by far the best way to prevent contamination.

We provided the weapons. With five FALs, a scoped .308, two genuine (as in, fully automatic) AK-47s, and three Rexio pump twelve-gauges, we not only had enough, but a decent mix of, firepower. Between the Taurus-built M9s and the Browning Hi-Powers, we also had enough backup pieces, particularly since we loaned the .44 to Prospero, who damn near went Dirty Harry on us, dry firing that wheel gun at imaginary zombies. And if they got closer than pistol-range? Well, the whaling machetes from Husvik were sturdy and effective. No reason to give them up now.

Once we got to the end of our checklist, we found one of the best local fishermen, put in a special order for fresh catch, and then went to check out our ride and choose our ambush site.

Chloe stood in front of the off-white Range Rover Defender 110 with her hands on her hips. "Really? I'm the only one who knows how to drive a stick? *And* who knows how to shoot for real?" Without waiting for an answer—we guys were all trying to look somewhere else—she yanked open the driver's door.

And stared. The steering wheel was on the other side of the car. "Erm...and the pedals, are they, um, reversed too?"

"No worries," Jeeza said brightly, slipping around her. "I drove some in Jamaica, whenever my family went—" She stopped, her voice faltering after the word "family." She was motionless for a moment, her hand on the side of the Range Rover's doorframe. She blew out a long shuddering breath. "Yeah, I can drive the fucking truck. Get in."

"You liking the view, Chloe?"

She glanced down at me from her perch atop the Range Rover, smiling. The way a wolf might. "Oh, I'm liking this view just fine."

We were at the only intersection on the south road out of Georgetown. It was about half a mile beyond the outskirts. Go another half mile or so, and you were on a long slope down that went straight past the barracks of the U.S. base. From there, you were on the same flatland as the airfield, which was a mile and a half farther on. On foot, it would have been a modest hike. In a vehicle, blink a few times and you'd miss most of the ride.

Chloe was about level with what Prospero had touted as the best position around: a small hillock of volcanic rock—barely seven feet high—that was set back a few yards from the northwest corner of the intersection. But I was keeping an eye on that other road, the one that branched off due east and ascended toward Cross Hill. From there it wound south and east, toward the higher center and then the southern skirts of Green Mountain.

"You know," Prospero chuckled, "that's not where the stalkers will be coming from. They'll be running up at us from there." He pointed down the gentle southern slope toward the base.

"That's the plan," I agreed.

But I wasn't as happy about the lay of the land as Chloe was. I mean, I could see why she liked where we were going to set up. You could see along both roads, and from the top of the little hillock, the southern stretch of highway was—literally and figuratively—a straight shot. To the west, the side that the airfield and the base were on, the land fell away from the road except for the hill where the Air Force had built their GPS station and the target tracking radar that everyone called the Golf Ball. Because that's just what it looked like. Except for the almost pyramidal hill that it was perched on, the rest of the ground on that side of the road was a flat fan of scrub and low, wind-bent trees that fell slowly down toward the sea. The brush wasn't great for visibility, but anything approaching from that direction would spend more time out of cover than in it, unless they were crouching or, in some places, crawling.

I looked over my shoulder again. The road to Cross Hill went through far more tricky terrain, with more and taller brush as it ascended to a modest plateau. An arm of that higher ground flanked the road all the way to intersection's southwest corner. If a stalker followed along the crest of that elevated stretch, no one would see it until it profiled itself on the ten-foot rise that was less than thirty feet from our position.

Chloe's voice jarred me out of my grim imaginings. "You seein' ghosts, Alvaro?"

"Not exactly. More like premonitions."

Her fine, dark eyebrows straightened. "Whaddya mean?"

I turned and hooked a thumb over my shoulder. "Tell me, if something was coming from there, could you see it?"

She glanced in the direction of my thumb, focused on the terrain. "Not sure." A dainty cuspid came down on her very full lower lip. "It would depend."

"Yeah," I said.

"Now, Alvaro," said Prospero, putting an uninvited arm around my shoulder, "do not spook our one and only sniper. Build confidence, not anxiety!"

I removed his arm gently but firmly. "Sorry. That's not my job."

"But it is. Our objective is to kill as many stalkers as—"

"That's *not* my job." When Prospero stopped, puzzled, mouth still open, I set him straight. "My job is to make sure that everyone who got off *Voyager* gets back on. Alive, intact, healthy. Having enough to eat is a bonus. Anything more is icing on the cake. So my first concern is not how to kill infected, but how to keep my friends from getting killed *by* them." I pointed back up the east road. "There are a lot of places along that stretch of highway we can't see. Which means it's a place we can't really control. If something reaches the top of that rise across the intersection undetected, it's just one long jump and a short sprint away from us."

Prospero shook his head; he pointed south toward the base and the airfield. "Down there is one of the two major concentrations of stalkers." He swung his arm around until it pointed at Green Mountain. "There's the other. Almost three miles away. No direct road. Rugged ground. Even assuming that gunfire might attract them here, we'll still be long gone by the time any from the mountain arrive."

I crossed my arms. "You sure? And you still think the best way to bait the infected from the airfield up to us is with a live, thrashing fish?"

Prospero crossed his arms, too. "That remains my suggestion. You have a better one, perhaps?"

"No, I think it's promising. But 'splain this to me; assuming they can't smell their lunch from that far away, how are you gonna let the infected know we're even up here tomorrow?"

"We'll blow the Range Rover's horn a few times. It's always attracted them in the past."

"Right. And then we assume that, without any delay, they'll

run up the southern road toward the fish we've got hanging from the traffic sign about fifty yards away."

"Correct."

"And you're not concerned that there might be some other infected, just prowling around, that could get here first—or at the same time—from a different direction?"

"That's why I agreed with your suggestion that you and Steve carry the two AK-47s instead of FALs. If we have unexpected guests, or any get too close, the automatic fire should be more than sufficient to deal with them."

I nodded. "Yeah, let's hope."

Rod shrugged and smiled, as if to say, "hey, don't worry so much." Steve was Steve; couldn't tell what the hell he was thinking. Chloe was smiling too, but more like she was trying to reassure me.

Jeeza, however, was *not* smiling. She was just looking at me, like she wanted to say something but didn't know what—or maybe, couldn't find the words. She just nodded slightly and looked past me.

Up the eastern road.

## October 18

It wasn't a perfect day. The clouds had socked in. No rain, but reduced long-range visibility.

And then there was the wind. There's usually a stiff breeze blowing on Ascension, and the higher you go, the more noticeable it becomes. But we'd made landfall during a period of relative calm, and Chloe had estimated her long-range accuracy based on what we'd experienced since then.

Those estimates had changed with the weather. Her mood had changed too, as well as the frequency with which she was cussing under her breath. And then more loudly.

When Rod asked her what was wrong, she damn near bit his head off. "What is wrong is that the wind speed and direction is going to make the first three or four shots pretty much a crapshoot. And since we don't want to alert the zombies until we're ready for them, I can't get the windage until right before we ring their dinner—well, lunch—bell." She resumed her string of muttered obscenities. Chloe may be the most creative curser I have ever met.

It didn't help that the wind was also shifting as much as two points every few minutes.

Jeeza, who was on top of the Range Rover to work as spotter (and driver, if we needed to bug out), turned to Prospero. "Do we, uh, abort the mission?"

He shrugged, nodded down to where Rod was pouring water over the tuna that had mostly stopped thrashing. "Might as well carry on."

We'd lashed a fish-gutting rack to the traffic sign down the road and had hung a live tuna from it, the one that had been caught the day before and kept in a tank until this morning. For the past fifteen minutes, I'd been glad fish don't have vocal cords, because if they had, this one would have been screaming.

I half-agreed with Jeeza; maybe we should wait for a better day. Which made me wonder what would happen if I said so. Who was really in charge? And not knowing the answer pissed me off because I couldn't believe I hadn't thought that through beforehand.

Prospero kind of acted like he was, probably because we were the outsiders and he was military. A Senior Aircraftman, Technical, whatever that is. Certainly didn't sound very impressive. I mean, maybe he is super hot shit with radios and computers, but that title doesn't exactly scream "I am a badass zombie killer." And he didn't hold his FAL much more confidently than the rest of us.

I guess we found ourselves in that situation for a bunch of reasons. Coming up with the plan had genuinely been a group effort, so we were kind of in a collaboration groove. Then, when we met with the council, it was Prospero who got us in, who introduced us, and got us taken seriously. So, he had the local juice, even though all the locals treated him like he was a living, breathing bad-luck charm. And despite all we'd been through, the bottom line is that the five of us still think of ourselves as kids when we're around older people. Or we did when we got up today.

But right at that moment, as I kept my AK sighted down the south road, and well to the side of Rod's silhouette, I just breathed out my frustration. We were six people without any backup, clustered behind a Range Rover tricked out for a Mad Max movie. And yeah, we'd picked an okay spot for our little surprise party, but it wasn't perfect and the wide-open spaces of this near-desert island were making us all very aware of just how easily we could be overrun.

This was especially true since we really didn't know how the infected would act in this kind of situation or this kind of terrain. Our only experience was dealing with them as they tried to get off a trawler in an icy subarctic inlet. Prospero had seen more of how they acted, but that was people who'd just turned, in town. It wasn't out in the open, where we could only guess where they'd come from, when, and whether it would be as small scattered groups or one big horde.

Rod stepped back from the wide-gilled tuna, careful not to be in range in case it found enough strength to start thrashing again. Prospero leaned over into the Range Rover. Only thing left to do was honk the horn.

Yeah, the day wasn't perfect, and it was an awful idea to start a life-and-death activity without knowing—*knowing*—who was in charge. But on the other hand, the fishermen had caught exactly what we needed, followed us to the intersection, hung the critter up, and then rolled back down toward Georgetown in neutral to minimize sound. No random infected had appeared, which would have been—at the very least—a real pain in the ass. And best of all, no one, not even Jeeza, showed any sign of wigging out.

And still the horn hadn't blown. I looked over my left shoulder; Prospero was looking at me, then looked at the horn symbol on the middle of the steering wheel, and on down the hill.

I shrugged and nodded.

And wondered what would happen next.

What happened next is that we waited. Long enough to check our watches. Twice.

Then, way down the road, a couple of infected wandered into view from the housing section of the U.S. base. They veered in our direction. Jeeza, who was up on the roof of the Rover, swept through a three-sixty with our best binoculars. She shook her head. With our flanks and rear clear, those of us aiming down the slope hunkered down behind our cover: Chloe and Prospero prone up on the hillock just behind the Rover, Rod and I behind its hood. We leaned over our guns, waiting.

I don't know what we had been expecting. Maybe a mad rush like the human wave attacks that you see in old black-and-white Korean War flicks? Or maybe an angry mob in those "glorious revolution" movies that make it look noble and cool to be cut down in windrows by muskets or machine guns? Well, it wasn't that.

It was, at first, just a handful of infected ambling up the road, stooped forward like they were either half asleep on their feet, or trying to catch a scent. Maybe it was both, because as they neared three hundred yards (we had range markers every fifty), they started to perk up. But before that, it became obvious why the locals had taken to calling them "stalkers." What made them really scary, even at this long range, was that you could tell they were relentless. They'd keep coming no matter what. And at three hundred yards, they must have smelled the fish, because some of them started, well, speed-walking.

"Is this normal?" I heard Chloe ask as she snugged her eye to the scope of the .308.

"Slower than usual," Prospero allowed. "Must have been dormant for quite some time."

Which made sense, but also got my pulse up a little. We still had no idea how quickly stalkers went dormant, or how hard it was for them to remain that way. And if the answer to both was "easily," then the number that had survived this long might be significantly higher than even we had guessed. "Chloe—" I started.

"I get it," she assured me. "I'll stay ahead of the curve." Which sounded a little like the "plucky bravado" equivalent of whistling past a graveyard. But if anyone could thin the stalkers out before they got close, it was Chloe.

Still, I can't say I really enjoyed hearing the flat thunderclap of the .308 just four yards behind my right ear. Don't get me wrong; the sound of guns doesn't bother me. But when they're close, I don't like having them go off *right behind* me. Where I grew up, that was often the last sound unlucky gang-bangers heard.

Down the road, the closest of the stalkers sort of flinched to one side and then started running. No: that doesn't explain it correctly. One moment he was walking, the next he was in a full-out long-legged charge. And howling.

Behind me was the *clacketta-clack* sound of Chloe working the rifle's bolt, and also a lot of cursing about shitty wind conditions.

Rod had risen up from his sights to get a better look at the lead stalker and the other two who were keeping up, just behind him. "Hey, Chloe—" started Rod.

"Safety off," I told him, "and shut the hell up."

The .308 cracked again. Half a heartbeat later, the lead stalker took a final staggering step, and then fell toward the side of the road. The one right behind him glanced over but didn't stop; he was charging and yowling even more energetically than the first one had. The second paused long enough for hunger to overcome bloodlust, I guess; he swerved into a crouch alongside the fresh corpse, hands already a blur in anticipation of bloody reaping.

Chloe was reloading. Jeeza was calling out targets. "Three

morc behind. Five hundred yards. They're, uh, trotting. Getting faster. More behind. I think."

"You *think*?" Prospero's tone was high and ironic.

"There are more," she corrected. "And more behind that. But they're dirty as shit and—"

—*ker-rack!* declared the .308—

"—the light sucks, so—"

The new lead stalker, stumbled, righted herself, and charged even harder.

"—I can't give you precise headcounts until they're at about four hundred fifty yards. If that's okay with you."

The .308 spoke again and the charging stalker went down, about one hundred yards south of the tuna.

Not that I'm a gifted observer of stalker behavior, but it sure didn't look like that zombie, or the one before it, had been interested in the fish. Their impulse was pure aggression. They evidently knew they were being attacked, and the gunshots may have seemed like some kind of challenge—hell, who knows what goes on inside their broken brains? What I *do* know is that, hungry or not, they were being driven by insane, ragemonstering fury.

Maybe, if we had held fire until they got to the fish, it might have gone down differently. But the next spot where we could have hung any bait was too far away and too close to stalkertown. Besides, Prospero thought that if the stalkers were too far away to see us clearly, they might stop for food, and so we could pick them off. One at a time.

But he was dead wrong. I didn't know what he'd seen, or how he came to the conclusions he did, but they were in it for the kill. Feeding appeared to be an afterthought.

I heard the *clicka-snick, clicka-snick* of Chloe reloading the .308. "Suggestion," I shouted over my shoulder.

"Make it good and make it fast."

"The wind steadies, you take shots. Any you've got. Screw optimal range. Go with your gut."

"Already there, Alvaro," she said as I heard the bolt snap down.

If Prospero didn't approve of the modification to his plan, he didn't voice it.

"Targets approaching three-hundred-yard mark," Jeeza said loudly. "Big bunch. Coming fast. We'll need the long rifles, the Flahs—the, uh—"

"The FALs," I corrected loudly as Chloe's rifle barked again.

"Yeah—the FALs. We're going to need them. Good news is the stalkers are kinda bunched up. They're sticking to the road." She paused. "Mostly."

Prospero's voice was clipped: "Define 'mostly.'"

"Some are angling off into the brush to our right."

I could see why they might. The pack in the road was just thick enough that it probably frustrated some of the ones coming up behind them. They were eager to see their prey, and they were probably stupid enough to think that if they could see us, they could get to us faster. But not over that ground. Not even if they had wings.

"Two hundred fifty yards," Jeeza said, just before the rifle cracked again. "Nice shooting, Chloe."

"They're closer," she muttered back, "and the wind's steadier." She squeezed the trigger again. Another dropped. There were still a dozen, all charging now. And behind them—

"Another group coming," Jeeza said. "Gotta be at least twenty."

Chloe's next shot hit one in the sniper's triangle; messy. "One more and I'm going to the Captain's FAL."

I nodded at no one. Inside one hundred fifty yards, the scope was still a huge help to most people, but Chloe—rightly—asserted that at that distance, her ability to put *lots* of lethal rounds down range with the FAL was a better use of time and of her skills.

*But,* I thought, *if someone isn't using the hunting rifle to thin out the next wave*—and then I decided not to think about that. Rule one of combat: there is no time to optimize. Here's what I mean:

You know those role-playing games where you sit around the kitchen table and roll dice to fight battles? You know how the game kinda stops while everyone plans exactly what they're going to do next, when they're going to do it, and in what sequence? Yeah, well, real world combat is not like that. Not at all. It's the opposite. The guns are so loud, there's so much you can't see or don't know, and so much shit is going down in so many places, that you just go with what you think will work. And when training, common sense, and instinct are all telling you the same thing? You do *that* without question. It's like using aikido in a real fight; you've trained each move so much that when you need it, you don't have to think; it's your *reaction*.

So, yeah: Chloe was right to drop the hunting rifle and grab our best FAL to deal with the closest stalkers. We'd worry about the farther ones later. If we survived that long. But even so—

I turned, sprinting toward the hillock. "Chloe: rifle!"

She stared, but tossed it down to me. I caught it—barely—spun around, handed it up toward Jeeza. Who also stared. "Load it for Chloe." Then I went back to the front corner of the Rover, just behind the right headlight.

That was the furthest forward cover we had. To the side and behind me was Rod with a FAL. Chloe and Prospero had the two best ones up on the hillock. Steve was at the back end of the Rover with the other AK. From there, he could fire to the south, or, in case of a nasty surprise coming from the east road, he could swing back behind the Rover and hit them from there. Everything was in the right place; everything was going as we'd rehearsed it. I breathed a sigh of relief, even though eleven stalkers were coming closer on the southern road. If that long uphill run had tired them, they didn't show it. They were already at the one-hundred-yard range marker. Then they were *past* it. "Jeeza? Targets!"

"Oh, fuck!" she shouted; .308 rounds clinked as they fell out of her binocular-grabbing hands.

Which was *my* fault. By asking her to reload the hunting rifle, I'd pulled her off her main task: watching and reporting on everything going on around us. All because I couldn't resist slipping in a little bit of optimization. Prick that I am.

"Uh...uh...seventy yards. Fire!"

The three FALs started sending rounds down range, slow and steady. I swear, every time Chloe pulled the trigger, one of those gimping bastards went down. About half the time, they stayed down.

Our other two shooters—well, that was a different story. And while Senior Aircraftman Percival Halethorpe was doing better than Rod from the 'burbs, it wasn't by much.

I watched the reduced gang close on the fifty-yard mark. That's where my AK was supposed to come in; Steve would engage at twenty-five. But there were only three untagged stalkers by the time they reached my marker, and at the rate the FALs were taking them down, I decided to hold fire to Steve's mark.

One got to thirty before Rod double-tapped him in the center of mass.

I exhaled—maybe the first time since the battle rifles had started deafening me. "Jeeza," I shouted, "range to next group?"

"Two hundred. But—"

"Yeah?"

"Two, uh, 'leakers' from the first group: the ones that went into the brush on the east. They're coming up from that side. One going for the tuna. One is—"

"I've got it," Chloe interrupted. "Just call—"

"No. Chloe, start hitting the next group down the hill with the scoped rifle. Prospero, swap in a fresh mag on her FAL as well as your own. I'll get the leaker."

"Alvaro—!"

"Do it." I laid down the AK and picked up the shorter Rexio. "Jeeza, give me a range and bearing."

"The leaker is at your one o'clock. Forty yards."

We'd defined the southbound road as twelve o'clock, and after weeks at sea, responding to clock-face and compass calls to get bearings was second nature. I pushed into the road-lining bushes, got through, and headed toward open ground, away from the stalker's line of approach.

"Twenty yards. She'll come out right in front of—"

The stalker tore out of the bushes, screaming in the direction of the Rover—and at the sight of her long, black hair, I froze.

Up until now, the infected had been targets at range. Like enemies in a video game, you never had enough time or proximity to make out any defining features. But now I was seeing a human, not a stalker. A hideous human—seamed and seared-looking skin, sunken cheeks, wild eyes, caked blood and drool at the corners of cracked lips—but still a human. And a deeper reflex—the primal and cultural imperative to never harm a woman—froze my trigger finger as I took a step back and almost fell into the brush.

The stalker hadn't really noticed me until then; she'd been utterly intent upon the figures responsible for making all the aggressive noise atop the car and on the hillock. But now she spun toward me, let out a weird, warbling shriek, and charged.

"Alvaro!" Jeeza screamed. Chloe's curses were almost as loud as the stalker's yowls.

I started—suddenly, I wasn't seeing a woman anymore, wasn't reminded of all the women in my family who had the same long, black hair. I was back in the present-day of our dying world, a monster charging at me.

I raised the Rexio, sighted along its fifteen-inch barrel, and started firing and pumping. Firing and pumping. I stopped when the trigger clicked and nothing happened. I think the stalker was hit by the second round, went down with the third, and was finished by the fourth, but I don't really remember it that way. It was just shoot and cycle the action; kill or be killed. I remember her stumbling forward, because I had to shift my aim point downward. But that's all.

Next I knew I was clawing back through the bushes, realizing that I needed to reload the Rexio—when Steve shouted, "East flank! East flank!"

Suddenly, the world was all crisp and sharp again. I dropped the Rexio near the other one we had ready at the front of the Rover. I snatched up my AK and brought it up—but not to aim along the eastern road. I trained it on the high ground that ran up to the southeast corner of the intersection: the rocky spur that had been the focus of both my waking and sleeping nightmares.

And sure enough, there was a stalker's head, topping that long, low rise. But since the ground there was at least ten feet higher than the roadway—"Chloe?"

"Can't. No time." Her hunting rifle cracked, its report echoing down the southern road. I couldn't remember when she'd started picking off the leaders of the next northbound mass, but I wasn't about to interrupt her. She had to keep thinning those ranks or they might swamp us.

"Jeeza," I called, "to the east; got a head count?"

"Not really. At least half a dozen. Maybe more. That ground is too rough to get a good count."

By the time she was done reporting, it was all academic, anyway. Two of the stalkers had crawled over the lip of the embankment that was catty-corner to our position and were scuttling down like human beetles. "Steve—"

"I see 'em. Got some coming along the east road, too. Start the music?"

"The Russian waltz," I agreed and trained the AK on the stalker who'd crawled down the side of the spur far enough to leap to the roadway.

Sometimes in combat you get unlucky—like having a bunch of attackers come from where no one else thought they might. But then, sometimes, you get stupid lucky in the very next moment. Which happened as I squeezed the AK's trigger. To save ammo, I was keeping it on semi-auto, and figured I'd fire three fast rounds at this stalker. Except he was getting ready to jump right as I started. So I cheated the barrel lower, trying to catch him before he could leap down. I overcorrected, aimed *too* low.

But he jumped a split second earlier than I thought. So although the first round went under him, he fell straight into the path of the next two. Both center of mass hits. He fell, and lay, as limp and still as a bag of potatoes.

The effect on the second was that she got even more impatient, leaped early, stumbled as she landed—which gave me enough time to line her up and double-tap her. Although one of those taps hit the volcanic rock behind her instead. I won't write what I muttered at myself, just that the third shot put her down for good.

After that it gets a little blurry. Steve's AK went from aimed semiautomatic to quick *dut-dut-dut!* full auto bursts. I never had the time to look down his way, but it must have gotten pretty hairy; at one point, Jeeza started blasting away to the east with one of the Rexios.

That was about the same time that Chloe's hunting rifle stopped and all the FALs started competing with each other to be the first to deafen me. I dropped two more that came down the side of the embankment, caught movement out of the corner of my eye; two of the mass of stalkers from the south had somehow survived to get within a dozen yards of the Rover. I turned quickly, pulled up on the AK's selector switch: too hard. I'd engaged the safety. So I tightly controlled it back down into the middle, full auto position, and leaned forward into the weapon as I squeezed the trigger. I walked it across the two approaching torsos when they were about four yards shy of the Rover's hood. They went down, then so did the empty mag as I hit the ejector.

That was the moment that the AK's little reloading quirk—you kind of have to rock the mag into place before you can drive it up and home—got the better of my trembling hands. It was also the moment when eight or nine of the skinned-looking bastards came scrambling over the embankment. Half of them were on the ground before I could get the magazine seated properly and palm-rammed it into place. It was a waste to stay on full auto, but they were coming fast and, well, yeah, I panicked. Dumped the whole mag. Maybe half of them went down. Steve got the last one in line with flanking fire and Prospero's FAL started whacking the ones who had just reached the ground. But there was still one coming at me, straining claws only three yards from my face.

I don't remember pulling the Browning Hi-Power and dumping half its mag into that staggering, and already much-vented, skel.

And then—nothing. The battlefield wasn't silent, not hardly; lots of the infected were still dying, making weird guttural noises that were equal parts impatient distress and impotent fury. We were all panting. Jeeza puked. A lot of us started reloading our weapons. Or tried to: our hands were shaking that badly. But still, it seemed almost eerily quiet. Just a few moments before, the only sound was guns—hundreds, it seemed—going off all around me: a magic circle that kept out more of the shrieking, once-human demons than we'd been able to keep track of.

We all wanted to leave right then, before anything else could happen. We were happy—and goddamned surprised—to be alive and unbitten, and we didn't want to tempt fate. We just wanted to haul ass back to town, get into a house with thick walls and double-boarded windows, and hyperventilate until all the jitters and terror were out of us.

But first we had to count the bodies, and then anoint each with a pint of old, useless motor oil. No raging pyre; gas was too precious and there was no way we were going to risk contagion by gathering the bodies. Of which there were fifty-three. It seemed like there had been hundreds, and that the fight had gone on for hours.

When we finally thought to check our watches on the ride back, we learned the truth:

Chloe had taken her first shot only sixteen minutes earlier, and we'd spent the last ten—at least—counting and torching the bodies.

## October 18 (second entry, after dinner)

Had to take a break and eat dinner. About which: turtle is tasty, but like anything else, gets old pretty fast.

On returning to Georgetown and telling what happened on the south road—the "after action report," as Prospero put it—the council seemed ready to give us a victory parade. We smiled, thanked them, said we'd return tomorrow with our ideas for the next phase of the operation, and ran for home without actually sprinting.

As soon as we were through the door, Chloe threw down her rucksack and threw herself into a chair. "What a shitshow," she spat. She really did spit at the end of the word "shitshow."

I sighed, leaned back against the wall. "I made a lot of mistakes," I agreed.

She looked at me like I'd grown an extra head. "Alvaro. Get over yourself. This isn't about you. This is about the plan." She stared at Prospero.

Whose eyebrows jumped toward his hairline. "The plan which we came up with *as a group*," he said.

"Based on your information—*first-hand* information—of what the stalkers here were like."

I used my shoulder blades to push off the wall. "That's enough."

They both stared at me.

I didn't stop. "Assigning blame isn't going to help us finish the job."

"Finish the job?"

"Yeah. We're not done."

Chloe's mouth opened—

"And I'm not, either. Let's focus on what worked and what didn't."

"Fucking fish didn't work at all," Chloe grumped, crossing her arms. The way that modified the outlines of her torso almost made me forget what the hell I was talking about. "Maybe three—*three*—of them stopped to take a bite. And they were the lazier ones."

Prospero put up a hand. "I will own that. My idea; my bad. In my defense, you must understand: I've never seen them in a group like this. They behaved . . . differently."

"Yeah," Rod murmured. "Like they were pack animals."

"That's because they—*we*—*are* pack animals," Chloe fumed.

"Well, they *were*," I amended.

Jeeza looked over at me. "What do you mean, they *were* pack animals, Alvaro?"

"Just that the infected don't really seem—well, social anymore." I glanced at Chloe. "Certainly not on a par with wolves, right?"

Chloe, child of the Denali, perked right up. "Yeah. Wolves have a pretty complex society. There's a lot of mating control, a lot of cooperative hunting, and a really clear *chain of command*." She shot a quick glare at me, but focused a longer one on Prospero. "So you're right. The zombies really aren't pack animals anymore. They're more like a horde of psychopaths busting out of a nuthouse." She looked up at me. "Or a school of sharks, where the only 'social' rule is not to attack each other *too* often."

Jeeza was nodding. "Sure, because the infected don't have to cooperate. Not even as much as sharks do." She jabbed an index finger back in the direction of the south road. "The infected don't have a . . . a reproduction imperative anymore. It's gone."

Jeeza's nod spread to Prospero. "Which explains why we've never seen very old or very young persons as stalkers, even though we know some of each turned. They were too weak. The others ate them. Just as a school of sharks does with their own injured." He grew pale. "They probably do the same to new mothers."

"I doubt a pregnant stalker would reach her third trimester," I added quietly. "If the infected are all about killing and power—"

"—then a newly pregnant stalker is just a future meal for the rest," Steve finished while staring at a blank wall. "So is her child. Maybe for her." He felt our stares, turned, stared back. "Does it really make any sense that a stalker would care about her own, or any other, baby?"

I looked away. What could I say? He was probably right, and we all knew it. "So," I started, "our job is to do better than we did today. Rule one is to follow the plan. I didn't when I told

Jeeza to reload the hunting rifle. That pulled her off overwatch. And we almost got overrun because of it."

Chloe shook her head. "Not so fast, Alvaro. You may have given new orders, but if you hadn't, I would have had to load that rifle. Instead, I was able to pick it up and started thinning out that second group from the south. Big time. You were too busy to see, but that was probably why we weren't overrun. Anyhow"—she frowned—"I was the one who almost got us killed."

"What? How?"

She shrugged, looked away. "I should have said something about the conditions."

"The conditions?" Rod echoed.

"Weather conditions," she clarified. "Look, no offense, guys, but I'm the only one who knew what today's wind and clouds were going to do to my ability to reach out and touch the stalkers. I'm the shooter; you're not. It was my call, and I didn't even think to make it. Or maybe I was too proud. Either way, I was off. Way off making the number of hits that we needed—and that you all had reason to expect."

Jeeza raised her hand sheepishly, like she was in third grade. "And I got distracted too easily. And Alvaro, really: it was on me to tell you if I couldn't reload the rifle *and* do my job. Except that—"

I knew what was coming. "Except what?"

"I didn't know who was in charge. I knew *I* wasn't. I thought, maybe, you were. It sure sounded like it when you shoved that gun up at me."

"Not knowing who was in charge was most definitely *not* your fault, Jeeza."

"Yes," agreed Prospero, arms crossed. "We'll need to come back to that."

"Damn straight," I said, looking him in the eyes.

Rod shuffled his feet. "I got panicked."

I could not help smiling. "Are you kidding me? Man, we all nearly shit ourselves. There's no blame there."

He frowned. "But there is, Alvaro. Because—well, because I forgot how much of our plan was based on guesses, not facts. And when some of the guesses turned out to be wrong, I suddenly didn't know what to do. So I—I froze."

"Yeah," Chloe said, "but you came around. Fast enough to do your job. That's what counts."

Jeeza leaned forward like she was suddenly on the scent of something, "Yeah, but I know what Rod means. Our plan had too many assumptions that we started to treat like facts. For instance, we thought that the infected would stick to the roads, that they'd only come from the base." She turned toward me. "But you knew different."

"No, Jeeza," I answered, wanting to get off the topic. "I didn't *know*. I just didn't think that was their only possible behavior."

"Yeah," Chloe said, eyes on me and not blinking. "And you were right."

"Listen, *cariña*, when you worry about everything—the way I do—you're bound to be right *some* of the time."

Chloe leaned forward. She wasn't smiling. "Yeah, maybe. But maybe that's part of what we have to do better next time. Not trust the script we wrote. We wanted—maybe we needed—to trust it because that made us feel like we were in control." Her eyes were hard on me, but in the way that makes you, well, horny. "You were the one who remembered the lesson that the Captain tried to teach us again and again and again: that no plan lives past—er, no plan . . ."

"No plan survives contact with reality." Steve finished. "She's right, Alvaro. That's why we elected you captain for when we're at sea. Because you don't forget that."

Out of the corner of my eye, I could see Prospero's posture changing. Yeah, this was what I had wanted to put off for a while: a discussion about who should be in charge and why. That topic had to be left for last. *Had* to be. Because we had to have a plan in place—as a group—before we decided who was going to be in charge. That way, even if a person didn't like who was chosen to execute the plan, they'd at least know that they'd had an equal part in *making* the plan. Which is what we had to do right that minute: make a plan.

It was like Jeeza had read my mind. "So what we haven't done yet is list the things we got right. Because we don't want to take those for granted. We want to make sure we focus on those when we make our next plan." And she looked at me.

"Well," I said, "our basic tactics were solid."

Prospero nodded. "Solid enough that when fate threw a few googlies our way, we still got the job done."

I didn't know what a googlie was, but I nodded anyway.

"We had the right kind of firepower in the right places. Didn't overestimate our accuracy—"

"That ain't sayin' much," Chloe observed with a wry twist of her lips. And she was right: with the exception of her, our shooting at range pretty much sucked. It hadn't been a whole lot better at close quarters, but we'd had enough guns and enough ammo that it overcame our lack of skill.

"Tell you what I was happiest about, though," Chloe continued. "No one froze. Not really. Damn, when the shit hit the fan, even Jeeza picked up a twelve-gauge and went total redneck on those stalkers coming down the east road." They exchanged a smile.

Steve was looking at the wall again. "And everyone remembered the plan. So it hung together. And because it did, we did."

Rod was nodding. "It's because of the boat." We all looked at him. "The time we spent at sea, I mean. We learned to, had to, count on each other out there or we wouldn't have survived. We brought that with us today. That's what kept us together, kept us on the plan. Not because we knew it would work, but because we knew we could count on each other."

Well, Rod would probably never be our leader, but he had my vote for our official motivational speaker.

I leaned back against the wall. "So, we've got to improve, but we've got a solid foundation. That's why we won, and because we did, we came away with another big advantage."

"Which is?" Prospero's tone was what the English call "droll."

"We got to see how the infected really act in combat. That means we have a better, more accurate understanding of our enemy. And that means we can make better plans."

Nods all around. Even Prospero, who asked, "So: what changes do you suggest?"

I'm not tactful by nature, but I knew I had to do my best at that particular moment. "I think the tactical idea behind today's plan—of bringing the infected into a kill zone—is great. But I think it would work better if we could find a site where we're in less danger and they are more exposed to our fire."

Nods all around again. Prospero's was hesitant. As I expected.

"So how do we do that?" Jeeza asked. Looking straight at me. Again. Didn't even glance at Prospero. And he saw it.

Rather than leading with my ideas, I leaned back. "Suggestions?" I asked.

Chloe shrugged. "We need to find a more secure position. Someplace even the most crazy-ass infected can't get to easily. And it should be higher, if possible."

"With a clear field of fire in all directions," Rod added.

Chloe shook her head. "Not that important, against the infected. They've got no sense of caution. They don't even bother trying to hide. They just come straight at you. It actually makes their movement really predictable. If we can force them into a limited number of approaches, that will keep them bunched up and easier to hit." She smiled around at the rest of us, playful. "Or, should I say, harder to miss?"

"Okay," Steve said quietly. "But wherever we set up, we have to know all the approaches. Really well. Today, from the east, we couldn't see them until they were really close."

Rod frowned. "Didn't they come down the east road?"

Steve shrugged. "A bunch did. But a lot didn't."

Jeeza nodded. "Some of them seemed to just come in out of the fields."

"Any pattern that you noticed?"

"Only one. The ones who seemed to appear out of nowhere on the embankment came up out of the flats to the southeast." She stopped, thinking. "More were just starting to come around Lady Hill as we left, heading towards us across Donkey Plain."

Prospero looked at me. "Which means they were coming from Green Mountain. It's the only other place with enough water to support so many. So I was wrong. Again. They *did* hear us and they *did* come running straight for us. Didn't bother to use the road. They took the straightest path."

I nodded slowly, seriously. I was glad he'd owned that; it meant he wasn't a total prick. But I didn't want my reaction to have any "I-told-you-so" in it. "Do you think that they might follow us into town?"

Prospero's tone was cautious. "Earlier today, I might have said yes. Now, I doubt it."

"Why?"

"Frankly, like everyone here in Georgetown, I still believed they are guided by primitive thoughts and plans." He shook his head. "Now, I am thinking that they might simply be creatures of stimulus and response." He nodded at Chloe. "Like sharks. So, by the time any latecomers reach today's ambush site, there won't be much there to excite them, except for the unburnt parts of the stalkers we killed." He shrugged. "For all I know, they might consume the charred remains, motor oil and all. But unless we show lights or make noise here in Georgetown, there's nothing to bring them here. We didn't leave any trail they'd think to follow."

I nodded. "Okay. Then let's figure out how to put down the rest of the stalkers. First step?"

Rod shrugged. "We do the math. We killed fifty-three today. According to the council's estimates, that would leave about forty-seven."

I nodded. "Yep, but I'm going to roughly double that and assume that there are still ninety infected active on this island."

"So you're assuming they must be able to go into torpor really quickly and really effectively," Jeeza commented. "Because you just took forty-three of the ones we thought had been stalker-fodder and converted them back into walking, breathing, biting monsters. That have been snoozing for weeks. Maybe months."

I shrugged. "I'd rather overestimate their numbers rather than underestimate. Besides, you said the ones to the east were converging on us from all over."

Jeeza nodded, eyes widening. "So you think they're just... hibernating in burrows or something?"

"Or something," I agreed.

"It's quite possible," Prospero slid into a chair with sun-bleached upholstery. "The temperature is constant and mild. You don't need much shelter, and there are volcanic vents, caves, and crannies wherever you go."

"You mean," said Chloe, eyes suddenly like a startled cat's, "that these motherfuckers could be popping out of the ground like—like bugs in spring? So when we walk by, they smell break-fast, and bang—they're up and after us with teeth bared?"

Prospero sighed. "Might not be quite that rapid... but yes, that's the basic idea."

Chloe's look of horror had already turned into straight-browed, locked-jaw determination. "You know, it's getting to the point where I'm *looking forward* to killing them. Where do we find a better kill zone? Someplace they can't overrun us?"

Prospero held up his hands. "To attract them, we have to make noise or otherwise call attention to ourselves: something dramatic enough to bring them in useful numbers. But outside of Georgetown, we can't truly be sure that any place is safe."

Steve lay flat on the floor. "Which means," he said to the ceiling, "that no matter what, *we* always wind up being the bait."

"And they could arrive in such numbers that they'd surround us."

"Surround, yes," I muttered. "But that doesn't necessarily mean that they can *get to* us."

Chloe had a calculating look in her eyes. "What have you got in mind, Alvaro?" She almost smiled. "I know that look."

"Well, what kind of structure would be best for what we're trying to do?"

"You mean, if we could just snap our fingers and summon it?" asked Rod.

He really *had* played too much D&D. "Sure," I answered.

"A fortified tower. With a moat. And a drawbridge."

*Yup,* waaaay *too much D&D.* But he was right. "Anything else?"

"Enough room for supplies. And for ten times the ammo we think we might need. A well in the basement. No doors or windows on the ground level. Oh, and a way to make noise to bring them all to us."

"Need anything else in your designer keep?" Jeeza asked with a fond grin.

"Well...*you*. Of course." Rod grinned back at her.

Jeeza blinked, then blushed and beamed. Their compartment was going to be noisy tonight. Well, noisier.

I kept the focus where it had to remain. "Rod, what if I told you we can get you that tower?"

"I'd ask, 'where've you been hiding it?'"

"In plain sight."

Prospero rested his forehead on his index finger. "This should prove interesting."

I ignored him. "It's got an absolutely unobstructed three-hundred-sixty-degree field of fire. And the maps say we can get to it without exposing ourselves to stalkers."

Even Prospero was serious and focused, now.

Steve sighed. "Enough drama. Just tell."

I smiled. "The Golf Ball."

Except for Rod, everyone else just stared. Rod smiled, breathed, "Yeah." Like he was on the verge of having a nerdgasm.

Jeeza swallowed loud enough for everyone to hear. "Alvaro, that's on Cat Hill. Which is really close to the U.S. base housing. Really, really close."

I nodded. "At some points, less than one hundred yards. That's the beauty of the plan."

"Sorry," murmured Prospero, "but that's the *insanity* of the plan."

His tone had been even, but I couldn't let that kind of talk slide, especially not from him. "Is it insane, Percy?" He blinked. "The Golf Ball is separated from the base by a chain link fence topped by razor wire. According to the council's last survey two months ago, it's intact.

"Now, if the infected somehow get over that, Cat Hill is a smooth volcanic cone about eighty feet high with slopes that range from thirty to forty-five degrees. At least, that's what it showed on the topo maps you forced us to damn near memorize before today's ambush. And if the zombies manage to somehow scramble up that completely barren slope, the crest's perimeter is also ringed by chain link fencing, and has two solid buildings, one with a second story."

Prospero was frowning but did not look confident. "And just how do we get there? The only access road goes through the housing complex before it passes through a gate and winds back behind Cat Hill."

I smiled; it wasn't friendly, I admit it. "Percival, you really need to pay closer attention to the maps you wave under our noses. Have you looked closely at the fence that separates the Golf Ball from the base?" While he was still fumbling for a reply, I went back at him. "Well, I *have* looked at it. It actually starts at the fuel terminal on the western outskirts of Georgetown. It's got a patrol and access road all the way along its landward side."

"True. But that does not lead to the Golf Ball."

"Not directly, no. But there are two gates in that fence as you head south on the patrol road."

He nodded. "Which are padlocked."

"Yeah, until we take one of the police ATVs down along the other side of the fence and unlock the southernmost gate. With a pair of bolt cutters."

Chloe was looking excited and scared all at once. "So let me put the pieces together. We send someone to check the ocean-side of the fence, starting at the fuel terminal and going all the way down to the southernmost gate. If they don't run into any stalkers on the way, they signal that it's safe and cut the lock off the gate. Meanwhile, we drive our DeRanged Rover down the access road on the other side of the fence and they open the gate and then lock it behind us. At which point we are all on a back road to the Golf Ball."

I nodded. "An old construction road. Some of it is overgrown, now. We'll have to go slowly and carefully. With both Rovers."

"A second Rover?"

"Yep. Necessary."

"Why?"

I grinned and cocked my head toward Rod. "To bring all the gear the Master Wizard wants to have in his tower. And so that if one of the Rovers fails, we can get out in the other."

Prospero was nodding more seriously, now. "Inventive. But once you've clipped the padlock, you've opened up a point of access for the infected."

He'd walked into checkmate. "Three reasons why that's not a problem. First, we've got plenty more chains and padlocks here in town, and last I heard, the stalkers aren't real handy with bolt cutters. Secondly, if there are only a hundred of them left, they're not going to swarm into so large a pack that it starts streaming along the fence, trying to find another way in. Thirdly, if some of them *did* find a way in, most would head directly toward where they can see what's making all the noise. Namely, us. Which brings them to the same side of Cat Hill that overlooks the stalkers we'll be shooting down in the base. And if a few leakers wander the other direction, they still have to get up the back of Cat Hill and through the perimeter fence."

"Okay, but they could camp out all around us, couldn't they?" Jeeza asked, frowning. "And if they do, then what? How do we get out?"

I leaned back and crossed my arms, but before I could reply, Chloe must have read the answer on my face.

"We don't," she said, wide-eyed but smiling. "Alvaro, you are crazy."

"Like a fox," Rod added. "Sure. Given the numbers, it's the perfect solution."

Steve looked over. "Help. I'm lost."

Rod was jabbering so quickly, so excitedly, that I couldn't get a word in edgewise. "It really is the perfect wizard's tower, Steve. Think it through. We drive up to the top, re-padlock both the lower fence and upper fence behind us. We start honking the horns and doing the French knights' bit from Monty Python's *Holy Grail*."

"What?" asked Chloe.

Rod smiled. "We taunt them. Parade around. Make them crazy with hunger and rage. And they come to us. However many are left. But there aren't thousands of them. There aren't even hundreds."

"Yeah," Steve allowed. "But they'll be coming through the base. A lot of houses and other buildings down there."

Chloe nodded. "Yeah, but remember: they don't use cover. So actually, the buildings will funnel them into *completely predictable* kill-zones."

Jeeza was looking at all our faces. "But still—how do we get out?"

Prospero sighed. "A very sane question. But the answer is: they don't intend to."

"What?"

I nodded. "We stay on Cat Hill until there aren't any left to come at us. The ones in the base will hear and charge us right away. Any skulking around the airfield will come a little later. With all the gunfire and all the horns, even the ones on Green Mountain will come down to check it out. Mostly because it will sound a lot more exciting and promising than trying to hunt donkeys and sheep. That's the whole point of the plan: to make enough noise so that, within a day or two, almost every active stalker will try to attack Rod's tower."

Jeeza glanced at Prospero. "You okay with this?"

His grin looked broken. "'Okay' is not the word I would use. But it is an inspired bit of madness." He looked at me. "Even if I go along with it, there's one other problem."

"Which is?"

"The same one that almost got us killed today. I thought we knew how the infected would behave. I was wrong. Could we be wrong this time, too? Is it possible that if they take enough casualties trying to get up Cat Hill that will spark a new behavior? That they turn back to shelter behind the buildings of the camp?"

I shrugged. "You're the one who told us that no one here in Georgetown has ever seen infected turn tail. Neither have we. Today they took over fifty casualties and never stopped.

"But for argument's sake, let's say that fifty-five is their breaking point and at that point, the rest hide behind the buildings." I smiled. "They can't do that *and* camp out near the Golf Ball's back entrance at the same time. So they won't see or know if we climb into the Rovers and leave. At which point, we go back to town, rest, restock, and return to the Wizard's Tower for round two. Lather, rinse, repeat."

Steve was looking at the ceiling. "You're right. The numbers work. Let's say they only take fifty more casualties. Even if the rest were to follow us back here, there's enough firepower in town to finish them off."

Rod looked excited. "So, we're on? Operation Wizard's Tower is a go?"

"Looks like it," Chloe affirmed. "Just one last detail." She looked at Prospero. Not unfriendly, exactly, but like it could swing that way really easily. "We need to know who's in charge this time."

Prospero held up both hands. "Not me. This plan is your brainchild. But I'm happy to follow along." His eyes changed, got a little less friendly. "This time."

I nodded at him; he nodded back. We understood that we had mutually agreed to kick the can labeled "overall command" a little further down the road.

Because right now, we had to prepare for another stalker-killing mission.

## October 20

It's fucking 2 AM and I can't sleep. I was just lying there, thinking about tomorrow (well, today now). About all the things that could go wrong. About all the ways my plan could get my friends killed.

Yeah, we worked the details. Yeah, we've got all the gear ready. Yeah, everybody is sure this will be a big improvement.

But still, everyone is scared. And they're probably scared of the same thing I am: that the Captain is right. That no plan survives contact with reality. So maybe they're all lying awake and staring at the ceiling, too.

At least Chloe isn't. I don't know if it's in her genes or the way she learned to cope with her screwed up home life, but it's like she can take her worries, lock them in a mental box, and shove it aside. I don't know how she does that. God knows I can't.

So here I am writing in this stupid journal. Psychologists and social workers used to claim that saying something out loud, or writing it down, helps you see it more clearly. I'm not sure about that, but it definitely makes each waking minute feel like a minute instead of an hour. Unlike when you're worried that every minute might be your last; then, each one feels like forever.

The last time I felt time expand and stretch that way was on the journey here, in the middle of the storm. I tried to write about that weird state of mind, but it was more fluid than the water itself, probably because words can't hold it, can't pin it down. It was like trying to write about the way everything slowed down while fighting the pirates in Husvik. I gave that up after trying half a dozen times. I couldn't get my head, or words, around it.

See, when you start thinking back on an event that was short and crazy, you discover that all its different parts—the actions and reactions—have become a blur. And it's not just because the passage of time takes the edge off your memories. It's because when the shit hits the fan, the only thing you're thinking about is staying alive, and, if you can, sticking with the plan.

Which is why the Captain had us drill for the battle with the pirates over and over again. So that the plan and its rhythms wouldn't get drowned out by the blood pounding in your ears while you're trying to kill the other guy before he can kill you. So that, even when we did lose the rhythm and the plan started going sideways—as the Captain had assured us it would—the basic beat was still there and we riffed our way back to the finale. Which is the key to winning any battle, he said. And he was right.

That's why it was so hard to write down everything that happened when we fought the zombies at the crossroads, or how it felt while it was happening. We don't remember a battle or crisis as one, smooth story; we remember snatches and moments. Like waking up from a nightmare, you recall some things really clearly and other things just barely or not at all.

Maybe it's different for real soldiers. Maybe they get so accustomed to the chaos that they are able to remember more. Or maybe they just stop caring that they can't.

I also wonder if it's especially hard to remember the details of fighting the infected (and the ocean) because, unlike us, they're *not* following any plan. It's not like they're opponents in some game of chess, whose moves and counter-moves help us recall what happened and in what order. With stalkers, or the wind, or the sea, there's nothing to figure out, no logical sequence to reconstruct.

Sure, maybe if you were watching from a distance, you could perceive how all the forces come together with a kind of inevitability, like physics. But not when you're in the middle of waves so high that you can't see over them. Or trying to manage sails in a wind that runs halfway around the compass in less time than it took me to write that sentence. Or fighting swarms of stalkers on open ground. In each of those cases, you're not trying to defeat an enemy; you're striving against a force of nature.

Maybe writing all this has tired me out enough. Maybe I found the words for what I've been feeling since we came through that storm and since we came back from the intersection. Maybe I've just bored myself blurry.

Whichever it is, I'll take it and whatever sleep it brings.

## October 20

When you're a poor kid who lived in big cities all his life, you do get some things that kids from the 'burbs *don't* have. Like having a nonstop bullshit detector running in the back of your mind, street smarts, and familiarity with violence—particularly of the senseless and deadly kind. But there's a ton of things the kids from the 'burbs know how to do that you don't. And one of those things is driving.

So when it came to getting to the Golf Ball, I was totally fucking useless. Which was even worse because as the guy in charge, and also the one who pretty much sold the idea to everyone else, I couldn't help with the very first phase of it.

Yeah, sure, I was the lookout, riding shotgun—literally—in the lead Rover. But Chloe was going to do the driving because (once she got used to the steering wheel being on the right) she was by far the best at it and had already logged a lot of hours in four-wheel drive monsters like the DeRanged Rover. Jeeza followed with Rod, ready to steer the newer, less tricked-out Rover to follow in our tire tracks.

It was pre-dawn, just enough natural light to drive, so we went very, very slowly. I had an eighteen-inch Rexio at the ready but kept my eyes on the handheld radio we'd stuck in the dashboard cup holder. Steve and Prospero had left fifteen minutes before and we were waiting for a single squelch break from them. That signal meant that they'd reached the southernmost gate and that there hadn't been any sign of stalkers. None had ever been spotted on the ocean side of the fence, but we weren't assuming anything, this time.

But a few minutes after we thought they might get to the fence, the radio crackled and squeaked: squelch break.

It was one of those rides when you realize just how relative time and distance are. Following along the fence—no shortcuts— was just over a mile. In L.A., at any time other than rush hour, that meant sixty seconds of cruising just north of sixty mph.

On Ascension Island, driving a four-by-four zombie buster in the goose-grey post-apocalyptic predawn, it took twelve minutes. Which seemed more like two hours. Because if we were attacked by even a single stalker, all the dominoes would go down in the wrong direction. We'd have to shoot it, which would be like sounding reveille for any others that might be nearby. So we'd have to abort. And of course, that whole time, Steve and Prospero had to be standing ready with the bolt cutters: to use them quickly if we showed up, or if we didn't, to jump back on their ATVs and return to Georgetown's little tank farm. Because it was stupid to cut the padlocks away until the Rovers made it there. Otherwise, if we had to abort, we'd also have been invit- ing the stalkers to take a stroll on the ocean side of the fence, which would seriously compromise any subsequent attempts to commence Operation Wizard's Tower.

But no stalkers jumped out at the Rovers. Chloe and Jeeza kept their engine noise to a muted growl, and when we arrived at the south gate, Steve already had the bolt cutters in the loop of the padlock. Prospero was covering him with the fifteen- inch Rexio. Not a gun he liked, but given the low visibility, if a stalker popped up, you wouldn't see it until it was really close. And the super short Rexio was really good at tagging really close targets.

Steve clipped the loop, stowed the cutters, and pushed that half of the double-gate toward us.

Nothing.

He pulled it toward himself.

More nothing.

"Shit," Steve hissed, forgetting noise discipline.

"Bollocks," Prospero muttered, not much more quietly. "Bug- ger is stuck."

Why is it that in life-and-death situations, it's never the big things that get you? It's something as small and stupid and unpredictable as a jammed gate, with dawn coming on and the nearest stalkers curled up in their scat-littered warrens only a hundred yards away.

Prospero slung the Rexio, came over to help. Neither of them were big guys, and the gate was not impressed by their combined efforts.

"Bollocks," Prospero panted again.

Chloe leaned out the window. "Hssstt!!!"

Prospero looked up. "Not now. We're working on it."

Chloe's ironic, raised eyebrow was probably lost on them. "Yeah, sure. But just stand back."

"Why?"

"I'm going to let it argue with the Rover."

"Chloe, if you haven't noticed, the gate does not open towards us, but towards *you*."

"Yeah, but if *you* haven't noticed, there's nothing actually blocking it. It's probably just rust and grit. Lemme run the front bumper up against it and push. That should unjam it."

Prospero stood for a moment. It looked like he was trying to find some snappy comeback. But then he stepped away, motioning for Steve to do the same.

Chloe rolled the Rover up until the bumper kissed the place where the two halves of the gate came together. She tapped the gas pedal.

The upright bars groaned softly; the chain link stretched like it might break.

She backed off the gas, shifted into neutral. As the Rover rolled back, she muttered, "Try it now."

This time it budged, but not all the way. She waved them away, repeated the process.

This time, when Steve and Prospero gave a heave-ho and pushed, the right side of the gate groaned and swung toward us. They waved us through, pulling the gate shut after us and securing it with a new padlock just as the leaves of the bushes started glinting pink and copper. The sun would be up in fifteen minutes. At most.

We spent most of that time driving a grand total of three hundred yards. On this side of the fence, the only thing resembling a road was a tangle of paths that tracked construction vehicles had bashed through the brush when they built the Golf Ball. But that was half a century ago and those vehicles had just been moving crap around. So it wasn't like there had ever been a direct path; for us, it was a set of ungraded switchbacks.

Navigating those really put Chloe's driving skills to the test. But after fifteen minutes of bumping and jouncing over roots, low bushes, and rocks that looked like half-buried buffalos, we slid down onto the Golf Ball's rear access road. Chloe kept the Rover in first as we almost idled our way along one hundred and fifty yards of left-curving road that followed the base of Cat Hill. When we came abreast of the paved double-lane that led up to the crest, she swung into it slowly—no sudden, loud movements—and accelerated smoothly up to the rear gate. Which was a lot flimsier than we had thought. Steve rolled past us on the ATV, made with the bolt cutters again, and we were in.

Or I should say, we followed Prospero in. Which had not been part of the plan. To be fair, it wasn't *not* part of the plan, either. What I mean is this:

If we found Golf Ball's back gate locked, Prospero had assured us that the site would be secure. Operational protocols, he explained. Since his life would be on the line, just like the rest of ours, we didn't question him.

But the moment the gate was open and Steve was pulling out a new padlock, Prospero juiced his ATV. He zipped up the last rise to the two-story building on the west, unslung his Rexio, and went in. Using a key.

"What the fu—?" began Chloe.

Before she could get the Rover going, I bailed out; I could run after him faster than waiting for her to drive into the small parking lot.

I found the door to the building ajar. I snapped my own Rexio off safety and slipped in.

It didn't take long to find Prospero; it's not a big building and since it's a prefab government structure, it creaks whenever you move.

I found him staring into a maintenance closet, shotgun hanging loosely in his hand. "Percival," I said, keeping my tone low and completely non-ironic.

"He was my best mate," Prospero said in a strange voice, both sad and wistful. "Never had a lot of mates, you know."

I stepped closer, looked around him.

A corpse in a U.S. Airman's uniform was propped in a

splay-legged sitting position against the far wall. Its left arm was handcuffed to a water pipe; its right arm lay loose, an M-9 half-slipped from that hand. The faded brown splatter behind the now husklike head finished the story.

"You knew... knew that he'd be here," I ventured.

Prospero didn't look over, but he nodded. "He was the one who called me when the Security Forces lost control of the base. Secured the documents, the machines, the mainframe... well, whatever the leftenant didn't destroy. He was dying and he still carried out all the protocols for shuttering a compromised station."

As if I knew what the hell all that really meant. But he was mostly speaking to himself, now, anyway.

"Poor sod knew he'd been infected but didn't tell the rest. He made the others leave first, locked himself in, shut everything down. And then shackled himself here. Which is where he called me from."

"To say goodbye?"

Prospero nodded. "That, and to tell me the steps he'd taken. And that he'd sent a final communique to Kourou."

*Kourou?* The thing about having a photographic memory is that it really is a *visual* phenomenon. I remember conversations pretty well, too, but words on a page are what kick my recall into high gear. But when I read a word I've never heard pronounced, it can take a while for that circuit to close. It took about three seconds, this time. "You mean, Kourou in French Guiana? The ESA launch facility?"

He turned and looked at me as if I'd just revealed I was a Nobel laureate. "Yes. That one. He came up here hoping to relay the final data they needed, but the leftenant had knocked us off-line. So all he could do was preserve the data we'd received and to make sure he himself couldn't undo any of the good he'd done. The last thing he said to me was that he hoped he'd find the courage not to let the disease take him." He looked at the brown stain on the wall, and his head drooped. "Apparently he did." He turned abruptly and walked past me. "No time to mope about. I'll show you the facilities, and then get Chloe set up in the best overwatch position. She'll have a clear field of fire on almost the entire base."

According to several faded plaques, the Golf Ball was a NASA and Air Force Target Tracking Radar Station that was completed in 1961. The two-story building in which we set up had been built later for some U.S.-Brit collaboration called the NSA-GCHQ. All I know about that alphabet soup label is that NSA stands for exactly what you think it stands for, and the new array and facilities were for U.S. spooks and their British pals to snoop on communications from South America to Africa.

Now it was serving as a staging area and sniper's roost for a bunch of teenaged zombie-hunters. I never read any Greek philosophers, but I think one of them said that change is the only constant. Dude knew what he was talking about.

Anyway, we finished our set up pretty quickly. Rod and I lugged in the ammo, water, and food (in that order) and then carried ready rounds for Chloe up to the roof. Jeeza carried up a couple of sandbag-rests for the scoped .308 but stayed put; she was working spotter again and began surveying the base for movement. Prospero and Steve checked out the ground-level perimeter fence with binoculars, and then walked the thinner one lining the crest of Cat Hill. Both were intact. No surprise. The stalkers on Ascension never had the numbers, let alone any reason, to crowd against and push down fences.

Weapons were distributed, along with a two-way radio for each person. The radios didn't have much operating life; their rechargeable batteries barely deserved the name. So we kept our one real radio on, next to Jeeza and hooked up to a goofy power-source built from a car battery. That way, anyone could switch on their own handset and make a report to Jeeza on top of the Wizard's Tower. Equipped with a megaphone, she, in turn, could spread the word to everyone else.

And yes, we did all start referring to the main building as the Wizard's Tower. It was partially as a nod to Rod, but it was also a lame attempt at dark humor. Back when such things still mattered, the NSA had been memed as the real world's equivalent of the Dark Lords of the Sith, Sauron's minions, etc., etc.

Hey, making bad jokes is better than obsessing about the possibility of being surrounded by stalkers for days.

As Rod lugged his last load to the roof—a sound system that was guaranteed to attract the stalkers—he was smiling like an asylum inmate who'd missed meds three days in a row. I figured it was some private wizard joke, but when I asked, he just shook his head and grinned even more wildly. "You'll see—eh, hear—soon enough." I shrugged, snagged my FAL, and went outside to join Steve and Prospero while I waited for him to come back down.

It wasn't my intent to keep the guys on the ground and put the gals up on the roof. Hell, there was no margin of error to allow for chivalry when assigning tasks. We just put the right people in the right jobs. In this case, our best sniper and spotter were the two women. Three of us four guys would stand a rotating watch at three equidistant points on the crest of Cat Hill, the last one held as a ready reserve at the center. Our job: to watch for any stalkers that attempted to climb or knock down the fence. And if they tried—well, that's why we had the FALs. It was, depending upon the angle, anywhere from seventy-five to one hundred yards from our patrol positions to the base of the hill. We were good enough shots to weed out any stationary cluster of stalkers. Eventually I looked back at the second story. "Hey, Rod: you coming?"

"Right now!" he whooped. Loud enough to wake stalkers, but that hardly mattered, given that was why he was up there in the first place. "So, are you ready for it?"

"For what?"

"For this!"

The speakers on the roof crackled, and then sent a wave of sound out over the dilapidated military housing units: a single bell-toll, followed by an abrupt surge of marching music. The kind they used to play back in Victorian times. "What the hell—?" I started.

But Prospero groaned. "Oh no. Not that."

"Not what?"

But Jeeza was damn near squealing with laughter. "Perfect!" I heard her shout after Rod, who had started down toward us.

I repeated—and this time, completed—my question: "What the hell is that?"

"That," said Ron as he came down the stairs of the Wizard's Tower, "is the Monty Python theme song!"

"Okay"—I vaguely recognized it from the old TV show—"but why?"

Rod stopped in mid-step. "Remember what I said about taunting the stalkers? Like, from *Monty Python and the Holy Grail*? I guess I looked as confused as I felt. "You know, the French knights on the castle wall?"

"Yeah, Rod, I remember you saying that, but it's—it's been a long time since I saw that movie. And I might have been high."

"But I thought you—? Well, whatever." He jogged toward his watch post on the south side of the hilltop, trying not to look disappointed.

Prospero looked after him, smiled at me. "Clearly, you are not a True Fan."

"Clearly," I agreed, and went to my post.

Fans or not, the stalkers sure did respond to that music. They came stumbling from various buildings around the base, looking like they'd just awakened. Which was probably the case for a lot of them; they were pretty gaunt.

Chloe let the first one get to one hundred twenty yards before putting the hammer down. The rifle barked; the stalker fell. Tried to get up. I heard the distant clatter of Chloe working the bolt and then, two seconds later, a second bark. The stalker, just rising, went back and was still.

We were all equally still. This was the moment of truth: how would they react when one of their number went down? More energetic? More aggressive? More likely to gather and come as a mass?

A few started moving a little faster and with a little more focus. They zeroed in on the sound of the rifle, ran toward that. If you could call what they were doing running. I mean, they were going through the motions now, but it was like they had ten-pound weights on every limb. But other than that, no change.

Even if you wanted to know how every one of the stalkers was shot that morning, I couldn't tell you. On two occasions, several got to the same stretch of fence at roughly the same time. Those of us with FALs took our time and took them down. After only three hours, fifty-two dead stalkers were scattered along the various approaches between the buildings below us. Chloe spent a little over eighty rounds achieving that feat, not because she missed a bunch, but because one of the things we were learning about the infected is that they don't stop coming. Even when they can't really run anymore. It's not determination or anything like that. They just aren't wired to do anything else.

A few latecomers didn't show themselves until all the others had died. Four or five had been hanging back in the last morning shadows. When they emerged, they did so in a careful crouch, but they didn't head for the Wizard's Tower. In fact, they were clearly trying to stay as far away from Cat Hill as they could while creeping toward the most distant corpses.

Chloe let each of them come all the way out, thinking they'd be easier to hit once they were trying to drag a body away. But these stalkers weren't any smarter than the others. I guess because they didn't see us or hear new gunshots, they thought the danger was past and started gnawing on the dead right in the middle of the street. Three made that same mistake before noon, one right after the other. Like I said, no smarter than the other stalkers.

However, one or two remained in the shadows, watching. After Chloe took down the third, they went to ground. At any rate, we didn't see any movement. So maybe some stalkers *can* learn some simple lessons, after all.

We were thinking that this had all been too easy and were about to start pestering Chloe to give us a try at the .308 like tweens at a shooting gallery, when Jeeza sat very straight on her observer's stool, binoculars aimed southwest. "Movement," she announced.

We hustled back to our positions.

Chloe gave one last try at working the kink out of her neck. "Where?"

"Coming across Donkey Plain. Straight at us. Not a mass. They're all strung out. Looks like they started from Green Mountain."

It made sense. Some would have heard the noise earlier than others. They'd be the first to arrive. The ones on the back of the mountain would bring up the rear. But— "Jeeza," I called up, "Are these stalkers going slowly, or—?"

"They are nonstop charging, Alvaro." She sounded surprised, worried.

I nodded. "Just like at the intersection. The ones to the east were fully active because they were getting game on the mountain. And the first who came charging up the south road must have been the most successful hunters here, around the base and the airfield."

"Pretty much what we expected," Jeeza agreed. "The ones that are still eating don't go dormant."

"Well," muttered Chloe, "no reason to be coy about where they should look for us. Time to turn on that corny music again."

These stalkers had a lot more energy than the ones from the base, even after loping through the rugged terrain between them and Cat Hill. But it also strung them out even more. The weaker ones couldn't maintain the pace set by the stronger ones.

When the leaders started arriving about twenty minutes later, it was creepy watching their manic movement while the Monty Python theme was playing in the background. There was something extra grotesque about the way they rushed and jerked toward us, as if intentionally trying to stay out of sync with the marching beat.

The first to arrive hit the fence in ones and twos. But eventually, statistical inevitability—the middle of the performance bell curve—produced an impressive pack of stalkers, who charged wildly through the gates into the base. But the buildings broke them up. They never hit in clumps greater than four and five, although, at the peak, several such clusters did run headlong against the chain link fence within the same minute.

But we'd been refining our aim all morning long, and Chloe shifted to the Captain's FAL for a few minutes to break that small wave. All those 7.62x51mm NATO rounds pretty much washed them away, their bodies piling on top of those few from the base who'd reached the fence.

Which was a bit of a problem. There were now some places where the corpses were two or even three deep and some of the stragglers from Green Mountain tried to use the highest one as a launch ramp. Two survived long enough to try that leap but wound up snarled in the razor wire that ran along the top of the fence. Which must have hurt like the torture that Father Hernando claimed was awaiting sodomizers, potheads, dropouts, and Giants fans in Satan's hottest regions of hell.

But the creepiest way that the virus rewires the infected is that just as it eliminates fear, it allows them to ignore pain. Instead, pain works like a shot of adrenaline: it supercharges their rage, makes them try just that much harder to get at you.

But none of them did. It was about 1600—that's 4 PM—when Chloe shot the last one who showed up. She was limping along with a compound fracture, just above the ankle. I would have sworn it was physically impossible for a human body to propel itself with that kind of injury (probably the result of a bad fall among the volcanic pits). But there she was, shrieking and clawing at the air as she stumbled along like some mad, gory reinvention of a peg-legged pirate.

Chloe's second bullet put her down. The Monty Python theme went on, brassy and bass-drummed, marching onward with such excessive Victorian zeal that it seemed like a deranged musical indictment of our dying world. It had been a black humor soundtrack up until that moment. Suddenly, it was grim mockery.

Jeeza reached over and turned it off.

The silence was better, but not much. As the shadows lengthened, we stared down from the top of the Wizard's Tower: ninety-four bodies that had been ravaged by disease before being drilled and bloodied by our bullets. That's probably what victory has always felt and looked like: sobering. I suppose the difference now is that you don't feel guilt.

Not after you've looked into those infection-mad eyes.

## October 21

The next day, we made our report to the council, Prospero silent and smirking behind us. On the one hand, what we told them was their dream come true: one hundred and forty-seven stalkers killed in two days. But on the other hand, it meant that all their math—and all their assurances to the rest of Georgetown—was pure shite, as Prospero pronounced it. And that meant their credibility was in the same crapper as their numbers.

We let Jeeza do the talking. She's good at it, and she has far more patience with idiots than the rest of us. For instance, I wanted to point out that since stalkers can obviously go dormant for long periods of time, all we really knew about the body count on Ascension island was that 270 people were survivors, who had disposed of 400 corpses, and in the past forty-eight hours, we'd killed 147 stalkers. Which meant that we could only account for 817 out of the roughly 1000 people that had been on the island when the plague hit. And there was no guessing about the last 183 because the whole "they are eating each other" assumption was a total crock.

Maybe I wouldn't have put it that bluntly if I had been talking to the councilors, but I'd have been tempted to. Big time. Not Jeeza. Her attitude and approach were like the lyrics of that old, old song come to life: "You've got to accentuate the positive,/ Eliminate the negative." She talked about how much safer the island was now, and how much had been achieved in just two days, and how much we appreciated the trust they'd shown us. Without which, this happy outcome would not have been possible.

Then she put a little edge of melancholy in her tone. "But," she started sadly, "this makes it necessary to reevaluate the assumptions under which we started." (Amazing that she managed to completely avoid any suggestion that *they* were to blame for that.) After all, now there were 187 persons who could not be accounted for. Certainly, she assured them, the great majority of those had been eaten (she actually used the word "removed," like they were a stain on the carpet or something). But we couldn't be sure how many, because the last two days had shown us that the behaviors and natural resilience of the stalkers were not, and could never have been, fully understood.

Which produced exactly the effect she—we—had been hoping for: the councilors asked us what we were going to do next.

Jeeza for the win.

It was clear that they were also coming to realize that, if we shared everything we'd learned, they were one impromptu town meeting away from being lynched for incompetence and endangering everyone with their bullshit theories. So while they were grateful, they were also uncomfortable; we could spill the beans anytime we chose.

On the other hand, I also got the feeling that one or two of the esteemed councilors were beginning to get greedy. With the stalkers so reduced, they no doubt regretted agreeing to give us first pick of the salvage from the base and the airfield. We now had both a deal and sensitive knowledge that they wished we didn't have: a potentially risky situation for us.

But Jeeza managed to make us seem totally trustworthy and nonpolitical while also implying how important it was that we complete what we started. After all, she finished, it's essential that we eliminate the last known cluster of the stalkers, those hiding out in the airfield's terminal, hangars, and warehouses. Because after that, she admitted, Ascension's locals would have to finish off any remaining infected on their own.

That rocked them back in their chairs. "U-us?" one of them gabbled.

She nodded sadly. "Everything suggests that the weaker stalkers do not remain close to the others when they go dormant. Probably to avoid becoming prey for the most aggressive of their kind. Unfortunately, there is no way to know how many lone stalkers might be in the volcanic rifts or vents all over this island." As new horror started draining the color out of their faces, Jeeza spun them around again. "But thankfully, you have the answer to that problem."

"We do?" gabbled another.

"Certainly," she said with a smile that was one-half angel and one-half homecoming queen. "The dogs. Once we remove the remaining, er, problem at the airbase, it's unlikely that any sizeable groups will remain. Given what we saw of the stragglers and margin-feeders, there will be lone, or maybe pairs, of hidden dormants. With the search grid that we've already plotted, and with firearms and ammunition from the airbase, and your own dogs, you can sweep the rest of the island."

"But would that be safe?" one elderly man quavered.

She shrugged. "The ones just coming out of dormancy will be no match for all your guns."

And so we walked out of the meeting to the sound of "thank yous" and "bless yous" and "tell us how it goes tomorrow." On the way to our loaner house, we got a few cheery waves and even more smiles.

Once in the house, though, it was back down to business. Planning the hit on the base was easy enough. It was mostly a modification of what we'd already done. And as long as we cleared our approach step by step and always had two avenues of retreat for the Range Rovers, it was hard to imagine getting swarmed anymore. Toward the end of Operation Wizard's Tower, the only stalkers we saw were thin as rails and stumbling as much as running. Besides, it wasn't really possible that all 187 unaccounted-for humans could be stalkers. There were dozens of eyewitness reports of them feeding on each other. And the weakest were probably so deep in torpor that the fight at Cat Hill hadn't roused them. But just to be sure, we had seeded the bodies there with old motor oil and other toxins—enough to make even a stalker sick, we figured. Bottom line: even my paranoia couldn't reasonably conjure up a scenario in which we would face more than twenty fully capable stalkers at a time on the huge airstrip. And we could always shoot a bunch of them, drive away, make the rest chase us, shoot some more, and etc. etc. lather, rinse, repeat. It was hard to envision a full-on disaster. Not during the first part of the clearing operation, anyhow.

Nobody else saw any strong possibility of our plan going sideways. In fact, they started talking almost like it was already a done deal.

"You know," Jeeza said wistfully, leaning against Rod, "once the base is cleared, and they've finished hunting down the last stalkers, the locals can plant new crops up on Green Mountain. There's probably lots still growing up there from the start of the season."

"Yeah," agreed Rod, arm around her shoulders, "that will change everything here."

Steve nodded. "And on St. Helena, too."

"Huh?"

I saw what Steve was getting at. "Sure. Once Ascension is stalker-free and a little time goes by, the Saints can lift the quarantine. Anyone who doesn't want to scratch out a living here can go back there."

Chloe shook her head, her smile ironic. "So, clearing this island of stalkers doesn't really mean that the locals will stay; it means they can leave. Damn, the post-apocalypse world is just as full of contradictory bullshit as the old one."

I glanced over at Prospero, who had been uncharacteristically quiet. "And what about you? Will you still want to get away from here, if everything works out? Hell, if you stop baiting the councilors—even though they *are* pricks—I think your reputation might be rehabilitated. Maybe into 'local hero.'"

Prospero shook his head. "Even if that were to happen, no; I can't stay here."

Chloe frowned. "Why?"

His explanation came out through a long, weary sigh. "Because if I did stay, then any month now, maybe any week, you'll need to learn how to make your way across the oceans—or deserts or plains or forests—using maps, a compass, and a sextant. Are you ready for that?"

Chloe heard it as a personal challenge. "Actually, I am. So's Alvaro. And the others are getting pretty damned good at it."

Prospero's response was a sad smile and a slow shake of his head.

I raised my chin. "What are you really getting at?"

He looked me in the eyes. "GPS will be dead soon. Frankly, I don't know how it has stayed active this long."

Prospero talks a lot of shit, a lot of which seems to come out of the weird, jolly irony that seems part of Brit culture. But this time, he was deadly serious. Both in his voice and his eyes. That was the moment I realized that the end of the world hadn't finished happening yet. There were still major pieces left to crumble, sources of light yet to be extinguished. And I had taken this one for granted. Like an idiot. I sat. "Explain," I said. "Why is GPS going to die?"

He nodded. "GPS satellites are not in regular orbits. Keeping them aligned involves constant coordination and—this is *key*—recalibration. Their orientation to the ground, and alignment with each other, undergo small changes with every passing day. In time, those changes result in unreliable data. When the data becomes too unreliable, GPS will shut down entirely."

Rod, whose mouth had been hanging open, gulped. "You mean, when they get far enough out of sync so that there's no data being exchanged, it would send you a message like . . . like 'no service.' Like when your cable box goes off-line."

"Exactly," Prospero sighed.

"So what does that have to do with your needing to leave here?"

"Because I just might have the means to preserve the system. At least for several years. Maybe a few decades." He glanced away. "It's hard to tell."

I nodded. "And how do you plan on doing that?"

He seemed surprised that I wasn't laughing in his face. I was kind of surprised at that, too. "By going to the ESA facility at Kourou," he answered slowly. "With its facilities, and with software specifically designed to compensate for the loss of alignment, GPS might have a longer lifespan."

"How?"

He grimaced. "The full explanation is long, complicated, and very technical. The short version is this: there are about fifteen primary GPS ground stations. The master control, as well as most of the others, were compromised early on. Three—those at Diego Garcia, Kwajalein, and here—remained operational longer. Probably because of their comparative isolation.

"Of these three, Diego Garcia was lost first and sustained considerable damage, from the sound of it. So far as I know, Kwajalein continues to operate, but its staff went dark shortly after Diego Garcia went down."

"Why?"

He shook his head. "Can't say. It could have been an order from what was left of your Joint Chiefs or NSC, part of an attempt to firewall the facility. I only know—well, *suspect*—that Kwajalein is still functioning because without it, there's no way GPS could have functioned this long." He frowned. "But in the last few weeks, it has shown subtle signs of degradation."

"And you fear that Kwajalein has finally been hit by the virus?"

"Or they were hit the same time as everybody else, but locked down the base, sealed the necessary parts of the facility, and held out as long as they had supplies. Or something else has occurred. I have no way of knowing."

"And here?"

Prospero sighed. "The damage done when the leftenant turned is not trivial, and I'm not familiar enough with the system to determine if it can be made fully functional. Even if it can, I don't have the codes or knowledge to operate it."

"Your friend—the one we saw in the NSA facility—did he know how?"

Prospero nodded. "Yes. Actually, he was part of the software development group for saving GPS."

Steve looked over. "Where does Kourou fit in all this? Is it one of these ground stations?"

Prospero shook his head. "No, but the staff there came up with the software concept. They shared their ideas with a group of colleagues—all around the globe—who decided to put aside secrecy oaths and classified restrictions in order to create a program which, if we can send it up to the correct satellites, will propagate across both GPS and other orbital platforms."

"What's it do?" Rod asked, eyes intent, head thrust forward.

Prospero held up a palm. "As I said, a real explanation would require a great deal of time. But in simplest terms, the program uses the orbital platforms to keep a watch on each other. It employs an observation-based algorithm that anticipates, checks, and adjusts for alignment loss in the GPS platforms."

"Wow! Is that even possible?"

Prospero smiled. "Won't know until we get to Kourou."

So, now we came to it. "Why there, if it's not a ground station for GPS?"

"Because, even after the plague hit, it had a functioning, world-class antenna: Diane. It was specifically designed to check telemetry and on-board systems of launch vehicles and their payloads. Such as satellites."

I nodded. "And it could send this software up to the GPS platforms?"

He nodded back. "Given the right instructions, and assuming it remains operational, yes."

"Whoa: 'Assuming it *remains* operational'? You just said it was."

He shrugged. "I have no particular reason to suspect it isn't. However, it's been months since my last contact with the ESA, and the region around Kourou was just as porous to the virus as the rest of the South American coast."

Jeeza frowned. "Yeah, but…isn't French Guiana pretty, well, remote?"

Prospero nodded. "It is a small country and not many people travel to Kourou other than to work at, or visit, the launch facility. But it is not completely isolated, so there are likely to be some stalkers either in or near the ESA complex.

"Fortunately, it has—or had—a dedicated regiment of the French Foreign Legion for base security and lockdown. When last I was in communication with the ESA staff, they were still coordinating the global programming efforts but had already locked themselves into an underground shelter with three months' worth of supplies."

"And?"

"And comms degraded. We were reduced to pings. Then everything went sidewise here. No more intercontinental transmitters or e-mail. I picked up their pings on our best maritime radio for a few weeks. After that, silence." He shrugged. "I stopped thinking about it. There was nothing I could do."

I crossed my arms. "And then we showed up. Heading in the right direction." He nodded but didn't say anything. "And you've been trying to figure out how to recruit us. To help you in Kourou."

He nodded again. "Something like that."

"Yeah, something like that, and a little more."

Rod frowned. "Whaddya mean, Alvaro?"

"He means," Chloe answered quickly, "that Percival here has been trying to position himself as head honcho, too. To be the boss when he steps on *Voyager.*" She smiled. "How do you think that's looking, Percy?"

To his credit, Prospero smiled. "Not bloody likely." He spread his hands. "Frankly, when I learned your ages, I couldn't imagine how you'd made it here at all. I supposed it was some combination of modest skill and profound good fortune. But I was wrong."

Chloe's chin came up proudly. "Yeah, we've gotten pretty good at what we do."

He nodded. "I wager that you have, but that's not what changed my mind."

Steve rolled his head over to stare at Prospero. "What did, then?"

"Seeing you work together. You've become a team. And I don't just mean a group of mates that get along and help each other. I mean that you've sorted out who's got what skills, and who takes what roles. And because you did it on your own, it flows naturally. Not like—well, not like the RAF. Or any other service."

Jeeza rested her chin on her hand. "I thought they would work better."

Prospero shrugged. "In many ways and under most circumstances, yes. There's never any question who is in charge. Well, not officially. Each person's role is clearly defined and strictly enforced. But some teams, some squads—they never gel. So it remains a bumpy ride."

"So," I said, "where does that leave us, Senior Aircraftman Halethorpe? How do we settle this? Pistols at dawn?"

He shook his head, dead serious. "You lot won't take me as your leader. I'm from the outside, even if I have a military rank and a few years on you."

"It's more than that, Percival," Chloe jumped in. "Tell me: do you sail as well as we do? Have you been trained by an SAS officer?" She was going too far with that one, but she was on a roll, so I didn't jump in. "Have you been in a firefight?"

Prospero's eyebrows and posture got a little straighter. "I seem to remember being alongside all of you for the last two."

Chloe's chin pushed toward him. "That's not a firefight, Percival. A firefight is when there are people shooting *back at you*. Like in Husvik. 'Cause if you think that the only things we have to worry about in this world are infected, then you may be in for a nasty surprise."

I leaned into the space between them. "Not that we're looking for a repeat of Husvik," I assured him and reminded her. "In general, humans with guns are a lot more dangerous than infected. But Chloe's right; an apocalypse doesn't seem to bring out the best in people."

He nodded. "Fair enough. And I agree: you have the skills that will get us to Kourou and keep us alive along the way. But once we're there, you won't know what to do. I will." He crossed his own arms. "How do we resolve that impasse?"

I'd seen this coming and had an answer ready; gaining the initiative is how you put yourself in charge of any conflict. "No impasse, Prospero. We just separate areas of authority."

"How so?"

"Simple. When we're at sea or scrounging on land—anything other than helping you at Kourou—we call the shots. But once we set foot in the facility, you're in charge. Presuming you know the layout and where we've got to go."

He nodded. "I do." A pause. "Mostly."

Chloe rolled her eyes. "So your actual answer is no, you don't know."

He reddened. "Before the secure net went down, I downloaded all the maps I could find. Granted, most of them were from archived Google Earth snapshots. But I didn't think everything would go pear-shaped so fast."

I could hardly blame him for that. The plague had outpaced almost everyone's worst-case scenarios. "The way I see it, our job at Kourou is to find a way not to fight infected but to get you to the control center so you can work your computer mojo."

Steve looked over at me. "Seriously? You think we should do this?"

I ignored him, kept my eyes on Prospero. "So you come up with the plan. We reserve veto power on the details. And once we've delivered you to the control center, our job is to keep you safe until the program is uploaded and activated."

He shrugged. "Acceptable." I could tell he had hoped for more authority when we got to Kourou, but I just couldn't accept putting my friends' lives in his hands.

Steve hadn't stopped looking at me. "Really?" he asked.

Now I looked at him. "Really. Think of how much we've relied on GPS, both getting to South Georgia and again since we left. We'd have been floundering around in the South Atlantic for months, might have starved out there." I saw Chloe about to object. "And yeah, maybe we could have navigated well enough with sextant, compass, maps, and clock. But that's a big maybe.

And since most people who've survived the plague don't have those navigation skills, keeping GPS up and running could be the difference between taking back this planet in ten years instead of a hundred. If ever."

Steve's eyes closed slowly. "Some of us won't survive Kourou, Alvaro."

Jeeza sat straighter. "Steve, you can't know—"

"He's right to point out the risk," Prospero said with a sad nod. "Getting out could be more difficult than getting in, depending on what we find there."

*A little help here, Prospero?* "One way or the other, the longer we wait to *really* fight back, the less likely we'll be able to do so effectively. And if there's even a slim chance of keeping GPS alive, that helps everyone who's still got electricity and a locator to stay alive and join the fight."

Rod nodded rapidly. "GPS isn't just about knowing where you are. It's about having a way to coordinate. To gather. To attack. Or defend. Or retreat. Without that, you're just lost in Infected Country, waiting for them to roll over you in waves. So, it's worth it. It's worth all of us, if it comes down to it."

I wondered if Rod would be as brave as his words. If any of us would, if we found ourselves surrounded by those howling monsters with distorted human faces. But all I said was, "Are we cool with helping Prospero save GPS?" I looked at Steve. "It's got to be all in or nothing. We can't split up."

Steve opened his eyes, glanced at me, then at Prospero. "I'm cool."

I nodded, felt good about making the decision, but felt sick to my stomach because Prospero was right: unless the Kourou facility was deserted, it was not likely that all of us would come back from that mission. "Okay," I said, "then let's get dinner and get to sleep early. Big day at the airfield tomorrow."


Right as I was pulling aside the sheets to climb into bed, I smacked my forehead.

"What?" Chloe asked.

"We didn't decide on music."

"Music?" She slid over to my side of the bed. "Babe, we don't need music. Besides, we don't have any."

"No, I mean for the speakers. For tomorrow. I can't take another whole day of shooting stalkers with the Monty Python theme as the soundtrack."

"Oh, that," she said with a flounce. "No worries. I've got that handled."

"Y-you do?" I stammered. Partly at her response, partly at the way she was looking at me.

"I've got it all taken care of." She smiled. "You'll see."

## October 22

"See?" Chloe yelled over the music. "All taken care of!"

I managed not to grit my teeth, but I couldn't help rolling my eyes.

She laughed, put her high cheekbone to the stock of the .308, peered down the scope, and fired.

I had a FAL, tried to do the same, but was tempted to swing it around and take out the speakers on top of the Rover just behind me. Anything to stop the idiotic repetition of the most idiotic lyrics in the world, howled by one of rock's most flamboyant front men.

An idiot song about a bicycle. A bicycle. About riding it where I like.

Holy crap, how I hate that friggin' song.

I aimed and fired. The stalker who'd just come stumping out of the shadows of Wideawake Field's small air terminal missed a step, fell, did not get up.

The rocker's voice, as dramatic as any operatic diva's, kept hammering away at my eardrums: something something about black or white. Bark or bite. But always back to that god-damned bicycle.

*Sweet mother of God.* I was so eager to drown it out, I probably fired a little early at the next stalker, only caught him in the arm. Before I could finish him off, Steve put a second round in his solar plexus.

"That's seventeen!" shouted Jeeza from atop the other Rover.

"What about the rear?" I shouted back.

She turned, scanned behind us. "Nothing. Wait. One. Still a kilometer off."

"Track him," I yelled.

"It's a 'her.' I'm on it, Alvaro."

And still, over all of that, I could still hear it—"*Bicycle!*
*Bicycle!*"—sung so loud and clear and high that no amount of
earpro would have been able to keep it out. Not that we could
wear any; we had to hear each other over his diva-crooning. So
I simply had to accept that today, Chloe's musical bliss was my
torment.

However, it was a positive sign that I had enough time and
focus to mentally bitch about her choice of musical stalker-bait.
Because if that's your worst problem when you're potshotting
ravenous zombies, it's a good day.

It had started with us driving into camp using a rear access
lane that skirted the housing area so we could check out the pile
of bodies at the base of Cat Hill. We'd expected some stalkers
to be scavenging there, and potted three of them doing just that,
but no others. Which was a little surprising, because we could
smell the corpses at fifty yards, and the infected seem to get
heightened senses when they turn.

We bypassed the housing complex and rolled up on the airfield at about 0545. The stalkers there are early risers; their only
fresh water source is whatever condenses on the runway. How
that taint of macadam doesn't kill them over time, I can't tell
you. I guess turning also toughens the digestive track. Regular
humans would have been puking their guts out. Or spending
half the day in the latrine.

We had the AKs and shotguns at hand, but we never needed
them. We parked out on the tarmac, about a hundred yards from
the dinky terminal and support buildings, cranked up the music
(if you can call it that), and waited with our FALs.

It was almost half an hour before the first came staggering
out. I didn't need Jeeza's binoculars or Chloe's scope to see that
this stalker was in pretty bad shape. Halfway-to-Dachau thin, and
not capable of running. Its movement was more like an annoyed
lope. So there was plenty of time for Rod, the first person in the
day's firing rota, to take him down. If any stalker got to within
fifty yards, Chloe was waiting with the bolt action. And if, by
some freakish chance, she missed or had a misfire, there were
always the shotguns and AKs.

The infected that emerged from the terminal were weak and

slow. Clearly, they'd been in torpor for a long time. Otherwise, it's certain they would have joined the mobs that attacked us at the intersection or the Wizard's Tower. But I'm betting that these stalkers—or, more accurately, stumblers—had to hide from their own kind or get eaten.

They staggered out at wide intervals and in ones and twos, which made them easy targets. We had the luxury to aim all our shots and pay attention to our mechanics, rather than just dropping threats as quickly as we could. In short, it was like having a live fire range with real live targets, but almost no risk. And because of that, we had the ability to take turns at learning what we were doing wrong, how to fix it, and become better marksmen.

Now, if you are reading this in some future where there are no more infected, and you have a balanced diet and a safe place to sleep every night, that might sound pretty cold. Damn near sociopathic, I guess. But teaching ourselves how to shoot at moving targets more accurately was the biggest boost to our survival odds since the Captain showed us how to sail, and then, set up an ambush.

I had the last place in the "training rota," and the rate at which infected were appearing was tapering off. But my spirits lifted because that asinine song concluded.

My relief was short-lived. Almost immediately, the musical void was filled by a torch-song piano riff that threatened to tumble over itself. It was joined a second later by the same diva-voice, crooning moody lyrics.

I knew what was coming. "Christ," I muttered, "dear Christ. Send me deliverance. Send me a stumbler to shoot. To drown that out. Right now. Please. Oh, please."

But no stick-thin silhouette came shambling out of the terminal, so I had no reason to use gunfire to drown out the sudden surging, melodramatic strains of the new song. One I hated almost as much. About champions. Who will keep on fighting to the end.

*Give me a break, you candy-ass. As if you were ever in the shit. Like we are.*

I scanned the other building exits: still nothing. *Sweet Jesus.*

Repetitive, moaned claims of being champions—*the* champions!—evoked two powerful reactions: to puke and laugh. Simultaneously. I thumped my forehead against the FAL's receiver. "Jeeza, is there *anything* to shoot?"

And now there was no time for losers because diva-boy and his pals were the champions. Champions...of the world!

Jeeza looked down. "What's wrong, Alvaro?"

"I friggin' hate this band. *Hate them!*"

Chloe's voice was loud, sharp. "Hey! My dad liked them!"

"Yeah?" I shot back without thinking. "Well, your dad—"

Then I saw her face. Her eyes.

"Your dad," I continued, "at least had the good taste to have the most outstanding and beautiful daughter in the world."

Chloe doesn't surprise easy, but I guess she hadn't seen that course change coming. Her mouth turned into a full-lipped "O." Then she got a look on her face which translated as, "You are SO getting laid tonight."

As I finish writing this in our very, very unmade bed, I have to say: diva-boy and his band still suck. But I suppose I can tolerate them.

So long as their music produces the right kind of outcome.

## October 23

The next day, as we climbed out of the Rovers, we had to keep the three dogs heeled in close on their leashes. They'd been growling and getting stiff-legged and puffy-furred from the time we turned into the base housing complex, the shadow of Cat Hill still a long lump pointing back toward the New World. Chloe had practical experience with dogs, but we didn't want her handling them instead of a gun. Because you really can't do both.

Besides, the dogs all decided that they really, *really* liked Rod; couldn't do enough to please him. Oh, they fawned all over Jeeza, but it was like she was the Queen-Mother to his King. Turns out Rod's suburban upbringing had involved dogs that could *not* fit in a lady's handbag, even when they were still blind puppies. I guess they caught vibe off him from the way he got right in among them and got them all excited about chasing sticks and charging around. He was smart about them, too. Example: if he played a game with them, it was one he was sure he could win. Otherwise, if they did things like rushing in and trying to bait him, to get him to grab for them, he always remained half-hearted about it. Like a big papa dog indulging pups.

They ate that stuff up just as eagerly as they ate fish and tortoise scraps from his hands. For a special treat, he'd let them get up on their hind legs and take the morsels from his teeth. Nothing made them happier.

But now it was time to put them to work. We moved the two Rovers to the center of the approximate main street of the housing section, Chloe on one car roof with the scoped .308, Jeeza on the other with her binoculars. The rest of us followed Rod and his mongrel horde up and down that stretch of road and the lanes that ran off from it, shotguns and AKs at the ready.

Nothing came out at us, but at three different buildings, the dogs got agitated, straining toward a particular doorway. Once we'd noted those, we pulled back into a position where we could keep all of the duplexes and barracks under observation. Then, with one of us always watching the rear, we put on our construction goggles, surgical masks, and gloves (for all the good they'd do), and wrestled our heads into the cricket helmets we'd scrounged from the locals.

We went back to the first building and set up in a triangle that gave all of us a clear shot on the door. We weren't quiet about it; better to make enough noise to bring the stalkers out into our kill zone than going in after them.

Except none came out.

Fine: we'd anticipated that. That's why we had also hit up the locals for a string of those little firecrackers that you see on the Fourth of July or Chinese New Year. We detached one, lit it, tossed it into the doorway: a loud enough pop to alert anything inside, but not in the other target buildings.

Still nothing.

"What the hell—?" Chloe started.

"Hang on," Prospero said softly, which in Brit doesn't mean "just give me a second," but rather, "wait; I've got an idea." He studied our position relative to the other two doorways. "Alvaro, I think these buggers may be too knackered to come out and play."

Which agreed with my own suspicions. "Okay. So, more stumblers, probably. What do you want to do?"

"Use the Rovers' horns. The other two doors are far enough that if anything does come out of them, we've got plenty of time to put them down."

I shrugged and nodded at Rod, who was now hanging back with the less modified vehicle. Since we had started using it to transport the dogs, we had called it the Rover Rover. One hand controlling the leashes, Rod slipped sideways into the interior and leaned on the horn.

It took about half a minute for one stalker to show up, lurching awkwardly out of the farthest doorway. As he came out of the shadows, we saw that most of his left foot was gone. So was his right hand. Looked like he'd lost an ear, too.

He was an easy target. Steve took him down with one round

of single-aught buck. The breath rushed out of the stumbler as he hit the ground, motionless. We walked over to check him.

Prospero kept his own Rexio trained on the corpse. "Well, it's plain to see why he stayed out of sight."

"He was prey, now," Steve nodded. "What about the other two doors?"

Prospero glanced back at them. "An excellent question, Steven."

I shrugged. "Let's get the answer." I let the AK slip into a cradle-carry and made my way to the next one, a barrack.

"Surely you don't mean to go in there?" Prospero muttered at my back.

"Don't really have a choice if we want to finish the job." I raised my voice: "Rod, bring one of your pups. One you can manage easily."

"What for?"

"Need a nose to tell us when we're about to run into trouble."

Rod met us at the doorway with the smartest of the dogs: a border collie-shepherd mix that was fast, steady, obedient, attentive. Just what we needed for going into a dark building. Along with the headlamps we slipped on.

"I'm in first," I muttered. "Just to make sure there's nothing right on the other side of the door. Then you bring the pup in, Rod, and we take our cues from him. Everyone, shoot high. Don't clip Rin Tin Tin. On three. One, two—"

On "three," I shoved the door sharply. It flew back hard; it had only been leaned closed. I wasn't the only one startled; I almost blew apart a bird that came flying out, and damn near had a heart attack as I swung my weapon up to do so. "We're clear," I shouted, both for my own benefit and the team's.

Rod brought the pooch in, who took two sniffs and started to growl, joints stiffening as it started to pull him down the hall. "I can hold him," Rod muttered, shortening the leash. "But I can't keep him quiet forever."

"Don't try. Let him bark."

Rod shrugged, leaned toward the dog and whispered in an excited tone. "Whatta you smell, boy? What's back there? Can you get it? Will you get it?"

The dog didn't bark; it let out a full-on Cujo-of-the-Baskervilles howl, broken up by bloodthirsty growlings.

Rod glanced at me. "Should we—?"

"Hold your ground. Weapons up."

About the same time I followed my own order, there was movement toward the end of the barrack's corridor: a figure scampered—*scampered?*—out of a doorway, headed toward the one across from it.

No one waited for my order—"Fire!"—not even me. Two shotgun blasts and a quick AK stutter deafened us, momentarily lighting up the interior like a weak strobe-light show.

The figure slipped, crawled. Steve put another round into it. The stalker howled—but not so much in anger as pain. It wasn't quite a human sound, but it also wasn't the insane raging-at-creation-itself snarl-shrieks of your typical infected.

Prospero started heading toward it, hand moving off his Rexio's grip and toward his pistol—

"Hold position," I snapped.

He looked at me, startled.

"We're in the dark. We don't know the floorplan. Rod, quiet that dog. If you can."

"But—" Steve started.

"We stay put. That stalker isn't going anywhere. We'll put it out of its—and our—misery when we've cleared this corridor by the numbers. No rushing. Leapfrog advance. Assuming Cujo there can pipe down."

It took another few seconds for Rod to get the now-renamed dog under control. Mostly.

It was just a thirty-foot corridor, but if I'd been able to bite my nails, I'd probably have chewed them clean off. Not because there was anything in the hall—there wasn't—but because of how vulnerable we were. No armor except ratty old cricket helmets and only a little daylight seeping in, here and there. After the first ten feet, every one of us was thinking the same thought: *What the hell are we doing? This is a job for professional soldiers!*

Except we didn't have any professional soldiers. It was up to us.

By the time we reached the stalker, it was dead or as good as. Prospero didn't take any chances; he pulled a Taurus M9 and put one in its skull. It didn't even flinch. We saw what it had been running for: a broken window in the room across the hall. The room it had burst out of—its lair—was a nasty stew of scat and rat carcasses. Some of the rats had been as big as groundhogs.

We continued, doorway by doorway to the far end of the barrack, and went out that door into the early morning mist.

I yanked off the cricket helmet. "Shit."

Rod came up alongside me, and Cujo sniffed gently at my hand. "Alvaro, what's wrong?"

"I'm *stupid*, that's what's wrong!" I remembered to bring my gun up and cover the open approaches as I headed back toward the Rovers.

"Stupid? How?"

Chloe and Jeeza were sitting bolt upright; I guess my posture told them I was pissed. "Stupid for not thinking to break all the fucking windows before we went in! Christ, we didn't *have* to go door-to-door in the dark. It's a single story. Every room has a window. Just put a shooter at the entry on each end. Then put another on the side of the building opposite while the fourth shooter just smashes the windows and clears each room from the *outside!*" I waved at the barrack behind me; I would have torched it if I could have. "Goddamn, it's like I'm Pavlov's fucking tactical dog, trained by fucking movies and video games. I could have gotten us all killed—or at least one of us bitten—by playing hide-and-go-seek in that hallway. I am a *moron.*"

"No," Chloe said from atop the Rover. "You're just not perfect. And no one expects you to be. Except you."

I looked up. Her eyes added, *and I love you*, more clearly than words could have.

I don't know how or why, but that steadied me. "Okay, I may be the only one who had to learn this lesson the hard way, but we can't simply trust pre-plague tactics. A lot still work, but a lot don't, mostly because they're based on assumptions that no longer apply. Like the tactics for entering an enemy building."

Prospero nodded. "Because the stalkers aren't really 'enemies' in the military sense of the word. They are not thinking opponents."

I nodded. "I'm sorry I put all of you through that," I said, looking individually at Rod, Steve, and Prospero.

Rod smiled, Steve shrugged, and the corners of Prospero's mouth crinkled as he admitted, "I hadn't thought it through either, mate. For good or for ill, we're all in the same boat."

I straightened up, wished I had a washcloth to wipe the sweat out of my armpits, headed toward the third and last building the dogs had tweaked to. "Now," I said, "let's go do this the *right* way."

The third and last housing unit was, as Steve put it, a slam dunk. The fourth window that I smashed revealed yet another cowering stalker. She loped weakly across the hall—and straight into two rounds of single-aught from Prospero's Rexio.

About thirty minutes later, we pulled up at the site of the prior day's musical massacre: the tarmac in front of Wideawake Airfield's passenger terminal. We knew this was likely to be a more dangerous environment in which to go room to room; it was mostly comprised of irregular, interior spaces that had no windows or other openings for daylight.

But actually, we'd started preparing for our entry the day before by giving ourselves an advantage that we hoped would compensate for the lack of light deep inside. When the stalkers had stopped emerging from the terminal, we'd poured a wide circle of (now useless) fabric softener around their corpses. And sure enough, a day later, it looked like at least a few of their pals had crossed that heavily scented barrier to snack on their remains.

But that protective circle (of lemony freshness, not magic) didn't figure in the first phase of our zombie-clearing plans. Instead, Prospero, Steve and I took up a flanking position to one side of the terminal's ruined entry while Chloe and Jeeza kept a three-sixty watch for unexpected visitors. Rod had the dogs back at the cars, trying to keep them quiet. I gave him a thumbs-up and he honked the horn. We waited.

After about a minute, three very strange-looking infected came bounding out of the deeper gloom. They had almost as much physical energy as fully active stalkers, but their bellies were grossly distended; they had probably gorged on the corpses we'd left behind. They rushed forward, blinking into the morning light. The dogs started baying at the same moment I gave Rod the second thumbs-up.

Jumping from one Rover to the other, he snapped on their high beams.

The stalkers screeched, threw their hands up against the light as they kept running forward. But their gait was unsteady now, and their focus was on the dogs. That ferocious barking was a clear challenge, and nothing attracts a stalker's attention faster than that.

I doubt they even knew the three of us were there until we opened up.

That big meal had definitely recharged them. It took three hits to put them down. All except the one that Steve hit high; a single aught ball punched through the bridge of her nose and she fell as fast and limp as a bag of wet laundry. None of them got within twenty feet of us. I couldn't tell if our marksmanship had notched up a bit or if we were just a little more calm and collected when firing in combat. Maybe a bit of both. Or maybe we just got lucky.

We waited. Nothing. Rod honked the horn again. Still nothing.

I rose from my kneeling position and waved him in. "Let's get the dogs working."

Despite how much the locals depended upon them, we hadn't realized how valuable dogs would be against the infected until we started thinking about having to clear the base and the airfield. At which point, their value became obvious. So when the police were prepping our back-up vehicle for Operation Wizard's Tower (the one we now call the Rover Rover), we went to the council and asked if we could borrow a few of the town's dogs. We were given our pick, and so, chose three that were known to be even-tempered, easy to work with, and above all, had good noses.

Those three dogs were now straining at their leashes as Rod joined us at the terminal's gaping entrance; there wasn't a bit of glass left in the doors or the ground-to-ceiling windows on either side of them. Rod held out a rag that he'd anointed with the fabric softener. The dogs got the scent and got busy, almost pulling him inside. Weapons in an assault carry, we followed.

It wasn't much of a terminal. The single baggage carousel appeared to be an afterthought that no one had ever used. There were fewer seats than you'd find in a large doctor's office. No amenities of any kind, except for a snack machine. It was the only object that had attracted the stalkers' attention and had done so in a very big way. It was on its side, glass front shattered. And—

And there were empty candy-bar wrappers all around it. I looked more closely, and discovered that they'd also devoured a crate's worth of those cheddar crackers with peanut butter fillings. My comment on this discovery was singularly insightful. "Huh." I said.

Prospero was frowning. "Some survivors claimed they'd seen evidence that the grotty bastards have a sweet tooth. I dismissed it, but—"

"Not just a sweet tooth," Rod corrected casually as the dogs kept tugging at their leashes. "Look: potato chip wrappers. The stalkers need carbs, too. Probably even more than we do."

Prospero pointed at the unmolested bags of sunflower seeds that were still in the vending machine. "How does your theory account for those?"

Rod shrugged. "They're not refined carbs. Doesn't smell the same. No animal fat, either." He hauled back on the taut leashes, tilted his head toward the far end of the combination arrivals and departures area. "Look, are we gonna do this or what?"

If the terminal's public spaces were small, the private/official sections were disproportionately large. According to Prospero, that was mostly to house security and support services for when and if the airfield ever became a logistics hub again, as it had been during the Falklands War. He'd been in those rear areas a few times and had been able to give us the basic layout, but not a detailed ground plan. He knew the major corridors and bigger rooms, but there were still plenty of question marks on the map.

The dogs, however, didn't need any map to find what they, and we, were looking for: the stalkers who'd gone through the fabric softener. Rod gave them the scent again, and once they were done nosing around (and growling) they resumed pulling him deeper into the terminal.

He didn't lengthen their leashes, though. For all we knew, there could be other, still torpid stalkers. They might rouse only when we came very near or otherwise disturbed their beauty sleep. And since they could pop up anywhere, we kept the dogs in close, working on clearing each new space we encountered. That way, there was no part of our rear or flanks that we'd overlooked.

In the outermost areas, we found the lair of the three that had rushed us near the entrance. Lots of still locked rooms, too, which promised lots of undamaged and unused stores of—well, everything. But no stalkers. We pushed deeper.

This is the part that could easily be told like a campfire ghost story: all the dark niches and blind corners. All the sweaty twists and turns in the darkness. Two of our headlamps flickered out because batteries that have been recharged half a dozen times really suck. Then there were all the moments the dogs got quiet and then started growling—sometimes at the walls. So yeah, it was kind of scary: by the time we were done, we were all putting out that especially rank fear-sweat.

But in hindsight, it really wasn't a big deal. The dogs did their job. They found four of the down-tuned stalkers we started calling "passives." Their only impulse was to get the hell away from us. We killed three of them outright and wounded the other. It almost escaped because one of the dogs (Daisy, a Newfie-Rottweiler mix) pulled so hard on her leash that Rod fell over. And when we came in to protect him, we stumbled into each other.

But if Daisy made the problem, she also fixed it. She didn't so much leap on that passive as she tackled him. By which time, Rod had gotten back to his feet and pulled her off as we finished the job.

That part—killing the passives—was kinda sad. I mean, these infected were entirely different. But even if they weren't aggressive now, I doubt they'd be so harmless if *we* were the ones who were vulnerable. They're probably a lot like rats: skittish when frightened, aggressive if they've got the upper hand. Besides, they were infectious. And these days, that's the bottom line.

Once we'd cleared every square foot of the terminal, we got out quickly. Jeeza was there with a bleach and water mixture for our bodies (including Daisy's) and a more human-friendly decon wipe for our faces. We hadn't gotten close to any of the stalkers, but we weren't about to take any chances. My biggest fear was that just being in the same enclosed space might be enough to infect us. But Prospero and the councilors had heard enough radio chatter during the start of what they called The Fall to feel pretty sure that there wasn't any real risk of that. Most infection was through direct contact or exposure to fluids. And if it was transmitted by air, we had taken care to stick to wide corridors and big rooms. The passives did prefer smaller spaces, though. Again, just like rats: they protect themselves by living in small, hard-to-get-to spaces.

It was at the airfield's warehouses that we found the only truly surreal scene of the day. Of the two that were no longer sealed, one had simply had both doors thrown wide and stalkers had torn half of the boxes and containers apart. Mostly to get at candy and snacks.

But at the other warehouse, only one door was slightly ajar. The dogs got a little lively when we approached, so we fastened a tow-line to it and hitched the other end to the lashing ring on the Rover Rover's front bumper. Jeeza eased the vehicle into reverse and as the warehouse door started opening, we did a silent three-count and then stormed in.

At first, we couldn't make out what we were seeing, it was such a crazy mess. There was a well-gnawed human skeleton in the middle of the floor, surrounded by heaps of dead rats. The super-sized groundhog kind. Looking more carefully, we realized that this had been some kind of last stand for a stalker, who had taken at least thirty of the rodents down with it. We closed the door.

"Well, that's how they survived here," Prospero muttered.

"You mean the rats or the infected?" Steve asked.

"Both. Because for every place the stalkers could get into, the rats must have wormed into a dozen more."

I nodded. "Makes sense. The rats fed on whatever stores only they could reach. Their population grew. The stalkers hunted them." I glanced backwards. "Maybe vice versa, sometimes."

"Yeah, sounds right," drawled Chloe. "Now what?" She was bored; there'd been nothing for her to shoot.

"Now," I grinned at her, "we do the dull stuff."

"You mean, the *more* dull stuff," she corrected with an eye roll.

The "dull stuff" took the rest of the day and part of the next. First, we got every window and door into every building wide open. Then, Steve and Prospero drove back to town to announce that, as expected, the clearance was complete and we were ready for the salvage teams. While the two of them were gone, Jeeza spotted two stalkers coming towards us from Lady Hill.

Chloe took them out at three hundred yards (showing off) just before the guys returned with the Rover Rover, and this time, it really did live up to its name: there were more than a dozen dogs crowded into it, sniffing and eager. We just let them loose on the airbase, where they terrorized—and significantly reduced—the local rat population and performed an independent sniff test for any remaining stalkers. Result: nada.

As we were regathering them to do the same job at the housing complex, the first of the salvage teams arrived: about twenty folks in pickup trucks and vans. The island has plenty, given all the military loads that had to be moved from one site to another.

Our first job was to compile a quick-and-dirty catalog of the contents of each building. Not that we didn't trust the council, or they us, but, well, if you start with an inventory, you are less likely to have anything disappear and then get into an argument about who should have gotten what.

If anyone who reads this is interested, the full inventory, and what we took from it, should be among the papers stored with this journal. I'll only mention a few highlights here.

Guns galore. Mostly M4s and M16A2s. A couple dozen M9s and a few Brit HP35s. We passed on the handful of Brit L1A1 uh, "bullpups," with Prospero strongly encouraging that decision. There was more 5.56x45mm ammo than you could shake a forest-worth of sticks at, and a good amount of belted 7.62x51 NATO, but no sign of a machine gun to fire it.

There wasn't much in the way of body armor, but enough so that everyone was able to have a full rig—except me, because I'm just that fucking small. A reasonable number of smoke and tear gas grenades, but nothing else except for a few frags. Plenty of personal medkits, but about half of them had been opened and used for wound management. Which meant that there was no way of telling if the dried blood on the packaging was infectious or if some invisibly small drop had contaminated the other contents. So everything that came in a waterproof container we boiled and saved; everything else had to go.

There was some surgical gear and anesthetics. Some really excellent maps. Clothing for all weather and climates. Milspec tactical gloves, knee and shoulder pads, face- and eye-pro, comm gear. SCBA and all the gear for the airstrip's fire and emergency response team—pieces of which *did* fit me. So while everybody else gets to walk around looking ready for combat, I get to walk around looking like I'm ready to put out fires. Honestly, I'm thinking that the others should go for fire coats as well. We need full body coverage if we want to be protected against bites and scratches. But if they want to spend a few days looking all tacticool, let them. I, the always-dull voice of reason, can wait that long.

Lots of meds, both OTC and prescription. However, (no surprise) we came up short on aspirin, NSAIDs, analgesics: all the stuff people gobble down when they're suffering from a cold or flu.

All sorts of handy containers; all sorts of toiletry items; all sorts of prophylactics. Tons and tons—literally—of fuel of all kinds. Tons and tons (again, literally) of food, and especially wonderful: a treasure trove of carbs, mostly in rooms or containers that neither the stalkers nor the rats could get into. We had already been rehearsing various cautionary mantras about reintroducing carbs slowly. Just like getting water after long dehydration, you may want to gulp down as much as you can, but you *will* regret it.

I know this list seems pretty long, but it barely scratches the surface. The super-short version is this: if there was something we needed, the odds were that it was there. Or that you could jury-rig an equivalent out of what was.

Back before the plague, you usually didn't have a lot of needs, really. Most of them were defined by what you were going to eat or do over the coming week. Some stuff, like clothes and sporting gear meant thinking ahead a little farther. But then the plague came and the only thing you had enough of was breathable air. Everything else was either in short supply or unavailable. So you either got used to doing without or building work-arounds. Or you died. I can't begin to tell you how many times since the Captain bypassed Valparaiso that we've had to improvise or cross our fingers and hope for the best.

But a military base is essentially a stockpile of ninety-five percent of the things you'd really want—really *need*—after the apocalypse. So when we suddenly had access to the mostly undiminished stores of a combined U.S. and RAF airbase? It was like Christmas and deliverance all rolled into one. Nothing I had ever experienced prepared me for the almost physical shock of relief I felt as all that gear got inventoried and trucked away.

In the weird new reality of the post-apocalypse, we had gone from being paupers to Warren Buffett in the blink of an eye.

## October 31

After a week back at sea, I am finally forcing myself to take up this journal again. Particularly since we'll soon see Fernando de Noronha on the western horizon and have been preparing to make our first landing in the dark of the night.

We left Ascension Island late on October 25, having spent all of the 24th and the morning of the 25th loading and haggling. We hadn't anticipated any deal-making but once we were done bagging stalkers, we had the time to think about next steps in detail. And Prospero felt enough a part of our group to make some really good suggestions.

Specifically, he pointed out that there were two items we could really use that hadn't been available at the base: a compact solar array and reverse osmosis membranes for our water purification unit. Fortunately, both were available from various locals, so we could use salvage to trade for them.

But then the council stuck their long noses in and ruled out a private trade. They hastily designated both solar panels and water purifiers as "critical technologies" that were necessary for the survival of the entire island. Consequently, all sales of such items had to be approved by the council who were also muttering about applying surcharges. The actual owners rolled their eyes but didn't complain. They weren't the ones who'd be paying the surcharges.

There was one little wrinkle in the council's shifty plan, however; we hadn't finished declaring our cut of the salvage. So we told them we were going to take all of the carb-rich foods—every bag, can, box, sack, and crate of it. The council cried foul. We shrugged and called those foodstuffs "critical to our survival" and folded our arms. At which point they relented about the solar set up and the purification membranes, and we, in turn, relented about taking all the carbs. The trades went through as originally planned. The only additional cost was in bruised feelings, which, in the post-apocalypse, isn't as unimportant as it might sound.

However, that was just the council. The rank and file locals proclaimed us heroes and were happy to trade for all sorts of other useful items (too many to list here). Then they hosted us at the Obsidian, where we suffered through a few rounds of their worse-than-death booze.

Some of the goods we picked up in trade were things we hadn't thought about until we were about to leave. For instance, we acquired quite a collection of Fodor's and other travel books that detailed (and included some maps of) almost every island in or near the Caribbean. Including our next destination: Fernando de Noronha. Since we'd ultimately need to grab supplies and salvage from those presumably stalker-infested islands, those stupid little guidebooks and port maps could prove the difference between life and death.

We also got a parting gift from the townsfolk: two of the dogs that had helped us clear the airbase. One was Cujo. The other was Daisy, who outweighed Cujo by at least twenty pounds, was totally dog-smitten with him, and was getting pretty round with their pups.

The idea that we'd soon be up to our collective asses in puppies did cause some muted grousing about food and water and space and how to train *any* dog not to crap or pee all over a boat. However, in the end, all those potential problems had solutions. In fact, what the airfield mission had taught us was that dogs *were* the solution when it came to living in a world teeming with infected. Whether as guards, detectors, or fighters, they had proven their worth so many times and in so many ways during the clearing of the airbase that no one seriously entertained the possibility of *not* taking them with us. If we didn't, the odds were much greater that, someplace along the way, one or more of us would be surprised by a stalker and that, as they say, would be that.

Which was totally unacceptable. There was nothing we wouldn't do or spend to minimize the chance of that happening. Because if one of us was bitten, the only thing we could do was provide a mercy bullet. And no matter who fired it, it would be like each of us putting the barrel right against our own hearts. Yeah, our crew was weird and sometimes dysfunctional, but we were a family: the one thing that felt a little bit like the way the world had been before. The one thing that just might keep us sane.

When we weighed anchor late on the 25th, there were a handful of people to see us off as we headed toward the setting sun.

Most were gone by the time we'd pulled out beyond the other boats riding in the shallows.

So much for being heroes.

The first day at sea, the solar panels proved to be a big help, particularly since we now have a new milspec radio, with a civilian back up, and a second (and better) radar set that was installed by locals with real skills. We'd also grabbed a bunch of other electronics, everything from laptops to CD players. Collectively, they made navigation a little more certain and life at sea a lot less monotonous. Rod had been like a kid in a Willy Wonka version of Radio Shack, finding the best, most rugged, least Internet-dependent programs and computers he could.

We were also able to begin recharging batteries and could tap the panels to boil the water before feeding it into both purifiers (yeah, we got a portable backup). We were told that this pre-cleansing step would extend the life of the reverse osmosis membranes. Maybe it will, maybe it won't. Either way, I figure it can't hurt.

And toilet paper. Even the stuff that had been water-damaged at the base—oh, the wonder that is toilet paper. By necessity, we'd gotten pretty used to living without it. You just get less fussy and keep reminding yourself that all the seawater surrounding you has lots of different hygiene applications. Until, eventually, you come to believe and accept that toilet paper is just a thing of days gone by, a past luxury to which you have become indifferent.

Until, that is, you get hold of some once again. On the one hand, you realize why people cut down hundreds of thousands of hectares of forest every year just to wipe their butts. But in the very next moment, you can get depressed, realizing that—even if we do take back this world, somehow—it's gonna be a long time before humans have the necessary luxuries of time, effort, and resources to produce Charmin again. And until we do, I'm not sure we can consider civilization to have been fully and firmly reestablished.

However, while the rest of us were droopy-eyed with delight over sufficient carbs and the return of what had once been called "bathroom tissue," Prospero was eagerly learning his way around every laptop and computer that technonerd Rod had cherry-picked for us. As soon as he finished that, he started burning CDs and copying data to thumb-drives like he'd been possessed by a digital demon.

A seventy-foot ketch may sound big, but it's not. So when Prospero started stalking feverishly back and forth between various special machines while muttering what sounded like incantations cribbed from his namesake, everybody knew it. We just figured it was his own (admittedly weird) business. But when he started showing up late for his shifts on deck or at the wheel, I had no choice but to drop by and ask, "Uh...whatcha doin'?"

"Protecting ephemeral reflex," he replied.

It was structured like a sentence, but it didn't make sense. "What?"

"Sorry. Just a tick." Which in English-English means, "just a sec." He finished messing with a Linus (Lynust? Line-uks? Linux?) machine that he had dubbed "the pick of the litter" and turned toward me. "The GPS rescue software was code-named Project Ephemeral Reflex. My copy may be the only one."

I looked at all the hardware. "Couldn't you have burned copies back in Georgetown? I mean, I know electricity was rationed, but—"

"Powering the computers wasn't the problem: storage media and formatting was."

"Huh?" muttered Chloe, who had drifted in behind me. I heard the others approaching.

"Is that why you needed the Linus machine?" I said, cocking my head at his "pick of the litter."

He stared, baffled for a moment, then looked away awkwardly. Like he was embarrassed for me.

Rod muttered, "It's a *Linux* machine, Alvaro. Probably much better for his purposes."

"What do you mean, 'his purposes'?" Steve asked.

"I mean that I'm pretty sure that the code for Ephemeral Reflex didn't start life in a Windows or Apple OS," Rod murmured. When he resorted to that extremely gentle tone, we knew that the discussion had just moved into the very special Twilight Zone where only compugeeks can live, work, and speak the language.

"Spot on," Prospero said with a quick nod. "I wanted to make sure we have plenty of backups on plenty of different media. There's no knowing which we might need when we get—"

"Prospero," I said.

He stopped, turned.

"Back up a bit. You said you may have 'the only copy' of Ephemeral Reflex? What about the team at Kourou?"

He shook his head. "Maybe, but we can't be certain they got a complete copy of it."

"What?" exclaimed Rod.

Prospero sighed. "The code for Ephemeral Reflex was being worked on around the globe. Everybody was on everybody else's distribution list, but the comms became unreliable. Stations stopped responding. My Yank friend got all the pieces just before—well, you saw how he wound up."

"And Kourou never confirmed receipt of the same, uh, pieces of, uh, code?" It was like I was trying to deliver a bad line from a bad spy flick.

Prospero shook his head. "No, and Dortmund—they sent the last bit—went dark minutes after we got it on Ascension. But it may be that they went permanently dark before they sent the packet to Kourou."

Rod nodded. "Makes sense."

I looked at him. "Explain that."

Rod shrugged. "Well, Kourou has that big dish—Diane—on-site. So if they got complete code, then they should have immediately uploaded it and made GPS safe. But since it isn't, they didn't. Upload the program, I mean."

"Clearly not," Prospero agreed. "Fortunately, the Kourou team had taken precautions for a worst-case scenario. They sent all the other teams technical details on Diane, their computer systems, the relevant power plants and backups."

"Typical nerds and computer jocks," Chloe muttered with rolled eyes.

Prospero frowned. "Scoff if you must, but that gives us a blueprint for how to load the program, power the array, and send it. Unfortunately, there's no way to know why *they* didn't. Could be that they lost containment, were breached and overrun, or had a severed data or power line. Or maybe, they never got the last bits of code from Dortmund. In which case, this copy"—he held up a thumb drive—"could be all that's needed to complete the mission."

"Or," said Jeeza, frowning, "maybe that antenna—Diane?—was damaged. In which case, nothing we do will fix the situation."

Prospero shrugged. "True, but we can be bloody sure of this: if we *don't* go and see if we can fix it, GPS *will* be lost. For good."

Jeeza nodded. Her eyes were wide, unblinking. "Meaning that, even if there's nothing to be done, some of us could still die. For nothing."

I nodded and stepped in between them. "Which is why Fernando de Noronha is more than just a water and salvage stop. It's a training opportunity."

Jeeza stared at me, not understanding. "A . . . a training opportunity?"

"That's right," I asserted, partly discovering the truth of what I was saying even as I made it up, word by word. "The only way we can reduce the danger of a mission to Kourou is by training for it. For real. More live ammo and more live stalkers. But in a slightly *less* controllable environment. Fernando de Noronha is perfect: small area, small buildings, small preplague population."

"Are you suggesting we—we cleanse it?" Chloe asked, eyes round. "Like Ascension Island?"

"No. We don't know enough about it to determine if that would even be possible. But we do need to restock water and top up on fuel. And while we're there, we should assess the island. At least to the extent we can do so at night."

"At night?" Jeeza's voice was louder and higher.

I nodded. "Think about it; daytime is worse. If enough stalkers see us coming, they'll dogpile us. But at night, we could sneak ashore, stay on the fringes, take a look around. The original population was only three thousand—"

"Three thousand?" Jeeza almost shouted.

"Yes," I answered, looking directly at her. "Three thousand. But it's been at least three months, and the stalkers there don't have anything to eat except each other."

Steve frowned. "What do you mean?"

"I mean that, according to the guide books, the biggest

animals there are feral cats. And we know the stalkers don't go fishing. So either a lot of them are in torpor or they tore each other to pieces, or both."

"And you want to go on a nighttime field trip to find out?" Jeeza's voice was hoarse. With fear.

Chloe shrugged. "Look: this is how it is now, Jeeza. And how it's going to be. Probably for a really long time. We've gone over this already. Right now, the only way for us to survive is by scavenging. Call it 'salvage,' if that makes you feel better. But it boils down to the same thing. We land on islands—because they're small and we can get back out to sea if shit goes sideways—and kill any stalkers between us and what we need to grab. And if there are too many, we run like hell. It is just that simple."

Jeeza nodded, then her eyes started getting bright. Despite the pitch of the deck, she rose hastily and swayed out of the commons. Rod jumped up, following her aft toward their cabin. Chloe sighed, nodded at Steve and Prospero, took my hand, and led the way forward to our own bunk.

Once we got there, she turned around and took me by the shoulders. "Damn, Alvaro: when did you come up with that stuff?"

"Uh . . . what stuff?"

"Y'know: 'Fernando de Noronha is a great training opportunity for Kourou, is a soft target, and we can use it to stock up on food and water.' When did you think that up?"

I shrugged. "Pretty much as it was coming out of my mouth."

"You shitting me? You sounded like a general." Her face darkened. "Or a politician."

"Wow," I murmured, "a great compliment and a killer insult all in the same sentence. You work fast."

"Yeah? You won't be saying that in fifteen minutes, lover. But for real, taking charge like that—it didn't come out of nowhere. So spill."

The way she curled up on the bunk just then, there was no way I was going to hold back any info. Or anything else. "It's not like I wanted to go all Master and Commander on anyone. Least of all Jeeza. But ever since we started dealing with Prospero—well, it was going to be him or me in charge. And since I can't let it be him . . . well, if people are getting scared, or doubtful, then I've got to be the one to step forward. Can't be a leader if you can't do that."

Chloe's eyes travelled down from my face, stopped someplace just south of my belt-buckle. She half-smiled. Which generated the reaction she knew it would. Her smile widened. "So who's number two on the totem pole?" She let her tongue linger on the word "pole."

"Prospero," I answered.

Her smile vanished, replaced by a frown that was heading toward full-on glower. An expression which did not actually produce any change in my growing...condition. "Why him?"

I shook my head. "I don't want it to be Prospero. But no one else will do."

"Hey—" she started.

I shook my head harder. "No. Hear me out. It's a process of elimination. Let's start with the easy choices. Can you see either Rod or Jeeza leading this crew?"

She shook her head before I was even done asking the question. "Steve neither," she added.

"Right. They're too timid, too quiet, too nice, or some combination of the three."

"So that leaves Prospero and me. And he gets the nod because—?"

"Because we need you leading from the front, Chloe. No one—self included—has as much in-your-face aggression as you do. And the person who's got to be thinking about the details of a mission cannot be the same person who is responsible for showing the sheer ferocity, guts, and will that gets people moving and makes things happen."

I hadn't said that with the intent of mollifying her. Making the right decisions meant our lives, now. Screw hurt feelings and a ruined night of wild sex.

But it worked like a charm. Her smile was back, even broader than before. "So I'm your top sergeant! I am your designated Kicker-of-Asses and Taker-of-Names!"

I laughed; I hadn't expected that reaction, but I guess I should have. I mean, she's Chloe. "Yeah," I said, "pretty much. Besides, I know that the Ephemeral Reflex stuff will bore you silly. And the person in charge has either got to be able to dive in and get the basics, like me, or be the expert, like Prospero. Who has done his share of fighting, has military training, and a rank."

Her smile became part-sneer. "Yeah, a Senior Aircraftman,

Technical! Be still my beating heart!" She reached out and pulled me toward her. I was glad to go with that flow. "Does he know? That he's number two?"

"Not yet. I needed to talk with you—all of you—first."

She nodded, looked up at me from under those long, straight eyebrows. "Is it really necessary, making him the number two?"

"Why? Don't you trust him?"

She shook her head. "Not entirely, no. I get a weird vibe off him. Like he hasn't told us everything."

I didn't disagree with her. "Yeah, but we need a clear chain of command. What if I suffered a head wound and couldn't speak?" She tried shushing me, but I held her hand and kept going. "Or just a leg wound? Like what happened on South Georgia? You and the others had to step in. Which was kind of natural because we'd been with each other for so long. But Prospero? He's—well, he's—"

"—an outsider," she finished with a nod. "Okay. I get it. You've got to make his position official because it won't ever happen *naturally*. I still don't *like* it, but I get it." She smiled that smile of hers and rose up on her elbows. "Speaking of getting it—"

## November 2 (just before dinner)

This morning we got our first sight of Fernando de Noronha. It looks like a genuine tropical island, not the burnt out remains of a sea-mount volcano (like Ascension) or a rock meatloaf (like St. Helena). But it does have some really weird rock formations. It's surrounded by coastal buttes that look like arthritic fingers accusing the sky for their deformities.

Fernando de Noronha (or FdN, as we've started calling it) is tapered at both ends, about six miles long and just over two miles wide. It is almost on the equator and to say that the sun here is strong is an insane understatement. It has some decently forested (well, I guess you'd say "jungled") rock-spur hills, but also a lot of smoother, rolling land toward the northeast. At that end of the island, there are also a bunch of much smaller islands trailing off in a line that follows Fernando de Noronha's ENE axis.

We didn't have a whole lot of information about it; just two entries in travel guides, each accompanied by a basic map. One entry focused on the island's "quaint charm." The other covered the same basic material, but from the opposite angle, citing the "utter lack of modern facilities and conveniences." Eye of the beholder and all that, I guess. However, between the two, we were able to piece together a lot of key information. Tactical intel, Prospero called it.

Assuming that the plague reached FdN about the same time as it infected the rest of the Atlantic rim, it hit during the tourist off-season. Given FdN's small population and limited services, the virus probably spread very quickly. Anything resembling normal life had likely stopped at the end of June or early July.

The island's three thousand full time residents had almost all been involved in its tourism industry in one way or another. Fishermen were the only other significant portion of its working population. Off-season tourists usually didn't number over a hundred, but we assumed there had been two hundred, just to be safe. Some unknown portion of those thirty-two hundred souls would have tried fleeing on boats, but usually, people made that decision too late. So we figured that maybe two hundred got the chance to leave, reducing the total population base back to the original three thousand.

If, therefore, the plague followed the same pattern that the radio hounds on Ascension and St. Helena had heard occurring elsewhere, about forty percent would have died of the disease or stalker attacks within the first month. So by late July, we guessed eighteen hundred infected had still been alive on the island.

But that was over twelve weeks ago, and FdN's feral cats weren't going to add much to the food supply for the turned. It was hard to imagine that more than half of the initial number of turned could have survived, since in just seventy days, they would have needed to eat three times the meat they could strip from the dead. So, while reminding ourselves that any estimates were just hypothetical bullshit dignified by a few semi-reliable numbers, we figured that there still might be as many as nine hundred infected, but probably not more than three hundred active.

FdN's infrastructure was pretty rudimentary. Local water came from either rain-collection or a small desalination plant. There was an actual spring on the island, just beyond the craggy bluffs that overlooked a small bay (and beach) labeled as Praia da Cacimba do Padre. However, the locals had always considered the spring too difficult to reach and too small to be worth the effort. Stocking up on water from it was probably not going to be a reasonable objective, at least not this trip.

Except for the modest output of the locals' kitchen gardens, all FdN's food (and most of its water) had been supplied by ship. There were only two tiny supermarkets, both described in the snooty guide as "reminiscent of overgrown bodegas." And since they were located in the more inhabited, central part of the island, they were not places we were willing to visit. It would be way too easy—and too likely—for us to get surrounded there.

Instead, our target was a pair of adjacent hotels near the south coast. They were by far the largest of the innumerable family-run *pousadas*. Although the closest translation is "hostel," most resembled a hybrid bed-and-breakfast/country inn. Usually, the guest rooms were still part of the house in which the owners lived, but some had expanded, boasting separate apartments with their own televisions, bathrooms, fridges, and air conditioning.

Therefore, since hundreds of the locals were also part-time innkeepers, they'd have always had a good supply of food on hand. So when the virus hit, we figured they had boarded up their houses and hunkered down with their overstocked pantries. That wouldn't have saved most of them, of course; they still had to come out for water, and the infected would have been relentless in their efforts to break into houses where they could detect prey. However, if a *pousada* was solidly built and furnished with a roof-top cistern—well, there was still a slim chance we might find survivors. And when you're sailing around a dead and dying world, little rays of hope like that can keep you going for a long time.

Lastly, FdN's "public hospital" was a glorified MedStop, and the few drugstores all warned travelers to "bring any medicines which you use constantly." So even if we could have reached them, we didn't expect that they would add to our supply of useful meds.

After I finished overviewing what Jeeza and I had gleaned from our two sources, Steve looked up from the maps. "Do you still think it's worth the risk?"

I had asked myself that same question and had come to the answer I gave him: "Yes, because the more I've looked at how the population was distributed, the more I believe we can control the risk. Not only should the number of stalkers be low, but since active infected remain in groups, there should be very few out on the peripheries. That's one of the reasons we're landing here." I put my finger on the map.

Chloe leaned to get a better look. "Baia Sueste. Why there? There are other out-of-the way beaches."

"True," Prospero replied, leaning over the map, "but this one has a paved, straight road that ascends evenly to the two largest *pousadas*. That means easy access and clear sight lines."

"Sight lines won't matter much if we're going in at night."

Prospero smiled. "You seem to forget we pulled two pairs of night vision goggles from Wideawake Airfield."

"Yeah, with unreliable batteries."

"Which we've charged. And you will have a moon just entering the third quarter in clear skies."

Chloe frowned, glanced at me. "You mean, we're going in *tonight?*"

I shrugged. "No clouds. We can't ask for better."

"Maybe not, but I could ask for a little more warning."

"Why?" asked Steve. "Wouldn't you just spend more time worrying?"

I'm not sure anyone else could have gotten away asking Chloe that question. But Steve spoke so rarely, and his questions were so blunt and guileless, that he got a special pass. She nodded. "You've got a point. Okay, we go tonight. What else?"

Prospero picked up without missing a beat. "Baia Sueste is a sheltered inlet that is not heavily forested nor developed. No houses or other buildings except for the two target *pousadas*. Which sound more like hotels."

"How large are they?" Rod asked, leaning over my shoulder for a better look.

"The one closest to the beach has five luxury bungalows and four apartments. The one farther up the road has seven apartments, sounds a bit less luxe."

Steve frowned at the unfamiliar word "That's still pretty small," he murmured.

Jeeza nodded. "Yeah, but that's good."

"Sounds like there won't be much to salvage," Steve persisted.

Jeeza smiled. "The way these kinds of resorts work, you'd be surprised."

Chloe leaned back, arms folded. "Dish, sister." She'd gotten over the fact that Jeeza had been a rich man's daughter and knew about things such as tropical resorts and managing money and resources. Probably because Jeeza had proven to be a damn good spotter and, when needed, didn't hesitate to use a shotgun. Turns out that she shot skeet with her parents a few times in Jamaica. Couldn't figure out if she had done it at a resort, at a private timeshare, or some place that her folks owned. Whichever it was, her dad—and/or her mom—had been very, *very* rich.

Jeeza explained the *pousada* situation in a quiet, almost clinical voice; she clearly didn't want to sound like a spoiled rich girl. "Look at what the guide book says about the one closer to the bay. Not only does it have separate buildings; it has an infinity pool."

"A what?" asked Chloe, a second before I could.

"An infinity pool," answered Prospero, "is designed with one side so low that the water runs out as a sculpted waterfall which feeds a second, lower pool, and is then pumped back up into the first one. An unbroken loop of water flow. So, 'infinity.' Usually built overlooking the sea."

"Damn," Chloe breathed, "that sounds cool. And really pricey."

"Yes. And yes," Jeeza muttered. "And here's what it tells us: this hotel catered to a very wealthy clientele. Notice the proximity to the beach at the bottom of the road and all the facilities there; water sports, restrooms, outdoor/indoor cafe with drinks and snacks. No other beach on the island has those. And neither of these super-sized *pousadas* have single rooms. They are all apartments or bungalows—but *without* kitchens. That means these are not 'seaside efficiencies.' These are high-end, totally private, luxury accommodations with restaurants on the premises. Which are going to have a lot more food and supplies than what they need for the coming week or two. They'll get their meat, fruit, and vegetables fresh, but will have lots of staples in storage because their needs change and they can buy in bulk."

While I was wondering if Jeeza's folks had been in the hotel business, Rod was staring at the map. Or, more accurately, the x-marked *pousadas* just north of Baia Sueste. "Pasta," he breathed hopefully.

Jeeza nodded. "Could be, but more likely tapioca and wheat flour, rice, dried beans. Canned goods. Condensed milk. Sugar."

"Tinned meats and ham," Prospero added.

I almost hummed "*hot sausage and mustard!*" but I'm not sure anyone else was familiar with the film *Oliver!* Suddenly I missed watching old movies on TV with my mom. Very much.

I dove back into the business at hand. "So, that's why checking out these two *pousada*-hotels is worth it. A nice smooth beach to land on, a direct approach to our objective, low to zero building density, long sightlines for our rifles and night vision goggles, and a decent chance of finding more carbs than we can carry."

"Yeah," Chloe said. "About all that food. I don't like that we'd be coming out heavy, even if it's carbs we're carrying."

"Well..." Prospero said, looking at me.

Suddenly, everyone else was looking at me, too.

I sighed. "So, one of the reasons I had us take the recharger and all those car batteries from Ascension was that I figured it might come in handy if we wanted to, you know, jump start cars and trucks."

"Hard to do without the keys," Steve observed.

I shrugged. "Well, yeah...unless you know how to hotwire a car."

All the eyes on me widened. Except Prospero's: he and I had worked out the plan together.

Chloe's expression was particularly interesting. A mixture of surprise and feral admiration. "Alvaro, you...you sweet bastard! You can hotwire cars?"

Well, the "bastard" part was true, anyhow. "Yeah. And no, I'm not going to tell you how I learned. Just accept that I did." It helps if you can memorize every technical schematic when you really want to.

Chloe was eyeing me like she wanted to jump my bones right on the chart table. "Okay," she murmured, "no questions." Her smile got wonderfully evil. "Don't ask, don't tell."

I did not know how I would get through the briefing with a boner, so I stopped looking at her. "If the parking lots have a few vehicles left—mostly carts or stodgy dune-buggies, according to the guidebook—we might be able to drive down to the bay with our entire haul. If not, we'll just carry what we can and mark the rest for later."

"We'd go back a second time?" Jeeza's voice was tight.

I nodded. "Yeah. Sooner rather than later."

"Why sooner?"

"Because if we come back later, a new bunch of stalkers might have moved in. But not if we do it in one trip. While the rest of us transfer the first load into the dinghy, someone watches the road through binoculars. And if no new infected come to check out any sounds we made during our first visit—"

"Like gunfire," Chloe drawled.

"—then the *pousadas* should be clear for a second run. Which will be faster, since we'll already know our way around and have chosen what we want to take. It's just in, grab, and out."

Jeeza looked reassured. Somewhat.

Prospero rubbed his hands together. "So, are we at an end?"

I looked around. No questions or frowns. "Seems like it."

"Brilliant. Then I'm off to see if the batteries are topped up for use in the NODs."

We all looked at him.

"Nods?" Steve asked.

Prospero smiled sheepishly. "Sorry, mates. I forget where I am, sometimes. NODs: night observation devices."

"Thanks," I said.

He headed out with a "Ta!" tossed over his shoulder.

The others were starting to rise. "Hold up a moment?" I asked.

They stopped and sat, wearing half-formed frowns. "What's up?" Rod asked.

I hadn't expected to have the opportunity to speak to them without setting it up, so I knew I'd have to roll it out quickly: "I've been thinking that the ship's log shouldn't be a—a collective record, anymore."

Jeeza rested her sharp chin in her palm. "Why?"

"Well, partly because I started it as a personal journal. To record my own thoughts...and feelings."

Chloe's poker face was absolute.

"But more importantly, I'm worried about the precedent we set at Husvik. About other people writing in it. Because that means that other people can read it."

Jeeza smiled. "We won't peek at your personal entries." Her smiled widened. "Promise."

I sat, lowered my voice. "Look, I don't care about you guys reading—that stuff." Which was only *kind of* true. "But now we've got someone, well, 'new' working and travelling with us."

"Don't you trust Perciv—Prospero?" Steve asked.

"For the most part, I do," I answered. "But that's not the point. The old logbook—well, it's about *us*. It describes how we get along as a group. And I'm not sure I want to share that."

Thankfully, I didn't have to take the next step alone. Chloe explained my misgivings as well as I could have. "Look," she began, "if what we found on St. Helena and Ascension are any clue to what lies ahead, we could be picking up more people as we sail from place to place. And I agree with Alvaro: it's not safe to let them read about us, to learn who we are, or—particularly—the disagreements we've had. We could bring a person on board who seems okay but turns out to be the kind of rat-bastard that would go through our journal trying to find stuff he, or she, could use to push our buttons. Maybe try to get us to argue by finding sore spots, say things that will set us against each other. All so they can gain power."

Chloe shook her head. "I'm not willing to take that chance. Besides, if we really want a ship's log, I say let's start a real one, without anything private in it. Just the facts about what happens, each day."

Murmurs of agreement all around.

"Okay, then," I said. "Who's going to make the entries?"

People started looking down at the tabletop. Chloe included. No one was fired up by the idea of keeping a ship's log. Color me shocked.

"I'll keep doing it," I volunteered. "Captain's job, anyway. But anyone can jump in whenever they want."

Given that no one was nodding, or even willing to look me in the eye. I was pretty sure I wouldn't be sharing the duty any time soon.

"Okay," I said, standing. "It will be dark in three hours. Time to get ready."

## November 3 (early morning)

I didn't know it would come in handy so soon, but I was wearing a face-full of the black camo paint from Ascension as we headed for shore. The waning half-moon picked out the brighter sand of the beach and the edges of the rocks, but for the most part, the steep, stony arms that cradled Baia Sueste were just looming black silhouettes. "See anything?" I asked over my shoulder.

Chloe, wearing NODs, shook her head. "Other than waves, trees, and the restaurant at the south end of the beach, nada."

"Any chance that restaurant could be a hideout for infected?" Jeeza's voice was steady but tense.

"Not unless they like living exposed to the weather. All the windows are busted and almost half the roof is gone. Looks like storm damage."

We finished motoring quietly around Ilha Chapéu do Sueste—the "Southeast Hat," which is a lot more lopsided and craggier than its name suggests. "Six hundred yards," I muttered. "Check your gear and paint."

Prospero, who was in the back of the dinghy near the outboard, sounded skeptical. "I wouldn't put too much faith in those camo sticks. The stalkers have excellent nighttime senses."

I shrugged. I'd heard that a lot while we were on Ascension. We hadn't been around to see it for ourselves. I suppose that, along with their senses of smell and hearing, turning might improve their night vision. But if there was any chance that the face paint could help us, I was all for trying it out.

Steve had a steady hand on the outboard's tiller, thanks to time spent with his dad on camping trips. He saw the tell-tale swirls and foam of submerged shallows that I would have missed completely. Hitting them would have been a disaster: *Voyager's* dinghy was a hard shell, not a Zodiac or partial inflatable. That made it better in rough water, but tougher in the shallows and a real bitch to get close to the beach. Assuming you didn't tear a hole in its bottom on the way in.

But his dad would have been proud. Steve timed our final approach so that we had a low cresting wave behind us. It pushed us far enough so that, when we hopped out, the water was no higher than our knees.

Prospero jumped over the dinghy's transom as soon as the outboard had guttered to a stop. "You did well," he said to Steve.

"I did better than that," Steve deadpanned—and then smiled. The first time since I'd known him.

Jeeza grinned a little as she climbed over the side and said, "Now don't leave me to do this myself before you all go and have your fun." Which was kind of silly because I don't think that even Chloe could have pushed that boat ashore by herself.

But the six of us together muscled it forward, waited for the next surge, and then charged it up the sand. After which Rod stood very straight and pointed toward the other end of the long arc of moonlit beach. "Well, whaddya know."

We followed his index finger: a Zodiac, tied off in a rock-sheltered tidal pool at the eastern end of the bay. There was a trawler motor still attached to its transom.

"That would be damn handy," Steve said with a hint of longing in his voice.

"It would," I agreed. I signaled for a huddle in the lee of the dinghy. "Small change of plans. Contact team advances as planned to secure the restaurant at this end of the bay. Once we know it's clear, I'll send you a squelch break, Jeeza."

"To do what?"

"To run to the other end of the beach with a tow-line. Once you've made sure the Zodiac is floating and free of obstructions, fasten the line and spool it out on the beach."

"Uh, okay. But why not wait until we're ready to *leave*?"

"Because that Zodiac is likely to be the most valuable thing we might find tonight. So even if we return with infected right behind us, I want it ready for towing."

Chloe frowned. "Tow line isn't long enough to reach."

I nodded. "If necessary, I'll run to the near end of the tow-line and swim it out beyond the surf while you're launching the dinghy. You motor to me, we hook up the line, pull the Zodiac out."

Chloe shook her head. Jeeza shrugged, smiled. "Aye aye, Captain!"

We stayed low as we left the cover of the dinghy, then kneeled. The cover team—Chloe and Prospero—aimed landward. The contact team—me, Steve, Rod—slipped water-tight bags off our backs. We unpacked our body armor and shotguns. Prospero handed the rifle bag forward. As the cover team watched over us, we unwrapped our weapons (M4s for them, an AK for me). Once we were in our armor (in my case, a fireman's coat) and our guns were ready, it was our turn to cover Chloe and Prospero as they geared up. I watched the dark line of vegetation waving along the back edge of the beach and tried not to feel guilty that I had the AK.

Let me be clear: Rod and Steve wanted the M4s. And I understood their reasons. The M4 is light, has super low recoil, and still has a laser-beam trajectory at ranges where the AK's rounds are starting to rainbow. But it was night, and we'd be in brush and between buildings: we'd be lucky to see a stalker coming at thirty yards. Might be more like thirty inches, and in those conditions, I didn't want an overpenetrating 5.56mm popgun. I wanted a human-stopping 7.62x39 round that was every bit as accurate at those ranges. Yeah, we had the shotguns on our backs, but their stopping power wouldn't do us any good if we didn't have enough time to unsling them.

Chloe and Prospero finished shrugging into their lighter gear and checking their pistols, then reshouldered their FALs. They looked at me.

I should have just given the word, but I hesitated. This was the moment where all our planning and preparation would be put to the only test that mattered: would it keep us alive when we walked into stalker-country? At night and without a town to fall back on if things went sideways? That was also the moment I realized that I had forgotten two final steps: what a great start.

Meanwhile, Chloe had started cursing and tugging at her NODs. She had a military helmet: not the best protection against stalkers, but it was designed for the night-vision gear. Although given Chloe's annoyance at the mounting mechanism, you'd never have known it. Even so, the helmet's open face gave her and Prospero the sight picture they needed in order to see enemies—and us—quickly and clearly.

Finished, Chloe gave an irritated thumbs-up. I nodded and signaled my team to seal the visors of their fire-helmets. The last thing any of us wanted was a slashing, shrieking stalker spraying infectious spittle—or blood—into our face. Once Rod had latched his in place, he angled his torso forward, ready to charge toward the restaurant.

I shook my head, pointing at his hands and mine. We still had to double-check that our sleeves were folded over our gloves and taped into place. Going room to room at the airbase had taught us that, when your enemies are zombies, the most vulnerable part of your body is your hands. I mean, yeah, we did have fire gloves, and there was no way a stalker was going to bite through *those*. But there was also no way we could have shot our weapons while wearing them. Squeezing a trigger, reloading, or cycling an action? Maybe, but everything else was pretty much impossible. Such as: flipping the safety (you *might* be able to with an AK), hitting the magazine release (forget it with a pistol), or clearing a jam (doubtful, and only if nothing is distracting you—like, say, a ravening stalker). So our gloves were all U.S. military issue, even though none of us were totally sure that they'd stop a stalker's teeth.

Prospero and Chloe had angled their FALs inland again, but their eyes were on me. I nodded to them, then my team, and rose up into a hunched run toward the restaurant. I stayed close to the surf; that kept us out of the cover team's landward sightlines.

Nothing came out of those shadows, and we reached the restaurant—or what was left of it. Rod, Steve, and I peered into the jumble of fallen timbers. We couldn't see squat.

Not for the first time, I wished there had been a way to bring the dogs. But we had no way of knowing what we'd find or how fast we might have to haul ass out of there. Too many scenarios ended with us either having to leave our pups behind or being mobbed as we tried to get them back into the dinghy.

Since the sightlines inside the ruined restaurant were very short, I laid my AK next to Rod, unslung the shotgun, snapped the safety off, and began moving forward. I kept my back to the left-hand interior wall, which gave Rod and Steve a free-fire zone into the rest of the place.

When it's dark, and the floor underfoot is littered with beams and other crap, and you're wearing a sealed fire helmet, and the air is coming in through an open SCBA tube, your situational awareness is pretty much zero. Yeah, you're well-protected, but you're also a bumbling *piñata* and the rest of the world is a baseball bat, just waiting to take a power swing at your blind side. Which is everywhere.

That's also when you realize that the hottest thing a human being can wear is a fire coat. Especially when you're playing hide-and-seek with stalkers. At night. On the equator.

By the time I walked every foot of that damn ruin and waved the all-clear, I swear I had sweated out at least two pounds of water. Which I put right back inside myself by draining one of my canteens. Yeah, I know: a shitty example. "Sip it." "Make it last." My words. But I didn't disregard them; I was so thirsty I didn't *remember* them.

After we'd crept to the landward side of the ruin, Rod handed my AK back to me. We spread out along the ragged remains of the rear wall, took a knee, and aimed our rifles into the dark brush beyond. I toggled my radio's send button.

That signal sent Jeeza down the beach to the Zodiac. She stayed at the edge of the surf; the infected weren't averse to water, but from what we had seen at Husvik, they lose any ability they had to swim. They're reduced to a frenzied dog-paddle. The locals on Ascension reported the same.

As Jeeza started back toward the dinghy, Rod leaned toward me. "Hssst. Lookit. In the parking lot."

I peered through the storm-shattered vertical planks of the bayside wall. Two of FdN's underfed dune-buggies were still parked there, a fallen tree screening them from the beach. "Yeah. I see them."

"Want to try hotwiring one?" Rod sounded eager, like a little kid urging a tween to do something daring. And stupid.

"Nope. For all we know, the storm that wrecked this place washed over them. Probably messed up their ignitions. Besides, we don't want any infected to hear an engine approaching. The only engine sounds we want them to hear is when we're leaving. And hopefully not then, either."

Steve motioned toward the beach. Jeeza was back, crouching in the moonshadow of the dinghy, shotgun out. Chloe and Prospero signaled they were ready.

I waved for them to advance and turned to watch the inland terrain over the muzzle of the AK.

Again, no reaction in all that darkness. As Chloe came up alongside, I nodded my head toward the up-sloping road: a straight shot to both *pousadas*. "All clear?" I asked.

She was scanning it. "No movement. And I mean nothing. Not even birds or little animals."

I wondered if that was normal for FdN, or whether the infected had learned how to hunt sparrows and mice. I didn't put it past them.

But we hadn't come to assess the state of the local wildlife. "Give us fifty yards head start," I said, reciting from the plan. "Then follow, maintaining that interval. We'll pause every fifty to give you a chance to scan for targets with your NODs. Let's go."

For the first hundred yards, the hill's slope was barely noticeable; maybe a five-degree incline. But after that? Twenty to twenty-five degrees. That may not sound like much, particularly when you're only doing it for two hundred and fifty yards. But when you're in the tropics, wrapped up in protective clothes and breathing masks, and wearing visors that prevent you from seeing what's right at your feet, it's nerve-wracking and exhausting. It also made me hope that the travel writer who had described this as a "smooth, steady slope" would die a horrible and painful death. Which (odds being what they are these days) he probably already had.

Chloe's impatience with her NODs wasn't helping the mood, either. "God *damn*. I am taking this flimsy thing off. It's a piece of—"

"Chloe, you're our eyes. Keep it on."

"Yeah? Well, you come back here and wear it, then."

"You're our best marksman. Uh, markswoman." *Marks*person? *Screw it*. "Look, you've gotta wear it."

"You think I can shoot with this thing on? I can barely see the sights. It's—"

"Chloe, you're not just wearing it for shooting. Your eyes are trained to hunt, will see things we might miss. We need those eyes watching over us."

It was a few seconds before she toggled to reply. "Okay, okay.

But damnit, I really don't like—Movement! Right ahead of you! I can't—"

I turned, saw a dim figure emerging from an overgrown lane about sixty yards ahead on the right-hand side of the road: the entrance to the first, and most luxurious, *pousada*.

"Contact," I muttered to the guys on either side of me. I knelt. They did likewise. "Chloe, do you have a shot?"

"Damn. I . . . I can't tell. And if I'm wrong, I could hit you guys!"

"Chloe, is it coming straight down the middle of the road?"

"No, it's on the right, but starting to veer center. Like it knows you might be there. It's starting to run."

"Contact team," I snapped, "shift: five left. Go." It sure sounded cool. But it must have looked like slapstick, the way the three of us bumped into each other. We'd never trained for moving as a group in the dark. But we got to the far left side of the road. "Chloe? Do you have—"

"Stay. *Right there!*" she interrupted, as a silhouette became visible ahead of us.

A breath later, the FAL barked three times. The figure stumbled, kept coming. Then a quick flurry of four shots. The stalker went down on the third.

"Christ, I *suck!*" Chloe shouted.

"You killed it," I said sharply. "Now swap in a fresh mag. And Chloe?"

"Yeah?"

"Infected might *not* assume that a gunshot—or a lot of them— means 'chow time.' But if you shout, they will *know* you're food."

"Yeah—delivery, in this case," Rod added.

Jeeza had toggled in, giggled before she could release.

Chloe didn't say anything. I could imagine her fuming fifty yards downslope. "Prospero, you having the same problem with the NODs?"

"I am," he admitted. "Never worked with them before. Thought it would be easier."

I nodded to no one. It was a nasty surprise. I had presumed that, being in the military, Prospero would have been familiar with them, and he never said otherwise. The rest of us knew only what we'd seen in movies and video games, both of which made it look pretty easy to use NODs in a gunfight. But, if we had to pop off half a dozen rounds for every infected that showed up, our night vision strategy would be way too expensive, both in terms of risk and ammunition. "Change of plans," I announced.

"Alvaro—" began Prospero in his almost-patronizing voice.

"Not now," I snapped. Damn it, when is Prospero going to learn that the middle of an operation is not the time for a debate? "Contact team goes to shotguns and enters the grounds of objective one. We stick close, find a choke point, set up, wait for any hostiles to come out. Cover team, advance to the lane leading into objective one. Keep a watch uphill to objective two."

"And maintain overwatch on you, too, right?"

"That is a secondary priority. Secure our rear."

"Alvaro!" It was Chloe. "We can't help you if—"

"Chloe, we just learned that NODs are only good for recon. Not your fault you can't aim with them. Now, get moving. The stalkers will be, if any heard that gunfire."

Steve and Rod were right behind as I sprinted up past the dead stalker and ducked under the heavy, overgrown boughs that used to arch over the lane into the first *pousada*.

One good thing about fighting the infected: they don't care about being quiet. If they know, or even suspect, that they have prey, they yowl like people in an asylum.

That's what happened at the first *pousada*. No sooner were we in that narrow, bushy lane than they started sounding like refugees from the psych ward. Which told us how many were coming, where from, and roughly how far off they were. Or so I thought.

Two came leaping down the stairs from the main building on the left, and we all swung that direction, raising our shotguns. But at the last second, another two came sprinting up from the pool area down a slight slope to the right.

There wasn't time to coordinate targets; we just started pumping and firing. It's not even like we were "engaging targets." If we saw something moving in our front one-hundred-and-eighty-degree arc, we fired and cycled and fired again until it went down. The range was never less than thirty feet, so there was no time to even see if you hit. There was just enough moonlight to see them coming, to see them fall down, and to see that there were a few more behind them.

I wish I could remember more details than that, but I don't. Maybe that's because it all happened so fast, or because I was so shit-scared. I do remember Rod, on my right flank, taking a step back. So I did too, yelling "Back one!" over the sound of Steve's shotgun and my own. I don't know if they heard me, or just noticed that I'd given ground. The net effect was that we kept a line, just in time to greet the new stalkers that came charging up from the pool and down from the house.

These infected were slower, like they were still waking up. One was limping. In between shots, I remember thinking that we wouldn't have survived if they had all come at once. I also remember thinking (in the same moment) that it was weird that none of them had come boiling out at us right after Chloe started firing. Or after she shouted.

Two more had gone down. The last two were almost on us. I thought I had one round left. Steve still had his shotgun up. Rod had dropped his Rexio, was reaching for his pistol—

"Coming in!" shouted Chloe, right as:

—I fired my last round and went for my flensing knife;

—Rod got his M9 unholstered and fired;

—Steve squeezed his shotgun's trigger, got a dry *click*, and hissed "Shit!";

—and Chloe, god love her, showed up beside me, NODs down like a bug-eyed monster and blasting away with her Browning Hi-Power.

I remember hacking at two different stalkers with the whaling tool. Only the first one had been moving. I'm not sure whether panic, adrenaline, or an excess of caution got me swinging at the second. At any rate, we accounted for all eight and they never did touch us, although they got within inches of doing so. Literally.

Not like it would have turned into a game of "tag, you're dead," because we were in pretty heavy protective gear. But it came way too close, and for me, effective leadership meant ensuring that physical contact wasn't even *possible*. That wasn't my gold standard; that was my definition of minimum acceptable performance. And I had just fucked up. Royally.

Which is why I only muttered a quick, "thanks" at Chloe before pushing past her.

I could feel her staring after me. "Alvaro, what—?"

"I fucked up. Which means we've got to finish this quickly. Everyone reload. While I listen."

"Listen for what?" Prospero chirped.

*For you to be quiet, asshole.* "For more infected. There were more than we guessed, and we made a lot of noise bringing them down. Which could bring in more from the towns on the other side of the airport." The runway was five hundred yards inland. A few hundred yards farther north was the main road along which all the island's tiny villages were clustered. It also led to FdN's one real town: Vila dos Remédios. I wasn't worried about the gunfire being heard that far off, but if the infected near the airport got excited, their yelling could trigger a chain reaction.

But like some corny old song says, all we heard were the sounds of silence. "Let's move," I said, starting toward the second *pousada*, only one hundred fifty yards farther up the slope. I say "only" because I was still cruising on adrenaline.

"Alvaro, is that a good idea?" Rod's voice was careful.

"It's better than any other," I shot back, not entirely sure of what I was saying. But I'd feed myself to a stalker before I'd let myself *sound* uncertain. "If we stop to grab stuff here, any new stalkers will show up while we're scavenging, distracted. Bad deal. We beat feet back to the dinghy? Then we did this for nothing. Because any infected that wander down here will eat these bodies. They'd be awake and strong by the time we return. Another bad deal."

We were halfway to the second *pousada*. I nodded toward it. "We hit this fast. Then survey and scavenge. Then back down to objective one and do the same. Always with two people on watch. If stalkers come, we drop everything and split." I crouched down beside the land leading into the second *pousada*. "Remember, once we leave here, we *always* move back toward the dinghy."

Steve nodded as he drew alongside me. "And we're ready to book it all the way if we have to."

Rod had joined us. "Okay. Let's do this."

Chloe and Prospero posted themselves at the right-hand curve just beyond us. From there, the road ascended in a straight shot to the airport. They nodded when they were set. We charged toward the *pousada*.

We'd taken only three steps when Chloe sent a quick message: the batteries on her NODs had petered out. Meaning that their operational life was to be measured in minutes, not hours. Welcome to the post-apocalypse, even if you have battery rechargers.

It also meant that Prospero's night-vision could fail any second, too. No time to waste. I got my team to the objective and into entry formation.

Prospero toggled in. "Update."

"Go."

"NODs shows what looks like base housing, one hundred fifty yards up the airport road."

*Shit!* "Describe."

"Better than barracks; more like a row of duplexes. Just south of the airport. Probably for crews, security, other personnel on temporary assignment or layover. Not uncommon on these small islands."

"Any sign of activity?"

"None. Looks a wreck, though."

"Hurricane-wreck or infected-wreck?"

"The latter, I'm afraid."

For a few moments, I thought real hard about turning around and heading for the dinghy. But my gut told me that the infected we'd killed at objective one were a pack that had successfully staked out their own territory. Between what they scrounged at the *pousada* and the occasional fish that washed up in the bay, they were able to stay active. Logically, then, potential rivals that were close to torpor wouldn't like the odds of tangling with them. Passives would run in the other direction. And any packs large enough to be a threat probably had better luck prowling among the buildings north of the airport, particularly after the passenger terminal had been picked clean of bodies and pre-packaged foods.

That decided me. "We stick with the plan. But no noise. Rod, you're on the lights."

"The lights" were our contingency for situations where we wanted to attract any nearby stalkers without alerting others that were farther away. High-power flashlights from the airbase at Ascension gave us just what we needed: a tight, focused beam that we could play over small target areas like windows, doorways, corridors.

No sooner had Rod aimed the light at the *pousada's* open doorway than we heard furniture falling over and, a moment later, a stumbler came out, blinking like an old geezer roused out of his nap. I nodded at Steve, who aimed and fired one round before the infected could even screech. The stumbler fell headlong down the stairs, didn't move. We waited. Really? Just one, lone—?

"Movement!" hissed Rod, swinging his light and Rexio to the side of the house.

A figure—actually, just its haunches—disappeared into the overgrown plantings that ran around the back of the building.

Steve aimed, but I waved him down. "It's a passive."

"Still a stalker," Steve pointed out.

I nodded. "Yeah, but tonight, we don't make any more noise than we have to."

"Is that all of them? Really?" Chloe asked, her voice high with disbelief. I wasn't aware she was even on the channel.

"Let's wait a minute and see. Rod, lights on the windows again."

Two minutes passed. No motion inside or outside the house. None up at the airfield housing, either, according to Prospero.

I breathed deeply. I still wanted to turn around, run down to the beach, jump in the dinghy, and keep the outboard's throttle wide open until we got back to *Voyager*. But what I said was, "Okay; entry formation. Let's clear the objective, then mark for salvage."

So then ... wedid we ... th ... and it w ...

## November 5

I meant to write more but I fell asleep over this damn journal. That was two days ago.

At least I recorded all the important stuff before I went face down in the gazpacho I was dreaming about. The weird thing is that although those events aren't even a hundred hours in the past, it feels like they're a million years—and a whole world—away.

And we really are in a different world, now. Yesterday we arrived at Rocas Atoll, which truly looks and feels like another planet. But I'm getting ahead of myself. Gotta finish the after action report from Fernando de Noronha.

So, we went into the second *pousada* with our limbs shivering from being whipsawed between adrenaline and fear...and discovered it was empty. Which sounds like it should be a relief, but it wasn't. Because if anticlimax is not a fun mental state, your body's version of it is friggin' awful.

When I went through that front door, and then leap-frogged room to room, my adrenaline levels must have been through the roof. Which is logical, because my lizard hindbrain was insisting there wouldn't *be* a tomorrow if my adrenal glands didn't keep me juiced. Only after we confirmed it was a dry hole did we let ourselves stand down. Except we couldn't. Not really.

We were all pumped up with no place to go apeshit. It's the whole-body equivalent of that moment when you step out of a car that's been speeding through the desert all night. The world slows down, but you don't. You *can't*. But then, when your head and heart finally come to stop, you really do crash; that's when you learn where that expression comes from. One minute you're cruising, the next you hit the wall. Done.

It's just like that when you're all amped up to kill or be killed. Except about a million times worse. Because it's not just a sensation in your head; it's a ragged, humming feeling all through your body. Like your limbs might lash out and do something—*any*thing—before you could stop them. You're not really out of control, but it sure doesn't feel like you're totally *in* control, either.

We'd all felt a little of that after clearing the passenger terminal on Ascension. But the stakes hadn't been so high and the risk hadn't been so absolute. Because we had all sorts of ways to get out of, or control, that situation.

Fernando de Noronha was completely different. It was in the middle of the night, in a place we'd never been before, using tactics we hadn't really tested, with unknown numbers of stalkers all around us. So yeah, it took a while for the adrenaline to ease off enough that our hands stopped trembling and the soundless hum faded out of our ears. Surveying objective two for salvage was what finally helped us come down from that awful high, because we had to focus if we wanted to find all the survival-crucial goods hidden there.

Unfortunately, this *pousada* was not a jackpot. Its so-called restaurant was more like a kitchen that could do buffets and breakfast. Everything had been trashed by the infected, who had soiled this place with extreme prejudice. We're talking scat all over, including the walls. We'd never seen that before. The same treatment was lavished on anything that looked like art or was visually creative in any way. In some cases, they hadn't merely flung, but hand-smeared, their own crap across it.

It made them seem more savage, because it made them seem more human; they hadn't been entirely random about what they shat on. I'm certainly not saying they were making a "statement," but on the other hand, you couldn't fault them for lack of clarity.

The guest rooms offered mute but clear testimony as to what had become of the tourists staying at the *pousada*. Intact suitcases and lack of forced entry, combined with blood patterns and gnawed remains, told the stories of each occupant's final moments. You didn't need to be a forensics expert to understand that they had all been surprised, either by recently turned locals, staff, or their own family/friends/lovers.

As we headed back for the front door, we were shaking again, but the reason had changed. We'd never seen that kind of aftermath. At Husvik, the infected we encountered were just rabid monsters. At Ascension, we saw the aftermath of a war between cannibals in a military asylum. But the corpses strewn throughout the second *pousada* were just regular people who, like most of the world, had become playthings for the plague's monstrous ironies. Parents had been attacked by their kids. Grooms had been gutted by brides. Octogenarians had leaped out of their z-frames to tear apart people who were one-fourth their age and four times their strength. The rules of the world had turned upside down and blood poured out.

We left that *pousada* at a run, racing down the front steps, panting and pushing up our visors. But we hadn't finished the job; we still had to comb through the outbuildings and sheds (even small hotels need a lot of storage space).

That walk-through produced some worthwhile finds: rope, jerricans of gasoline, some spare batteries and light bulbs, extension cords, flashlights. However, as we were leaving the gardener's shed, Steve, who has a pretty keen sense of smell, put his nose in the air and said, "Peppers."

He turned toward the land behind the *pousada*. As he did, I realized it wasn't just a wildly overgrown field; it was a big-ass garden. Another step and I was at the end of a crop line, looking down what was left of the rows. Lots of rows.

It wasn't a garden at all; it was a small farm. Probably the source of the *pousada's* high-priced "fresh-to-the-table" ingredients.

Steve edged toward one of the furrows of darkness between the half-erased crop lines just as I, too, began to smell fruits and vegetables. But the scent was *too* strong.

"It's rotting," Steve said. He probably knew the smell because his folks had owned "a cottage in farm country," whatever the hell that meant. I knew the odor because that's how "fresh produce" smells when it's been on sale for two days, just before it spoils. In other words, it smelled like the kind of fruit and vegetables I grew up on.

"Rotting on the vine," I added. My mom had always used that phrase, even for things that didn't grow on vines. And I always had to stop myself from pulling a smirk when she did, thinking, *WTF? You trying to be fancy?*

Suddenly I wanted to eat a bullet for every time I'd ever thought that, for being an ungrateful little wiseass shit. "It's rotting on the vine," I said again, louder. Like I was slapping my earlier self across the face. I missed my mom so bad I thought I might start bawling right there between the peppers and papayas.

We left the garden without saying another word.

Because it had a *real* restaurant, objective one was the goldmine, particularly for staple carbs: rice, beans, flour, cornmeal, even dehydrated milk. A treasure trove of canned goods, too. It was just what Jeeza had predicted.

And whereas the other *pousada's* roof cistern had become a breeding pool for algae, this one had been built with filters and special covers. Access was through a sturdy, locked door on the third floor. Nothing between it and the ground level had been of interest to stalkers: just linens, cleansers, cleaning equipment, spare furniture, and seasonal supplies.

All of that was in the main house, which had no guest rooms. Which in turn, explained why it was so much more intact than the second *pousada*: except for the few hours when the restaurant served meals, there was no prey to be found there. Oh, the stalkers had run through the place, grabbed ready-to-hand high energy foods like bread and meats, scatted in various places. But all the killing had taken place in (and wrecked) the high-end bungalows that dotted the property's grassy bayview slope.

Bottom line: between the untouched cistern and storerooms, we had more water and food than we could carry. The only other thing we did grab was the pool treatment chemicals and cleansers: key ingredients for our homemade decon bath. We had no way of knowing exactly what did or didn't kill the virus, but we were pretty sure that those chemicals would do the trick. Question was: how to get all that down to the dinghy?

The answer we'd been hoping for—a car—was, to coin a phrase, a non-starter. The buggies and small vans were too screwed up. The same storm that had roughed up the bayside restaurant had toppled trees that mashed or trapped half of the vehicles, including most of the ones that I might have been able to hotwire. A bunch of others had been trashed by humans, both normal and turned. And almost everything with wheels had a plastic tube hanging out past its unscrewed gas cap, its tank drained. I wondered how the hell we were going to get all the goods down the hill.

And that's when I stopped for a moment and realized, it's a *hill*. Duh.

I walked to the most intact car that was close to the road and opened the door.

Chloe, who still hadn't forgiven me for going stiff and brusque on her, muttered, "Hey, genius; that one has a tube sticking out of the gas tank."

"Yeah," I answered, leaning inside to check the basic controls, "I know."

"So?"

"So check the tires."

"For what?"

"Just make sure they have enough air."

Prospero heard us, left off organizing the salvage. "Alvaro, I don't know how you expect to get that car running—"

"I don't. I expect to get it rolling." When he didn't understand right away, I added: "It's a manual. I just checked the clutch. It slips into neutral no problem. Hand brake still works."

Prospero laughed, shook his head.

"What's so funny?"

"Really?" he asked. "You don't see? Here we are, half dozen people with IQs on the right side of the bell curve, and none of us see the obvious. Until now." He stared at the car and shook his head again. "I'll organize the loading." And off he went, still chuckling to himself.

Chloe was standing next to the car. "You want I should push?" I couldn't see her face with the moon behind her, so I couldn't tell if her voice was sullen, embarrassed, or both.

I smiled. "Let's get it loaded first."

It was a good thing we found the Zodiac and that it was in such good shape. If we had tried to put all of the salvage and ourselves in the dinghy, we'd have sunk. As it was, even with me and Jeeza making sure the overload stayed lashed down in the Zodiac (they are good for carrying people; not so much for cargo), both boats were riding low in the water and were about as responsive as garbage scows.

But it was a short run back and we off-loaded our haul before dawn. We got the boats up on deck just as the sun's rays started painting orange-gold ripples on the water to the east.

We'd anchored *Voyager* in a sheltered part of the bay, but that hadn't made us feel any better about the necessity of leaving her uncrewed. The dogs had been even less enthusiastic about that decision. We'd had to lock them below to make sure that they didn't try to swim after us. That was after Prospero suggested leaving them topside on leads, which Rod answered by going over to big, smiling, drooling Daisy and lifting her lip. He looked meaningfully at her exposed teeth, then at the leashes in Prospero's hand.

Who made the same comparison and nodded. "Right," he said, and took the leads back below.

Our consensus as we headed for our bunks that dawn was to never, ever, leave *Voyager* without an anchor watch again. But I wonder if that resolve will hold the next time we have to go on stalker-infested shores. There's strength in numbers, and when there are only six of you, everyone counts.

We slept past noon. Would probably have slept longer, but dogs are essentially big, furry, alarm clocks. When you've been in bed so long that their stomachs, bowels, or bladders are starting to complain, they let you know. Daisy is particularly effective in that role, as her tongue is almost as wide as our faces. Or at least it seems that way when you're being licked by it.

Frankly, I was grateful that she only let me sleep five hours. I don't usually have nightmares (my dreams are bad enough; like Dali on acid), but scenes from the second *pousada* were on endless loop in my head. Waking from that was a relief.

It seemed that no one else slept very well, either. We dragged ass until we hit our bunks again that evening, but by then all our new-gotten gains were secured for heavy weather and balanced so that *Voyager* wouldn't sail crank. The next day—yesterday—we weighed anchor and made for where we are now: Rocas Atoll.

We got two greetings upon arriving at Rocas Atoll: the raised claws of a bunch of defiant sand crabs, and the raised (but skeletal) hand of the human body they had literally stripped to the bones.

They were suitable introductions to what is probably the strangest place I've ever been to. Rocas Atoll is seemingly barren: just sand, coral powder, two buildings on stilts, and two "lighthouses" that more resemble the trusswork towers that hold up powerlines. You can count the number of palm trees without running out of fingers and toes. These features are all located on one of three islands that barely remain above water at high tide. Twelve feet is the maximum elevation above sea level.

At low tide, though, the atoll's oval shield wall of coral and ossified algae, buttressed by sand banks, rises almost five feet above the ocean swells. There are two inlets, one to the north, and a much smaller one to the west (leeward). The area inside the natural weather-wall is about one half wide-open lagoon with a depth of up to twenty feet, and one half coral maze pockmarked by tidal pools. The punishing equatorial sun heats the water trapped in the pools to as much as 99 degrees Fahrenheit. Meanwhile, the ocean just outside the coral reef hovers around eighty degrees.

When the sea rushes back in at high tide, so do the big fish, including some impressive sharks. As the water rises, the three islands look (and feel) like they are always just one big wave away from being smothered under the surging blue risers. The upper surface of the coral maze is submerged (barely) and the spaces between its craggy walls become deep-flow highways where a wide variety of critters come to eat—and often, be eaten. When the water begins to recede, the big fish retreat to the lagoon or back out to the waves.

According to a guidebook, the atoll is actually a coral accumulation on the peak of a seamount less than five fathoms down. The crest of that seamount extends in every direction and works like a baffled wave break, ensuring that the three islands don't get swamped by large swells or breakers. I swear, if I had invented Rocas Atoll as a setting for a science fiction novel, readers would have laughed and tossed it away: too many implausibilities.

As I write this, I'm sitting on the narrow porch of one of the shelter-shacks on the "big island" of Farol—which is a whopping eleven hundred yards long and two hundred twenty yards wide. About fifteen feet away, the one lifted finger on Mr. Skeleton's hand (the middle finger, of course) points to the west. As if reminding us that is the way to the destination we all decided upon: Kourou.

However Mr. Skeleton got here, Rocas Atoll didn't save his life. If he had any fishing gear, there's no sign of it. There were three desiccated lobster-shells around the biggest shack, but it's impossible to tell whether they'd been caught by him or prior visitors.

We, however, have had no problem grabbing all the lobsters we can eat, although we have to be careful when grabbing them from the tidal pools. Shark repellent is hit-and-miss, so we always keep the FALs handy, too.

So that's life on Rocas Atoll. We've rigged condensation collectors (we use the ship's purifiers as little as we can) and although our diet is still predominantly seafood, lobster is a pretty good change. We're almost caught up on sleep. When we are, we'll figure out where we should go next.

And if Kourou is still our final destination.

## November 10

Kourou scares the shit out of us. All of us. I mean, if the first *pousada* on FdN almost undid us, how are we going to make our way around a huge, flat facility and its buildings, all of which are probably infested with stalkers? Since leaving Ascension, most of us have talked with Prospero about what will be involved, but never as part of a group conversation, and never with enough time to drill down into the nitty-gritty details. Mostly because, at sea and on a small boat, there's always something else that needs doing.

That pattern of endlessly deferring the topic of Kourou stopped today. But not because we decided, as a group, that the time had come to grapple with it. Nope. Ironically, it came about because I was still spooked by what had happened on Fernando de Noronha.

Specifically, I'd been dealing with a bad case of pretender's syndrome ever since I almost got us killed on Fernando de Noronha. Of course, the biggest problem with my overcoming pretender syndrome is the fact that I really *am* a pretender. And for the foreseeable future, there's no way to change that. So the real question was: how skilled a pretender can I become?

To be clear: everybody was very cool about what happened on FdN. In fact, no one thought I did anything wrong. When I tried pointing out the mistakes I made, Jeeza sat me down like she was channeling Willow and demanded to know what I thought I could have done better. When I told her, she called my examples "toxic hindsight." It took me a few moments to unpack that and realize she meant that I was beating myself up with Monday-morning quarterbacking. She and the others had just chalked it up to "shit happens."

But to be frank, that attitude *will* get people killed. Because if you don't acknowledge that you could have done better, then you never will. It's simple logic: accepting the reality of failure is the only way to improve. And here's the reality of what happened on Fernando de Noronha: the only reason we all survived is because we got lucky. I know—I can *feel*—how much real training would have helped me be the kind of leader we needed. The kind of leader that the Captain had been—the full measure of which I am only now coming to realize.

Sure, we all knew that the SAS were among the baddest of bad-asses. But what we didn't—*couldn't*—understand is how much specialized training is required to produce, and maintain readiness in, that kind of soldier.

Take my current crisis of incompetence: the tactics and execution of what the older military manuals call "close quarters combat," or CQC. According to Prospero, even if you're trained to be an infantryman, you'll only get a few weeks of those drills. If that much. But SAS and other special units get many times that amount of training, with regular refreshers and updates along the way.

And then, there's me, who's trying to inform my (maybe?) common sense with the few relevant manuals we salvaged from Air Force lockers on Ascension Island. But if that doesn't work out, hey, no pressure. What's the worst that could happen? Maybe kill a few, or all, of my friends through incompetence? It would be really, really funny if it wasn't so fucking serious.

I think about it all the time, now. I try to write down everything I've ever read or seen about actual close combat, try to delete the bullshit that Hollywood and games hammered into my head, and try to remember that more than half of what's left just doesn't apply when you're fighting stalkers instead of soldiers.

But the hardest job of all is to keep working at it when you know, beyond a shadow of a doubt, that you are never going to be the leader that your friends deserve. Because no matter how hard you try, your lack of real training and experience is almost sure to get them killed, sooner or later.

Or when you get to Kourou.

So a few days after arriving at Rocas Atoll, I managed to pull my brainless head out of my despondent ass and work the basic problem: how can I materially and reliably improve our odds of surviving a CQC engagement?

First answer: avoid CQC engagements. Obviously. Operation Wizard's Tower was a product of that realization. But if the first *pousada* on FdN has proven anything, it's the invariable truth of the Captain's mantra: no plan survives contact with reality. So, even though we may *try* to avoid CQC, there's just no way to be sure we always will. Which means we have to get better at it.

Second answer: don't let what you'd *like* to achieve get in the way of what you *can* achieve. Just because I'll never be the Captain doesn't mean I can't keep improving. Which goes for any/everyone.

And, third answer: Getting better at CQC doesn't involve a mystical personal transformation. It involves drilling a finite set of skills until—just like aikido—those skills not only improve, but become second nature.

And that third answer was arguably the most important, because it pointed toward a concrete and immediate course of action. Since we were in a safe place, with enough food, water, time, and ammo, I proposed that we set up the best "run-and-gun" course we could on the closest island: Ilha do Cemitério. The crew didn't just agree; they were stoked. I got to work.

"Cemetery Island" is a perfectly flat ellipse of sand, four hundred yards long by two hundred yards wide, and, at high tide, only six feet above the water. We laid out both a basic practice range and a training area for live-fire exercises.

I kept the run-and-gun drills restricted to pistols, shotguns, and the M4s: our CQC go-to weapons and the ones for which we have the most ammunition. But we didn't start with loaded guns. The first few days were nothing but dry-fire run-throughs, first as individuals, then in two-person teams. That, and daily range work, didn't just produce modest gains in marksmanship; it helped me see each person's gifts and limitations more clearly.

For instance, Prospero's training, however modest, meant his skills came back quickly. So I put him in charge of creating and running the live-fire drills. The only time I've had to intervene is when he defaults to his by-the-book tendency and starts working on tactics that are pointless when you're facing the infected.

Steve's innate calm makes him really reliable. He is the person least likely to get excited and sweep a teammate or forget trigger discipline. He's also really comfortable with a pistol, arguably as good as Chloe.

At first, Jeeza got easily flustered during the drills, but overcame that pretty quickly. She's still most comfortable with a shotgun, because it "feels further away" from her. I'm still not sure what she means by that, but she eventually got into the groove of the drills and has proven to be the most graceful of us. I don't mean she does leaps and pirouettes as she goes around the imaginary corners we've staked out in the sand, but she moves smoothly. Once she knows what she's doing, there's no wasted motion.

Rod is not a natural at CQC, never will be. He has a tendency to overthink everything. So do I, but when it's time to act, I can slide Mr. Brain over into the copilot seat. He remains alert enough to mutter the occasional suggestion, but mostly, he knows to shut up so that Captain Action can fly the plane. But with Rod, Mr. Brain is in charge. All. The. Time. And the closer the enemy approaches, the more of a deficit that becomes.

I've learned that being small can sometimes be an advantage in CQC. Not for knocking down the doors, obviously, but when it comes to going low and fast, hugging corners, and still being able to recover and fire quickly—well, when your body is smaller and limbs are shorter, you can change position more easily, more quickly.

Unfortunately, Chloe got more and more pissed as she learned the opposite: that her size and strength come at the expense of flexibility and agility. She isn't actually heavy, anymore, but she's still built like—well, yeah; she's built. Solid; low center of gravity; strong, thick limbs—but not great for the kind of hide-and-go-seek-on-acid moves that can help you in CQC. Also, while she's still better than the rest of us with guns, that advantage is not as great when it comes to shotguns and pistols. Hardly a surprise: she grew up shooting medium and big game at three hundred yards or more. Only a certain amount of that skill translates into the snap-shot/duck-and-go craziness of clearing rooms and hallways.

So days passed and progress was made. Then, today, after returning to Farol from only our second set of live fire exercises, Prospero skipped cleaning his weapons and instead, just passed by with a nod and waded back out to *Voyager*. When we were done cleaning our own weapons, we followed, thinking that maybe he'd gone ahead and fixed lunch for us.

He had. After a fashion.

Around the chart table were small plates and fish patties. Cold fish patties. Not a delicacy, I assure you.

In the center were our nav charts of northern Brazil and the Guianas. There was a pin in the small state labeled, "French Guiana."

We looked at Prospero, then at the fish patties, then at the pin. I suspect we were all thinking the same thing: "Which do I dread the most, right now?"

Prospero didn't give us a chance to decide; he pointed at the pin. "Kourou. You've read the files, I take it?"

Silence.

Prospero cleared his throat. "By which I mean, the folder of information I put in the 'to read' box."

More silence.

"I see." He sat. "Then here are the basics." We took our seats. The fish was looking more appealing with every passing second.

Prospero consulted one of his larger laptops. "Kourou is the third largest city in French Guiana. It is also the second largest port, after the capital at Cayenne, approximately forty miles to the southeast. The Kourou River provides the flow for the city's deep-water anchorages, since there is no bay to speak of."

"So, the rest of the coast is . . . what?" Chloe asked. "Beaches?"

"Mangrove swamps and mudflats, mostly," Prospero answered. "The latter shift constantly. Pre-plague, they were recharted every few years."

"Sounds like we go in by river, then," Steve observed.

"Yes. If we can."

Jeeza raised an eyebrow. "And what, exactly, does *that* mean?"

Prospero sighed. "It means that Kourou is no different from any other place on this planet; we have no way of knowing how much it has changed, or how much damage has been done."

Rod was staring at the map. "So how big is French Guiana's third biggest city?"

Prospero's prominent Adam's apple bobbed. "Just over twenty-five thousand."

The table was silent. Then Jeeza shook her head and said, "That's insane."

Prospero looked puzzled. "You think the population estimate is incorrect?"

"No, I think the idea of going there at all is *nuts*! God only knows how many stalkers are still prowling around. Probably still in packs."

Even Chloe looked worried. "Damn, I'm not even sure we

have enough bullets. Assuming we could bait them all to us. Which doesn't seem likely."

Rod was frowning. "Man, I dunno, Prospero. When you said the ESA facility was remote, I was imagining that it was, you know, out in the boonies. But this..." He looked at the map; the little rocket-ship symbol was right next to the red circle denoting Kourou. "It looks like we'd have to go through Stalker Central to get there."

Prospero cleared his throat. "The percentage of surviving infected might be considerably lower than we expect."

"Why's that?"

"Because, as I told you at the outset, the Third Regiment of the French Foreign Legion was permanently assigned to ensure the security of the launch facility. Logically, they would have inflicted heavy losses on any stalker hordes."

Chloe sneered. "You mean the way the military units on Ascension Island took care of business there? The same units that actually became the majority of the stalkers we had to deal with? The same kind of units that weren't able to stop the stalkers anywhere in the whole world? You mean *those* military units?"

Prospero looked at me, desperate.

I shrugged. "She's right. Nothing indicates that military units were any less susceptible to the virus than civilian communities. They probably spread it more than they contained it; they were engaging the infected at close range before anyone understood just how easily the virus was transmitted."

"But if we don't help preserve the GPS sys—"

I held up a hand. "Prospero, why are you bringing up Kourou *now*?"

He blinked like an owl. "Isn't that why you initiated the CQC training? To improve mission readiness?"

I could have kicked myself. "Yes, eventually. But look at what happened at Fernando de Noronha. And that was a cake walk compared to what we'll run into at Kourou.

"I'm not saying we shouldn't continue to plan for the mission"— Jeeza looked at me like I had lost my mind; she might have been right—"but look around." I indicated the table. "Six of us. Yeah, we've got more guns, better armor and are eating a damn sight better than we were four weeks ago. But against a city of twenty-five thousand? Without direct water access or a vehicle to plough through hordes of infected, how are we even going to get to the launch facility?"

Prospero looked slightly grey. "So what are you saying?"

"I'm saying we need to get more information—"

"—It's there in the folder," he objected. "For anyone to look—"

But I didn't stop: "—*and* we need more resources. Maybe we'll find the access is easy. Or protected, like a tunnel. Or maybe we'll find a working armored personnel carrier in our travels. Or there will be some other change in the tactical equation. Because I am still sold on the importance of going to Kourou. I am convinced that keeping GPS alive may be a crucial factor in keeping humanity alive. But as we are today?" I shook my head. "Until things change, we have no way forward. For now, this is the end of the line: we have to table Ephemeral Reflex."

Prospero just nodded, didn't try any other arguments. I suspect he understood why I had jumped in and closed down the discussion: the longer the debate continued, the more the others were going to dig in against the plan. In the end, they might have turned their backs on it permanently. That's what happens when you push people to agree with you when they've already decided they don't. They just become more and more opposed. And frankly, the mission to Kourou didn't just seem impossible; it sounded like suicide.

An alarm rang up in the pilot house. Rod reached over and powered up the radio; time to do our daily frequency sweep.

I looked around the table. Nothing but long faces. And I knew there was no way to ease the pain of the wound we'd just suffered.

I don't mean the bruising that any group gets from a sharp argument. I'm not even referring to the deeper cut of telling Prospero that, no, even though we'd agreed to take him to Kourou, we'd changed our minds—at least for now. No, we had just amputated, and thereby killed, our best hope for a fast track back to a better world.

There had never been any argument about whether GPS was as important as Prospero said it was. I mean, how could there be? With it, you always knew where you were and got where you were going and avoided the places that you shouldn't go near. Without it, you were blind in a world filled with the infected, which was simply a death sentence with an unknown date of execution.

So in killing GPS, we'd killed all the unspoken hopes we'd placed in it. Sure, we might eventually find more people like us, and (if we could trust them) maybe one day we'd have the numbers, and the resources, to take on Kourou.

Except, by then, GPS would be gone. Which I had purposely glossed over to preserve the one thing we *did* have left: us. A group of people who not only worked well with, but cared for, each other. But we wouldn't have remained that way if we had kept arguing over whether or not to commit noble suicide by going to save GPS.

Ending a meeting on a note of despair or defeat is a really bad idea, so after a few seconds of silence, I side-shifted topics: "In the meantime, we keep training for Kourou." I turned to Steve. "Speaking of training, you are a bad mutha with a pistol. But you don't even bother to tell us?"

He shrugged. "I guess that's why you call me Silent Steve."

*Oops. He'd* heard *that?*

He smiled. "As nicknames go, it isn't bad. I learned about pistols from my dad. At our cottage." He shrugged. "We bonded over plinking. Sorta." His smile became brittle. "I was a disappointment."

I didn't know if he meant a disappointment as a marksman or more broadly. But that wasn't my business, and even if it had been, it was hardly the time or place to ask.

Instead, it was time to listen to this week's Top Forty selection of static, automated distress beacons, and occasional coded exchanges that Prospero was sure were military. Sometimes we heard snatches of speech, but it was so garbled that we couldn't even tell what language it was. On the one hand, it was nice to know that there were people alive beyond Ascension and St. Helena. But on the other hand, there was no way of telling if those people on the radio were potential friends or just more pirates like those we'd fought at Husvik.

So we pretty much lost our shit when, precisely thirty minutes after the hour, we heard the pattern of squelch-breaks that was the "we're okay" code we'd arranged with Willow.

## November 10 (second entry)

"Damn," Chloe breathed, "is the send-time correct—?"

"It is," I said.

The squelch pattern repeated.

Jeeza was literally biting her nails. "Aren't you going to answer?"

"Not yet," I muttered. "It might not be them."

"Who else would it be?" Jeeza asked, nails forgotten.

I swear, Chloe's glower could be used as a weapon. "Maybe some bastard pirates. Maybe they followed behind the bunch we killed at Husvik. Could have tortured Willow and Johnnie, got the code. If so, they're just trying to lure us back."

Prospero lifted his chin from where he'd rested it in his palm. "So let's set a trap for them."

"A trap?" Steve asked. "How?"

"By responding as they expect; we try to set up a rendezvous. But when we make the inevitable exchange of coordinates, we give a false string. In fact"—a malign grin slowly curled his lips—"if they *are* pirates, we might be able to trick them into making our lives a little easier."

"What do you mean?" Jeeza said with a frown.

"You'll see. For now, let's just respond. Rod, would you do the honors?"

Rod was already hovering near the radio; he jumped to comply.

"Remember," I warned, "If they're pirates trying to con us, they *won't* want us to go back to South Georgia. They'd have to be pretty desperate to wait that long."

Steve shrugged, gestured to the world around us. "You see any shortage of desperation lately?"

"Fair point," I nodded, discovering that my palms were sweaty. I could not afford to allow myself to believe that it was really, really Willow—and probably Johnnie, too. Because if it wasn't them, it would be like scaling yet another high mountain of hope just to get pushed off. I wasn't sure if I could handle that twice in one day. But if it *was* them? Oh, if it was, then—"Send the coded response, Rod."

He did so.

We waited several seconds, and then Morse code started coming in. Fast.

Way faster than Willow could signal. And Johnnie had never learned how.

"It's not them," Jeeza whispered, her eyes growing red.

Prospero, eyes closed as he listened, spoke the message aloud as it came in. "Authentication received. Please send secondary authentication."

"What?" said Rod. "There is no 'secondary authentication.'"

I nodded. "Send that."

He did.

The dits and dahs streamed back at us. Prospero spoke each word as it completed. "'Very good. Now, what's my bra size?'" His left eyebrow curled sharply.

We looked around at each other. Rod frowned. "How the hell would we kno—?"

"34 B," Chloe muttered. "We rotated laundry, remember? Guys, then girls? She was such a twig."

Rod, his own eyebrows raised, tapped that information in. A short wait—then a torrent of Morse code: "'So it is you! Where are you? We are totally, totally overjoyed!'"

Chloe rolled her eyes, but her voice was thick. "She is such a ditz."

"Yeah, a ditz who would have been a doctoral candidate by the time she was twenty-five," Rod said, grinning. Then he saw my face, frowned, looked at Prospero's, frowned more. "What? What's wrong?"

"Whoever is sending that signal hasn't given us any way to verify that it is, indeed, Willow," Prospero murmured like someone announcing a death in the family. "If they have her, they have her underwear."

Rod gulped, looked from him to me. "So—what do I send?"

I glanced at Prospero. "What's your plan for that trap?"

His evil smile was back. "To get them do some of our work. At Kourou."

Rod looked shocked. I just smiled at Prospero. "Go to it, then."

Prospero dictated the message slowly, carefully. "Happy to hear you, too. In French Guiana. Currently four miles upriver from Kourou, anchored at safe-haven near ESA facility."

The silence after that send grew longer and longer still. I nodded at Prospero. "Nice try, though."

He shrugged. "It is, as you Yanks say, a 'win-win.' At this point they will either start shedding their charade or will ultimately stroll into Kourou and do some of our dirty work for us."

"It's a long way to come," Steve pointed out.

"That assumes they're still in South Georgia, rather than just a few days away." He hooked a thumb at the radio. "We've no way to gauge range, much less direction."

Rod nodded—just as a new stream of signals gushed forth.

Prospero translated. "'Alvaro, you are being very silly. Ask us anything about you that we could reasonably answer. Or about anyone that is still'"—a long pause—"'there.'"

"How's life at Husvik?"

The reply was fast; you could almost hear the indignant, schoolmarm scolding: "Alvaro! We agreed never to send that word in the clear!"

Prospero nodded at me. "Good strategy you two came up with. She could have given any normal answer and a captor would have no way of knowing that it was code signifying that she wasn't speaking as a free agent."

I nodded. "But it's not decisive."

Prospero shook his head. "No, it's not. I can't think of anything that would—"

Jeeza got up. "Rod, send this very slowly. Big gaps between each word."

"Uh—okay. But why?"

"Because you need to give her the chance to interrupt you."

"Huh?"

"Rod, darling: just do it."

Rod nodded.

Jeeza closed her eyes. "Willow. Do. You. Remember. What. You. Told. Me. About. The. First. Time. That. You. Saw. Johnnie. Naked?" Pause. "Do. You. Remember. What. You. Said. About. His—"

The radio vomited out a rush of signals so swift that I couldn't keep up with them—and I'm no slouch.

But Prospero could, grinning as he went: "'Stop right there, Jeeza! Choose another question. Anything.'" A pause. "'Please.'"

"No need for any more questions." Jeeza opened her eyes, smiling like an impossibly smug Cheshire cat. "That was proof positive." She noticed our curious stares and made an "ewwww!" face at us. "Private between the girls, jerks. Back off!"

We made various placating gestures as Rod typed in Jeeza's reply and then added his own flood of greetings, happiness, disbelief, and eagerness to rejoin—

A sharp spurt of code interrupted him. "Further messaging in the clear is unwise. Our monitoring indicates various ships active your part of the world."

*Our part of the world?* I blinked. "Where—*how*—the hell did they get directional- and range-gauging comms?"

Prospero nodded, but leaned closer to listen to the continuing message.

"Sending three strings, using day of week codes. Choose one of the values to indicate closest location."

The strings started coming in. Prospero looked up. "I have no way to know what they mean. Is it—"

"Hush," I told him as I listened. "They're sending coded coordinates." We'd set up a cypher that used a changing mix of navigation, trig, and log tables, specific to different days of the week. That gave us one set of values that we then converted (using yet another day code) into latitude and longitude values. Chloe pulled out a paper and pencil and nav map. Rod jumped up to get the code books. But I could see the day's tables floating in my mind. Sorta.

I converted the tabular references. "Seven degrees fifty-six minutes south by fourteen degrees twenty-five minutes west."

Chloe slid the grid arms. "Ascension Island."

Jeeza nodded. "She and Johnnie knew we were headed there."

The next string was, "Fourteen degrees fifty-four minutes south by twenty-three degrees thirty minutes east."

Chloe had to move slightly to locate that one. "Further north. Cape Verde."

Steve frowned slightly. "We never said we were going there."

"No," I agreed, "but if their comm array shows them basic range and direction, they may simply be listing off likely rendezvous points, going from east to west." More code came in; I translated. "Three degrees fifty-three minutes south by thirty-two degrees twenty-six minutes west."

"Bingo!" Chloe looked up with the most radiant smile I had ever seen on her face. Maybe *any* face. "Fernando de Noronha. Yup; they were checking likely coordinates, running east to west."

I nodded to Rod and discovered that my calves were trembling. This was really happening. We were really going to see Willow and Johnnie again. And I guess the trawler. A part of me wanted to head straight toward them, not take any chances. I tamped that down. "Rod, indicate we confirm option three."

"Acknowledged," Prospero translated. After a pause, a shorter set of signals rolled out of the speaker.

Eyes turned toward me. I converted the two strings into values—a smaller and a larger. I divided them by twenty-four and announced, "ETA is between twenty-two and twenty-four days from now." No one said anything. "Rod, confirm that we'll be there." I smiled. "Waiting with open arms."

He sent. A pause. Then: "Acknowledged. Will resume daily squelch check as per original calendar. Will convey ETA adjustments by original preset changes in squelch intervals. Counting the days. Bringing friends. Message ends."

The radio fell silent. We did, too. We stayed motionless, waiting, listening, for five seconds.

Then Jeeza screamed and grabbed Rod; I couldn't tell if she was hugging or mauling him. Chloe came over so slowly and quietly it reminded me of the way I was taught to enter a church as a kid. Her eyes opened wider and she whispered. "I don't believe it."

I hugged her—one of my favorite activities—and smiled. "Believe it; they're really coming."

"No, stupid. I know that." She glanced over my shoulder. "I mean *them*!"

I turned. Steve was hugging Prospero. And then I realized that wasn't just because he was the closest person. And then I realized how often Steve and Prospero stood close to each other. I think my mouth started to open with a mute "ohhhh—" of realization, but I snapped it shut.

Prospero was facing me over Steve's shoulder. First he looked abashed; I don't think Prospero is a PDA sort of guy, regardless of the situation. Then he looked defiant, and then, when he didn't spot anything but surprised smiles, he kind of melted and looked as though he might be as happy as he had ever been in his whole life.

There was a lot of noise. Steve slid down the companionway, running forward to get celebratory carbs; Twinkies and Hershey bars, I think. Prospero scooped up the cold fish cakes, ran out the pilot house's starboard door and started flinging them to the birds, kind of dancing as he did.

Chloe shook her head looking after one and then the other of them. "Who knew?" she asked rhetorically.

I repeated it, but seriously: "Really—who knew about, well, *them*?"

Rod grinned like a maniac. "Who cares?"

Jeeza nodded, may have dabbed away a tear. "I do."

Chloe started. "You? *You* have a problem with—with them?"

Jeeza's smile became beatific. "I didn't say I have a problem. I said I *cared*."

"Why?" I asked.

Jeeza shrugged and wept. "Because now, everybody has somebody."

When the impromptu party wound down, I found myself on deck along with Prospero, who was watching fish nibble at the cakes. I grinned. "What a bunch of cannibals."

He grinned, too, but thoughtfully. "Not as though we have any right to criticize them for that, anymore."

"True enough." I glanced sideways. He'd made a pretty rapid transition from giddy to reflective. "What's on your mind?"

He nodded at the waves, but I suspected that gesture was really aimed beyond the horizon. "I'm thinking about the job—the lifelong job—that lies before us."

I felt a flash of guilt. "Hey, was that cannibal crack a major buzz-kill? I'm sorry if it—"

He waved away my concern. "No, Alvaro. I was just reflecting upon my own reaction to the news that Willow and Johnnie are coming. How I was every bit as happy as the rest of you, even though I've never met them." He stared out at the ocean again. "These days, every healthy human being is a gift, is another reason to hope that we might survive and prevail."

I nodded. "Yeah. Kind of ironic."

He raised an eyebrow. "Ironic? How?"

I shrugged. "Ironic because I know the other thoughts that must have been going through your head when we confirmed it was Willow. Because those thoughts were going through my head, too."

His lips crinkled into a faint smile. "Oh? So you are a mind-reader, now?"

"I don't have to be. You and I know that Ephemeral Reflex is essential, the same way we know that the others are right to call the mission suicide." He started to reply; I held up a hand. "I read through all the files as soon as you put them out, just after we left Ascension. Kourou will be a stone-cold bitch. Impossible for the six of us."

I sighed. "But then Willow calls, and now we've got another ship, another crew, and more resources. And with them, we might be able to locate and gather even more. Meaning that Ephemeral Reflex might be possible after all."

Prospero shook his head, stared at the swells again. "So, you really *do* read minds."

"Yeah, maybe I do. Because my ESP is telling me that's not the only thought we had in common."

He frowned. "Do tell."

I needed to look at the water as I told him. "The same second you realized Willow's arrival might make it possible to save GPS, you also realized that by joining us, she's also ensuring that some of us will die. Because if we go to Kourou, people *are* going to die. People who are our friends. People who would *not* die if we never went there."

Prospero got a little pale. "Reading minds is one thing, Alvaro, but that . . . that sounds more like prophesy."

I nodded, wishing it wasn't true. But I knew better.

I stared out at the waves again. Or rather, beyond them, the way Prospero had when we started chatting. And although I had no idea where we would wind up if we were to follow along the line defined by both our gazes, I could feel us coming closer to that unseen destination with every passing mile, every passing second.

We were looking toward the same place, far beyond the horizon. Toward the place where the twinned trajectories of our fate and hope converged, became the vanishing point that awaited us at the end of both lines.

We were looking toward Kourou.